Carlo

took a few steps toward them and ~~~~~~
sharp pinch from Michael snapped her out of her
flustered state, and she offered hers. Carlo's hand was
cool and dry, sending a tremor through her as he
wrapped it around hers.

"Simone."

"Mr...Carlevaro." She cleared her throat as he let
go. She couldn't help but rub her sweaty palm against
her jeans. Touching his cool skin had felt like a
disgrace.

"I'm glad you've finally arrived." Carlo's gaze
traveled over her face. It rested on her lips for a
moment before it shot back to her eyes. "I want to take
off in the next thirty minutes."

Simone's heart, which had, for those treacherous
few seconds, stood still, started to pound.

"I just landed from a long-haul flight. I'd like to
take a quick shower."

Carlo raised an eyebrow. "A quick shower?" His
gaze traveled over her body, mapping the route the
water would take.

God, he remembered.

Heat rushed to her cheeks at the potent memories
that flooded in her mind. Years ago, they had shared
many showers that were everything but quick.

Perfect Mistake

by

Sophia Karlson

Sophia Karlson

Perfect Mistake

Cover Art by *Debbie Taylor*

The Wild Rose Press, Inc.
PO Box 708
Adams Basin, NY 14410-0708
Visit us at www.thewildrosepress.com

Publishing History
First Crimson Rose Edition, 2018
Print ISBN 978-1-5092-2023-6
Digital ISBN 978-1-5092-2024-3

Published in the United States of America

Dedication

To my husband and his unwavering faith in me

Chapter One

Landing on her feet came as naturally to Simone Levin as landing a plane, but this time...dread stirred in her stomach as she glanced down at her phone again.

The pilots' schedule she had downloaded minutes before boarding her international flight to Dar es Salaam didn't specify where she'd be flying to this week, but the solid orange block mocking her from the screen was crystal clear. She was *on* for the next three weeks straight.

Ten minutes to landing. She swallowed the curse that hovered on her lips and leaned back against the seat. Her schedule hadn't been the only bad news. Peppe had suffered a heart attack a few days ago. She held a deep affection for the Italian owner of the Tanzanian safari airline she piloted for. Peppe had taken a chance on her, given her a job, at a time when her life had been in shambles. For the past three years he'd always been in her corner regarding the schedule she needed. But now...

She glared a last time at the solid orange block and sighed as she switched off her phone. There was no way she could have foreseen this mess, but right now she wished she'd never gone on vacation. She would have flown home had the news of Peppe's heart attack reached her sooner, would have been making sure whoever took over in his absence understood her

1

scheduling needs. An orange block meant she would spend an overnight at a safari lodge, somewhere in the sticks. The new schedule was crazy, and it wasn't as if any of her fellow pilots would stand up for her in her absence.

Shit. Forget about landing on her feet this time. She'd settle for landing at all.

A warm little hand covered hers and she turned to her three-year-old, who sat next to her. She leaned in and wrapped her arm around her daughter's shoulders and pulled her into a hug to settle her frayed nerves. The economy class seat's armrest was a pain in the midriff, but hugs were important. Especially today, when after two weeks of vacation she'd be leaving Sarah with her nanny again.

"Love you, Mommy."

Sarah always picked up on her mood. She was too quiet today. Ever since she'd discovered talking, it had been as if the radio were tuned in to a talk show for toddlers. Forcing herself to unclench her muscles, she exhaled her nerves and smiled as she brushed a few rogue curls from Sarah's forehead. "Love you too, darling."

Sarah had it more spot-on than she cared to admit. She was nervous as hell for their future. There was no way she could manage three weeks away from her daughter. She hardly managed the two nights she had to spend away during a week, when she had to fly guests to some far-flung safari lodge. But it wasn't just Peppe and the schedule.

Before she'd gone on leave, she'd applied for the airline's fleet manager position. It would be a promotion, but more importantly, an office job, which meant no overnights. She'd never wanted an office job, but over the past few years, it had started to make too much sense. But Peppe had suffered his heart attack before he had finalized the promotion. Simone liked to be up in the air, but not like this.

She itched to get her messages. She'd sent Michael Flynn, a co-pilot and friend at Carlevaro Air, a message just before take-off from Heathrow, asking him what he knew about the schedule changes.

They undoubtedly had to do with Peppe Carlevaro's subsequent medical evacuation to Rome. One of the cons of living in a third-world country was that the medical facilities were not always up to scratch.

A replacement from somewhere in the Carlevaro International swamp had probably already descended on them to throw his weight around. Some idiot who had no idea about flying a paper plane, never mind a real aircraft.

She still had to tell Sarah that she might have to spend one evening away. She'd thought that Sarah had become used to her traveling for work, but lately she had started to throw tantrums. For her fellow passengers' sake she would wait until they disembarked the Airbus before breaking the news.

"Look, Mommy." Sarah smiled at her.

Simone leaned over Sarah to peek out of the cabin window with her. Below them Dar es Salaam was a patchwork of shacks and dirt tracks, separated by the odd tar road. The rusty hues of the quilt were not misleading. Down there it was a chaotic Third World that pulsed with vibrant life. Coming back to Dar es Salaam after a break in a First World country always made her heart beat to a different rhythm.

She tore her eyes away from the landscape and leaned back in her seat. Once at the office, she would talk to whoever had changed the schedule. As much as she liked to keep her private life private, she might have to play the *Sarah-card* for the first time in three years to get her way.

As the Airbus landed, she switched on her phone.

Sarah squeezed her hand and Simone smiled at her. "Home sweet home."

"Ruthie's here?" Sarah questioned with her gray eyes, so different from her own. But Sarah's rowdy blonde curls were as wild as Simone's.

"Yes, she's picking you up."

Sarah beamed. "We go to beach?"

"Yes, darling."

"But you put me bed tonight?" It was as if Sarah conjured a dark cloud in her gray eyes, their color intensifying.

Simone looked away. She didn't want to go into the whole explanation right now. Why did it have to be so bloody difficult? She could only spread herself so thin, pleasing everyone at work, while being there for Sarah. The knot in her stomach tightened. It would be so much easier if she got the fleet management position. She hadn't thought of a plan B yet, in case she didn't get the promotion.

"I'm scheduled for a stay-over tonight." She couldn't fathom the idea of more than one night. "I think they've made a mistake. I'll ask at the office if I can change it." The chances were slim if she left Sarah out of the equation.

Sarah pouted, her lip trembling as if on command.

"Please, Sarah, let's just get off the plane."

Sarah seemed to understand that now wasn't the time to push the issue as she turned to stare out of the window, still sulky, but distracted by the activity on the tarmac. Simone breathed out and checked her watch. She had ample time to get through customs, get their luggage and then catch a taxi to the first terminal, where the light aircraft departed and landed. She would have time to shower before flying her mystery flight for the day.

Simone gathered their things, and the two of them joined the crush of passengers waiting to disembark. As they stepped outside, the wall of humid heat settled on her skin in a sticky film. She pulled Sarah along, the heat wrapping around them like a blanket—too hot, but comfortable in its familiarity. After three years of expat life in Tanzania, Dar es Salaam had become home.

It had been such a subtle change that had crept up on her. *Home is where the heart is.* It was here where the bulk of her heart kept beating, despite being thoroughly broken four years ago. She'd returned three years ago as a single parent. With the US Dollar salary and most living expenses covered, she would have been stupid not to take a chance with Peppe after she'd had Sarah.

As they walked across the tarmac, her phone beeped through a text from Michael.

Prepare yourself for a shitshow. The big boss arrived yesterday and he isn't a happy camper. I'm in the lounge.

She had no idea who the big boss was. For this branch of Carlevaro International the buck had always stopped with Peppe. Simone didn't have time to contemplate this news further, because Sarah immediately set to asking where Ruth was. "Customs and luggage first, darling. Ruthie's waiting on the other side."

Sarah bounced along happily, oblivious to the heat. After the long journey, Sarah's relentless energy worked on the nerves. The day was still long, and she had to be focused at work. With every step, she was emotionally detaching herself from her daughter. During their vacation they'd spent every minute together, and she disliked the inevitable separation. Hopefully, Sarah would grin and bear it.

They cleared customs, collected their luggage, and exited the terminal to meet with Ruth, who waited at their agreed meeting point close to the taxis.

With a joyful shriek Sarah was in her nanny's arms, tugging at the older woman's braids.

"You're a blessing, Sarah missed you so much," Simone said as she hugged Ruth close.

"I missed you too." Ruth gave her a wide smile. She gestured at Simone's heavy backpack. "Is that all you need?"

"Hope so." Simone laughed. "Can you manage everything?" It was a silly question because Ruth always managed.

"Sarah can help. What do you say, honey?" Ruth put her down.

"Yes-yes-yes." Sarah was trying to maneuver a suitcase in the direction of the parking lot.

It was time for a quick exit before Sarah noticed she'd be gone for the rest of the day.

Simone caught her daughter around the waist, planting a kiss on her chubby cheek. "I'll see you later. Love you." She glanced up at Ruth. "I'm scheduled for an overnight tonight, but I think the admin assistant made a mistake. I'll let you know if I don't manage to change it…otherwise I should be home by five." Simone straightened up. "Be good, Sarah."

"Bye-bye." Sarah waved at her, and Simone walked away in the opposite direction. She held her breath, waiting for the inevitable wail. But Ruth had drawn Sarah into an enthusiastic conversation to distract her. Simone turned and followed their progress. She trusted Ruth to take care of Sarah. Her job would have been impossible if it weren't for Ruth. Simone closed her eyes in a silent prayer of gratitude.

Twenty minutes later she rushed through the ill-lit corridor of the first terminal toward the Carlevaro Air staff lounge. She rolled her shoulders, consciously putting on her work face. Being back on Carlevaro turf made her rethink her strategy. For some reason she sensed she had to go around this flight schedule business with caution.

Two pilots sat in the staff lounge, killing time before their next flight. The lounge smelled dusty, and old, olive green couches circled a stained coffee table. A water cooler stood in the corner, and a double row of lockers lined one wall. The room was in stark contrast to the luxury safari lodges Carlevaro owned, putting the pilots right in their place.

She tossed her backpack on the couch next to Michael. "Hey, guys. Any news on how Peppe's doing?"

"Hey, Sweet Cheeks." Ross O'Connor gave her the once-over before carrying on with his phone.

She ignored Ross and looked expectantly at Michael for his response.

"No news since he got evacuated out of Tanzania," Michael said, running his fingers through his cropped red hair and down his sunburnt face.

"A shipment of Carlevaros and hangers-on arrived yesterday to take over operations," Ross said. His English held a more localized drawl, and he carried the deep tan of a white man who had lived in Africa for a long time.

She needed a sense of the lay of the land, for much hinged on Peppe's return. "Any chance he's coming back to work?" she asked.

Ross snorted. "The bloke's sixty-five and had a heart attack. With all the money this place is churning, he could've retired a long time ago. Not sure why he didn't. Personally, I plan for an early retirement."

"Peppe loves his job," she murmured, trying to calm her inner tremors. "He built most of the lodges Carlevaro has here, expanded the business. You don't just let go like that."

And I'll miss him. Her stomach pulled tight at the thought. Peppe had given her a second chance. No other man would have employed a single mother with a six-month-old baby as a pilot. Peppe had taken her on without any questions when she'd asked for her old position with Carlevaro Air. He'd offered her the job on the promise that this time she'd stick around longer than the three-month probation period. He'd been unaware of the many ways in which he'd helped her. A knot jumped to her throat, swelling.

"I guess we'll all miss Peppe. His nephew is taking over." Ross slipped his mobile into his pocket. "*Angelo.*" He oozed the word with a mock Italian accent. "I believe that means angel. His brother, though,

8

the CEO, looks like the devil himself."

"Oh." She swallowed, hoping for more pertinent details. The Italian family business would have a row of heirs waiting in line to take over operations. Someone new, who didn't know her and her situation. Her hands stilled. "And the fleet management position?" She forced her voice to sound calm and tried to look uninterested, but her pulse fluttered in her neck, right where anyone who cared to look would see it skipping against her skin.

"No decisions yet," Ross said. "Peppe would've made the promotion announcement this week. Now we have to go through another round with this new lot."

Frustration grated in her. Peppe had had the candidates narrowed down to her and Ross. She had work experience and the support of the current fleet manager, who'd written an impeccable referral for her. For the past year, she'd worked every minute she could spare in the administration office to learn the ropes. Ross had a smooth tongue and an MBA.

"You've seen the updated schedule?" Ross pointed to the whiteboard.

"Yes." She leaned closer to decipher the hard copy, which had more details than what she'd downloaded on her phone.

"A bit inconvenient, isn't it?" Ross muttered as he came to stand next to her. He was as tall as her and scrawny. "I wouldn't complain if I were you. Not everyone gets handpicked to fly the Carlevaro contingent across Tanzania on a private site inspection."

She almost smiled at the bitterness lacing his voice, but was too annoyed by what he'd said.

"A stupid site inspection?" The words blurted out before she could stop them. She would be at their beck and call, flying from one lodge to the other, then waiting for them with nothing to do. And that with Sarah at home with Ruth, for three weeks. "Why must I fly them?"

"I think it was easier to just roll the schedule for another three weeks," said Michael, standing on her other side, scratching his head. "This all happened last minute, so instead of shuffling everything to accommodate the Carlevaros, we're all flying the same destinations for another three weeks and you got assigned to charter the big boss around. Worst of all, no one will be granted leave for the next month."

She ignored his last sentence. "But the schedule— I'd possibly be away from home for three weeks. I have no clean clothes…" Her suitcases were gone with Ruth and she only had her uniform and what she was wearing.

Michael avoided her gaze. "We're not in a position to say anything, Simone."

Ross smiled, but his eyes were cold. *What about Sarah?* The question hovered between them. It was her against Ross. It was her against a company full of men. And they all felt the same. She had privileges none of them enjoyed, because of Sarah.

Had nobody mentioned Sarah to the new Carlevaro management? She ignored the niggly thought that the pilots and other employees had been speculating about her exact relationship with Peppe for the past three years.

No, this was a test, surely, of her commitment to the company. "How long is this stupid site inspection going to take?" Simone asked, more to herself than anybody in general.

"At least two weeks, more likely three, if they're going to visit all their properties," Ross answered. "It's high season. They're having problems sorting out their accommodation." His tone said he was relishing every second of her anxiety, as if he'd already pocketed the promotion.

Worst-case scenario, she would be hopping from one lodge to the next, only returning to Dar es Salaam to refuel. She leaned closer to read the fine print in the orange blocks that hadn't been included in her email version.

"I'm flying the DHC? Who is going to co-pilot this plane with me?" The De Havilland Canada DHC-6 Twin Otter was the biggest aircraft in the Carlevaro fleet. The other aircraft were Cessna Caravans or smaller, licensed to be flown by one pilot only.

"The CEO," Ross said, hitching his eyebrows at her.

"What? The CEO?" This wasn't getting any better. Now she'd have to smooch up to some hotshot for three weeks. Probably the big boss Michael kept referring to in ominous tones. An older Carlevaro, who'd been uprooted from his beach house in Thailand, or his penthouse in Singapore, possibly his little vineyard in Tuscany.

With the unfounded rumors of her and Peppe going around, she couldn't afford to smooch up to anybody.

"Mr. C.F.L. Carlevaro. He has a commercial pilot's license," Ross said. "Apparently."

"So why the hell doesn't he fly them around himself?" she blurted out.

Michael snorted. "During high season it's the only airplane we can shuffle around—"

"Ugh, Simone," Ross muttered, "can't you see the opportunity? You can prove yourself to them. If that fails, let your other assets do the job."

His words bulldozed her and her stomach jolted. God. He was really implying she should sleep with the new boss to get promoted.

"Jeez, man." Michael stepped in between them. "We're all stressed about the situation, no need to be a dick about it."

"Well, we all wonder why she got that nice apartment which the company pays for. Would be interesting to see if she gets to keep it under the new executive management."

Heat crept up her neck and spread to her cheeks. She bit her tongue to keep back a stinging retort. She still didn't understand how living a quiet life with her daughter, not mixing with the other expatriate staff, had resulted in her being rumored as Peppe's bit-on-the-side.

Spending most of her working time with a bunch of cocksure men had made her immune to a lot of things, but Ross O'Connor had been trying to get under her skin and into her bed for some time. And now things were going sour at speed. The battle for promotion was *on*.

"Game on, Ross. I don't feel threatened." *Unlike you.* There was no other reason why he would've made that comment. She was a better candidate for the promotion than Ross and he knew it.

Michael's hand was on her arm. "They're starting off in Rufiji. That's a short flight," he said, to divert the conversation.

Exhaling, she turned her gaze away from Ross.

Her life was meticulously planned, her overnights arranged in advance with Ruth on a three-weekly basis with each new rotational schedule. It was a juggle, and keeping the balls in the air was possible as long as she knew what was coming. She wasn't prepared for this mess, and only had one extra ironed uniform in her locker. She glanced at her backpack, wilted from two weeks of travel in the UK. Nothing in there was fit for an African safari.

"Get Ruth to pack some clothes for you and I can collect and forward them to the lodge by tomorrow, or the day after," Michael said, as if he'd read her mind.

"Liz won't mind doing your washing at Rufiji," Ross said in a conciliatory tone, as if his previous comment had evaporated. He surely had a short attention span, but mentioning Liz, his sister, made her rethink her situation. Liz would be able to lend her some clothes.

Either way, three weeks were impossible. "I need to talk to the idiot who authorized the bloody schedule changes at the last minute."

"That would be me."

The voice spoke polished British English with a smidgen of an Italian accent. A chill of recognition shot down her back. She would've known that deep voice anywhere. She closed her eyes, begging it to be a dream, a trick of her imagination.

She swerved around in unison with Michael and Ross. A man leaned in the doorframe, looking as if he'd been there for ages. Tall, with broad shoulders, he wore a white short-sleeved shirt that revealed the slight brush of dark hair on his forearms. His black hair was short and sprinkled with gray at the temples. As Simone met his gaze her heart stuttered. Her pulse slowed in shock, then rushed with a burst of adrenaline.

Yet here he was. Carlo. The man who'd disappeared from her life four years ago.

Her gaze took in his face, comparing it to the memory that haunted her empty nights. He had a healthy tan, but wrinkles at the corners of his eyes spoke of more than days spent in the sun. Where four years ago the lines that cupped his mouth were often pulled into a laugh, they were now permanently set, like his frown, the lines burrowing deep. He was not to be messed with.

And those eyes, the color of a gray sea with a storm melting into it. *Sarah's eyes.* She wanted to drop her gaze, scared of what he might read in her own eyes, but he stared at her blankly, as if he didn't recognize her.

"Mr. Carlevaro," Ross said. "This is Simone Levin, your pilot."

Her tongue stuck to her palate in her suddenly parched mouth. Carlo hadn't moved. His gaze still rested on her, taking all of her in, in a wordless greeting. A softness had settled around his mouth, but from his gaze…he was trying to conceal that he knew her. Had known her. *Intimately.*

She sensed he was doing her a favor by not acknowledging her in front of Ross and Michael. It had been the same four years ago…what they'd had, they'd kept to themselves. It had cost her dearly in the end.

Carlo pushed away from the doorframe, took a few steps toward them and stuck out his hand. A sharp pinch from Michael snapped her out of her flustered state, and she offered hers. Carlo's hand was cool and dry, sending a tremor through her as he wrapped it around hers.

"Simone."

"Mr…Carlevaro." She cleared her throat as he let go. She couldn't help but rub her sweaty palm against her jeans. Touching his cool skin had felt like a disgrace.

"I'm glad you've finally arrived." Carlo's gaze traveled over her face. It rested on her lips for a moment before it shot back to her eyes. "I want to take off in the next thirty minutes."

Simone's heart, which had, for those treacherous few seconds, stood still, started to pound.

"I just landed from a long-haul flight. I'd like to take a quick shower."

Carlo raised an eyebrow. "A quick shower?" His gaze traveled over her body, mapping the route the water would take.

God, he remembered.

Heat rushed to her cheeks at the potent memories that flooded in her mind. Years ago, they had shared many showers that were everything but quick. She opened her mouth but no words came out.

"We're waiting in the guest lounge." With a nod to her companions he turned and strode out of the lounge.

Simone became aware of movement next to her.

"Yeah, he's bloody intimidating," said Michael in answer to something Ross had said.

"Snap out of it, Simone, you can't let the CEO of Carlevaro International wait," Ross said. "I bet *he* meets your exacting standards."

"Go to hell, will you, Ross O'Connor." Simone strode past him and grabbed her ironed uniform out of her locker with her work shoes. She resisted the temptation to slam the door when she entered the pilots' restroom.

Chapter Two

Simone's hands trembled so much she struggled to lock the bathroom door. She dropped her toiletry bag and banged her head against the hand basin as she bent to pick it up. A blinding sting settled behind her eyes, and she blinked it back. How was it that after all this time, this man, who had broken her heart and almost her spirit, had arrived at the Carlevaro pilots' lounge out of the blue?

Their intense six-week relationship flashed by her mind's eye—those halcyon days, colored in turquoise and gold, which she'd thought would never end. They'd ended as they'd started, abruptly, with a phone call. The call's repercussions had only hit her weeks later. He'd left her with the promise he would phone her again, that he'd be back in a couple of weeks. Those promises had been broken, one by one.

He hadn't even had the decency to break up with her via a text message. A knot pushed up her throat, making it hard to breathe.

Sarah.

She paused, closing her eyes for a moment as she leaned against the wall. There was no way she could deal with this on her own. She grappled for her phone, which she'd stuffed in her back pocket after getting off the plane, and pressed the speed dial for her sister.

"Landed safely?" Gabi asked as she answered. "I

just got my luggage."

They had traveled together, but Gabi had flown back to South Africa, whereas Simone and Sarah had returned to Tanzania.

"Yes." Her voice trembled and she let herself slide against the wall as her legs all but caved in. "Oh God, Gabi." Her voice broke and she had to swallow.

"Are you okay? What's happened?" Gabi's tone picked up, sitting up straight.

"He's back." She didn't need to explain anything more.

"You've got to be kidding me." There was a short pause in which she could hear Gabi's mind doing the math. "It's been what? Four years? Holy crap, I'd love to have the job that gives me that much leave."

"He's no longer a pilot. He's the freaking CEO," Simone groaned, the reality newly settling on her. How the hell did that happen?

"CEO of Carlevaro East Africa?"

"Carlevaro *International*." The words sank in slowly. *Mr. C.F.L. Carlevaro.* It was the long-drawn name that had started appearing on the directors' list on the company documents after the original CEO had passed away. "He's a Carlevaro. He never told me he was a *Carlevaro*."

"What?"

"He'd told me his name was Carlo Laurentia." For weeks, after he'd left, she'd searched for him on social sites on the internet. She unobtrusively tried to trace him via the company, but he'd vanished into thin air. Now it made sense why she couldn't track him down. She never got his private email or his phone number because it was never necessary. They lived in the same pilots' digs on the Peninsula, went to work together, flew together. They made love whenever they were alone, which was as often as they could contrive it. Then one day he had left without a trace for a crisis at home.

She dropped her forehead into the palm of her hand. It was too much, and afresh the tears pricked behind her eyes.

"Does he know about Sarah?"

He couldn't know. There was no way he could know about Sarah's existence.

What would he do if he found out? Her fingers trembled so much she balled her hand into a fist, pressing it to her mouth to check its quivering.

"Simone? Stop breathing into the phone like a psychopath. Does he know about Sarah?" Gabi repeated, her voice urgent.

She blew out a sigh. "I don't think so."

"Oh, for fuck's sake. Just don't cry. You look horrible when you cry." Gabi's voice was cool, calm. She could almost see her sister pull herself together, her mind ticking over. "Where are you?"

"In the staff bathroom. I'm supposed to be taking a shower. He wants to fly out in half an hour." A cold shudder rushed through her body. "The freaking schedule!" She almost cursed.

"You've gone mad. Slow down and tell me exactly what's happened."

She would have to explain everything to Gabi from the start. She took a deep breath and filled Gabi in on Peppe's heart attack, the changed schedule she'd received after they'd already parted ways at Heathrow and Carlo's arrival at the staff lounge that morning.

"I can't ask him to change the schedule, not without bringing Sarah up as my reason," she finished off. Her hands were bound. She had no control over the situation and helplessness threatened to overwhelm her.

Gabi sighed into the phone. "You don't want him to know about Sarah?"

"No." It was an impulsive decision and she had no idea where it came from. But she had no doubt that it was the best thing to do.

"I don't blame you. He has no right to your daughter."

"Not only that. The Carlevaros are stinking rich. All their hotels…East Africa is not even a quarter of their properties."

Gabi had grown silent on the other side. They both knew that men with money were dangerous, deceptive things. They'd learned that from their father a long time ago. He came and went, leaving a trail of debris in his wake that would be cleaned up by money. She swallowed at the bile rising up her throat. Money meant lawsuits, parental custody battles…each thought fed the ulcer that had popped up in her stomach over the past few minutes. Carlo could take Sarah.

"Can you keep her a secret?" Gabi asked eventually.

She took a deep breath to subdue the pitch of panic in her chest. "I don't know if anybody at the office has told him about Sarah."

"Doesn't sound like it. In any case, what right do the other pilots have to tell him about your daughter? It's your private life."

Trust Gabi to be calm and clearheaded in the situation. Medicine as a career fitted her like a glove.

"You're right. I didn't think about that."

"And if he is the CEO at the top of the food chain he won't be in East Africa forever. He might only be there to oversee the handover to someone else now that Peppe is gone."

"Peppe's nephew is taking over. But it's not Carlo."

"There, see? He might even be gone by tomorrow," Gabi said in a positive tone, and then she added, with a bit of sarcasm, "No surprises there."

A dry laugh scraped up her throat, but she plugged it. "What if he's here for my full three-week assignment? I don't know if I can do it. I'm terrible at acting."

"Agreed."

Gabi's response wasn't very hopeful. But the image of her daughter invaded her mind. Sarah was her life. The idea of being separated from Sarah sent pins and needles crawling under her skin. "I'd have to ask Ruth to stick it out until I'm back at home."

The situation was hopeless and nothing made sense. The only thing that made any sense at that moment was that Carlo mustn't find out about Sarah. She steeled herself.

As if she read her mind, Gabi said, "As we say, put the white coat on, Simone, and act the part. You can do it."

"It's going to be hell."

"You've been through worse—thanks to him, may I remind you."

"True." Being a single mom with a student loan to pay off at the age of twenty-three had been no walk in the park. Her learning curve had been so bloody steep at times it had given her vertigo.

She'd come this far on her own, and she wouldn't let him mess with her life. She didn't need him, and neither did Sarah. She ignored the little voice nagging her that Sarah had some right to know who her father was, now that he'd crash-landed back into her life. The only solution was to get a grip, quickly, do her job, and let Carlo Carlevaro return to where he came from, none the wiser.

"Give me your action plan," Gabi prompted her.

"Take charge, act the part, stay away from him as much as possible, no idle conversations, uh…" She exhaled deeply after each point.

"Do what you do best. Be a pilot, put every emotion to the side and deal with the situation," Gabi completed. "No tears. Walking around red-eyed and blotchy with snot everywhere would be a dead give-away."

The image was so spot-on Simone laughed. "Yes, Dr. Levin. Anything else you want to prescribe?"

"Nothing else, except…don't let him get under your skin. There's no cure for that."

Simone glanced to the ceiling. *Carlo touching her skin*…her stomach quivered as if butterflies were stirring their wings, warming up for flight. No. Never. "Okay, I'll keep you posted."

They rang off and Simone stared at the screen for a full minute before getting up.

Relieved by her younger sister's injection of common sense, she opened the cold water to the max, stripped her clothes off and stepped into the shower. For a long moment, she let the water run down her body, slithering down her heated skin, calming her heart as it beat down on the valley between her breasts.

Silent tears trickled down her cheeks. They'd been sitting on the rim so long, they just needed a little push to flow. But they were tears of anger. Carlo had resurfaced as the CEO of Carlevaro International. He'd been close all this time but yet so far, on the top of the corporate Carlevaro International pyramid, heading a company that employed over twelve thousand people in nine different countries. If only she'd known.

As she got out of the shower, she chuckled mirthlessly. That hadn't gone as anticipated. How many times had she visualized seeing him again? She'd dreamed of it, begged and prayed for it. In her dreams, she always strolled on an empty beach, wearing her white spaghetti-strap dress. Today she'd been dirty, sweaty, in jeans and hot shoes she'd wanted to kick off since getting off the plane, her teeth furry and her hair a mess. In her dreams, they'd been alone with no audience; he'd gathered her into the haven of his arms and kissed her in his slow intoxicating way. Sarah had been clinging to his leg, asking to be lifted into their embrace.

Did he still smell of espresso and the aftershave he always wore? It was subtle but distinctive. Had he stood close enough she would've known it was Carlo, even if his voice hadn't given him away. She rested her palm against her cheek, recalling the tingling of his skin against hers as he had shaken her hand earlier.

Over the years, she'd accepted she had just been a fun fuck. But, for her, there had been much more between them during those six weeks. He might have fathered Sarah, but he hadn't been around to find out about the pregnancy, hadn't cared enough to call her, to find out what had been going on.

She shuddered. Acting for a couple of weeks was all it was going to take. She could keep her distance, and he had pretty much proved he could keep his. How hard could this be?

She dressed with quick, aggressive pulls of her trousers and shirt. Then she combed out her wet hair until the curls bounced back in equal anger. By the time she'd sorted her things she was exhausted. After he'd left her, acceptance had taken a long time to come, but she'd moved on with her life. And now he was back, throwing everything into turmoil again.

He can't, he won't *get under my skin. For Sarah's sake, but also for my own.*

Chapter Three

Carlo watched Simone as she hastened up to the glass door of the Carlevaro Air Departure Lounge. With her sun-streaked hair tied in a ponytail, her white shirt tucked into her cargo pants, and the wide brown belt circling her narrow waist, she looked just like she had four years ago. But something stirred in him as the company logo on her shirt's front pocket drew his eyes to her full breasts. She was still long-limbed but somehow she was more woman, as if her curves had come of age.

Who had brought the change on her? It was more than physical. It was in the way she carried herself— somehow taller, prouder; she no longer slumped to hide her height. Something contracted in him. Had she been with someone else the past four years? She'd moved on swiftly after their intense relationship, something that he'd never thought possible. The heartache of losing her had burnt like hell, but he'd only noticed it much later because at the time he'd already been burnt to the bone.

She's no longer yours. He had to shrug off the memories, but for six weeks she'd been his. He'd known every inch of her. It felt like decades ago and not a mere four years that had flown past in a mad rush.

He walked up to her to meet her away from the rest of the group. She wore the tourist smile, the one all staff had ready for guests at a moment's notice, and her face was flushed. His arrival had been a shock, and from the glance she shot at him, it had been an unpleasant one. At least he'd had half a day to get used to the idea that he would see her again. He'd been able to school his thoughts, although it had taken him most of a sleepless night. For once he'd been tossing and turning over something other than the business. When he'd met her the first time she was on her first expatriate job away from home. That stint hadn't lasted very long, but he hadn't known she'd returned to Tanzania to fly again for his uncle's airline. To find her on the list of pilots employed by Carlevaro Air the day before was the last thing he'd expected.

She didn't even look in his direction, but continued her decisive stride through the lounge to the exit that led to the tarmac and runway.

"Are you up to it?" Carlo asked as he blocked her way.

Her gaze shot up to his, and her eyes widened. "Up to what?"

"Flying."

She shrugged. "Why wouldn't I be?"

"You look tired."

She glanced away with pursed lips. "I did spend the night in an economy class seat on an eleven-hour flight."

He regretted putting her in this position. Any Carlevaro pilot could fly with him, but this trip was about more than flying and he needed someone he could trust. Looking at the bigger picture, he'd had no other option but allocating Simone to their three-week schedule. He hoped it would take much less time than that. He was fighting against the clock. It had always been ticking in the background, but now it was as if gunshots announced the hours, going off in his ears. "A day off after an international flight is standard, but we don't have time."

She sighed, lifting her hands up. "Look, Ca…Mr. Carlevaro. I'm six hours into my eight-hour duty day, taking into account the long-haul flight. It's not as if I piloted the Airbus from London." The glare she shot at him told him he should know better than to doubt her professionalism. "It's my job. I'm trained. I won't notice forty-five minutes."

She walked toward the stairs leading to the exit, but he had to stop her. He needed to bridge this gap. Her coldness was unjustified and so unlike the Simone he'd known four years ago. Maybe her reaction was not entirely unexpected, given the fact that he'd descended on her from nowhere. He clasped a hand around her wrist. It was a mistake to touch her, but he could not help himself. Her wrist was slender and warm, and her pulse raced underneath the delicate skin. The urge to pull her to his chest and trap her willful mouth under his heaved up and he had to check himself. He let go of her as she jerked away with an angry murmur. Her eyes shot daggers at him and he shoved his hands into his pockets.

"I want to introduce you to some of our group."

She stopped midstride. "Whatever for? I'm only the pilot." She checked her watch. "You wanted to leave as soon as possible. I still need to do the pre-flight inspections."

Carlo sighed. There was a wall, thick and high, and he had laid many of the bricks. "Just my brother. He's taking over from Peppe."

Her gaze darted over the group, and when she glanced back at him, there was ill-disguised interest in her eyes.

He turned to call Angelo, whom he sensed had observed their interchange. "My younger brother, Angelo Carlevaro," he introduced them as Angelo stepped forward.

Inside him, a slow heat rose as Angelo shook Simone's hand with his eyes on her beautiful face. A stab of possessiveness made him put his hand on Angelo's shoulder, gripping in silent warning. Angelo let go of Simone's hand. His brother was a playboy and although not into blondes, Carlo wouldn't let Angelo within ten meters of Simone if he could help it.

"I hope you'll find a warm welcome, Mr. Carlevaro." Simone shifted on her feet, but she didn't drop her gaze as she darted it to him and then back to Angelo. She was measuring them up, comparing.

"Hot as hell, actually," Angelo laughed, shooting him a quizzical glance.

Simone smiled. It was the first natural smile he'd seen from her and she'd saved it for Angelo. He would have laughed too if the sensation in his gut didn't feel like jealousy warmed up.

"You'll get used to it," Simone said then turned to him. "If you are to co-pilot our flight, Mr. C.F.L. Carlevaro, you can make yourself useful and get the pre-departure documentation in order." She nodded at Angelo. "Excuse me."

She was out of the door and down the stairs before he could reply.

"Feisty." Angelo scratched at his stubble. "What

was all that about?"

Carlo couldn't help grinning. He had no idea where the new Simone came from, but he loved this new spark in her. "She's captaining the flight. I suppose she needs to make sure I follow the co-pilot rules."

"Rules are there to be broken," Angelo mused.

Carlo watched Simone as she strode over the tarmac to the parked DHC-6 Twin Otter. Her hips still had that seductive sway to them. A twinge of lust stirred in his groin. It was a reaction he had been trying to suppress ever since he'd seen her in the pilot's lounge, defying O'Connor. He hadn't heard what O'Connor had said but Simone had put him in his place.

When he looked at Angelo again, his brother's gaze was still glued to Simone. He shook his head. "Stay away from the staff, Angelo. With everything else, we can't afford a sexual harassment suit."

"Who says it's going to be harassment?" Angelo smiled at him.

Carlo's fingers itched to curl into fists. Handsome as hell, Angelo hardly ever spent a night alone but never kept a woman for longer than a month. Being away from his grazing grounds was going to be a challenge for his younger brother. He took a deep breath and dropped his gaze away from Angelo's eyes. He'd be damned if he let Simone fall prey to Angelo's antics.

"If you're to manage this branch, you're going to have to toe the line, Angelo. If you are unable to do it, I will hire an outsider."

"Calm down, Carlo, one pretty woman and you think I'm eating her knickers. I know what's at stake."

"Do you?" Carlo wasn't sure Angelo understood what Peppe's heart attack meant. Peppe's heart attack had been caused by shock and was by no means just an issue of age or health. Dealing with the issue that had triggered the heart attack was going to be difficult. He was thankful that Dino Viggio, his own right-hand man and one of their executive directors, had volunteered to uproot himself from Rome for a year to come and kill the proverbial fires and hold Angelo's hand.

At least this was not the head office and the whole house of cards underneath it. But this Carlevaro branch was made of straw, and someone was holding a flame to it.

****

Simone sat in the pilot's seat, waiting for the group to climb up the narrow air stairs and into the nineteen-seat aircraft. She studied each person as they waited their turn. There were a few people she recognized, so they weren't all from the Rome-based Carlevaro International head office.

The Kenya-based conservation manager, Noel Peters, was getting on the plane. There were three auditors, sweating in their suits behind him. Still on the tarmac were four Tanzanians in khaki clothes and hiking boots that gave them away as game rangers, even though they weren't carrying their hats and rifles. Then there was the Italian group which included Carlo, his brother Angelo, an older man she'd never seen before, and a tall woman, dressed in elegant white trousers and shirt, with a zebra-print scarf in an intricate knot. She looked familiar, but Simone couldn't remember where she'd seen her before.

The group lacked the usual buzz the tourists she

flew around had—they were too quiet. No thrill of flying in a small plane, no excitement for their first safari or a long-anticipated holiday. This was no site inspection party. It was as if they were heading for a funeral.

Carlo stepped up to make sure the door was closed properly. She lost sight of him as he went around the plane. Soon he would squeeze into the space next to her. Just the idea made her heart beat faster. She signaled to the ground staff that all was in order, put on her headset and spoke to the control tower. Carlo heaved himself into the plane, bending his long legs as he slid into the co-pilot seat next to her. His heat filled the space, his familiar scent drifting over to her in a gentle lure.

God, no one should be allowed to smell so good. Especially not in the tropics.

He buckled up and picked up the flight documentation.

She talked them through the routine pre-departure checks. Between checks she allowed him time to tick off the items on the flight documentation.

"Have you kept up with your flight hours in the past few years?" she asked. Being CEO of Carlevaro International didn't sound like a job that allowed time for flying.

"Sort of," Carlo replied as he adjusted the fan behind his head.

"What does that mean?"

"I still need to fly some hours this year."

"Are you still licensed to fly?"

"Yes."

If it was anybody else she would've insisted on

checking his papers, but she didn't doubt his word. Not when it came to flying. She taxied to the runway, then switched on the recorded message with the flight safety instructions. A calm male voice told the passengers how to fasten their seatbelts and what to do in an emergency. She could recite it in her sleep.

Carlo gave a short laugh and she glanced at him.

"Some things haven't changed."

Memories rushed back in a flash. When she'd come to Carlevaro Air in Tanzania for her first job, he had been her mentor for her probation period. At twenty-two she was younger than the average rookie, but Carlo put her at ease those first few days. He made her laugh; there was no ice to break.

He flew with her on every flight, made sure she was comfortable flying to each lodge, landing and taking off on each dirt runway in faraway places like Ruaha and the Ugalla River Game Reserve. They started off with the short flights to Zanzibar, Mafia and Pemba, then to Mikumi. She stretched her wings with him by her side, got to know the aircraft in the fleet, the runways, the lay of the land from the air and GPS coordinates. By the time they'd flown together for a week and a day off loomed, it was as if they'd known each other for years.

On their mutual day off he offered to show her around town, and together they set off in a three-wheeled taxi, called a tuk-tuk, to the few shops around the Peninsula. Afterward, they ate a languid late lunch at an Italian place that overlooked the bay. It was a weekday and they were alone that afternoon in the restaurant. They sat on the comfy lounger, and when he hooked a windswept curl and tucked it in behind her ear she leaned into the circle of his arm as if she belonged there from the first moment. They sat, silent, for a long time, watching the tide come in, a kite surfer catching the wind some distance away. When he brushed her temple with his lips, it was the most natural thing to turn and kiss him back.

"Simone." Her name sounded so beautiful as it escaped his mouth in a tortured groan. "I shouldn't. We shouldn't. Please. Help me resist you."

She was in no position to resist him. It was really an unfair request. She was herself with him, as she'd never dared to be with any man before him. He made her aware of every inch of her female form, drawing her out of her cocoon as if she'd waited for him her entire life.

He didn't hurry her but went about it as if they had all the time in the world. "There are no virgins where I come from, Simone. I want to treasure you, every moment with you," he said, but she was so eager, which made him laugh. He had tried to slow them down, but it was the honeymoon she'd dreamt of, with the man she'd fallen in love with.

She swallowed the sweet memories, but they caught like a big, dry pill, too painful to even choke down.

How the hell had he gone from mere pilot to CEO of Carlevaro International?

"From where I sit a huge number of things have changed." She nipped any comment from him in the bud by picking up communications with the control tower.

They reached the runway and her palms were sweating. Soon would come that moment where he needed to help her push the overhead throttle. If she could avoid him touching her, she would, but there was no getting out of this one.

"Ready for takeoff," she said when she got the all clear. She pushed the throttle. Other pilots would place their fingers over hers on the metal throttle, touching as little of her as possible, but Carlo's fingers stroked over the back of her hand, found their grip, then settled over hers, his palm caressing her knuckles, pushing the throttle hard, bringing the airplane to the required speed for takeoff. The warmth of his hand, the sudden intimate caress of his fingers as he touched her skin sent a shudder down her arm, and it settled in her stomach, from where it spread a warm tide of desire that pooled in the space between her legs.

She wanted to close her eyes and savor the feeling, hating herself for reacting to him, knowing that it had been too long since someone had touched her like that. She kept her eyes open and withdrew her burning hand as soon as the plane was safely in the air. She forced herself to concentrate on flying, putting all emotion aside. She was trained, all right. How arrogant she must have sounded, only to feel jelly-legged after a simple touch of his hand. That was how it had started four years ago.

She peered out of the side window, doing anything to avoid having him in her peripheral. Dar es Salaam spread underneath them and the sea dominated the rest of the view, with its Persian blue waters, dotted with islands, which were surrounded by turquoise waters and circles of sand enclosed with reef.

"I forgot how beautiful it is here." His voice came to her through her headset.

"Yes," she said curtly, not wanting to talk to him. She was rattled. She needed space and time. His arrival had ripped open wounds that had taken years to heal.

He was quiet for a long time, staring out of the window at the changing landscape as they flew inland. She knew the exact moment he turned to her; she could feel the way he touched her with his gaze.

"We need to talk, Simone."

"There's nothing to talk about," she snapped at him like a dog.

He took a deep breath and sighed. "We'll talk, at some point, whether you like it or not."

She pursed her lips together. "As long as it's strictly about work. No digging into the past." She didn't dare go there. How would such a conversation end? She'd decided he would never know about Sarah. Any innocent or not-so-innocent conversation could give her away. The best strategy would be to stay away from Carlo Carlevaro.

"It's about work. I never talk about anything else." He sighed and raked his hand through his hair, but stopped midway as his headset blocked his hand. He dropped it to his thigh where he clenched and unclenched his fist.

She blinked with a slow sigh. "Good." Then why the hell did she feel deflated?

They flew in silence until they approached the Selous landing strip at the Carlevaros' Rufiji Camp. The Rufiji River resembled a swollen brown artery, fed by hundreds of smaller veins, wrinkles at the corner of an eye, that flowed into the bigger water mass. There were a few lodges in this part of the Selous, but the Carlevaros' camp was situated kilometers away from the rest, in a private concession on an elevated bank of the river.

She landed the aircraft and faced the passengers. They were already unbuckling and wanted to get up. Carlo didn't move but sat staring at the bush. Two Land Rovers, converted to game drive vehicles, waited next to the airstrip for them.

"Please remain seated," she called to the back. "How long are we staying?" Simone asked as she took off her headset.

"Two days, maybe more. You need to be on stand-by."

Her heart plummeted at his words and she closed her eyes. He didn't know about Sarah. He wouldn't be so cruel as to intentionally force her to stay if he'd known she had a child at home. That much she would give him.

She was going to be shackled to him for the next few weeks. Why hadn't she realized it this morning before she even set foot out on the tarmac? She wouldn't be able to fly this plane anywhere without him. She swore under her breath. Her mind had been too occupied with everything else.

She'd have to beg Ruth to stay with Sarah until she got home. She glared at him. "It would be nice to have some type of schedule. Where are we going next?"

"That depends on the lodge that can accommodate us. Hopefully Ruaha."

She suppressed a groan. The exclusive Carlevaro lodges were small, with the biggest having forty rooms, able to accommodate up to eighty guests. They could be crisscrossing the country for weeks, flying after availability during high season. It meant she might not go home even for one overnight.

He was still not moving. She opened her door and unbuckled, ready to climb down and open the air stair. Technically it was his duty, but he sat frozen in space.

"Please remember we'll need to refuel at some point," she said, reminding herself to keep it business, to keep it practical. And hatch a plan to get home as soon as possible, without making the excuse of having a gorgeous little gray-eyed girl at home who lately had been asking where her daddy was.

He leaned toward her. "Join us for lunch."

She bit back a retort. A fuel leak could be very useful right now. "No, thank you." He was so close; it would only take a slight shift for their bodies to touch.

"Simone—"

"You know where to find me once you've decided on a departure date and time. Please inform me in time to make the necessary preparations."

She clambered down and let down the air stair. Being away from his intoxicating scent was a relief. She signaled to the passengers that they could get out and opened the hold. Greeting the rangers who stood close, ready to unload the luggage, she turned to meet and assist the passengers as they descended.

The sun was bright, baking down on the sandy, grass-patched runway. A plover ran with its long legs along the edge, heading for the short cut grass next to it. The noise of the bush filled her numb mind, the buzz of the cicadas and the constant low chatter of weaving birds in a nearby tree. She took a deep breath, savoring the smell of dew-covered grass drying in the sun. Anything to take her mind off *him*.

"Thank you, Simone, good flying." Angelo stepped

down the stair, put on his sunglasses, and strolled off in the direction of the game drive vehicles. Recognition flashed through her mind as she realized she'd flown him before and on more than one occasion. The image came back in a split second. That same rakish smile, the designer sunglasses—the thing that was missing was the flavor of the month by his side. He'd come to Tanzania a few times over the past few years, taking his girlfriend on exotic vacations.

The rest of the group followed, and she greeted them as they continued to the vehicles. With the hold now empty, the rangers were packing the row of small suitcases and duffle bags, laptops and camera bags into the game drive vehicles. She closed the door of the hold and locked it.

Carlo descended the stairs last, meeting her gaze. "You will join us for the meeting at three. Whether you join us for lunch beforehand is up to you."

He stalked off, plucking his laptop bag from the remaining luggage next to the vehicles.

She turned to lift the air stairs up, trying not to roll her eyes. She'd say "no thank you" to that polite lunch invitation, but she couldn't shake the feeling that she'd gotten off lightly.

Chapter Four

Simone slumped down onto the rickety single bed in her allocated staff tent. Carlevaro East Africa kept to their promise of a light footprint on African soil, and with tented camps, the staff and guest accommodation were built with as little cement possible, on wood stilts and platforms.

She took a deep breath and tried to rub the cramps from her shoulders. She'd sent a message to Gabi, notifying her that all was going as planned. Then she'd phoned Ruth and had spoken to Sarah. Her daughter's disappointment had stung. Worst had been the admission that she had no idea when she'd be home. Sarah's internal mommy clock had started to click vigorously lately; it was as if Sarah had sensed she'd be gone, and the idea that it could be forever had become a raw reality. Maybe telling Sarah that her daddy was "gone forever" hadn't been the best idea. If Sarah had realized that her mommy could be gone "forever" from one day to the next, she could only blame herself.

"Simone?"

She recognized Liz's husky voice and wished her away. But she couldn't avoid her, as they'd become friends over the past two years. There were few enough expatriate women working for Carlevaro in Tanzania that they stuck together like peas in a pod. Liz was married to James King and together they managed the

Carlevaro Rufiji Camp. She stood up and zipped open the tent.

"James was right when he said you looked like roadkill." Liz grinned as she scanned Simone's face. She held a thermal cup and a bowl of biscotti in her hands. "I shouldn't let my husband abuse any of my friends like that."

Simone smiled as she dropped down on the bed again. "Thank you. I suppose my holiday has worn off pretty quickly."

Liz ambled in and sat down on the folding chair, putting the coffee and biscotti on the bedside table. She glowed and something in her expression told Simone this was more than a social visit.

"Flying the Carlevaros...it sounds stressful."

"It wasn't on my agenda," Simone said as she picked up the coffee, taking a cautious sip. "Thanks for the coffee. Could I borrow some clothes? I didn't have time to pack anything for this trip."

"Sure, I'll send something over after lunch." Liz searched her face. "From what I've heard they're staying for some time, allocating you solely to flying them?"

She nodded, keeping busy with the coffee. The grapevine was clearly in top form.

"What are you doing with Sarah?" Liz asked softly.

Simone shrugged. "The usual. I've already phoned Ruth, she can help. For now."

"Why don't you tell them? Surely they won't—"

"I don't—I won't—bring Sarah into this equation, Liz." She wanted to plead, but not sound desperate. "And please, don't you or James say anything."

"The promotion means this much to you?"

Since Carlo's surprise arrival the promotion had been the last thing on her mind. "Yes."

"But if they know about Sarah it would work in your favor? After all, it's mostly an office job."

Simone dropped her gaze, not wanting to give Liz a chance to read anything in her eyes. "I want to get this on my own steam. Call it my rediscovered feministic streak."

Liz chuckled. "Okay, whatever. I get it. So, do you know why they're all here?"

"No idea. With Peppe gone…"

"There's more to it than that. James said there's a meeting this afternoon." Liz took a biscotti and started crumbling it.

"Which Carlevaro told me to attend, heaven knows why." Simone glanced at her, and then again at Liz's fingers, which were trembling.

"You mean Mr. Carlevaro, the Italian Stallion, or his hot-as-hell-and-definitely-no-angel brother?" Liz joked.

"Carlo Carlevaro. The man himself." Mutiny rose in her.

"He's gorgeous. I would happily do anything he tells me to." Liz winked at her, a dimple in her cheek as she smiled, her earlier nerves dispelled.

Only Liz would bring up the idea of casually sleeping with the boss. "You're married, take out your hormones on James." Simone shifted on the bed. The tent felt ten degrees too hot.

"Don't worry, I do." Liz chuckled. "They're going bonkers at the moment."

Simone raised her eyebrows. "What's up?"

"I'm pregnant!" Liz burst with the news. Her eyes

sparkled, joy overflowing her features.

"No wonder you're looking so rosy." Simone smiled. She was so relieved for some happy news in Liz's court. "Congratulations. How far are you?"

"Two months. I should wait until the three-month mark but I can't keep it to myself anymore." She grinned. "You're the first to know, besides our families." She took a bite of the biscotti and grimaced. "Orange peel? Seriously? What was I thinking?"

"Thank you for telling me." Simone mustered a smile and held out her hand to take the offending biscotti from Liz. Cleary, she didn't have the appetite for orange peel right now.

"We visited the clinic in Dar es Salaam last week for a checkup. And all's fine. There's this little heart beating, oh my goodness, it's the cutest thing."

She looked away from Liz's glowing face, toying with the lid of the thermal cup. It *was* the cutest thing, especially if it was wanted, planned. "Your folks must be so happy."

As Simone glanced up Liz turned her face away, but she spotted the involuntary swallow.

"Yes…I really hope Dad will be able to see this little one." Liz sighed.

Simone squeezed Liz's shoulder. "Did the last treatment work?"

"Yes, but living with leukemia for ten years has drained everything…from pockets to…the fight in him. The last two treatments cost a fortune. If he could just hold on a few more months—"

"It's going to be okay, Liz," Simone promised, wishing she could comfort her friend by saying something less clichéd. "What are you going to do

42

work-wise?"

Liz lifted her lips in disgust. "I'm exhausted. To be honest I can't stomach food at the moment. I want to vomit every time I need to cook bloody tilapia."

"At least you're not alone in the kitchen," Simone said.

"I still need to make sure everything is up to the Carlevaro standards. Without garnishing it with puke."

"And where're you having the baby?"

"Not here—I might be mad but I'm not stir crazy yet. We'll go back to London for that." Liz patted her flat tummy. "I wanted to ask you about maternity leave."

"What about it?"

"My contract says four months paid maternity leave, but I would need to leave for England at thirty-five weeks. I hope to take unpaid leave. What does your contract say?"

Simone swallowed, forcing her fingers to relax their grip around the cup. She dunked the biscotti in the coffee, stopping short of scalding her fingers in the steaming liquid.

"Pregnant pilots don't fly. My contract doesn't make allowances for maternity leave."

"Blimey, that's out of the backwaters, ain't it?" Liz shook her head with a frown.

"Carlevaro Air's rules," Simone said, the back of her throat contracting. She took a nibble of her soaked biscotti but it clogged in her mouth.

"But you had Sarah before you started to work here?"

Simone wished Liz would stop probing. Few of the current expatriate staff knew about her aborted stint four years ago. Those who did were older and knew better than to ask too many questions. "Yes. Best you email HR in Dar to see how you're going to manage it."

"I haven't told HR yet. James would also need to take time off."

"Better sooner than later, to give them time to sort out temps. Lodge managers and chefs don't grow on trees in this place."

"I know," Liz said.

A moment of silence passed between them as Simone studied her face. She had dark circles under her eyes, and under the pregnancy glow there was disquiet in her being.

"Have you had...?" Simone started. She hated raising this topic, adding to Liz's worries. "Have there been any more mice?"

Liz shot her a nervous glance. "We've progressed. We've also had a bird, and a bushbaby." She rubbed her nose, which had started running out of the blue. "All the same, headless, waiting for me on the chopping block as if I'm to cook them! It makes me sick."

"God." Simone shook her head. That someone had been planting beheaded animals in Liz's kitchen, stalking her as such, had been a quiet concern for weeks.

"I told James I'm leaving if they get any bigger," Liz said. "He has been reporting it but there is no figuring this one out. Yet."

"Someone is trying to intimidate you."

"Yes, but who? And why?" Liz snorted. "I know James can be an ass but bloody hell, he has to run this place and with the type of guests we get, *nothing* can go wrong."

"I know." Simone swallowed down the acid that brushed up her throat. Running a Carlevaro lodge was tense enough without embellishment.

"We won't win any popularity contests with some of the staff, but our ratings make up for it." Liz sighed. "I hope it's worth it."

"You're not scared to stay here, are you?"

"Not yet. Not with James around." Liz checked her watch. "An hour to lunch. I best get going. Are you coming over?"

Between the image of a beheaded bushbaby splayed on Liz's kitchen counter and Carlo there was only one answer. "No thanks, my airline breakfast is still haunting me."

"As they do. James is taking the Carlevaro boys around the lodge for inspection, they better not run late. There's nothing less appetizing than wilted microgreens."

As Liz left Simone dropped a hand to her knotted stomach. Poor Liz. What if the stalking didn't stop before her maternity leave?

Her mind returned to her own problems. She couldn't imagine a day getting any worse. Then she laughed, but it sounded more like a sob. She took her phone and connected to the lodge's Wi-Fi. She searched for Carlo Laurentia, the name she'd known Carlo by four years ago. The search spat out nothing but the same arbitrary hotel in Italy that she'd checked out a thousand times. Then she typed in Carlo Carlevaro and pressed search. In seconds images of Carlo appeared with links to business-related websites.

Her innards cramped. It was easy to find him knowing his real name. If only she *had* known. She'd wanted to tell him that she'd fallen pregnant. Having a baby had been the last thing on either of their minds at the time. Carlo hadn't struck her as the type to leave a woman high and dry. And yet he had. She suppressed the urge to throw her phone into the corner of the tent. Everything could have been so different.

Chapter Five

Carlo watched the in-house guests leave for their afternoon safari activity. They would be gone at least three hours, giving the group enough time to sit down in the dining area for their meeting. All the game rangers and trackers would also be gone from the lodge, which was essential for privacy.

He raked his hands through his hair, feeling dispirited. His father and uncle's company had over decades evolved into an exclusive, boutique hotel chain with branches throughout Southeast Asia and Africa. Their East Africa operations consisted mostly of high-end safari lodges. The airline, previously a sideline, used to fly guests to their lodges. But over the past thirty years, Carlevaro Air had developed into one of the most competitive light aircraft airlines in East Africa, out-earning the safari lodges. That the airline would be the one to hang the noose around their necks...

This lodge was at ninety-five percent occupancy all year and well managed. The tented accommodation was glamorous, stylishly colonial and gleamed with polished wood. Comfortable loungers and deck chairs overlooked the Rufiji River. The lunch had been exceptional and later, for dinner, the staff would light lanterns, creating a magical atmosphere. With the generator running for only a few hours at night, the stars in the sky would have no competition for their brilliance.

From where he stood on the deck he could see hippos in the river, and farther down a herd of elephants came to drink. He clenched the railing tighter as he observed the elephants. There were several young ones playing with each other, not much different from human children. They scuffled and ran around in circles, following each other in what looked like a game of tag. Every now and again they would disappear between their mothers' legs, just to burst out again in the clearing. They were a treat to observe, yet bile rose to his throat. One day, each of those elephants would be in danger of being killed for their tusks. The idea made him physically sick.

He took a deep breath to contain his anger. Peppe had failed, and if he and Angelo didn't get their act together there would be nothing left in thirty years' time.

Noel Peters walked over, brushing some sweat from his brow. "The head ranger tells me there are two sites where we can go and see the carcasses. Both recent."

Carlo suppressed the queasy twist in his stomach, the anger pulsing stronger through his veins. He checked his watch. "Let's get this meeting done with. We'll go tomorrow morning." He took a seat at the head of the table.

The rest of the group filtered over from where they were sitting by the pool relaxing after lunch. Simone wasn't there. As everybody took their seats Carlo sat down and indicated that they would wait.

Two minutes later she rushed in, wearing a pair of

khaki shorts and a white strappy top. Her hair was a rumple of curls, hanging loose around her shoulders. She stifled a yawn as she sat down next to the rangers, whispering an excuse for being late. It was obvious that she'd been sleeping, and if he weren't so annoyed he would've loved to kiss the sleepiness from her eyes, see them sparkle with life and lust. Angelo sat across from her, his gaze dropping to the neckline of her top, which hinted at the fullness of her breasts. Involuntary arousal surfaced and he clenched his jaw. *Damn Angelo, he was stripping her naked with his eyes.*

He forced his gaze away from his younger brother and Simone. He had to get through this meeting without giving in to the distraction Simone had always supplied. From the first day he'd set eyes on her it had been like this. The magnetic tug, as unavoidable as the earth's gravitational pull on a meteorite.

He studied the people around the table. Some of them looked uncomfortable—notably James King, the lodge manager. James's wife couldn't join the meeting, as she was busy with dinner preparations. He'd started to collect data on every single person who worked at the lodge, and the Kings had only been with Carlevaro East Africa for a couple of years. He cleared his throat to get the full attention of the group. "As you know, Peppe Carlevaro retired. Angelo Carlevaro," he paused as Angelo nodded to the group, "will be taking over as managing director of Carlevaro East Africa."

"How's Peppe doing?" Simone interrupted.

Carlo sighed. Everybody must be worried. Change and uncertainty made people nervous. "He's doing well under the circumstances, and we hope he will recover well."

"He won't be back?" There was sincere concern in her voice.

"No."

She lowered her gaze to her lap.

"Dino Viggio, my right-hand man in Rome, will assist Angelo. Dino will be here for six months or so, depending on how things go." Carlo paused while Dino shook hands with those he didn't know.

"Two days before Peppe had his heart attack, he emailed me about a situation that was brought to his attention." He looked at Simone as he spoke. He wanted to see her reaction, judge it for himself. She didn't look up at him, but fiddled with the wristband of her watch.

"Poaching has been a problem in the Selous and Ruaha for decades now. But it has escalated in the past six months in the areas where our lodges are situated." This wouldn't be news to most of the people around the table. He suppressed a sigh knowing he was about to drop a bomb. "Now it has come to light that Carlevaro Air has been flying the illicit goods out of the reserves."

Simone jerked her head up, her eyes wide. "What?"

The people at the table murmured to each other, uttering their shock, then glanced at Simone, before turning back to where he was sitting at the head of the table. All color in James King's face drained away and then he flushed red, looking as guilty as sin. Carlo warned himself not to jump to conclusions.

Simone grew pale under the scrutiny of the group and glanced at James, who didn't meet her gaze. Were either of them involved or were all three, with James's wife Liz in tow?

"A syndicate seems to be operating in this area, and is connecting with our lodges in the Ruaha. We suspect elephant tusks are being flown out of Ruaha and the Selous almost on a weekly basis."

"How do you know this?" Simone asked, frowning. Her eyes were bright and her earlier sleepiness was gone, her voice quavering.

He tossed the incriminating photos they had received on the table.

"These arrived two days before Peppe's heart attack. Someone shoved them under the door of the Dar es Salaam office. Addressed to Peppe."

Simone reached across the table to pick up the photos.

He searched her face, but except for having paled, Simone revealed nothing. "The photo quality is bad, taken at either dawn or dusk. But you can identify a Carlevaro Cessna Caravan being loaded with what resembles an elephant tusk wrapped in some fabric."

Carlo knew there was no denying it. The wrapped object being lifted into the hold of the airplane had the distinct curve of a tusk, and judging by its size must have weighed almost thirty kilograms.

Simone looked up at him before studying the photos again. Finally, she shuffled through them, somewhat dismissively. She shook her head in denial. "Is this all you have?" She passed the photos to James, who held out his hand, fingers trembling as he took the photos.

"It's enough." He tried to stay calm and keep the anger from his voice, but Simone shot up, her chair scraping cruelly along the wooden deck.

"I don't believe it. How do you know where these

were taken?"

Carlo's gaze swept over the group, as they passed photos from one to the other, expressions grim. Unlike them, he'd had time to study the photos, to go through each image, trying to see if there was enough to identify a person or the location. In the few photos with people in them, faces were turned away from the camera. Whoever had taken the photos had done so on the sly and in a rush. In one picture he'd recognized the signpost at Rufiji Camp's landing strip, cut off three-quarters of the way. The sign was in the standard Carlevaro font used throughout their lodges, in their brochures, and on the menus, logos, signs and stationery. The branding was a dead giveaway.

"Sit down, Simone," he said.

Her hands were resting on the table, pushing onto the surface so hard her knuckles and fingertips had turned white. She slumped down in the chair, defeated as she raked her hair away from her face.

"I've called in Noel Peters, whom all of you know, to lead an investigation. For now, it seems nothing has leaked to the media. The damage to our company's reputation, should this come out, might be irreversible," Carlo said. "If our staff are involved in poaching activities, it could break our Tanzanian operations."

"Why would that be?" James asked, leaning forward.

"We could lose our concessions from the Tanzanian government and Carlevaro Air's operating license could be revoked," Angelo said.

"If that happens we might as well close shop." Carlo let the comment hang like a sword over the group but it felt as if the blade's weight was pressing into his own neck. If Carlevaro East Africa closed down, Peppe's conservation efforts of the past decades would be washed away and where the elephants had been grazing there would be nothing.

Shocked silence followed. James raised his eyebrows at this and Simone paled even more.

"Noel, together with our anti-poaching unit from Kenya," Carlo nodded to the four game rangers who sat on either side of Noel, "will be investigating. The forensic auditors will be going through everything at the lodges and the head office in Dar to see if they can uncover anything."

He waited a moment before continuing. "It's imperative that we sort this out before anything leaks to the Tanzanian government or tourist board—need I mention the EAWS, WWF or any other conservation NGO we've supported over the past thirty-odd years?"

He handed the meeting over to Noel, who was much more informed about what was happening on the ground in regards to their East Africa operations. He trusted Noel. He was one of Peppe's best and oldest friends, and had worked for over forty years in the conservation business. Carlo didn't think Noel would ever take up smuggling illicit goods.

Noel didn't elaborate on the Carlevaro's plan of action but detailed how the perpetrators would be dealt with. He told the group that customs police had found a pile of elephant tusks in a container in the Dar es Salaam airport, ready to be shipped off to Asia.

Carlo studied each member at the table, knowing that they might have given too much away, that the perpetrators might well freeze their operations. But at some point, they would take the chance again, because the money was too good to refuse. He seethed and could happily wring any poacher's neck.

Simone avoided meeting his eyes as his gaze rested on her. If she were not involved it would've been a shock to hear about the air trafficking. But what if she was guilty? It was a nagging thought and one he chose to ignore for the moment. Where had she been these past few years? He had never come back to Dar es Salaam after he'd terminated his contract as a pilot. If he'd known that he would find her here he might have returned.

"Do you have anything to add, Carlo?" Noel asked.

He'd lost track of the conversation. "No."

Everybody stared at him, and he swore under his breath, annoyed with himself for losing focus. It was something he hadn't fallen prey to for years. It could be the heat, but if he was honest with himself, it was because she was there, sitting deep in thought across the table.

He adjourned the meeting, stood up and strode to the railing at the end of the deck.

"Join us for dinner," Angelo said, in that musical voice which had just enough accent to make the average woman's knees weak.

"No, thank you. I'd like an early night."

"As if you're tired. You rolled out of bed earlier," Angelo teased her.

Simone didn't respond, probably blushing as she used to. He turned to see her response to his brother's charms.

Simone's eyes were downcast, but she didn't blush. She pulled up even taller. "Mr. Carlevaro—"

"Call me Angelo. You know by declining you're

offending our Italian obsession with food and feasting."

She smiled, but her eyes were cold. "Mr. Carlevaro. I know my place. I would like to stick to it." She chipped the words with precision. No message could be clearer.

"Nonsense. Come have a drink. If we're to fly together for the next few weeks we might as well get to know each other." Angelo was taking hold of her hand to tug her to the bar. She stood her ground and retracted her hand.

"The last time I saw you, there was a redhead at your side. I don't think she would care to see you drinking with another woman," Simone said, challenging him softly.

Carlo wanted to laugh at the expression on his brother's face. Angelo wasn't used to being snubbed. And clearly, Simone had evolved into much more than the average woman. She'd always been different, but he loved this new, spirited side of her.

"Back off, Angelo. Simone doesn't want a drink," Carlo said, turning away from them to look at the river. Her footsteps beat on the deck as she walked away.

Angelo came to stand next to him. "What the hell's up with you?" he asked in Italian.

"As I said this morning, you need to stay away from the staff."

"By the looks you've been giving her your hands are itching to get into her—"

"Angelo," Carlo sighed, raking his hand through his hair.

"What?"

"There's more to it than that."

Carlo stomped off, annoyed that he'd left his

expressions unguarded to those who knew how to read
him.

Chapter Six

Simone fled to the kitchen. Dealing with Carlo was enough; having to deal with his brother, a *charmer*, would be more than she could handle. Especially not with Carlo's silent presence, watching her every move, analyzing it, as if she had somehow overstepped the boundaries by talking to Angelo.

Maybe she had. She swallowed at the thought. Angelo was Carlo's brother and he was going to manage Carlevaro East Africa. A stab of fear shot through her and she paused outside the kitchen door. If Angelo found out about Sarah and told Carlo… To Angelo her little girl could have been fathered by anybody, but Carlo had a sharp mind and did math for breakfast. A simple thing like Sarah's date of birth would give her away.

She slumped into the kitchen, where she found Liz surrounded by her four assistants.

"Try this, will you?" She pushed a spoon with soup into Simone's hand. "It's gazpacho. I cringe at the thought."

Simone tasted. "At least you haven't lost your touch, it's yummy."

"Phew," Liz said, turning to the kitchen assistants, giving them a rush of instructions in Swahili. "How was the meeting?"

Simone scanned the kitchen and pursed her lips.

There was no way she could bring the topic of discussion up in front of the kitchen staff. James would fill Liz in. "Fine. They gave us some interesting stats on the lodge."

"Oh. How dull," Liz said, "So, how're we doing?"

"Just great." There was a pinch of sarcasm in her voice, but Liz didn't pick up on it as she took fresh bread rolls out of the oven.

She couldn't get her head around Carlo's disclosure. Poaching and trafficking were crimes and serious enough to put every other employee's livelihood at stake. If Carlevaro East Africa closed shop, more than a thousand people would lose their jobs. A domino effect would spill over to the reserves where they had lodges, and at the thought of the animals involved her stomach tightened. The Carlevaro conservation philosophy was the reason she worked for the company. Companies like Carlevaro were often the last barrier between animals and their extinction. What was Liz's view on conservation? No one worked in the bush without having or obtaining a deep love for it.

Simone leaned against the counter, picking up a bread roll. Breaking it open, it steamed out some heat and she nibbled at it, trying to digest what had happened that day.

"Do you want anything else with that?"

"No thank you, I—"

"You've eaten nothing today. Not pregnant too, are you?" Liz joked, winking at her. She had hardly uttered the words when she snapped her mouth shut, eyes widening as she stared at the kitchen door. Simone's hair on her back stood on end. Only one person could shock Liz into subordinated silence.

"Can we help you?" Liz asked before turning away, getting busy with some plates on another counter.

"You're having dinner in the kitchen," Carlo said.

"Sort of," Simone retorted with defiance. He could command her to join the group for dinner, and they both knew it. He just had to ask nicely; he was the big boss, after all. One did not say no.

"When you're done here," he said in a level tone, waving at the kitchen in general, "meet me outside, Simone." He turned on his heel and was out of the kitchen before she'd even registered that he was there.

She watched the kitchen door stop its pendulum swing. There was a tangible silence as the kitchen staff, horrified at having the CEO of the company in their domain, held their breaths. She read consternation on everyone's faces—what if Carlo Carlevaro walked back in? A minute passed before a collective sigh of relief escaped and everyone scrambled on with what they had been doing before Carlo had marched in uninvited.

"Blimey. I know it's his kitchen but he could give a girl a bit of warning," Liz spat out as she continued clattering plates around.

Liz's gaze bore through her and Simone could read her mind. Before falling into besotted love with James, Liz had not been shy about opening her legs to anything half handsome and male. Working with a bunch of men, she'd known Liz by reputation before she'd even had a chance to meet her. To Liz, Carlo's words just now had probably sounded a lot like *come naked and be quick about it*. Simone sighed. She hoped Liz knew her better by now. She was not the bed-hopping type.

"I wouldn't keep him waiting. By the look he gave you you're knee-deep in it," Liz scolded, when Simone still stood glued to the counter.

"Any chance you need someone to wash dishes?" Simone begged, wishing for any excuse to avoid Carlo. As she left the kitchen she repeated her mantra about not letting him get under her skin.

****

Simone walked into the guest lounge, her eyes adjusting to the darker interior. The lounge was decorated in the opulent colonial style of the later explorers. Persian carpets covered the wooden floors, cozy reading corners were cordoned off with wing chairs and sofas, and a billiards table stood under an elaborate stained glass light. An antique glass bookcase with Africana graced one canvas wall.

Carlo stood by the bookcase, studying its contents in the twilight. A waiter padded through the lounge, lighting and hanging lamps.

Simone went to stand next to him. "Why am I here?"

He turned to her. The dark shadows under his eyes were somehow more accentuated in the play of lamplight than in the bright sunshine.

"Let's talk somewhere else," he said.

"Where do you suggest? The guests are bound to arrive soon and you know we can't walk around by ourselves after dark."

"Come to my room."

She inhaled sharply, her hands clenching into fists. "Is that why I'm here? Do you really think—"

With a soft groan, he curled his fingers around her arm and pulled her onto the deck, away from the other people sitting in the lounge. None of them had noticed their interchange. Noel Peters was talking to the woman in the zebra scarf. Further away Angelo leaned over the deck's railing with his back to her, a drink in his hand, talking to Dino and James.

"To your room then," he whispered, "although I much prefer mine. And no scenes, if you please." His hand was a ring of fire around her arm, propelling her to the wooden walkway.

"*Askari*," Carlo called to the security guard, who escorted guests to their tents after dark, and kept an eye out for any animals entering the camp. The tall man in the Maasai dress of rich, red-colored fabric stepped out of the dark, torch in hand.

"To the staff camp, please," Carlo ordered softly. After a few steps he let go of her arm and she exhaled, forcing her shoulders to drop their square stance.

"That was unnecessary," she said as she rubbed her arm. He hadn't hurt her, but the feeling was there, his touch burning.

"I'm not so sure."

He walked next to her, but she kept her eyes on the torchlight that swayed left and right into the darkness, catching the glimmer of any animal eyes that might be watching them.

She stopped short a few steps from Carlo when they arrived at her tent. "I don't care who hears this. If you think we're going to carry on where we left off four years ago you are very much mistaken."

He didn't blink an eye. Instead, he turned to the *askari* and asked him to come back in fifteen minutes. The man sauntered off, leaving them alone, with Carlo glaring at her. A slow heat kindled to life in his eyes as his gaze traveled over her. He lowered his lids, barely hiding the smoldering look that made her glow deep in her core. "You seem to be singularly one-track-minded, Simone."

Heat rose to her cheeks; it spread down her chest to her treacherous heart, which pounded at the thought of him. Why was he still able to do this to her? Being alone with him was the worst possible idea.

"Well, if not for that, why march me to my tent as if you would have your way—"

"Now you make me sound like a *libertino*. You may still be devilishly tempting, Simone, but now that I'm your boss you're completely off limits."

She stood frozen outside the tent as he zipped it open in one swift jerk and disappeared into the dark interior. And how exactly did that happen, she wanted to shout at him. He murmured some Italian under his breath but she caught his last words, in English, as if he intended her to hear them. "It makes life so much easier."

He came out with the folding chair and placed it next to the one under the vestibule of the tent.

The full extent of his words hit her and her racing heart stalled. His last words had either been a compliment or a set-down.

She hadn't asked him here. Did he just put her in her place, as if she'd made eyes at the boss and HR called her in for a disciplinary hearing? She brushed her hair out of her face and slumped into the camping chair, utterly rebellious, but too stunned to do anything else.

"Now, if we were in my tent, we could've raided the mini bar and this would've been much more civilized," he said as he sat down.

She shook her head, exhaling. "Don't snub your own shitty staff accommodation. Knowing that you used to stay here yourself, you could've done something about it by now."

"It's on the to-do list."

"Clearly at the bottom end of it." She put as much bite as she could into her last words.

He chuckled, then sighed, as he dropped back deeper into the chair to gaze at the stars glittering in the sky. "From here nothing looks shitty at all."

He seemed so relaxed; it took the wind out of her sails. She closed her eyes and let the sounds of the bush penetrate her buzzing mind and slow her drumming heart. Something scuttled through the tall grass on the outskirts of the camp, and somewhere an owl hooted. She inhaled deeply to calm her nerves, but instead she took a deep breath of his intoxicating maleness, laced with espresso and his aftershave. This was so like the old days. Any moment he would reach out for her hand to lace his fingers with hers. Tears were closer than she cared to admit but she swallowed them down.

"Why did you apply for the fleet management position?"

His question catapulted her out of her moment of reverie. How had he stumbled upon the one question, which would make her reveal all, within just two minutes? She wasn't scared of Carlo, but she was weary of what he could do to her heart. And then to Sarah, once the truth was out.

She had to buy time, to gather her scattered nerves. She glanced at him. "Is this an interview?"

"No, I'm curious."

She clenched her teeth and racked her brain for any answer that would quiet him. "I need a change, a new challenge."

He said nothing. She chewed her lip, sensing that he wasn't satisfied with her answer. "I plan to settle down at some point and flying isn't a family-friendly occupation." There, the truth was half-out. Did she have to be so bloody weak? She could almost hear Gabi saying the words.

"That's debatable. It will depend on your husband."

"Not once there are children involved." She nearly spat out the answer, for what would he know about it?

He shrugged. "Possibly."

The relief drained her. She regurgitated his every word to see if he'd somehow learned about Sarah. If he'd known it would have surfaced by now.

He shifted in his chair and the gravel on the ground crunched underneath his weight. "Are you seeing someone?"

The question caught her off guard. "I…no. Not at the moment."

He cleared his throat. "I suppose we all have our five-year plan."

Yes, and mine didn't involve ever bumping into you again.

"Simone." He sighed. "You are the only person on the pilot payroll I still know and can rely on. With the exception of the management couples at some of our lodges and older staff, people who've been with us for ages and who share the Carlevaro passion, there is no one else I can trust."

She turned to face him; the topic had changed very quickly, but she instinctively knew where he was heading. Getting off personal turf was essential, and she went with the flow. "Surely you don't think I'm involved in this poaching syndicate?"

"No—" He hesitated. "But you're the only person I know and trust in Carlevaro Air."

"You think you know me? Time changes people." *Except if you never knew them in the first place.*

He groaned. "Don't make this personal, it's about the business."

She bit on her tongue to fight the tears and the simultaneous urge to slap him. He'd just poked around her private life and now he was accusing her of making it personal. It *was* personal. Half of her wanted to have it out with him, to tell him in detail what had happened in his four-year absence from her life; the other half wanted to grab her daughter and run.

"Do you know of anybody that could be involved in this? Someone who has been acting strangely? Anything, really?"

His questions ripped her back to reality. "No." She'd been wondering the same thing.

"Think about it. We have twenty-two pilots on our payroll. At least one of them must be involved."

"I can't think of anybody."

"You hang out with these people, you live with them." He was raking his hand through his hair.

"No, I don't."

Carlo turned to her with a questioning look.

"I no longer live in the pilots' digs, and I don't socialize with them anymore," Simone said.

"Why not?"

"Peppe authorized alternative accommodation since I'm the only woman on the team."

"He never passed that by me." He paused. "Not that he would have. Where are you staying?"

"In a new block of flats next to the Hilton Hotel. It overlooks the yacht club and the sea."

Carlo frowned. "It must cost the company a bloody fortune."

She bristled. "It's worth every cent to me not to be surrounded by a bunch of horny bastards who think all I'm good for is a quick fuck."

Shock registered in his eyes. She never used to swear. Initially living and forever working at close quarters with a bunch of men had rubbed off on her. Talking about sex in such a degrading way had also never been part of her vocabulary. Neither had it been her experience with him for those six weeks, irrespective of what she'd convinced herself of afterward. When had she become like this?

He tilted his head in question, frowning. His eyelids closed further as he leaned toward her. "That's what it was like for you? When we were together?" He cursed. "It explains a lot."

She didn't want to go there, and yet she wanted to go there. But not now, not like this. Her heart was in her throat, constricting her breathing with every thud.

The torchlight of the *askari* swung its way toward them.

"Wasn't it for you?" she asked as she stood up. She dashed into the tent and zipped it closed. His chair scraped on the gravel and indented the canvas as he shot up. He murmured something in Italian she equated with her own awful words. She closed her eyes and waited until she heard two pairs of footsteps go down the path. Silent tears streamed down her face. Only when she could hear them no more did she sob, releasing the pressure in her chest.

Chapter Seven

Simone had grown up on a piece of ill-managed farmland in South Africa and the dawn noises were part of her internal clock. She loved the chatter of birds that woke her up when she stayed at a Carlevaro tented camp, where the barrier between her and nature was thin. Unzipping the tent, she stepped outside. The promise of first light was in the velvet sky that took on a lighter shade of midnight blue in the east.

Human noises could be discerned for those who cared to listen for them; the hum of the generator, voices, someone laughing.

"Going on the game drive, Simone?" James, already dressed, was coming from the bigger cluster of tents where the permanent staff had more settled housing.

Simone wanted to crawl back into bed. She'd tossed around most of the night, spinning things in her head and overanalyzing. But it had been months since she'd been on a game drive. Few opportunities came her way and she always took up an invitation. Plus it would get her mind off everything else.

"I'd love to go—how much time do I have?"

"Twenty minutes. I'll send an *askari* over."

"Thanks."

She switched on the light and went to the small bathroom at the back of her tent. The mornings were cooler in June and she blessed the soul who had gotten up even earlier to stoke the boiler for hot water for the staff. She took a quick shower, ran a comb through her curls and dressed in her uniform pants and a clean top Liz had lent her. She grabbed her fleece jacket, for in the wind of the moving safari vehicle she would be cold.

The *askari* waited outside and escorted her to the deck. A number of guests had already gathered around a long table set with tea, coffee, some fruit and muffins. The Carlevaro brothers weren't there, and she let her shoulders hitch down a knot. She spotted Dino Viggio talking to Noel Peters and the unknown woman, who stood at Dino's side.

They called her over.

"I don't believe you've been introduced," Dino said, turning to the woman next to him. "This is my wife, Natalia. She's also part of the Carlevaro team."

Simone smiled and shook Natalia's warm hand in greeting. "It's chillier than normal," she said, not sure what else to say.

"Warm up with some coffee. It's really good, can I get you some?" asked Natalia, her accent very American. There was unexpected warmth in her voice and Simone met Natalia's gaze. She looked concerned, as if she knew every inch of turmoil Simone had gone through during the previous day and night.

"Thank you, I..." Before Simone could finish Natalia had stepped up to the table and poured steaming coffee from a silver coffee pot into a mug. The waiter smiled and put the cream and sugar forward.

"Please pour another, Talia." Carlo spoke behind her, and Simone's insides quivered upon hearing his voice, her earlier calm evaporating. Their unfinished conversation from the previous evening shot back into her mind, their angry words echoing between her ears.

Carlo came to stand right next to her, his arm brushing her naked elbow. It was a soft, intentional movement, and its effect rippled through her.

"Slept okay?" Carlo asked as he turned and searched her face with a soft gaze. Two days' worth of beard on his cheeks and his still-rumpled hair made him look as if he'd tumbled from a cloud. She smelled the sleep on him, and her whole body wanted to wrap around him and snuggle up in his long-lost, yet familiar scent. He had forgotten her outburst, or at least had written it off. Clearly, he'd slept better than her.

"Staff quarters can do with new mattresses," she mumbled as she took the coffee from Natalia. "Thank you."

Natalia smiled. "Last time Peppe was in Rome he did mention staff accommodation upgrades, didn't he, Carlo? We mustn't let that fall through the cracks."

"Best I come test them out for myself," Carlo said. "To make sure." He had a barely perceptible smile and she could kick herself for the nuance she'd introduced.

She broke their locked gazes, heat rising to her cheeks. They'd always hoped, on flying to a lodge, that they would be offered guest accommodation instead of the usual staff quarters. Once settled in their staff rooms Carlo would go off to chat to management about getting guest rooms. He joked that he charmed them into giving them available rooms, telling them they could test the mattresses. He always got what he wanted. Little had she known he could have commanded the most expensive Carlevaro suite on a whim. She couldn't meet his gaze. Every conversation with him was going to spark a memory. A hot stone, which she'd be dragging with her until Carlo flew back to Rome, settled in her stomach.

James ambled up to their group. "If you're ready to go, the vehicle is waiting."

The regular guests had left and their excited chatter faded in the distance. *Damn.* She couldn't extract herself from the Carlevaros' company without being extremely rude.

As they got to the vehicles Angelo took the front seat next to the ranger. By the time Dino, Natalia and Noel got into the Land Rover only the last row at the back was open. Simone climbed up and sat down, hoping James would sit between her and Carlo. But James stood back as Carlo got into the Land Rover and waved them off. As Carlo dropped down next to her, he inhaled deeply. He threw his arms back over the seat and grinned at her. "I really missed this. All of it."

She edged away from him, not knowing what to make of his statement. It was bordering on flirting and was definitely in the no-go zone. She prayed that Carlo wouldn't turn on the charm because she wouldn't be able to resist him if he carried on like that for three long weeks.

****

Carlo lifted his face to the sun that rose in an orange glow. The air was nippier than he remembered, smelling of earth and bush, a raw freshness that had long disappeared in built-up Europe. As he took another deep breath he regretted that he hadn't come sooner. He'd spent time on safari often enough, but in the two years he'd flown for Carlevaro Air something in him had taken root in the African soil. He'd always felt he'd left a part of him behind and he'd been haunted by an intense desire to come back. If he hadn't been so busy, he would have made time. But four years had passed in the blink of an eye and work had always interfered with any plans. As soon as he thought he'd be able to travel, another meeting had been scheduled, or another crisis had erupted. Instead of flying to Nairobi or Dar es Salaam he invariably found himself on a plane to Southeast Asia where Carlevaro had the bulk of their hotels.

Those last few weeks with Simone before his father's illness, while he'd still had the luxury of choice, had been the happiest of his life. When the universally dreaded phone call came, yanking him from his chosen life, he'd had no clue what had waited for him on the other side. Ten weeks later his father was dead, and he had lost a part of his past forever. Little had he known at the time that he'd also lost a part of his future. The future he'd envisioned for himself with Simone. He'd never thought that far ahead, but with Simone it had been a case of not knowing what he'd had until it had been lost.

When he'd come back for a short business meeting six months later, Simone had resigned from Carlevaro Air, and nobody had known where she'd gone. By then he'd understood that she'd moved on and he'd let go, if only by pure mental force.

Simone shifted, and not for the first time he wished he could reverse the clock and go back to those weeks he'd spent with her.

"Why didn't you ever tell me your real name?" Simone asked softly, her voice hardly audible as the

71

vehicle droned off into the dawn.

He sighed at his singular most stupid mistake, but he'd done so on his father's and Peppe's insistence. A spate of high-profile kidnappings in Kenya had threatened to cross the border, and his uncle wasn't taking any risks with him flying around East Africa, visible bait with such a recognizable name as Carlevaro. The ransom money hadn't been the problem, but the opportunity to pay it over rarely presented itself before a body surfaced. "I did tell you my name, just not all of it."

"Carlo Fabbri di Laurentia Carlevaro. I found you on some business profile websites yesterday. It's quite a mouthful," she said. "You're on no social sites, but with a name like that—" She broke off, and took a breath. "No wonder I couldn't find you years ago."

His heart skipped a beat at her last words. "You looked for me?" He'd never heard from her again, had never imagined that she might be searching for him. She leaned in to avoid a few branches that stretched into the open vehicle and blood rushed south to his groin as her arm brushed against his.

"I wanted to know how you were doing...if you were going to renew your contract with Carlevaro Air. I didn't know that you were going to..." She made a halfhearted wave with her hand. "Inherit...*this*."

He sensed that his answer was important. If the decision had been up to him he would've stayed another year, at least.

"I hardly inherited *this*." He cut short a deep sigh. It had been foisted onto him at a time when he couldn't have been less prepared. "The decision to stop flying was made for me when my dad fell ill."

"Really?"

"I had my chance to get hands-on experience. I had to manage some of our hotels in Thailand and Vietnam before I got to fly for Carlevaro Air. When my dad fell ill, my years of freedom, as he liked to call it, were over."

"Poor you."

"I apologize for deceiving you." He grunted inwardly. He regretted not coming clean with her within the first few weeks of their relationship. Somehow the opportunity had never come up, probably because he'd consciously avoided finding one. He hadn't wanted to ruin what they'd had by tagging himself and bringing the business into the mix. "Understand that working for Carlevaro under my full name would've infringed the work experience I was aiming to get." *Dio*, it sounded weak.

"Yes, to be one of the boys is key to flying a plane and making sure passengers get there safely. I get you." Her tone was bitter and it made him wince. His lie had put the bitterness there.

But what was in a name? It had never defined him with her. Which was maybe why it had been so different. "Simone—"

She shook her head. "I feel like…I never knew you. As if everything was fake."

Her words sent a chill down his spine. He'd never imagined she would feel this way. He leaned toward her, close to her ear. "It wasn't fake," he whispered. "Deep down you know more of me than anybody else."

He glanced at her but she stared into the bush. The vehicle's headlights caught the dark bulk of a hippo in the road and the vehicle slowed to a stop. Everybody quieted upon sighting the animal, and whispered conversations were put on hold. The hippo stomped further down the road, then paused to give them a quizzical look before disappearing into the foliage.

They drove on, and the front rows fell back into their companionable chatter. Carlo stroked his chin, uncertain how to bridge this gap with her. When Simone tugged on her fleece jacket he leaned over to help her, but she shook her head and struggled on. Still, he couldn't stop himself from turning up the collar as she zipped it up, so it protected her neck from the wind. His knuckles brushed her cheek and she flinched. His heart raced faster at touching her and his fingers itched to caress the soft line of her cheek, but the look she gave him chilled him to the bone.

After a moment of silence, he breathed out heavily. "Would you had been with me if you'd known I was the owner's son? Peppe's nephew?" It was a soft-spoken challenge. The wind carried his question away from the people sitting in front of them. It was a recurring question he wanted answered by every woman who crossed his path. Were they in it for him or for his money? Would they still be interested in him if it all went belly-up and he was stripped of his status? He'd come to read the female mind quite well. He was no longer interested in digging deep in the hope of finding a heart.

She turned to him, then lowered her gaze, licking her lips. "It was all just you. There was never anything else. I thought you knew that."

Yes, he'd known. That was why it had been different…real, with her. There had been no ulterior motive, no long-term plan to ensnare him. For the first and only time in his life he'd truly been himself with a woman.

"And now?" He couldn't stop himself. He had to know what she was thinking. In his own mind everything was drifting out of focus. His physical attraction to her was overwhelming—it was even stronger than when they'd first met. He told himself it was because their physical attraction had never satiated itself, but he hadn't expected feeling like this. Being separated for years had done nothing to change his intense primal desire for her. He wanted to touch her all the time. He craved her warmth, her breath on his skin. He wanted to possess her, to have her right there, on the Land Rover's bonnet, and nothing he told his head or nether anatomy would change that.

"I won't come close to you with a ten-foot pole," Simone said as she inched away to make even more space between them. "There's the fleet management position up for grabs. The other pilots will spread the poison that I got the promotion because I ogled you or worse. So keep your distance."

She was right; he should stay as far away from her as possible. Yet in her eyes there was something unresolved. He saw it in her gaze when she looked at him, sensed it in the way she edged away from him. Their relationship had been short, but intense. Every woman before and after her had become a weightless fog burnt away by memories of her.

It was the anger and resentment that bounced off her that he couldn't place.

"I phoned you as soon as I got things under control," he said at last, knowing what her response was going to be. That it had been too little, too late.

"Did you now?" She sounded so skeptical her words might just as well have been nails scraping at his face.

"For the first weeks of my father's illness time stood still, Simone. I didn't realize that it had been—" *Dio*, in his mind it sounded pathetically selfish. He understood that it was hard to forgive. "A whole ten weeks had flown by before I got my mind around my dad's illness and was able to think." Purely because by that time he'd realized there was nothing they could do to save his dad. The world he'd been plummeted into had been so warped that everything else had become unreal. Accepting that his dad would die had come just days before he had passed away.

She didn't react immediately, but after a good half minute she laughed joylessly. "By then I was long gone."

"I tried to track you down, but you'd disappeared."

She'd turned her face completely from him; he had difficulty hearing her last words. "I learned from the best."

The ranger slowed the vehicle and changed gears. "We're going off road so hold on. The first one's down here."

As the Land Rover crawled forward he felt Simone's gaze on him. He glanced at her. She stared at him with eyebrows raised, her head tilted in question.

"If you wanted the tourist safari you should have gone with the guests. We're going to see two sites of poaching." He wasn't in the mood for it. The only thing that could possibly get him into a better mood right now was to have a release of the tension with Simone. Since that wasn't an option it would have to be a half-marathon sprint, or a bottle or two of Chianti.

She swallowed, shoving her hands into the pockets of her fleece. "That would've been nice to know beforehand," she said, staring straight ahead.

"You would've stayed at the lodge?"

"Yes."

If she were involved in the poaching she wouldn't want to see her handiwork. He deleted the thought but knew it would leave a trace in his mind. The group quieted now that they realized where they were headed.

After the rainy season the grass was long and thick, making the off-road driving more difficult. Some patches of grass were drier and shorter, but there were the shrubs and trees to navigate. The vehicle bumped its way across the veldt, making franklins scatter and guinea fowl chatter their discontent.

The ranger didn't seem to drive in any specific direction but was confident of where he was going. After a good ten minutes' drive, the stench of rot hit them and then they saw the carcass of an elephant. Scavengers had pecked at it here and there, and a few vultures perched in nearby trees. A hyena slinked away, hovering close to some shrubs, turning to see what the intruders were going to do.

"I'll turn the vehicle upwind," the ranger said to the group. As he drove around the carcass everyone gasped in horror on seeing the remains of the slaughter. The face was hacked away; there was no trunk and the tusks were missing. The carcass was a few days old and carrion, covered with flies, gleamed in the morning sun.

Carlo got up as the vehicle slowed to a standstill a few meters away, then jumped down with Noel, Dino, and Angelo. The ranger followed, rifle in hand. Natalia wanted to get down, but Carlo raised his hand to stop her. He glanced at Simone; she hadn't moved but had paled.

"This was a head shot with a .458 rifle, or something similar," said Noel Peters as the men came full circle to the front of the carcass.

As he circled the carcass, Carlo's stomach curdled and he forced his fists to relax. "How did you find this?"

"Usual way, following the vulture trail," the ranger answered.

"We always follow up on all kills," Noel said, "to see which ones are natural predator kills and which ones are poaching."

"And how old is this one?" Angelo asked.

"Four days."

Carlo met Angelo's gaze and saw him repress the same anger. He pursed his lips, shaking his head. Did Angelo finally grasp the weight of the responsibility that was now his?

"You never hear them firing the shots?" Carlo asked.

"They use silencers. They have very modern equipment and they poach with the wind, so the gunfire is carried away from the lodges."

Carlo started climbing back into the vehicle with the others following.

"Where's the next one?" Angelo asked.

"About one kilometer from here."

Carlo turned to Simone. Her hand trembled against her mouth, covering her nostrils. "Can you stomach more?"

Simone shrugged, the nausea rising up her throat.

How could she feel like this—relieved that seeing and smelling the dreadful sites of poaching disguised her inner turmoil? Ever since Carlo had said that he'd searched for her, even if only ten weeks after he'd left Tanzania, there had been a slow churn in her stomach.

As they continued in silence across the veldt back to the road, she clamped her fists to her stomach, breathing in the fresh air, trying to focus on everything except Carlo's words.

The vehicle swayed over the two dirt tracks for a while until the ranger turned it into the bush. This carcass was closer to the road and nobody got out of the vehicle. She couldn't take it in. That it was an elephant was hardly clear, the head was so mutilated. Shreds of skin kept the form of the body together, hanging on the giant ribcage like a gray winter coat.

Simone glanced at the eerie scene. A carcass rotted in the sun, but the surrounding noise of birds and flies, the scuttle of franklins in the long grass, belied the murder that had taken place. Life in the bush carried on regardless.

A vulture, sitting in a nearby tree, spread its wings and dropped off the branch, seeming too heavy for flight.

"When the vultures are no longer interested then you know there's too much killing going around," the ranger said as he put the vehicle in reverse.

She wouldn't be able to contain the meager contents of her stomach. Not with the bumpy driving, the stench invading her every sense, and the notion that there could have been a chance for them had she been able to stick around for his call. *Ten weeks.*

Ten weeks after he'd left she'd already been nearly

four months pregnant. She must have fallen pregnant within the first few days of being with him, despite using protection. She had been too stupid to know the signs, too out of tune with her own body to notice that her period had been late.

She reached for Carlo, but stopped short of grabbing his arm. "Stop the car, I'm going to be sick."

Carlo called for the ranger to stop, but he was too late; she convulsed. The ranger braked and Simone jumped down, just in time to retch up her morning coffee behind the vehicle.

"Are you okay?" Carlo was there, his hand on her back, warm, stroking.

Did he have to touch her? It made her feel a hundred times worse. "Yes." She straightened, forcing his hand off her back. But instead of letting go he caressed her arm as he searched her face. She wiped her mouth with the back of her hand, blinking with a sniff.

She stepped away from him, closer to the thicket, conscious of the heavy silence from the vehicle. Everybody waited for her to hurl again.

"We can't stop here," the ranger called to them. "The bush is too dense."

Carlo cursed. "Come. Anything can be hiding in these bushes."

He grabbed her hand and pulled her back to the side of the car. "Up with you."

She followed the instruction of his hands, which circled her waist, nudging her up. She stepped on the tire, grabbed the railing, and heaved. His hand was on her behind, shoving her not so gently, but a final stroke traveled down her leg. A second later he leaned over her to get into the back seat. With fire burning to the roots of her hair, she scuttled to her side.

"Sorry," he mouthed, the concern in his eyes merging with what could only be consternation.

He had stroked her leg in a most loving, possessive, caring way. And he'd clearly been unable to stop himself.

She glanced at the others in the car, her heart thudding in her ears. Natalia rummaged through her handbag; Dino was engaged with Noel, who pointed to something in the road ahead. Only Angelo met her gaze for an instant, before he closed his door. He had been ready to jump out...to witness her vomiting and then usher her back into the vehicle. Had he seen how Carlo had touched her? God, what if anyone saw?

Natalia turned and handed her a tissue and a bottle of water.

"Thank you," she murmured, having to grab onto the railing as the ranger got the vehicle back on the road.

"I'll take us to the lookout point," called the ranger above the droning of the Land Rover. "It's a safe spot to regroup and have coffee."

She didn't have to look Carlo's way—his gaze was on her, hot, simmering with hundreds of unsaid words. She could regroup; she'd been regrouping every five minutes since landing in this mess yesterday.

Chapter Eight

As the Land Rover stopped, Simone scrambled out and marched to the edge of the lookout. She took a deep breath of clean air that held no hint of Carlo or of the carcasses, and stared at the Rufiji River snaking its way across the plains into the distance. On the other side a herd of buffalo grazed. She could not lose her focus, not with Sarah's future in the balance. Carlo might be overstepping the line but she couldn't allow it to affect her.

Behind her the ranger was busy setting up for coffee and tea with the squeaking of the fold-up table and the rattling of the cooler box.

"Here." Natalia held out a silver thermal mug of steaming coffee.

"Thank you," Simone said guiltily as she took the coffee. Natalia served her coffee all the time.

"That was awful. I felt sick myself." Natalia turned her back on the men and stepped a few paces away.

Simone edged closer. "Yes. Thank you for the water."

"We're going to need to do much more than I expected to eradicate this." Dino's words fell heavy in the silent pause. She glanced toward the men where they stood with their steaming coffees in a half circle, staring out at the vista beyond.

"I didn't realize this was happening so close to our

lodge—it's within walking distance." Carlo's voice sounded tired.

Simone looked at Natalia. "It's never been like this. When I started with Carlevaro Air there was no poaching in this part of the Selous."

Natalia tightened her lips in a grim line and nodded toward the men. "They'll sort out the problem. They must." She took a sip of her coffee. "How long have you been working for Carlevaro?"

"Three years." She never included her probation period during which she'd had the stupidity to fall pregnant.

"I don't think he meant to tell me," Natalia said as she shot a glance at the men, "but Carlo let slip he knew you from when he worked here a few years ago."

She glanced at Natalia, not sure how much she knew. Natalia was part of team Carlevaro, but it wouldn't be fair to write her off on that basis. And yet a lot was at stake. "We hardly knew each other." She took a sip of coffee to swallow down the lie. "I had to go home, health issues…that couldn't be treated here, you know."

Natalia sighed. "That covers most things, doesn't it? For us Westerners, that is. We were so happy with Peppe's treatment when he had the heart attack. Thank God the doctors at the clinic were on the ball."

They sipped their coffee in silence.

"I hope everything is resolved? Health-wise, I mean," Natalia asked.

She was probing, without asking directly.

Simone's heart thudded in her throat as she considered her answer. "Yes, thank you, otherwise I wouldn't be flying." She had to stop this conversation from going any further. Natalia didn't need to know anything more. "How long have you been with Carlevaro International?"

Natalia chuckled. "I'm going to give my age away when I tell you. It will be thirty years next year. Right now, I'm taking a few days' leave."

Simone shook her head in disbelief. "You can't be older than forty."

"Thank you, but I'm closer to sixty than I'd like to admit. I've known Carlo and Angelo since they were children. Dino is Peppe's cousin, on his mother's side."

"This is really a family business." She almost wanted to sigh her relief at not telling Natalia more about her past stint at Carlevaro Air. She wouldn't be able to let her guard down with anybody. She'd resigned herself to the fact that she would have to deal with Carlo, but she wasn't sure if she had it in her to keep up the pretense for three weeks with Natalia. Not when the older woman was so sincere and easy to talk to.

"It works for us Italians."

"What do you do?" Inwardly she warned herself not to get too familiar with Natalia, but joining the men where they were tossing ideas around was even less appealing.

"I head the marketing department. I work with Julia, Carlo and Angelo's sister. She's supposed to take over from me in a year or two."

Carlo had told her that he had a sister and a brother, but she never got anything else out of him. Now she understood why. If he'd started telling her about his family it would have led to revealing who he was. For the first time she asked herself if it would have made a difference. Would she have been with him if she'd known?

Reflecting back on her younger self she knew she would have been petrified, blunted by intimidation, too shy to talk. Not knowing who he was, she'd been herself with him, as she'd never dared to be with another man. He hadn't been C.F.L. Carlevaro, and it struck her that he could've been different with her too. She'd seen glimpses of the old tease in him since he'd returned, but it was disguised, the nuances known only to them. They'd been so carefree during their time together, as if nothing could ever come between them.

She paused her thoughts, not wanting to delve deeper. "Is Julia older than Carlo?"

Natalia looked at her. "She's six years younger than Carlo. She's recently turned twenty-nine," Natalia sighed. "I'm worried that Julia may be too young for the position, but I'll be there for some time to guide her. We learned a hard lesson regarding succession planning when Tonio fell ill four years ago. If Peppe wasn't such a stubborn man, Angelo would've been working here last year already."

Simone shifted on her feet. Tonio Carlevaro must have been Peppe's brother, and Carlo's father. The intimate conversation was going places she didn't want to, yet every inch of her needed to know more. She clung tighter to her cup.

Natalia chuckled. "Julia has a passion for the work, for the Carlevaro legacy. Honestly, I should be more worried about Angelo; he is two years younger than Julia and has to deal with this mess."

"Aren't they groomed to take over from a young age?"

"Not really—Angelo and Julia maybe more so than Carlo was when his father fell ill. We didn't foresee that. Who wants to? In retrospect Carlo did an amazing job."

Simone recalled what had happened at the office those weeks after Carlo had left. There had been a Carlevaro International email about Tonio Carlevaro, then the CEO, being ill. She hadn't paid much attention; she'd had enough of her own problems having been pregnant. "I don't remember much about Mr. Carlevaro's illness."

"Peppe ran East Africa, so Tonio was less involved on this side. He had his eye on Southeast Asia his whole life. It happened so fast. It took no longer than three months." Natalia sighed and then took a sip of her coffee. "It was after the operation to remove the brain tumor that the gravity of the situation hit us. We all thought it was going to be benign, but it was advanced cancer."

Simone faltered. She'd left Tanzania before she could learn what had happened to Tonio. That Natalia was indirectly talking about Carlo and what he'd gone through with his father's illness made her ache. The feeling was unexpected, cramping around her heart. "I'm sorry."

Natalia sighed. "There was a point, days before Tonio passed away, that I thought Carlo wasn't going to make it. He was thrown into a very deep end. Then by some miracle he pulled himself together and got us all through."

The nausea that had yet to settle surged again.

Natalia touched her arm. "I'm sorry. I shouldn't tell you these things." She blinked with a sniff, and pulled a tissue from her pocket. "Sometimes it's easier to talk to a stranger, an outsider. In a family business there's no one to turn to. Everybody's involved. Being here brings all these memories back, and now with Peppe…"

Simone looked down, embarrassed at the urge to pull Natalia into a tight hug that nearly made her overstep the boundaries. "Don't worry, I understand."

Natalia's words were scratching at her conscience. She wasn't the outsider Natalia believed her to be, not when Sarah linked them. Four years ago, she'd only been aware of her own misery. That Carlo had had a pile of his own problems at the time didn't make everything right, but knowing more about that time in his life put a new perspective on things.

****

Carlo noticed that Simone kept her distance from him as they walked back to the Land Rover—she got in the front passenger seat, next to the ranger, from where he could only see her blonde curls.

He suppressed a sigh as Angelo sat down next to him, taking up the poaching issue again.

When the ranger slowed down for a leopard climbing into a tree, Carlo gave the group two minutes to admire the animal before he said, "We've got to get back to the lodge. Sitting here isn't going to solve our poaching issues."

They stopped at the lodge's entrance half an hour later. Carlo got out of the vehicle, deflated. The group ambled through the reception area to the deck, with Simone hovering on the outskirts. He glanced at her. She would dash off to that confining tent given half a chance. But Natalia had caught her in conversation again, and she would find it hard to leave without being rude. Natalia had that effect on people.

The in-house guests had returned from their safari and were enjoying their breakfast.

"You should eat something," he said to Simone as she approached the group's table with Natalia. She'd regained some of her color, if not her calm. She was nervous, her gaze jumping, avoiding his.

"I think I would rather not join your family breakfast." Simone stepped away from the buffet, ready to rush off.

"This is a business trip," Angelo said. "As far as I'm aware you're part of our investigation team."

Simone's stomach growled on cue and she looked like she wished she could evaporate.

"I think that's a sign." Natalia gave her a little smile.

Simone raised her hands, her face flushed, but Angelo was already pulling a chair out. "You've missed the staff breakfast, we all know that." Angelo smiled at her. "And Noel will be joining us too."

Carlo turned his back on the little scene unfolding between Simone and Angelo. It was a battle between Angelo's steel-strong charm and Simone's sheer will to resist him luring her in. A will, he suspected, that hadn't been fed a decent meal in twenty-four hours.

He was relieved when she sat down, the scraping of chairs and Angelo's chuckle giving the win away. As he helped himself to some fruit from the buffet, Angelo whispered something unintelligible to Simone and she laughed at what he'd said. It was the first time he'd heard her laugh since seeing her again, and he wanted to turn and look at her. Instead he murmured a string of

Italian swear words, because annoyance at Angelo and relief for Simone grated on him in equal measures.

The waiter took their orders for a hot breakfast, and the group settled down with freshly made watermelon juice, spiced with ginger. Carlo sat down at the opposite end of the table with Noel and Dino. They were talking bird sightings, their voices droning on. He focused on the banter between Angelo and Natalia, trying not to stare at Simone, who sat like a stone pillar across from him.

"So, how did you become a pilot, Simone?" Angelo asked.

His question drew the attention of the rest of the table, for it was intriguing. Carlo glanced at Simone. Her body tensed more and she lowered her lashes.

"After school I wasn't sure which direction to take, but I enjoyed flying, so I ended up going to an aviation college in South Africa."

"That's an interesting option for someone so young," Dino said.

"I started to fly when I was sixteen," Simone said. "By the time I enrolled for college I had enough hours clocked to enter the commercial pilot program. It was natural to continue, given the work opportunities in Africa."

Her hands were trembling as she spread butter on a slice of toast.

"Why did you start so young?" Natalia asked. "And taking it so seriously?"

Simone glanced away, toward the buffet, avoiding the gazes the rest were giving her. "The flying lessons were a belated sixteenth birthday gift from my dad. He asked me what I wanted for my birthday." She paused, then said with a wry smile, "He took me literally when I told him I wanted to fly away, all by myself."

The others around the table laughed, but as he met her gaze the hurt was as raw in her eyes as when he'd asked her the same question years ago. The *belated* had been the issue. Simone's dad had been more absent than present in her life. She dropped her gaze to her plate, busying herself with the toast.

Noel laughed. "Sounds like your typical teenager. I've survived my two kids' teenage years, but barely. My pocket, not so much."

Carlo looked at Dino and Natalia and with the slightest nod he indicated for them to stop the interrogation. He couldn't catch Angelo's eye.

"You're lucky to do what you love," Angelo said, staring at her. "Not everybody is that fortunate."

"Yes," Simone said. "I love flying, the sense of freedom it gives me." She blushed as everybody looked from their plates to her. "I'd be terrible at a desk job." Her last words were fumbled, as if she needed to explain more under their scrutiny.

Carlo locked eyes with her across the table. Was she unhappy as a pilot?

"Yet you are applying for one?" he asked, wanting to add that he didn't see her sitting behind a desk all day because she'd find it dull, but her knife clattered onto her plate as it slipped from her hand.

She paled, then swallowed, shaking her head. "Managing the fleet would be different. It's still about flying." She picked at a random curl before tucking it behind her ear. Her eyes darted around the table. "It's not bookkeeping...I mean. You know?"

Natalia chuckled. "I completely understand."

He met her gaze steadily, wanting to kick himself. He steered the conversation away from Angelo and everybody else's insensitive remarks, as oblivious as they were to them. But putting her in the spotlight about the fleet management position was equally unforgivable.

Simone's eyes widened, the tips of her teeth peeking out as she bit her lip. Had she just realized the breakfast was an interview in front of the board of directors? And she'd just put her foot in it?

Carlo glanced at Dino, who hadn't raised an eyebrow. They still had to make the final decision about the promotion, but he couldn't imagine Simone ever giving up flying.

The previous evening her excuse had been that she wanted a change, to settle down. She was only, what, twenty-six? Twenty-seven? Way too young to start feathering some unknown man's nest. He bit down on his jaw; he didn't know which one riled him up the most—Simone's nesting instincts or the idea that they were for another man.

During those weeks he'd mentored her at Carlevaro Air her enthusiasm for life had been as addictive as heroin, and it had given him a high that he couldn't get enough of. She'd been a little bird who'd escaped the cage, tasting freedom for the first time. It had been all or nothing, and she had been going for all of it.

He met her flustered gaze. Now the sparkle in her eyes was gone, and she had none of the sweet tease she'd had about her four years ago. Simone had changed, and the gorgeous virgin he'd taken to bed in an uncontrollable moment of lust was gone forever. That *his* Simone was gone was hard to accept, now that he'd stumbled across her again. Something had stolen her inner radiance, and it hadn't been the dull routine of a desk job. He shifted in his chair as she looked away.

Angelo put down his coffee cup with a clang that broke the silence. "Don't worry, Simone, you're not alone when it comes to office jobs." He grinned. "Now Carlo, he's a man made for the Carlevaro International office in Rome." Angelo waved his hand toward him. "You should see him behind his desk, or even better, during directors' meetings, reigning over his domain."

Carlo wished Angelo would cut it out. Simone knew his passion was flying; he'd been at it since he could legally learn how to get a plane in the air. He'd given up his dreams to keep those of his father and Peppe soaring. There were things bigger than his dreams, and he'd known early on that he'd be the first in line to lead the company one day. He'd never anticipated that it would happen so soon. Inwardly he sighed. He hoped Simone wouldn't let any of this slip out to his ignorant family.

He glanced at her. How had it been that he'd shared so many things with her in the time they'd spent together, things he'd never shared with anyone else?

Simone had closed her mouth and was shredding the toast with her fingers. She didn't eat much, and he resented himself and the others around the table who'd continuously put her on the spot. She was nervous in their company, and he couldn't blame her with the questions they'd asked. Simone's flying had been an escape from an unhappy childhood.

This was only the beginning of a long trip. She was going to starve if this carried on, and he decided he'd rather not watch her fade away over the next few weeks. He would no longer subject her to his family's interrogations by inviting her to meals with them.

To take the focus away from her, he changed the subject. "We'll sit after breakfast to see if we can make out any pattern for trafficking. The auditors might've come up with some information by now."

"How do you plan to find a pattern?" Simone asked as she looked up, her hands quieting over her plate.

Carlo met her gaze. She was intrigued. For a split second he hesitated. Should he explain how they planned to catch the traffickers? He exhaled and relaxed. Simone might have changed, but his fundamental trust in her still stood firm. He needed her in his camp during this investigation, her brainpower and her intimate knowledge of how things worked at Carlevaro Air. He took the plunge. "Take the rotation schedules of the lodge staff, pilots and rangers, see what movements there are and enter the data into a spreadsheet. Do some graphs. Something will come up." He drew his fingers through his hair, huffing out a breath. *Something* must *come up*. "The rangers have been logging the poaching in the Rufiji since we opened our lodge here in the eighties. If we can match a poaching pattern with someone from the outside's movements we could have a link to the head of the syndicate."

"If there's a poaching pattern, why don't you stop them?" Simone asked.

"It's not that easy, and their rhythm changes frequently," Noel said. "We might have an idea when they will poach, but *where* is the problem. James and the rangers here have been going out some nights, in an attempt to stop the poaching, but—" He broke off for a second, then sighed deeply. "We don't have the feet to track the ten-kilometer radius around the lodge or keep an eye on every elephant roaming our concession. And some of the poaching happens on neighboring properties."

Simone shook her head. "I still don't get how these poachers would get tusks on a plane. That means they need to get it to the airstrip—"

"Which is a much shorter walk or drive than to the Tanzania-Zambia highway," Noel interrupted her. "Plus, they avoid potential discovery at roadblocks, never mind scanning at the airport. From our aircraft the goods don't even enter a terminal building or any form of customs. It's been going into an export container without a trace."

"It's the perfect solution," Carlo said, pushing his plate away. That such a scheme could develop under their noses had given him sleepless nights. "Simone, I was hoping you could give us some insight into how they could get the tusks loaded and unloaded, given that pilots are supposed to lock the aircraft when they park overnight."

She hitched her shoulders. "I've no idea. I lock up. It's part of our procedures and must be done for insurance purposes. But I can't vouch for any of the other pilots. Nobody checks up on us at the lodges. Even at the airport, no one checks these small things."

It was the small things that triggered the landslide. "Whoever is involved either opened up for the poachers, or the poachers themselves have a key to whichever aircraft they've been using."

Simone frowned, then shook her head. "Peppe had Medeco locks fitted on all the older aircraft. Medeco locks are a standard feature on the new aircraft," Simone said. "It's not so simple to get copies, they must be ordered from the States."

Carlo raised his eyebrows. He hadn't been aware that Peppe had had high security locks fitted to the Carlevaro fleet. Peppe had run his own show at Carlevaro Air. When he'd taken over the position as CEO, Peppe had made it clear that he wouldn't tolerate unwarranted involvement from Carlevaro International. So, Carlo had kept his distance, continuing his father's tradition of quarterly meetings in Rome, which Peppe attended. If he'd been more involved it would've been easier to get on top of things now. He shook his head. They would have to work with what they had.

"I think if we can catch the Carlevaro Air staff involved in the trafficking, we'll be able to expose the poaching ring. I've all the flight schedules for the past eight months on my laptop." He checked his watch and sighed. It was ten-thirty and he still needed to shower.

"Please sit with me and Noel at eleven, Simone," Carlo said. He looked at Angelo and Dino. "Can you check up on the auditors? They are with James in the office."

The others nodded. He stood up and stretched. As he dropped his hands to his hair to comb his fingers through it, he glanced at Simone. She averted her eyes, and he realized she'd been peeking at his happy trail as he'd stretched. Her slight blush and the way she toyed with her table napkin confirmed it. Desire pulsed through him. *You may stare all you want,* cara. He closed his eyes for a fraction of a second as he put his chair back in place. Such a pity his shower had to be solo. The idea of soaping her down, massaging those

hitched shoulders until she relaxed against him, his hands sliding over her breasts...*Dio*. He opened his eyes to the bright sunlight and harsh reality.

Did she feel the same intense pull to him as he felt toward her? She was an employee and she'd already asked him to keep his distance. He had no right to jeopardize her career by even looking at her in a way that might suggest something to onlookers. Angelo had already noticed, and Natalia was as sharp as wit. But to have touched her earlier was like breathing fresh air coming out of a confined, claustrophobic space.

He was so fucked. If nothing else he should respect her wishes, but feeling like this could make things go very wrong, very quickly.

Chapter Nine

Simone needed a break. She hadn't expected this. For three grueling hours, Carlo had dissected every Rufiji Camp employee's movements for the past eight months. All the staff worked on some rotation basis. Carlo had gathered data into spreadsheets at an alarming rate, letting the spreadsheet program spit out pivot tables and graphs. Simone was unfamiliar with this side of the business, but the novelty of it wore off quickly.

The afternoon heat combined with her sleepless nights had made her drowsy. So far, they'd managed to gather data for only a quarter of the pilots. Carlo had interrogated her on every pilot working for Carlevaro Air. He would pick up on the strangest things and drill deeper with more questions, picking her brain. With Sarah on her mind, she had to constantly check her words and it had been exhausting. She could tell him a hundred things about each pilot who flew for Carlevaro, but most of the information was irrelevant to their investigation.

When he peered up from his computer screen Carlo met her gaze. He searched her face before scrubbing his own with his hands. "Let's take a break. Have some coffee."

"I need to check up on my team, they're busy in the field so I'll radio them from the office." Noel got up, took his laptop and walked off.

Simone stifled a yawn and walked to the deck, stretching. She cocked her ear. A low hum droned from the east.

Carlo came to stand next to her.

"Our Dar flight is approaching," she said, pointing to the aircraft that shimmered on the horizon.

They followed the plane as it flew closer and turned over the river toward the short airstrip two kilometers away.

Carlo cleared his throat. "I got an email from our reservations department. Tomorrow morning, we fly to the Crater. I was hoping to go to Ruaha first, but there's no accommodation available. Noel and the rangers are staying behind here to carry on their investigation, so they have sufficient space for us in the Crater."

Inside her the threads of hope that kept her going stretched to snapping point. "That's a long flight. Are you going to all three lodges in the Serengeti and Crater before we fly back?" she asked.

"We've got one night at the Ngorongoro Crater, then two nights in Seronera, but nothing at the Grumeti River; it's fully booked." He sighed. "After that I hope for Ruaha. Solving the poaching problem is more important than anything else. I can skip these site inspections, but we need to go for Angelo's and Dino's sake."

Simone counted. It would be five consecutive nights that she'd be away from Sarah. Her darling girl would feel abandoned. It was the last thing she wanted Sarah to feel, because that hurt never went away.

She had to do something, say something. She needed to get home and spend some time with Sarah.

"I'll need to refuel after the flight to Seronera. We won't make it to Ruaha and back to Dar es Salaam."

Carlo glanced at her. "I know. We'll make a plan."

"If we had taken a smaller aircraft I could've gone alone." The bite in her voice was tangible.

He didn't respond. Did he relish the power he had over her? She couldn't go anywhere without him co-piloting at her side.

"Can't we refuel at Arusha? Even Mwanza?" He rubbed at his chin. "Flying to Dar to refuel is a waste of time. Time I don't have."

She swore silently. Time. It was all about time and money. Clinging to the last straw she said, "I can ask, but you know how it goes in this place. They might not have enough fuel for a last-minute charter. I would rather fly to Dar es Salaam."

"Has fuel supply become so unreliable? I hadn't realized." He frowned. "If Peppe let that side of things slip…" He shoved his hands in his pockets. "Please see if we can save ourselves the trip to Dar es Salaam."

She bit her tongue, the pain distracting her from the sting behind her eyes. Of course Peppe hadn't let anything slip. She had to keep her mouth shut; she had to keep her poise, for Sarah's sake. She nodded, turning away as the aircraft landed and disappeared.

"We'd best pack up here," Carlo said, right behind her.

She took a deep breath, telling herself that it would all be over in a couple of weeks. In silence they packed up his things, Carlo shoving his laptop into its bag, notes and printouts following.

She sensed his frustration; there was not enough time in the day. She'd spent more time with him than she'd bargained on and she desperately needed to get away from him. "I'm waiting for a delivery that comes with that plane. I'd best see if it's arrived."

She followed his gaze as he spotted Natalia, who was lounging next to the pool in a swimsuit, sitting up as a waiter served her a cocktail. "Going to see if those boys packed your bikini, are you?"

He was teasing her, and her stomach turned. How much of the conversation between her, Ross and Michael had he heard the first day?

"We might as well make the most of it." He summoned a waiter. "Join us once you've unpacked?"

"You've got to be kidding me," she hissed. What was he thinking? That nobody would notice, that nobody would talk? She longed to dive into the azure waters, but staff swimming in the guest pool was a big no-no. Half the staff already thought she'd been sleeping with Peppe; the tongues would be wagging if she misplaced a foot and tumbled into the guest pool with Carlo. Even worse, as much as she wanted to cool off, getting into a pool with Carlo would be like stripping down naked and rewinding the clock.

"Sorry," he said, a wry smile playing on his lips. "It's unreasonable of me to invite you to...overstep the boundaries."

His apology was sincere, and somehow it diluted her wrath. She swore under her breath as she stomped away. Gabi was so not going to like her progress report.

She walked to the entrance of the lodge, listening for the droning of the Land Rovers. James caught up with her, sweat pearling on his forehead. He wiped it off with a handkerchief, ready to meet the new guests. "We got so engrossed that I forgot the time."

She smiled. "Can't say that for myself. Did you manage to find anything with the auditors?"

"Not on the poaching, but the curio shop suffered some theft these past months."

"And who's the guilty party?"

"Someone I fired some weeks ago," James said as he indicated that the waiter with the welcome cocktails and cool hand towels must stand closer. "At least I won't have to fire him again." He stopped short, a frown furrowing his brow. "That makes me think."

"What?"

He looked at her. "I've had so much going on...but it makes no sense. I'm not sure if Liz told you about the bushbaby?"

A shudder rushed down her spine. "She did."

"That delivery was made that same morning, before I fired the curio shop assistant." He cursed. "I thought there was some connection, but time-wise there could be no link between the two." He shook his head, looking away with pursed lips at the two vehicles that arrived.

Simone stepped behind the trunk of the big acacia tree that spread a wide shadow over the entry to the camp, unable to make any sense of James's ramblings. James met each guest with enthusiasm and made sure the porters knew which bags belonged to which tent. Simone knew the spiel he'd give them about the lodge not being fenced. Guests should never walk around unaccompanied by a guard after sunset as they might bump into a hippo or worse.

At last a lone cabin bag remained baking in the sun, with a scribbled note attached to its handle, her name printed in capitals on it.

I went to your digs to pick up your stuff. Michael could not go. Your nanny and kid were not home, so I had to phone Tawanda to come open up. Took me an hour to get this for you. The suitcase was not even closed, so I was not sure if everything you needed was packed. I added a few things.

Cute bikini. :-) Ross.

A slow chill spread over her skin. She had to read the message twice. How was it that Ruth hadn't been at home? She'd arranged with Ruth to have her suitcase ready, so Michael could pick it up. The tone of the first part of the message said it all; Ross had been irritated about fetching her things and he would hold it against her.

It was the last two sentences with the little smiley face that freaked her out.

Ross knew she had a bikini. It roamed somewhere in her closet, but Ruth would never pack her a swimsuit for a business trip. Her hands stilled, but the little piece of paper quivered.

The notion of Ross stalking around her apartment and digging through her things made her stomach jolt in revolt. Never mind that it bordered on invasion of privacy, it grossed her out.

Tawanda's presence hardly helped. The administration assistant, who was also the custodian of spare keys to the buildings owned by Carlevaro East Africa, was a complete walk-over. Ross would eat Tawanda for breakfast. He'd probably gone through every last drawer in her closet. She shuddered as if a voyeur was watching her, his creepy gaze traveling over her skin.

She grabbed the bag's handle and tugged the

suitcase along. When she got to her tent she zipped the bag open to find three uniforms folded up in military precision. A pair of beaded sandals was in the shoe space with some extra work socks. Two sets of shorts and T-shirts. Underneath it was her white silk pajama set, which consisted of a pair of shorts with a thinly strapped top. When she reached the bottom, she found her bikini and underwear, meticulously folded.

Ruth would never have packed her such underwear. Her everyday underwear was practical, skin-toned and invisible under her uniform. Ross's hands on these delicate, lacy things... *Yuck*. Some of the lingerie still had tags on it. The embroidered sheer fabric burned her fingers. This was Ross's idea of a joke. Did he really think she'd wear this to work? She swallowed as she recalled his last words. *Let your other assets do the job.*

Been there, done that. Got the baby.

She sniggered at her own joke. If only Ross knew. God, what would she give to see his face!

Swearing, she hung a Carlevaro shirt on a hanger to let out the few creases.

She glared at the contents of her suitcase. The lingerie was gorgeous and had been stupidly expensive. She'd bought it on holiday a year ago when Gabi had urged her to start dating again. She hadn't tried the dating scene; Sarah had been the most convenient excuse to avoid going out, and nobody had been there to coerce her or to arrange blind dates.

But it had been more than that, and as the physical proof of her dating failure stared at her from the suitcase, the real reason was lounging next to the pool. She'd never gotten over Carlo.

Her fingers traced the pattern of a sheer bra's embroidered detail, the sensation on her sensitive fingertips pulsing desire from her skin to deep between her thighs. His touch had been like this on her body, soft, gentle, slow, titillating until he'd had her at the point of sweet release, just to draw her back from the edge. Again and again, until she'd broken into an orgasm so intense that it had left her wet and trembling.

"Simone?"

She jumped and closed the suitcase in mortification. Inhaling sharply, she realized she'd been holding her breath. She closed her eyes for a few seconds, intensely conscious of feet scraping on the gravel outside. She brushed a few rogue curls from her face, composing herself. When she stepped out of the tent Angelo stood a couple of meters from her, looking like a naughty schoolboy sneaking around where he shouldn't.

"I tracked you down." He smiled at her, and his eyes shone as if the world was made of fairy lights that reflected on him. To call him beautiful would be an insult. Every detail of his face and body had such perfect proportion, and such noble bearing, that he could be the closest living relation to God's Adam on earth at that moment.

"Can I help you, Mr. Carlevaro?" Her subconscious already nagged her that this was a bad idea.

"Please, call me Angelo." His gaze flashed a warning, and she sensed she'd pushed her new boss too far. The day had been exhausting, and as she sighed the fight went out of her.

"Okay, Angelo, what's up?" She stared him square

in the eye, unfazed.

He grinned right back. "You're flushed. Are you all right?"

She'd never been worse. "Yes, I'm fine, thanks."

He still scrutinized her. "We're going out for the afternoon game drive. Come with?"

She shouldn't, but having a sauna in her tent in the afternoon heat, thinking of Carlo and reminiscing was a bad idea. Sitting in the kitchen with Liz, talking babies, didn't appeal. Liz would poke and prod at her until every last secret was out.

Even worse, Carlo could come search her out and put her through another one of his interrogations like the previous night. Her stomach twisted. Right now, she would do anything to avoid Carlo. If she wasn't here he couldn't talk to her.

She dropped her gaze, trying to look uninterested. "Who's going?" If Carlo wasn't going then she could relax and enjoy the game drive and be sure not to see him for at least four hours. Then it would be bedtime and a whole twelve hours would have passed without her seeing him. With Angelo she'd be able to control the conversation. He might be hot as hell, but he didn't embody every single sexual memory like Carlo.

"Natalia and I."

"A drive like this morning?" She couldn't stomach that again.

"Nope, the tourist version." He searched her face. "Noel has gone bushwhacking with some of the rangers. Carlo and Dino are staying to do some work while the guests are out."

She digested the information. *Shouldn't you be doing the same?* She bit back the retort and looked away.

As if he read her mind he added, "They're working on Southeast Asia stuff. Carlo's baby."

A ripple went up her back and spread like cold fingers over her scalp. Nothing in his expression gave her the idea that he was toying with her, testing her.

She gave an elaborate sigh. "Twisting my arm, are you?" she said, before smiling at him. "Give me a minute."

She went to the bathroom at the back of the tent and stared at the mirror.

God, she was in so much trouble.

She rinsed her face, brushed her hair into a fresh ponytail, and grabbed her fleece. She met Angelo outside and together they set off toward the entrance where the Land Rovers waited.

As they walked she tried to recall if Peppe had ever seen Sarah. He'd known about her child, but hadn't made enquiries beyond approving her accommodation outside of the pilots' digs. There had been no reason for Peppe to believe Sarah was Carlo's child. She glanced at Angelo. He had no reason to come find her in the staff camp. She wouldn't be surprised if a couple of weeks down the line Angelo knocked on her apartment's door. That would be dangerous, because if Angelo ever saw Sarah, he'd almost certainly recognize his brother's eyes in that little pixie face.

For the first time since Carlo's arrival, resigning and leaving Dar es Salaam seemed unavoidable. She'd already had one Carlevaro mess up her life; she didn't need the complimentary services of his brother to boot. It would be polite to resign with the sixty days' notice requested by her contract, but she'd be willing to run. It would be the only option, really. Mentally preparing herself for a quick exit, she sat back as the Land Rover drove off.

Chapter Ten

Simone enjoyed the game drive. Angelo was attentive in a date-like way, which she liked more than she'd expected she would. But she couldn't relax with him and he kept his comments impersonal. With Natalia in the vehicle, the banter was light.

How had Carlo been with her in the beginning, during those first few days of her mentorship? Carlo had fought their mutual attraction, and although he had been warm and friendly, he'd admitted struggling to keep away from her. In itself, this internal battle had fueled her desire for him, that forbidden something that had to be savored. She'd never thought it would be so good.

She sighed. Angelo had his own brand of Carlevaro charm, and probably treated every woman that crossed his path like this. She glanced at him; he was quiet, at ease. Both brothers were tall and dark, the handsome, broody type. Angelo's hair was longer than Carlo's, an obstinate curl falling over his forehead. He was sexy in his white T-shirt and cargo shorts, and a far cry from the hardcore executive Carlo had turned into. Carlo radiated power, while Angelo gave off a different vibe. He was rich, good-looking, and she got the impression he couldn't give a damn about any of it. He had the same hands as Carlo though—long, strong fingers with trim cut nails and fine dark hair covering the backs of his hands where they sloped down to his palms. She swallowed. Those hands were so familiar, and yet they weren't *his*.

His gaze rested on her, and when meeting his searching eyes, she had to look away. His signals were clear. If she had Liz's nonchalance regarding sex, their trip could have taken an interesting turn. Especially if she'd been willing to do as Ross had insinuated and sleep her way to the top. She groaned inwardly. Maybe she was misinterpreting his body language because parts of him were like Carlo. Some relief from the built-up tension, sexual and otherwise, would be welcome.

Mentally she withdrew from the conversation and sat silently through the rest of the game drive. Angelo might be Carlo's brother, but he hadn't yet cultivated Carlo's sacred segregation of work from pleasure.

Her thoughts kept turning to Sarah, and her heart contracted with longing. She checked her watch; it was the time she'd usually be home after an overnight flight. Sarah would help her cook dinner, something mommy and toddler friendly, which they would eat together at the low coffee table in the lounge. Sarah would sit in her small pink plastic chair, and she would sit cross-legged on a cushion on the floor. Afterward, Sarah would have her bath, and she would sit with her, just chatting along. Bedtime would follow with a story and her daughter falling asleep almost as soon as the light was switched off. She loved their little evening routine, and Ruth kept to it when she stayed with Sarah. Soon it would be the longest she'd ever been separated from Sarah, and she couldn't bear thinking of it.

Angelo held his hand out to help her off the vehicle when they returned to the lodge after dark. When he held it for longer than necessary she pulled away and stuffed her hands into her pockets.

An *askari* waited for them at the entrance to the lodge. "You are eating in the *boma* tonight. Please follow me."

There was only one *askari*, and Simone seeped out a slow breath. She had no choice but to follow him with Angelo and Natalia to the enclosure on the outer edge of the lodge. So much for her twelve-hour escape plan. Carlo would be in the *boma*. She couldn't even sneak off to the kitchen for dinner, because it would be empty—the cooking would be happening over the barbeque that night. Even worse, she might stumble upon the latest sacrifice on Liz's chopping board whilst all alone.

She shivered and took a deep breath to calm herself. *He won't get under my skin.*

Glancing to the stars, she begged for strength. They were packed so tightly across the sky, there seemed to be no space for even one more. At her feet a snake of lamps showed the path to the wooden enclosure and she stepped inside the *boma* with fresh determination.

It felt like she'd landed in a nest of fireflies. She'd seen it so many times, yet every time the sight took her breath away. Hundreds of lamps hung at different heights from the trees inside the *boma*, and a campfire burned in the middle. Tables were set in crisp white linen with silver cutlery catching the light of the lamps like sparks. It was glamorously over the top, made more spectacular by the wild setting that surrounded them.

A waiter handed them warm, moist cloths for their hands, and another waiter was already standing nearby with cocktails.

Carlo stood at the fire, drink in hand, talking to Dino. Her skin tingled and her pulse quickened as he looked at her, and they locked eyes for a moment before Carlo glanced at his brother. Angelo stood by her side, so close that their shoulders touched. When Angelo brushed against her he didn't move away. *Marking his territory.* She took a small step away from him. Carlo glared at her and pressed his lips in a firm line before emptying his glass.

"Excuse me," she said to Natalia. "I'll be back."

"Can I get you some wine?" asked Angelo.

She didn't want to hang around having drinks with anybody, least of all Carlo. "I...no, thank you. We're flying tomorrow. I never drink the night before."

As she walked to the opening leading to the restrooms she caught Angelo's words to Natalia. "She can do with a drink, I've never come across such an uptight blonde before."

Natalia shot something back at him in Italian. By the tone of her voice, it sounded like a mother's reprimand. Simone would have laughed if she hadn't been too busy wishing that the night would swallow her and transport her to the other side of the world.

An enclosed walkway led to the restrooms, the way lit by lamps. It opened to communal twin hand basins, male and female toilets on either side with lamps lighting the basin and hand towels arranged in a hand-woven basket. She took her phone from her pocket. She wanted to phone Sarah and say good night, but there was no reception this far from the main areas of the camp. An *askari* would have to escort her back to the staff quarters—she couldn't sit through dinner with the Carlevaros. Not with that look of murder Carlo had in his eyes, Angelo with his charm on tap, and the rest of the group observing in silent amusement. At that moment, no distance was enough between her and the Carlevaros—all of them.

When she stepped out of the restroom footsteps sounded behind her, but she continued to wash her hands.

"How was the game drive?"

Her heart skipped a beat upon hearing Carlo's voice. This was a very bad idea. To be alone with him in a dark enclosure had always been...fun. Tonight, there was no allure in his voice, no soft promise to seduce her first with words, then hands, then lips. She took a shallow breath. Just the thought of him had desire pooling in her lower belly, a slow throb pulsing to her core. Even angry he was getting under her skin.

I'm so fucked.

Sarah, Sarah, Sarah.

She finished washing her shaking hands with care, using the time to get a grip. "It was great, we saw—"

"Spare me the details, please. I've stopped counting lions a long time ago." He cursed. "Stay away from Angelo." He spat out the words one by one, with undue emphasis.

She froze for a fraction of a second, and then plunged her hand down to grab a rolled hand towel from the basket. Did he think she had so little discretion and self-control? He really thought he had a right to meddle in her life? She sucked her breath in as she turned, tilting her head. "What?"

He stood a meter from her with arms folded and brows knitted. In the dark shadows of the lamps he could be the devil himself, he was so angry.

"Angelo will not respect your wishes to be left alone, employee or not," Carlo said.

She wanted to be left alone, all right, but not by Angelo. That Carlo was standing here warning her off his brother meant that he was jealous. That he could be jealous of Angelo was ridiculous. Didn't he know that he still had a hold over her, after four bloody miserable years? He actually cared. It meant he wouldn't leave her alone, and where would that leave her with Sarah?

"My brother is bad news, Simone." His tone was softer.

Bad news is better than no news, Mr. C.F.L. Carlevaro, she wanted to spit at him, but stopped herself just in time. That was no longer entirely true. Better late than never. She wasn't sure if this applied in her situation.

"Angelo's a reckless loner, used to getting what he wants." Carlo tossed up his hands in a frustrated gesture. "And disposes of women as if they have an expiry date."

Talking about Angelo would keep Sarah and their past from the conversation. "A spoilt brat, is he?"

Carlo raked his hands through his hair before he stuffed his fists into his pockets. He pursed his lips. "He has more than one girlfriend in Rome."

"That doesn't surprise me," she retorted. She could hardly imagine Carlo judging Angelo as a womanizer. She'd seen photos of Carlo with several women on the internet when she'd Googled him earlier. Just how busy had he been over the past four years? Most of the photos were of him with a toned, beautiful brunette, elegantly dressed with such an air of grace about her that the images had made Simone, with her long,

113

gangling limbs, feel like an oaf.

Carlo shook his head. "They're never of long standing."

"It runs in the family then," she challenged him. He was the first to drop his gaze.

"*Merda* Simone, Angelo has…issues."

Who didn't? Half of hers stemmed from the man in front of her.

He took a small step toward her. "I don't want you to get hurt."

"Too late for that," she murmured.

She dropped the twisted hand towel into the basket on the ground and tried to push past him. He stopped her with a hand on her arm.

"Simone, I honestly did try to phone you," he said, letting go of her. "I know it was too late, I know it's too late now, but I tried to track you down." His voice had reduced to a murmur. "I even phoned the contact on your employee health insurance form. Your next of kin was a dead end. I left messages for you, but you never called me back."

Her stomach twisted in a slow, agonizing coil, tighter than the hand towel she had wrung in her hands a moment ago. She could say nothing; her voice would give her away.

"Simone—" He gripped her shoulders.

She had no idea what he wanted from her. Whether it was forgiveness, closure, or a restart, she wasn't ready to give it to him.

She yanked away and rushed down the path, bumping into Natalia.

"Oh, sorry!" Natalia said, reaching out to steady her as she stumbled. "Nature calls."

Simone couldn't look at her. Natalia had eyes that saw everything, even in the dim light provided by the lanterns.

She swallowed hard and flashed her tourist smile. "Sorry, Natalia." She forced a chuckle. "That was close."

Natalia frowned, but let her go.

Simone stomped to the *boma*'s entrance, her breathing coming hard and fast. She stopped, took a deep breath, and released it. To wait for him to come back down the path would be even worse. She managed to contain her helpless, frustrated anger, pulled back her shoulders and stepped inside.

Back in the warm circle of the *boma* Simone searched for James but didn't spot him. Liz was behind the grill barbequing imported T-bone steaks and lobsters flown in from Dar es Salaam. Waiters circled around with silver plates of appetizers. She walked over to Liz, who was dressed in full chef's attire, appearing tired and wilting in the heat of the barbeque.

"I'm calling it a night." Simone wiped her brow where her agitation had settled in a burst of sweat. "I need to be up early tomorrow for our flight out."

"Lucky you," Liz said. "I must have your breakfast ready at seven for your departure at eight."

She glanced at the fire pit and then at the exit to the restrooms. There was no sign of Carlo. *Yet.* Her stomach was knotted into a ball of unmanaged stress. She needed to spend at least forty minutes running. There was nothing else legitimate to make the tension go away. "I'd like to go for a jog beforehand. Can you spare a ranger to go with me?"

"You'll have to ask James. Your group isn't going

on the game drive so someone should be available."

She pointed with her prong to the fire where James stood with Dino.

He saw them and Liz signaled to him with a wink. He introduced Dino to one of the guests who'd come to stand by the fire and came over.

"We can get you out at six for a jog, no problem," James said after a short discussion.

"Thanks, I owe you one."

Carlo entered the *boma*, looking straight at her as if his gaze was drawn by some magnetic force. She rushed off, meeting the *askari* who waited to escort guests back to their rooms. She couldn't get away from him quickly enough.

****

Carlo cursed as Simone disappeared with the *askari*. If he could just get her to talk, but every time he'd approached her she'd clammed up. His anger at being unable to connect with her had surged when he'd seen Angelo standing next to her, so close they'd touched. He had known Angelo would toy around, because that was what he did. Games. It was all just games. Would Simone play? *Dio*, the idea made his hands itch to wring his brother's neck.

He must change his approach and come up with a new strategy. He had to subdue the crazy need to take Simone into his arms every time he saw her, stop fantasizing about her long legs circling his hips, those soft lips yielding to his. For once he couldn't blame Angelo for having his mind in the gutter, for he wanted to oust him from his territory.

He shoved a hand through his hair. He hadn't needed Natalia to walk into his tête-à-tête with Simone either. It had been hard to come by; getting Simone cornered alone had become impossible after their first exchanges, when he'd been forced on the defense every time. Natalia knew more than she should, and it left him with an unwelcome feeling of foreboding. Eliminating Natalia and her sixth sense from his mind, he stared at Liz where she stood talking to James.

He'd observed the short conversation between Simone, Liz, and James from the dark entrance, and they'd looked so much in cahoots that his whole being rioted. He sensed Simone was hiding something from him. That it could have to do with the poaching syndicate left him filled with dread.

He planned to intercept James, who was approaching some guests who stood alone. James didn't know about the grilling he'd subjected Simone to that afternoon, unless she'd told him. He had probed her for information about everyone, and she'd given him information about everyone else, except herself. James King could be just the man to cast some light on the evasive Simone Levin.

Chapter Eleven

Simone stepped out of her tent in a makeshift running ensemble. She took a breath of dew-filled air, trying to restore a sense of calm and control that she'd lacked ever since Carlo had barged back into her life. After their aborted conversation, she'd gone to her tent, had a short chat with Sarah, and a longer one with Ruth. She'd questioned Ruth about her suitcase, and Ross having to get into her apartment to pick it up. Ruth had gone with Sarah to the music group they joined on Tuesday afternoons, expecting one of the pilots to come around early in the evening. Simone could have kicked herself. Between Carlo and everything else she'd forgotten about Sarah's schedule.

At least Sarah had sounded happy to spend another few nights with Ruth, so she had nothing to worry about on that score. She was thankful for the prior few weeks together on vacation. They had given Sarah some time away from Ruth, and the two were playing catch-up.

She'd chickened out of giving Gabi a real account of what had been happening between her and Carlo and only sent her a message stating that all was panning out as planned. She was quietly grateful that university was back in full swing. Between classes, studying, and an attempt at a social life Gabi would let the report pass for another day.

She'd toyed with the idea of phoning her mom after she'd spoken to Sarah and Ruth, but she couldn't do it, not yet. For the rest of the night she'd dozed off, waking up with a jolt every few hours, Carlo's words loud in her mind as if he'd said them right into her ear in the silence of the night. Her next of kin contact had been a dead end.

At that time, there had only been one next of kin. Her mother.

With a sigh she gave a quick glance around the camp. There was no *askari* in sight, but some things were worth the risk. She hoped to exhaust herself to such an extent that she could manage to sleep. In the early morning light, she walked alone to the main guest areas.

The game drives had departed, and quiet had settled over Carlevaro Rufiji Camp. The dawn chorus had dispersed to find food, and when she got to the lodge's entrance a ranger waited for her in his Land Rover.

She greeted the ranger and clambered into the row behind him. She'd hardly settled when Carlo stepped up and heaved himself into the seat next to her.

Her blood drained to her feet, numbness settling over her as her heartbeat lurched in panic. How could he? Couldn't he just leave her alone? She couldn't move; she couldn't run. There was no eject button that would by magic launch her back to her tent.

"We're good to go," said the ranger as he switched on the ignition and pulled away.

"Slept well?" Carlo's voice was soft, pleasant, and his gaze burned on her.

With her faux pas from the day before still fresh,

she grimaced. "Of course, always."

"Mind if I join you?" He was painfully polite.

She had no choice. "Not as long as you keep up."

"I can keep it up, don't you worry." He grinned.

Blood rushed to her cheeks. *Damn the man for teasing me.*

"I do a kilometer under four minutes. The airstrip is four hundred and fifty meters, so we need to go up and down twenty-three times."

"No problem."

"In forty minutes." She hoped he would pass out on the first round.

"Got it."

He gazed into the bush and they fell silent as the vehicle hit the road to the airstrip. She glanced at him. Carlo had packed for running. He wore running shoes and shorts, exposing his well-toned calves and thighs. Dark stubble carpeted his cheeks. Her fingers itched to touch it, to feel the roughness of it under her fingertips, to explore his face and let her fingers wander to the smooth skin behind his ear and down his neck. A wave of desire engulfed her. She knew what was under those clothes, and she wanted every inch of it. She shifted closer to the edge of the seat, away from him.

When they arrived at the airstrip twenty minutes later they drove the length of it to make sure there were no animals on it or grazing nearby. Already adrenaline rushed through her. Lions lay so flat in the grass here that they could go unnoticed until they swished their tails or lifted their heads.

"All clear for now." The ranger smiled as he stopped the vehicle so they could get out.

They stretched for a minute. The morning air was

still cool, and she was thankful for it. Her gut told her she was about to be tortured.

He yawned and shrugged off a final stretch. "Shall we?"

She nodded and they took off at a moderate pace toward the airplane parked on the other side. The ranger drove in their wake, ready for them to jump in at any given moment should something come charging through the bush. They continued in silence, building up speed with each lap they took.

Simone had to give it to Carlo. Not only was he keeping up, he was outpacing her. At the end of forty minutes they stopped by the DHC Twin Otter, which was parked off the runway. She felt sick from the exertion, lightheaded from forcing herself to continue on an empty stomach. Sweat trickled down her back; her hair was wet at the base of her neck. Carlo had seen her like this before, for they'd run together in the past. Facing him again like this—tomato red with wilted hair—was liberating. There was no more pretense—except that she was trying not to collapse.

Thank God he didn't seem to notice that she was about to die.

"You still give a good chase, Mona," he said, grinning as he bent down to stretch.

Hearing him call her by his nickname for her didn't help the churn in her stomach. Surprised by the rush of heat to her cheeks, she stretched down to hide her raw emotions. To hear him call her Mona, his voice endearing with just that dusting of an Italian accent, was a pure pleasure.

She dropped her head lower, aiming to get her nausea under control, but she had to blink several times to stop the welling of tears. It was just this sick feeling, she told herself, but it was much more than that.

She might have signed up for a lot, but she hadn't signed up for this. Carlo was turning on the charm and it would weaken her defenses. Worst of all, she only had her cocky self to blame, spitting out some random running data for him to chew on.

"You're not slow yourself," she murmured eventually, wishing she could lie down on the dirt of the runway to catch her breath. There was no way she could admit she'd had to work to keep up, and that she'd ran herself to death's door the past half hour, repeating *Sarah* in her head with every step she'd taken. She'd never gotten her fitness level back to what it had been pre-Sarah.

Slowing down during the run would have given Carlo food for thought. She had, after all, run marathons before pregnancy and motherhood interfered. She didn't want to tell him a tall tale about why she didn't run like she used to; one lie usually led to another and she had no intention of getting entangled with them. She might just as well show him the C-section scar, which graced her pubic hairline, and make him prod the wobble of skin that wouldn't go away.

He walked off, stretching his arms, and she let out a shaky breath, relieved that he was no longer staring at her. A few meters from the airplane he stopped abruptly. She straightened up as he went down on his haunches, staring at something on the ground.

"Look at this, Simone," he called and indicated to the ranger that he must join them.

Simone stepped closer and saw shoe tracks in the sand.

"How old do you think these are?" Carlo pointed them out to the ranger as he joined them.

"They're fresh, from last night or early this morning," the ranger said without hesitation.

Simone frowned. "That can't be possible, I parked the plane two days ago. Nobody—"

She looked down at Carlo, shaking her head. He straightened, eyebrows knitted.

"Are you sure these are from last night?" Carlo asked the ranger.

"Yes," he said. Squatting, he pointed with his finger. "They can't be more than, say, three or four hours old. See, the silhouette is still sharp and nothing walked here since. The sand hasn't crumbled or blown in. No evidence of wind movement. These are fresh. If it were a leopard's prints we could've tracked it down."

Carlo muttered something indiscernible as he walked around, following the tracks but not stepping on them.

The ranger walked with him, deciphering. "There are two sets of footprints here, see." He pointed to a different type of sole imprinted in the sand. It was smaller than the other. "This was a skinny guy. The other one, well, heavier boot, heavier man, deeper groove in the sand."

Simone followed the men, not sure what to make of it. Someone had been here, stalking around her plane. A pang of dread shot through her.

The ranger strode to the edge of the airstrip and followed the tracks from there. "They came from this corner, someone waited here." He pointed to another track, which was barely perceptible except for a soft ridge in the sand. "But the other two went here.

Something was lying in the grass here where the one waited. See how flat it is? Then two walked here to the plane, and there was a scuffle. Notice how the tracks overlap each other?"

Simone followed the tracks with Carlo; now that the ranger pointed it out it was clear. Feet crisscrossed over each other, indecisive in their movement. It was right at the hold of the DHC Twin Otter. She locked eyes with Carlo. *The poachers?* She mouthed to him, but Carlo, with the smallest shake of his head, indicated she shouldn't say anything.

"And what happened then?" he asked the ranger.

"Well, they walked back into the bush. Going around the plane. Why, I don't know."

"Do you have your mobile with you?" Carlo asked.

"Me? No." Simone shook her head.

Carlo checked his watch. "We better get going, it's already quarter past seven."

"I think we should—" she started, but Carlo stopped her by taking hold of her arm with a warning squeeze.

"Get back for a shower and breakfast. We're running late." He smiled at the ranger, but didn't let go of her arm; instead, his hand reached for her elbow where it nestled in a possessive clasp. They walked to the vehicle, and as much as she wanted to shrug him off, she couldn't. His sure touch calmed her as much as the idea of someone sneaking around her plane in the dead of night freaked her out.

When the ranger stopped in front of the lodge's entrance they both got out and rushed down the path. At the split toward the staff quarters and the guest areas, they stopped. There was a new energy between them and they both spoke at the same time. Carlo stopped and let her talk.

"I'm going to have to do a very thorough pre-flight inspection. If anybody tampered with our aircraft—"

He nodded. "We'll go earlier. I want to take some photos of those footprints before they get trampled."

"I can't believe it. They are risking their lives walking around the bush in the dead of night."

"These poachers grew up in the bush. They know what they're doing." Carlo raked his hands through his hair. "I'm sure they wanted to plant the tusks of the elephant we saw yesterday."

Simone shook her head. "I'd be surprised if they got into the aircraft. I've got the key."

He searched her face before he looked toward the path leading to the guest areas. "I'll meet you on the deck in thirty minutes."

"Sure," she said, glad that she wasn't one for elaborate morning routines.

Back at her tent she took a quick shower and then tossed all her things into her cabin bag and backpack. She carried her luggage to the deck. Natalia and Dino were already eating breakfast and she greeted them. She hovered; her stomach yelled that it needed to be fed, especially after her exercise.

"Do join us, please, Simone," Natalia said, waving for her to sit down.

"I'm waiting for Carlo," Simone said. "We need to do some paperwork before we can fly out."

"I'm sure he'll be here soon," Dino said. "It's unusual for him to be late. Please have something to eat."

"We went running this morning—" Simone

clamped her mouth shut. It wasn't her place to elaborate.

Dino stood and pulled out a chair. She caved in, sat down with a murmured thank you and took a croissant to busy her mouth.

"A run?" Natalia sounded surprised. "I hoped that Carlo would leave his running shoes behind for a bit of downtime."

Dino sighed, gesturing with his hands. "You know that's how he deals with the stress, Talia. It's either running or flying or working. There's nothing in between."

Simone digested this tidbit. Did this mean he had no partner? He'd told her once that sex with her was his favorite workout. She'd always been the one to drag him out for a run. Maybe the lack of action would explain why he ran like a demon.

She forced her mind away from the thought and the glowing heat that had settled in her core since seeing him again and focused on her croissant. It tasted so good, the buttery, feather-light consistency melting in her mouth. She could eat a mountain of those.

She took in the empty chairs around the table. "Where's Angelo?" she asked between bites.

There was a brief exchange of glances between Natalia and Dino.

"He'll be here soon, he tends to be a late riser," Natalia said.

"We're behind schedule too." She smiled, wanting to reassure them. "If our pre-flight checks are fine we should be leaving at around eight forty-five."

They ate in silence.

When Carlo walked in a couple of minutes later his

lips were set in a straight line, cutting deep brackets around his mouth. He was so thoroughly pissed off, her pulse quickened. At first he seemed too deep in thought to acknowledge the others, but when he sat down at the table, he gave Dino and Natalia a curt nod. He stared at her for a long moment. Heat rose to her cheeks and she dropped her gaze to avoid his open scrutiny. Why was he this angry? He studied her as if she fisted all the answers in her hand, if only she would unfurl her fingers and show him. She dropped her gaze. Half of that was true.

Dino and Natalia sipped at their coffees and ignored Carlo. Simone had never seen him angry. Unsure of what to do she busied herself with her own breakfast, eating at double speed and wishing she were in the staff mess. She felt uncomfortable eating with the Carlevaro clan, not because of Natalia and Dino, but because of Carlo.

"Are you ready, Simone?" Carlo asked. He took a tentative sip of his double espresso.

"Yes, all packed and ready to go."

"Good," he said as he stood. He drained his cup and took a croissant from the basket on the table. "Let's go. We'll meet you at the airstrip," he said to Natalia and Dino. "I've tried to wake Angelo up. Make sure he's there or we leave without him."

There was an awkward silence around the table, and Natalia nodded. Dino didn't respond. Simone fell in next to Carlo as he strode to the entrance.

"What's wrong?" she asked. "Besides the obvious?" She hoped he understood that she referred to the poaching issues.

"Angelo has never graduated from his teenage

years," he said shortly. "Allowing him to take over this branch is probably the biggest mistake. Maybe it's the kick in the butt he needs. Time will tell."

"I see." There was nothing else to say, as Carlo fell back into contemplation, his brow dark and furrowed.

As they passed the kitchen she mumbled a soft excuse to say goodbye to Liz.

She peeked in past the swinging door. "We're off, I'll see you soon."

Liz looked up from where she was discussing a menu with her staff. "Sure, let's hope we have more time to catch up next time."

"Take care and don't overdo it."

"What a laugh," Liz said, shaking her head. "I have sleepless nights already and it's only the beginning of high season."

She caught up with Carlo at the entrance, where the Land Rover waited for them. Noel sat in the driver's seat with one of the Kenyan rangers next to him. Carlo must have arranged for Noel to drive them to the airstrip.

When they got to the runway, Noel got out with his camera. The ranger inspected the tracks, going on his haunches. After a few minutes he came back, interpreting the tracks to Carlo, who listened attentively. The two different rangers' stories were the same.

Simone waited for Noel to take pictures of the tracks. When he was finished she unlocked the pilot's door of the plane and pulled herself into the pilot's seat. For a moment she stared at the cockpit. Everything looked normal, just as she'd left it. Carlo came to stand next to her and she looked down at him. "Everything seems fine. Is Noel finished with the photos? Can we start?" she asked.

He shook his head and stroked through his hair in frustration. "There are fingerprints on the hold's door."

"They could be anybody's. Mine, or the staff loading the luggage." But they could also belong to those who'd stalked around the plane earlier.

"I know." He scrubbed at his face with his hands. "Either way I won't get the police involved. We can't afford to have this leak."

"It's going to get out at some point, Carlo. People talk. Employees talk even more." They were talking about the poaching, but it applied equally to her inherent fear of him finding out about Sarah. A mere slip of the tongue by someone who knew about Sarah could reveal everything. If Carlo discovered her secret via the grapevine... If he'd been angry this morning... She swallowed but forced herself to hold his gaze as a cold shiver shot down her spine.

He pursed his lips, seeming to struggle to contain his frustration. "Unlock the hold, please."

"Sure." She hadn't forgotten about the possibility of elephant tusks being in the hold. She climbed down the small protruding step and Carlo stepped aside to allow her to get down.

Noel and the ranger stood close as she walked underneath the wing to the hold. As she pushed the key into the hole she paused. The area around the lock was newly scratched. "Look at these," she said, tracing the fresh scratches with her fingers.

"I've noticed," Carlo said, his gaze lingering on her hand. His eyes darted to hers and the tips of her fingers burned, as if she'd pressed them to a hot stove. She snatched her hand away. God, he would be thinking she was trying to press fresh prints over the old ones, ruining evidence.

Her hands trembled now, but she managed to swing the door open and everybody drew closer to peek into the dark space.

It was empty.

"Let me get inside." Carlo nudged her aside with a soft squeeze on her shoulder.

He jumped and clambered in and on all fours to inspect the whole space.

"There's nothing," he said, sighing.

"I think they tried to stow the tusks last night, but for some reason they were unsuccessful," Noel said. "I'll send a team out to see how far they can follow these tracks and where they lead."

"They failed last night, but they'll try again soon enough. When will the cameras be up?" Carlo asked.

"We're rigging them. This location is the problem. We don't want animals to trample the expensive equipment." Noel looked around at the airstrip. "We camouflage the cameras and will use the trees we have here, though the good ones are a bit far off. We know what to do. We'll catch them sooner or later, don't worry about it."

"I don't care about the expense. Just get me some footage of what's happening here," Carlo said.

"Can't you put someone on guard at night to watch the planes?" Simone asked. Didn't that make the most sense? She didn't want to fly a plane that had been tampered with.

"That would defeat the purpose. We want to catch them, not just put their little project on hold." Carlo shook his head.

"The poachers won't come close if they think there is a welcoming party." Noel added. "We catch them on camera and we'll have a legal foot to stand on."

The men shook hands. Noel and the anti-poaching ranger got in the Land Rover to return to the lodge. Simone retrieved the checklist she had left on her seat. As the dust cloud from the vehicle settled she joined Carlo. He stood by the hold, arms folded, staring into the dark space.

"They left us alone in the middle of nowhere without a ranger." Simone liked the bush, but had spent enough time in it to have a healthy respect for it. If she'd been alone she would've waited in the plane until the rest arrived. That Carlo was there didn't help; it wasn't exactly safe to be alone with him either.

He shook his head. "Best we get cracking then. The others will be here soon enough."

Simone scanned the bush but couldn't see or sense anything dangerous. She blindly stared at her checklist, her hands still trembling slightly. She had to keep it business, and with what had passed that morning nothing could be simpler. There was no need to return to their unfinished conversation from last night. "I call and you check?"

"Yes, ma'am."

In twenty minutes they checked the fuel, oil, lights, doors and wheels, and made sure that nothing was dripping or dangling. Carlo was polite and efficient, acting like a star colleague instead of her ex-lover turned boss. It was confusing, and a superficial calm settled over them.

Simone laughed when Carlo swung the propeller

then hung on the wing strut to make sure it was solid. "Still attached or must I get the duct tape?" she quizzed.

He chuckled, having relaxed a bit after the morning's upheaval. He came to stand next to her. "That's all for the exterior of the plane, let's get inside before that lion strolls too close."

Her head jerked up and she glanced to where he nodded. There was nothing but an empty dirt runway, lined with a swath of short grass and a flock of guinea fowl scuffling through it.

He laughed. "Got you there, Mona."

She exhaled a raspy breath but her heart drummed in her chest. "Don't do that! Hell." She burst out laughing. "You might have forgotten Joshua and his stalking leopard stories, but I haven't."

His gray eyes, still bright with laughter, turned serious. "You're right. I forgot about Josh...*buon Dio*, it's been so long."

The atmosphere had changed between them. He stood too close; his scent teased her. His shirt fell open at the collar and the thatch of dark hair on his muscled chest tempted her to caress his skin. This was more dangerous than any leopard that could ambush them.

"Sign this." She shoved the checklist out to him.

As he took it from her his fingers brushed against hers and her breath hitched. He took the pen from her and she made sure he couldn't touch her again.

Carlo signed the checklist and when he passed the document back to her didn't let go immediately. "I regret many things, Mona. But I never regretted those six weeks."

Simone looked away, not wanting to meet his gaze. She hadn't regretted them either. Not until later.

Him being sweet was hard to stomach. If he continued to carry on like this she would crumble into a heap, begging him to make love to her. Her body craved his touch with an intensity she could not subdue. It was a need that became more overpowering with each passing hour in his presence. The tension of their unresolved past was layered, at times rather thinly, between pure sexual lust and the need to start with a blank page.

Her love for him had been real four years ago but she was no longer the naïve girl who had fallen in love with him. Her younger self had been so desperate for a man's unconditional love that she'd given him everything without thinking ahead. She sighed, a deep, silent sigh that made the stone in her stomach feel heavier. She had to put Sarah first. She couldn't subject her daughter to the same upbringing she'd had. If Carlo learned about Sarah and laid a claim to their daughter, his would be a whimsical presence, in and out, off and on. It would be gratifying to tell him about Sarah, have a good head-butting with him for leaving her, but it would not lead to a happy ending for anybody, least of all her daughter.

"Please don't call me Mona," she whispered. She took the papers and turned away from him. "The others are coming. Let's wrap up."

Chapter Twelve

Carlo sat back as the plane flew on autopilot. Next to him, Simone shifted in her seat, and he shot a glance at her. Openly staring at her didn't work—it made her so bloody nervous. Her eyes, which had always shone with lightness of life, had become permanently guarded and the laughter had burned out of them. She appeared haunted.

This morning she'd almost passed out after their run, and he couldn't shake the feeling that she was hiding something from him with measured intention. Suspicion had started to grind into his very bones. Why had she gone for a run in the first place? She hadn't been up to it. She'd lagged behind on the flat course, which would have been a stroll in the park for her years ago.

James King had been useless the previous evening, turning the conversation around every time he'd asked him something about Simone. When James had explained that Simone had planned to go for a run that morning it was natural for him to tell King he'd go with. He ran every day at home, and his body felt edgy from the lack of exercise.

The dark half-moons under Simone's eyes were more than sleepless nights; he'd figured that much out. What if she'd been trying to get rid of the last of the incriminating evidence, sneaking around the bush in the middle of the night, meeting up with the poachers to stow those tusks, or intentionally stopping them from putting them on the plane? He couldn't stomach the thought, and that the one footprint in the sand was just about her size...in his mind's eye the vision of her fingers tracing those scratches around the keyhole popped up. *Fuck.*

A pilot had to be involved, but that it could be her...he closed his eyes for a second, then stared out of the side window. Why had she left Carlevaro Air in the first place? And why had she returned? He hadn't had time to look at her employee file, but he might ask one of the HR people to scan its contents for him. In the meantime, he wouldn't think her guilty of anything until it had been proven otherwise.

He should ask Julia to get some information out of Peppe.

Thinking of Peppe, he sighed and glanced back at the cabin where Dino and Angelo sat next to each other. Angelo appeared worse for wear and he cursed under his breath. He had his doubts about Angelo's ability to oversee this branch of the company. Angelo didn't have it in him, but he had been so keen to try, so desperate to prove himself.

When Carlo had taken over from his father, it had been a rough ride until he'd found his feet. He'd paused his entire life to come to grips with the job, which still kept slipping from his grasp, like it was doing now. Angelo had had a late-night drinking binge with James King, with the usual side effects. Earlier he'd tried to drag Angelo out of bed to ensure he got up in time for their flight. How was it going to work when no one was there to kick his ass?

At least Julia was back in their lives, but an understanding sister was not the solution Angelo needed. If only there was a woman who could get through to Angelo, he could have some peace of mind. But Angelo hadn't ever let anybody close.

Carlo glanced at Simone. She'd been the only woman he'd ever let in, and she'd walked away. Physically the distance between them wasn't even half a meter, but on every other level it was miles. She stared out of the front window, regularly checking the instrument panel in front of them. They hadn't spoken since take-off. True, it had taken him ten weeks to make that godforsaken phone call, but she could give him a break.

In the past days his attraction to her had intensified, as had his confusion at the vigor with which she fought their mutual attraction. It was still there between them, tangible and dense. She hadn't been giving him mixed signals. She didn't want anything to do with him. In that moment, he would forgive her anything if he could just have one bit of her back. He sighed with a grunt. Just a taste of the woman she'd been four years ago.

"Pardon?" Simone cast him a sidelong glance.

He blinked and pulled away from his tangled thoughts. "Nothing."

She didn't look at him again. "I was thinking about this trafficking situation," she said, staring at the instruments. "I suspect they won't try to plant those tusks soon. Someone will warn them."

He shrugged off the thought that it could have been her who rang the warning bells. "They've probably been warned already. Noel is trying to keep it undercover, with the anti-poaching rangers from

Kenya." He shook his head. "At some point, they'll try to move it. Either by air or road."

The landscape on the ground changed as they flew northwest over the green valleys of Morogoro, to the duller landscape of Dodoma and the farmlands. They were flying low enough to see individual settlements that spread along the few roads they flew over. For kilometers it was untouched earth that stretched beneath them, with sisal plantations edging along the mountains.

"If you think about it, the only time they could plant those tusks is when a plane is parked unattended. This happens three times a week at Rufiji, when the pilot who does the island route to the Serengeti overnights at the Selous the next day." She glanced at him. "I'm not sure whether pilots who fly the day flights ever leave the plane unattended. It would be the exception and not the rule. I never do. There's no time."

He rubbed his chin, missing his stubble. "Which route is that?"

"It's a new one, about one and a half years old." She twisted a curl behind her ear. "We fly to Mafia, Zanzibar, Pemba, then directly to the Serengeti for an overnight. So island tourists can hop to the safari destinations. The next day we fly from the Serengeti to Ugalla, Ruaha and then to the Selous, for tourists who want both a northern and southern Tanzania experience. Kigosi is an optional stop. The third day we fly from the Selous to Dar es Salaam in time for most international flights."

He recalled Peppe mentioning the new route in a quarterly meeting some time ago. "This is over and above the normal Ruaha and Selous flight that doesn't overnight?"

"Yes. The route is always full because it suits the safari circuit so well."

"We need to investigate that," he said. "I wondered whether they would dare do it in broad daylight, maybe storing the poached goods in the refrigerators we use for food supplies. Those are empty during return flights."

"Maybe, but moving something of that shape would be difficult with the pilot overseeing the loading. And it would involve the kitchen staff at Rufiji—"

She'd cut her sentence short.

"And?" he prompted. The implication had hit her.

She hesitated. "That would mean that…"

She trailed off and he glanced at her.

That the chef and lodge manager at Rufiji could be involved in this poaching syndicate had been his first gut feeling. James was nervous during their meeting, but after spending time with him he thought it unlikely.

Maybe he had lost his human instinct. "You've known the Kings for long?"

She turned to look at him, but he kept his eyes on the controls.

"Liz started at Carlevaro East Africa ages ago. I've only got to know her since they've been at Rufiji." She paused, possibly gauging how much he needed to know. "She grew up in Kenya. James came from England to manage a neighboring lodge in the Serengeti and that's where they met. His parents have old money. I don't think—"

"They've been at Rufiji for two years. The poaching escalated in the past six months, so it doesn't add up." He held her gaze. "But to get such an operation going takes time."

"I suppose so." Simone nibbled at her bottom lip. "I can't imagine them being involved."

"Changes in family circumstances can make people do strange things." He shrugged. "Maybe James isn't as well off as you believe and he is worried about the future of his family."

She frowned. "What do you mean?"

"We pay our staff well, but you never know why people feel a financial strain, especially at home, with changes coming."

Simone shifted in her seat. Why did such an everyday conversation make her feel uncomfortable?

"So, you know?" she asked, eventually.

"Know what? That Liz is pregnant?" He gave her a sheepish grin. "Yes."

He kept his gaze on her, warming to the topic. "I caught her words when I walked into the kitchen two nights ago." His smile deepened. "Then I saw her face last night as she barbequed the lobster. She looked as if she was going to be sick. It adds up."

Simone didn't smile, but looked away. "Poor Liz. She's suffering from morning sickness. I hope it passes soon for her sake. But it's still early days."

He sighed. Simone was withdrawing again, this time from a conversation that, for once, wasn't a minefield of their past. He tried to suppress the undercurrent of frustration.

"Tell her she must take time off, we can always find a replacement."

He searched her face. She didn't answer, but a blush flushed her cheeks.

Her hand had curled into a fist where it rested on

her thigh. He would have reached for her hand and covered it with his own if he'd dared. "This is a Third World country, I'd hate for her to risk her health and that of her baby because of work...or anything really." He sighed. "It's not worth it, don't you agree?"

She fiddled with the switches on the overhead panel for the air conditioning in the cabin and directed the fan into her back, letting her curls dance in the wind. "I'll pass on those instructions from the big boss."

****

Simone turned the aircraft to align it with the airstrip of the Ngorongoro Crater. She couldn't wait for the flight to be over. She was no stranger to family changes and strain on one's pocket, but it hadn't been her place to let slip that Liz was pregnant.

After they'd dropped the subject of Liz and the poaching, Carlo had sat next to her, his mouth pursed in a grim, thoughtful line, his hand rubbing his cheek in a repetitive, pensive way. She worried he was going to ask her something—anything—that would cause her to incriminate the Kings, herself, or somebody else, never mind Sarah, who was always on her mind. She had yet to meet a mother with a three-year-old whose universe didn't revolve around her child. That she'd managed not to spill the beans yet was a miracle in itself.

She couldn't write off his words, that Liz shouldn't take a risk with her baby. What would it have been like if he'd been there during her pregnancy? If he'd known about the pregnancy, he would have cared very much. His genuine concern for Liz, a person whom he'd never met before, made her think, for a few weak moments, that she should tell him about Sarah. But once she told him there could be no erasing the words and she'd have to deal with the consequences.

Through a break in the clouds she got an eagle's view over the caldera. There was no mist and they landed smoothly, if she disregarded Carlo's hand on hers, which had become even more possessive since the first day. Before he let go he'd given her hand a soft squeeze.

Carlo opened his door and the cold hit her. They were no longer on the warm plains of the greater Selous, but over two thousand meters above sea level during winter. She got off the plane and put on her fleece.

The others disembarked, pulling on jackets. Simone watched the camp driver unpack the hold as she tried to avoid Natalia's ever-present, searching gaze.

"Can I close here?" Carlo asked from the top of the air stair, looking at her where she stood at the bottom.

"Yes, I'll lock up on my side." She felt uneasy. The plane would be parked for the night at an airstrip a forty-minute drive from the lodge. It was in the middle of nowhere by any standards. Since the revelations in the Selous, she feared that someone watched every move made by a Carlevaro pilot, with the intention of stowing poached goods.

She double-checked that they locked every door and hold, Carlo following in her wake.

"She'll be all right." Carlo gave the aircraft a pat on the wing strut.

"I'm just nervous," Simone said.

"I know." He glanced at her. "It's only one night, and it's not the Selous. Come."

They continued to the car, where the others were

seated out of the nippy wind. Carlo held the door for her to slide in next to Angelo. She had no choice, and as Carlo got in next to her she slumped in the warm hollow between the brothers. It was almost cozy, if she wasn't aware of the raucous pounding of her heart, which surely both of the Carlevaros could hear.

The road to the camp was a red mud track following the rim of the crater. Occasionally the dense foliage parted, giving them a peek to the caldera, but mostly the path contoured along tall trees, which faded into the rising mist. It was impossible to see far into the caldera, and after a discussion of the weather the group fell silent.

"We'll finish the data we started collating, Simone," Carlo said after a while.

She grasped her hands together, inwardly protesting. She dreaded sitting through another dissection of the staff's rotational schedules. "Sure."

"We'll be able to put in a decent couple of hours' work." Carlo sighed as he leaned back in his seat, brushing his shoulder with hers, sending a ripple down her arm, which spread to the rest of her body.

"I need to catch up with Rome," said Dino. "Our month-end figures from Southeast Asia came through this morning."

"Yes, I saw the emails," said Carlo. "I must focus on what's happening in the Selous and Ruaha. We'll talk about those numbers later today."

"No problem," Dino said.

Simone suppressed a groan; she'd be cornered with Carlo the whole afternoon.

The Ngorongoro Crater Lodge was the biggest hotel in the group's East Africa portfolio and she'd never stayed there before. It was not one of their overnight stops, and with the airstrip so far from the lodge it had always been a case of landing and taking off directly.

On arrival the lodge manager directed them to the lounge area, where tall floor-to-ceiling windows opened over the vista of the crater. Double volume windows stretched the impressive length of the lounge and dining room. She could not step closer to admire the view, as the manager approached them, but she felt giddy with seeing the lodge for the first time. She hovered with the group, uncertain of where to go.

"I only have the family house available for you," the manager addressed the group. "But it has three en suite rooms." The manager gave her a quizzical stare. Why give her that look? She was in no position to probe about her own bed for the night—yet.

"That's perfect, we don't need more." Carlo looked around the empty lounge area. All the guests had departed to the crater for a full day's game drive.

"It doesn't have views—" the manager started to apologize.

"We don't need views, we'll be working. Please put some tables together for us in the dining room and we can get started."

The manager got the message not to dawdle and strode to the reception area to give his orders to the staff, then came back to their party.

"We'll serve lunch at one." He indicated the dining room, where the staff was putting together the tables.

Carlo nodded and the manager took Angelo and Dino off on their site inspection.

"I'm going to have a look outside, I haven't been

here for ages." Natalia followed the porters outside, leaving her and Carlo alone.

Simone waited, not yet dismissed and with nowhere to go.

Her luggage had left with the porters and she had no idea where it had gone. She hoped it wasn't the family house. It sounded too intimate. The house was separated from the rest of the hotel, and used by small groups or families traveling to the Crater.

She sighed deeply, zipping her fleece jacket up to her chin, hoping they would kindle fires in all the fireplaces in the lounge and dining area.

Carlo stood next to her, staring at the vista as the mist rolled over the rim in patches. "Don't sound so agonized. If we focus we should be done by the end of the day." He didn't turn to talk to her, but stood with his arms folded.

"It's not that," she said quickly, maybe too quickly. "I don't know where to go."

He glanced at her. "You've been here before?"

She shook her head.

Frowning, he looked at her. "We never flew here together?"

"Only to the airstrip. I've never been to the lodge."

He nodded absentmindedly, but he dropped his arms and reached for her hand. His fingers were warm as they curled around hers. She wanted to pull away but he had taken hold of her in a grip so gentle it felt as if they had melted into each other. "Come see," he said as he led her toward the massive windows that overlooked the vista. "My father's masterpiece. He won so many architectural awards for this lodge's design. It launched Carlevaro International, to be honest."

It was the first time he'd spoken of his father and the pride in his tone was tangible.

She let him tug her along, unable to let go of the soft grip that bound them. "Your father designed this lodge?"

"All of the Carlevaro hotels. He was an architect, didn't you know?" He glanced at her and shook his head. "I never spoke about my family, did I?" He sighed a curse. "How did I manage to not mention him? He was a brilliant man, a visionary."

She could remind him that talking had not always been first on their agenda four years ago. He had her chatting day in and out, but she'd never gotten to probe him about anything. He'd been as guarded with her then as she was with him now.

The urge to wipe the slate clean engulfed her. The only bit of warmth in her body had settled where their fingers locked. If only he would take her into his arms, the world would straighten. If he would hold her, kiss her...she would be unable to resist him. Deep down she didn't *want* to resist him, and that was the problem. One bubble at a time, he was pushing her to the boiling point. And with that would come the truth about Sarah.

They'd reached a glass-enclosed deck, which seemed to protrude out over the sheer plunge off the crater rim, giving way to unsurpassed views of the caldera below. The world dropped away, and thousands of feet below the green curve of the valleys flattened into the plains of the crater. Slow mist rose and parted, allowing glimpses of the wide expanse of grasslands and Lake Magadi with its pale pink stand of flamingoes. They were so high up that the world below seemed as untouched and unreachable as a watercolor painting.

He gave her fingers a soft squeeze. "How's that for a view?"

She sucked in a soft breath. "There's nothing like it in the entire world."

"No." He was staring at her. He'd been staring at her and not through the window at all.

She glanced at him but had to look away from the intensity of his eyes, which held her with such dearness that she knew he'd spoken of her. Inwardly she trembled, her murmur of need escalating to an oscillating quake.

"Simone, there's something you're not telling me. If you are in trouble, please—"

She extracted her fingers from his, but he cupped her elbow in his hand. She felt like crying, but the only sound that slipped out was a strangled choke as she jerked away from him. "I'm in no trouble, thank you."
Four years too late for that one.

She wanted to laugh but it hurt too much. She had to phone her mom, but it would only be to confirm her suspicions. Her mother had never passed on the message that Carlo had phoned. Her eyes misted over and she had to blink, looking away. "I just wish someone could show me where I'm to sleep tonight."

With me. He didn't say the words, but they hung between them, heavy and drenched.

She curled her fingers into her palms, her nails cutting into her skin. Any physical pain that would stop her from showing him where it truly ached. "It's such a fine bloody line, Carlo. Please understand." She swallowed the last words, biting hard on her lip to transfer the pain that had settled underneath her heart.

"I know."

Footsteps on the polished floor echoed through the room. She glanced over her shoulder.

"We've prepared a table for you in the dining area on the other side, Mr. Carlevaro. There's tea, coffee and scones," said the waiter, who gestured for them to move to the other side of the lounge.

She breathed out in relief that the intense atmosphere between them had been shattered with the waiter's arrival. She couldn't go on like this.

"Thank you." Carlo turned to her, his frustration barely disguised in the pull of his mouth. "There is a room for you in the house, Simone. There was nothing else available, and I didn't want you go to a neighboring lodge."

Of course not. He had to keep an eye on her—like he had since the moment she caught him staring at her from the doorway of the pilot's lounge. A shiver shot through her like an electric shock, leaving her cold to the bone. She was being watched…she was a suspect in their investigation, despite him saying she was the only one he trusted that first night. Maybe she was their prime suspect. Why else would she be here?

Was this the reason why he'd come for a run this morning? He'd hardly left her alone since their paths had crossed again. She'd been so blind, thinking only of Sarah, she hadn't seen the bigger picture.

"You're cold—I'll ask them to stoke the fires." Carlo nodded toward the dining room. "Do you need a break? It was a long flight."

She needed so much more than a break. "No, I want to get this done and dusted as much as you do." Did he really think she would meddle with poaching and smuggling?

Swearing under her breath she followed him to the other side of the lounge where the dining room was situated. A circular bar separated the two areas.

Carlo took his laptop from his bag and plugged it into the extension cord. She had no armor, no laptop that could be a screen between him and her.

"Coffee?" she asked, for the silence was too tense and she needed to do something with her hands, hold something between them.

"Please. No milk, no sugar."

"Yes, I know." She could have bitten her tongue at those last two words, for he stared at her with a soft gaze, admitting the intimate knowledge a shared past held. His gaze shifted to someone behind her, and she glanced up to see Natalia strolling past the bar into the dining room.

"*Dio*, Carlo, that must be the most horrid family suite in our whole portfolio. Have you seen it?" Natalia had her laptop bag over her shoulder.

"Not since I worked here, and then it was a quick in and out," he answered as he sat down.

"It's in dire need of a soft refurbishment, I can't believe Peppe let it go like that. I hope we don't charge more than three thousand dollars for that hole a night." Natalia plunked down her laptop bag on the table.

"It's not used often as far as I know," Carlo said.

Simone sat down, gripping her cup with cold, cramping fingers, like a lifeline. With Natalia here at least she could breathe.

"You're on leave, Talia?"

"I need to let Julia know." She smiled at Carlo. "And I want to hear if she's coping."

"Julia's doing fine. She must cope by herself."

A funny looked passed between Carlo and Natalia. Carlo shrugged as if he had to let something go, and Natalia gave a deep sigh.

"My turn to make you a coffee?" Simone asked, eager to get away from the silent discussion between the two.

"Thank you, that would be lovely. I like it black," Natalia said. "And see, now I can enjoy the view, which the house doesn't have."

Simone handed a cup to Natalia. *And help us ignore the elephant in the room.*

Four hours later they still sat together, Carlo shooting questions at her sporadically, while he manipulated data on his computer, interspersed with times of silence as he read and responded to some emails. He got up to make calls in between, pacing the room, speaking mostly in Italian.

Angelo and Dino joined them and the whole business became more rowdy as the family tossed ideas around for the lodge. Then they studied and pulled apart the numbers from their Southeast Asian operations. Angelo peppered both Carlo and Dino with questions and she was grateful for her own reprieve.

She wanted to see what Carlo was going to do with the pilot data once they had it all loaded in the spreadsheet, but it was past five o'clock in the afternoon and she struggled to suppress her yawns.

"There you go," Carlo said, pointing to something on his computer's screen.

Simone woke up from the dull numbness that had settled over her. He had generated several graphs that tracked staff movement for the past eight months.

She leaned into the screen, but couldn't make sense of it. She'd lost track of what he'd been doing.

"What should I be searching for?" She frowned. Ribbons of different colors tracked lines over the graphs, crossing, others coming together at one point before splitting again. It looked muddled.

"I've made data talk in pictures. All we need to do is put the story together."

"How?" Simone asked, embarrassed as both Dino and Angelo stared at her as if she were a nitwit who'd missed the boat. Natalia was typing on her laptop, reading glasses perched on the end of her nose.

"Identify matching patterns, for starters." Carlo sighed as he leaned back in his chair, rubbing at his eyes. "I'm too tired to look at it now. The basics are there and we can build on it." He dragged his fingers through his hair. "We can sit with it tonight, or even better, tomorrow."

He stood and closed his laptop, then raised his arms over his head and twisted in a giant stretch. His fleece shirt rode up to reveal his taut stomach and navel in its bed of dark hair, which travelled south to the buttons of his Levi's before disappearing beneath the waistband of his jeans. Simone dropped her gaze as he lowered his arms and a wave of heat hit her cheeks. Her fingers burned with the desire to touch him. He walked toward the window and came to a standstill with his arms folded, his back to the rest of the group.

"I think we should call it a day." Dino's words drilled through to her.

When she looked up Angelo was watching her, one eyebrow cocked and his lips twitching in a wry smile.

Her blush deepened and she stood abruptly. *Yes,*

Angelo, that's the lay of the land.

Angelo also got up, his chair screeching. He shook his head. "I think I'll try and call Madeleine for a change."

Carlo turned at his words, glancing at her before his gaze caught Angelo's, straight in the eye. "About time, too. When is she back from her modeling shoot in the Maldives?"

"I'm not sure, but I think I'll ask her to fly over for a couple of days." Angelo's monotone voice sounded indifferent. He packed up his laptop and swung the bag over his shoulder.

Why would he invite a woman over if he weren't in the mood for her company?

"Join us for a drink afterward?" Carlo called after him.

"Sure." Angelo strode toward the glass doors and the exit to the verandah.

Simone felt Natalia looking at her, but she didn't want to talk. The need to be alone overwhelmed her. "I think I'll find my way to our accommodation. Good evening."

Carlo looked at her, raising his hand to stop her, but she rushed away, not looking back.

Chapter Thirteen

Simone walked faster, getting away from Carlo, but no footsteps sounded behind her. Once out of the entrance hall of the hotel she followed the receptionist's directions to the homestead. It was a refreshing walk, out in the cold, away from all those eyes. She could have walked for miles, but it was a short distance to the old farmhouse. It was a simple house—one of the first built in the area—and had some historic value but was lost after the glass and glamour of the main Carlevaro Crater Lodge.

Natalia must have sky-high standards because the interior was much more up-market than she'd expected. Embers glowed in the fireplace, warming the penetrating chill of the late winter afternoon. Her suitcase and backpack were already allocated to a room, so she closed the door and collapsed on the bed. Inhaling deeply, she took her phone from her pocket. She rubbed her face and breathed into her hand, taking a moment to gather herself.

Her finger hovered over the speed dial number, but instead of calling her mom she ended up dialing Ruth. After a short chat Ruth passed the phone to Sarah. "Hello, darling."

"When you home, Mommy?"

Simone swallowed. "I'm not sure. This is hard for me too." Pain tightened in her throat. She couldn't let

Sarah hear tears in her voice. "What did you do today?"

Sarah was quiet for a moment, and Simone smiled through the burn behind her eyes. That little brain was churning, probably trying to put things in order.

"School, nap, and play with Tim," Sarah said, her words not perfect, but the picture was there.

"Sounds like a fun day. What are you having for dinner?" Simone asked, imagining Ruth pottering around the kitchen with Sarah.

"Ruthie's making fishy chips."

"Sounds yummy."

"You must have some too," Sarah said, as if everything could be transported over the phone line.

Tears spilled from the corners of her eyes, but she forced a laugh. "Next time." She sat up straight with a sniff and leaned forward, dropping her head in her hand.

"What you do, Mommy?"

"Oh, the usual. I flew people around."

"A pwincess?"

"No." Simone chuckled. She'd flown the odd celebrity—film stars, musicians, and European royalty—a little excitement she'd tell Sarah about when she got home. The royalty had clung to Sarah's make-believe world of castles and kingdoms.

"A pwince then?"

Sarah's innocent question choked her up. *Your daddy.* She dropped the phone to her chest to kill the sound of her sobs and took a breath. She sniffed. "Nobody special, just the big boss."

"He scary?"

For a second Carlo's face appeared in her mind's eye, the permanent scowl he wore, so different from the man she'd known four years ago. "Very." She laughed. "No, he's not scary at all. Not deep down. You might get to meet him." The words just slipped out. She had no idea where they'd come from.

"No, thank you."

She had to pause at Sarah's retort. Sarah wouldn't say that if she knew he was her father.

Through the slit of light under the door, she saw movement in the adjacent lounge, and voices speaking in Italian penetrated her room. Sarah's frank response was sobering. "Yes, maybe not. Just you and me, okay?"

"You and me, Mommy. I love you."

Someone knocked on her door. "I love you too." She didn't have time for a proper goodbye. "I've got to go."

"Love you, Mommy."

She cut the call with Sarah and went to open the door, wiping her face in the crook of her arm. Angelo's voice sounded from the adjacent bedroom and a door shut further down. Natalia and Dino laughed in their room; their voices were soft, but distinct. Whatever changes were made to accommodate three en suite bedrooms in the old farmhouse weren't solid. She'd make no more phone calls until she was sure of privacy.

She opened her bedroom door. Carlo stared at her and every nerve in her body tightened. How much had he heard? By the expression on his face, he'd heard her whole conversation with Sarah.

How could she have been so stupid? She'd come to the house alone but the rest would have followed at some point. Everything she'd said to Sarah echoed through her mind, but she couldn't pinpoint any words that would give her world away.

Carlo held out a stack of papers. "A printout of the work we did."

She'd gone blank.

"The graphs." He searched her face. "Have a look, please."

She brushed some stray wisps of hair from her face and took the printouts from him. "Sure."

"Let me know if you uncover something."

She nodded. "I'll see you in the morning." She wanted to close the door, but he opened his mouth as if he would say something.

She had to cut him off. "What time are we leaving?"

"We're driving to the mobile safari once we're at Seronera." He sighed. "Fly out at nine? Leave here around eight?"

She nodded, burning for him to go. To stay. To take her home, to Sarah.

He blocked her view into the rest of the lounge with his bulk, but they were as alone as they could be with the others in their rooms.

"Mona." When he lifted his hand and stroked at her cheek with a forefinger knuckle she wanted to lean into his hand. Instead she pulled her chin away from him and avoided his storm gray eyes that peered right into her, seeking. He knew something was amiss with her, and the notion of him seeing straight to the heart of her secret was as scary as it was suddenly inevitable.

She dropped her gaze and wiped at her cheek with the back of her hand, drying the stray tear he'd caught on his finger.

"Don't," she whispered with a glare. They'd

discussed his nickname for her that morning, and this was not helping her keep things business-focused.

At least the next day's flight was a short one. Once at Seronera he'd be gone, along with his gentle hands and caring caresses which knew just how to make her yield. "I'll check the weather and let you know if we need to make changes. Good night." She pushed the door closed but a swift hand blocked her from shutting it.

"Come have dinner?" He spoke softly, as if he really cared. "You hardly eat, Simone."

No. A sense of vulnerability had shot through her at his touch, at the soft tone in his voice. And now his eyes questioned quietly, as if he would wait for her to talk when she was ready, making her want to collapse into his arms and tell him everything. "I was shredded at breakfast and lunch, Carlo. Spare serving me to your clan for dinner."

He put pressure on the door, and it widened, her hand weak. He was leaning in, centimeters from her face. She would've stepped back if her legs hadn't been so wobbly.

"Don't feel like that. I—" His gaze rested on her mouth, and for one sweet second she thought he was going to kiss her. Then he lifted his eyes. He stared into the room and at the double bed with a sigh. He cleared his throat. "You'll be okay here? Alone?"

The stupid question made her smirk. "Sure. Unless security is not what it should be. I'm starting to have my doubts with all the things happening."

It was a stab at him, the company, and everything he stood for. The barb hit home, for he stepped back, dropping his hand and gaze. "Lock your door then. As if it would…help."

She closed the door and turned the key. The twisting of metal rang through the room, and she peered down to see the two shadows of his feet at the door, which she'd basically shut in his face. She rested her forehead on the door, breathing shallowly until he'd stepped away.

God, she was one mean bitch. She slumped on the bed, scattering his stack of papers to the floor.

She hadn't locked the door to keep him out, but to keep herself in. The last thing she needed right now was to turn into that wanton, needy girl she'd been four years ago, burning with the desire to please him, to love him. Her self-assured independence was being undermined by her body, which had its own underhanded agenda. Every pulse centered on her own need, distracting her focus from Sarah. Her willpower to stay away from Carlo was evaporating.

****

Carlo let the hot water beat down on his tense shoulders and naked back. He leaned with arms outstretched against the shower wall, trying to shake his anger. He was slowly losing his footing on this situation with Simone, and it was the last thing he needed.

Spending the whole day next to her hadn't helped. He'd caught himself reliving snatches of those six weeks as if they'd just passed. The weirdest things surfaced in his mind, small things, everyday things. The way she tapped with the pen on her nose during the pre-flight checklist as they went through each step. Her almost manly scrawl of a signature at the bottom of the checklist where she had to sign. The way she tugged at a curl from her temple when she was self-conscious.

How excited she was when he took her to the bookstore at the Slipway for the first time. How quickly they settled into a routine during their days off, mostly lounging in bed, reading and making love between chapters, before eventually getting up and going for a late lunch at the Italian restaurant where it had all started. He could even recall what she wore that day, because he had the pleasure of picking each bit of clothing off her in a slow, provoking game that left her so aroused, she came in his hand.

He didn't guess she was a virgin, she had it written in her eyes, and in her sweet laugh when she told him that she'd "never gone this far with anybody" and that her "mother would kill her." That her mother was thousands of miles away was an antidote.

For the first two nights he enjoyed teasing her, because it was as novel for him as it was for her. In the circles he frequented in at school and later at university, and in the elitist circles of Rome, virginity was not valued or expected. He'd never been with a virgin before, but by the third night they spent together she was begging him to go all the way and he had no control left.

When asking her how she managed to hold out so long, she laughed it off. "I was that unwanted baby that ruined my mom's life, you know, pre-marriage, pre-abortion, pre-everything."

She never told him more, but between the lines he gathered that she grew up running wild on some neglected farm in South Africa. She was always taller than the boys in the class, but when puberty struck and the boys started catching up, her mother, who never cared what she was about, all but locked her up.

There was a proper rift between her and her mom when she uprooted to go fly tourists, unsupervised, in Tanzania. She told him he could do what he wanted to her, as long as he didn't get her pregnant. Babies had been one of the last things on his mind too, and he'd taken every precaution possible.

He'd been such an asshole that first night, arrogantly telling her that now that she was his employee she was off limits. He was eating those words, one by one, and they crunched in his mouth like sand. At least Angelo had backed off. He wasn't sure what had passed between the two, but Simone had managed to put his brother off. That would be a first. A warmth spread through his chest at the thought that she might have done it for him.

"Leave some hot water, will you?" Angelo called from the bedroom.

Carlo sighed as he closed the tap. He wasn't keen for his family's company. He'd make the excuse of more work to do after dinner. There were always unread emails in his inbox. Especially the one from the HR department in Dar es Salaam. Simone was hiding something from him but he didn't want her to see him spying on her. Reading that email while her eyes were on his laptop screen would have been wrong. He still trusted her, and deep down it was treacherous to even think she could be involved in something illegal. He groaned. The situation was making him sink to new lows.

****

Simone exhaled the breath she'd been holding as the Carlevaros left the house for dinner. There was a coffee and tea station in the lounge with a mini bar, and

159

she would forage dinner from there. She didn't know the lodge manager and wasn't in the mood to stroll around the hotel in search of the kitchen or staff mess.

She unlocked her door and peeked out to be sure no one was left in the lounge, then made tea and took a packet of chips, some cookies and a chocolate from the display. She returned to her room and put the makeshift meal down on the bedside table. She locked her bedroom door with one final twist of the key. For good measure she took it out of the lock and put it on the vanity. Sleepwalking was definitely not an option.

Gathering the stack of scattered papers from the floor she considered her bedtime reading. She sat down on the bed, kicking her shoes off and plumping the cushions up behind her back. She fingered the graphs, reading the titles, studying the axes and reading names, dates and places. The longer she stared at it, the clearer it became. It was indeed a picture. It showed the pattern each pilot had flown over the preceding eight months, and at the end of twenty-four pages a comparison with the poaching data. There were the staccato line graphs of the short flights, the longer waves of the pilots who flew the longer destinations. She'd never kept track of staff movement like this.

The overnight flight from the Serengeti to the Selous, which stopped in Ugalla and Ruaha, was a wave replicated by the flight schedules of only five of the twenty-two Carlevaro pilots. Simone sat up straight, because her name was on the list. She turned to the last page where the poaching graph was depicted in a thin red line. A chill ran down her spine as she saw the perfect visual replica of the five pilots' flight schedules matched to that of the poaching activity.

Chapter Fourteen

Carlo let go of Simone's hand with a last squeeze. She retracted her hand from the throttle, her annoyance bouncing through the cockpit. He shifted in his seat. He wanted her to trust him, and had held on to her hand during take-off as if trust could be transmitted through touch.

He'd read through everything the HR department had sent him, and although they'd sent only the general information, it had been insightful.

Simone had a dependent.

Automatically he wanted to delve into the various scenarios again. He glanced at her; she was twitchy. She might appear calm on the surface, but tension ricocheted through her, making her movements jerky.

Who could her dependent be? The options had been running through his mind since yesterday when he'd read the information from the HR department. Dependents were usually children. He'd deleted the idea right off the bat. Surely, if Simone had a child it would have surfaced by now. The image of her with a baby kept popping up in his mind's eye…she would be a wonderful mother. He stifled the deep, novel feeling of longing that stirred in his belly at the image.

It could be a family member, her mother maybe, or her father or her sister. It could be someone else's child. Maybe her sister's baby. From what he understood it wasn't uncommon for schoolgirls to fall pregnant in the neighborhood she'd grown up in. Simone had consciously pulled herself out of that pit, but her sister… Carlevaro East Africa had one of the best international medical plans for their expatriate staff but he didn't know the details of their medical insurance policies or how someone classified as a dependent.

He closed the mental circle and got back to the family member. The spike in his perfect infinite loop was the notion that Simone needed money to keep someone going. Someone with a health problem or a nasty habit. The type of problem only money could feed…and solve. She'd hinted in the past that her mom had a habit. Alcohol or drugs. He couldn't recall which because she'd always talked around it. The notion was too close to home and he rattled out a breath, deleting the thought.

It all hung around him like an itch he couldn't quite reach to scratch.

He hovered over how to approach the situation because he didn't want to interrogate Simone about her family life. Since he'd never shared anything about his own family with her it was unfair to expect her to bare herself to him now.

The bottom line was that poaching meant money. Simone had a dependent. She would need money. One plus one equaled two. He cursed inwardly as he shot her another glance. The flight was short, and he had to make most of the time with her. Once at Seronera, they'd be driving to the Carlevaro mobile safari camp and that was a whole day excursion. Why had he signed up for it at all?

She cleared her throat and shot him a glance. "I

studied those graphs last night."

Her words drew him out of his wasteful speculation. "And?"

"It boils down to five pilots if I interpreted the data correctly." She shifted in her seat. "Those of us who've been flying the route that overnights in both the Serengeti and Selous, at Rufiji Camp."

"Well done. I haven't had time to look closer yet." He rubbed at his chin. He'd get to the bottom of this, soon. "Who are the five pilots?"

She took a deep breath and sighed it out. "Me, Michael Flynn, Ted Barker, Samuel Msinga and Benedict Lucas."

There was some relief in her admitting that she was one of the five pilots. If she were guilty she might have kept that information from him until he'd discovered it.

"I've only met Michael Flynn." He recalled the redhead he'd spoken to on the day they'd arrived. He'd liked Michael; he was the straightforward, easy-going type. "Samuel Msinga and Benedict Lucas are locals?" he asked. After two days investigating the pilots he remembered the names, but he didn't have all the faces on the company profiles connected to the names yet.

"Yes." Simone hesitated. "They understand how things work in Tanzania."

"And?" He had to dig. For these men, there would be no language barrier, and they'd have a network and relationships that would ease their way.

"Just because they're local doesn't make them the obvious culprits, does it?" Simone sighed, frustrated. "Between the two of them they won't kill a fly. Ted Barker is an American and new to Carlevaro Air."

Barker had only been working for them for eight

163

months, which was a time match if nothing else. That left Simone and Michael. "What's going on in your mind, Simone?" He tried to read her face, but there was nothing but a frown to work on.

"I don't know. That's what the picture says, but my instinct tells me it couldn't be any of them." She glanced at him. "Ted maybe…you should have a look in his employee file. I'm not sure where he worked before. It could've been with another local airline and he switched to Carlevaro to implement the trafficking."

Carlo nodded. He churned the information over in his mind, the silence between them stretching. She'd introduced the idea of going through employee files. There couldn't be a better moment. He glanced at her. She seemed even more nervous than before. "I'll look at the graphs later." He rubbed at his brow with his forefinger and thumb. "Simone."

He stared at her, forcing her to meet his gaze.

Simone gave him a fleeting look, and her heart skipped a beat at the question in his eyes as he held her gaze. There had also been something in his tone that made the hair on her neck prickle. "Yes?" If she weren't strapped to an aircraft's pilot seat and hundreds of meters up in the air she would have bolted.

"You know I can't exclude you from our investigations."

"No…yes, I mean. I know you can't." Her fingers had started to tremble. Exhaling in obvious panic would give everything away, and to grip her hands to her thighs wouldn't help either. Carlo had been sending funny glances in her direction since they'd gotten in the car and headed for the airstrip that morning. "There is no reason why you should, and given the evidence—"

"The graphs aren't evidence. I'll look at them later," he repeated. He stared at her.

He knows. Her stomach tightened around the twisted cramp she'd be walking around with for days, and her mouth went dry. Somehow, overnight, he'd learned about Sarah.

"I've asked for your employee file, as part of our investigation." He lifted his hands as if in excuse, but he didn't have to. He was the owner. He could get any information he wanted. "It's not that I don't trust you."

She chewed her lip, staring out of the side window. The trust between them had become rather fickle. Why didn't he just say it?

"Who is the dependent on your employee file?" he asked. "There are no details, except that you have one dependent?"

Her mind charged back to three years ago and every single employee form she'd had to fill in for Carlevaro East Africa. She recalled every detail clearly, every little box she had to tick—they were flashing by in her mind's eye as if she was about to die.

"It's my sister." She swallowed and blinked. "Gabi." The lie had slipped from her tongue so smoothly. "I'm helping her pay for her studies, and she is on my medical plan." The first bit was at least true. She immediately regretted lying but it was too late.

Carlo might have asked for her employee information, but as soon as he had her medical aid file, which was locked away with the salary information for confidentiality, he would see that her dependent was Sarah Carla Levin. A little girl with a date of birth that solidly put her in the nursery phase and not in her second year of medical school. Hopefully, he would believe her and not ask to see those damning documents.

He nodded and looked away. "How's Gabi doing? You always spoke of her." His hands had relaxed and he pulled the flight documentation from his door's pocket. "You missed her when you moved here."

She almost burst with the quake of relief that vibrated in her. She wiped the sudden sweat on her palms off on her pants, making as if she were stroking out a crease or two. "Gabi's doing fine. She's on her way to becoming a gynecologist."

Oh, for fuck's sake. The next thing she was going to tell him was how Gabi had cut Sarah's umbilical cord at birth and had ever since wanted to become a doctor. She worked hard, to such an extent that she was first in her class. Gabi had only been seventeen at Sarah's birth and had been unsure of what she wanted to do with her life. Cutting Sarah's umbilical cord had been an intensely emotional, if not spiritual, experience for her sister.

"She's lucky to have you to look out for her." There was a tremor in his voice, and she glanced at him. He was staring blindly at the documents he'd balanced on the yoke in front of him. A minute passed before he met her gaze without wavering. "I've failed my sister completely. It's not a guilt you want to live with." He sighed. "You must do for Gabi what you can."

He hadn't tried to hide the pain in his eyes; not for the first time she wanted to prod him further. Something had happened to Carlo, which had left him isolated, despite being surrounded by family and work. She wanted to know more, but he'd started to fill in the documents. And probing Carlo was not on her list of *how to keep things focused on business*, so she consciously turned cold toward him, shutting her mouth.

But her mind and her heart weren't so easily switched off, and their conversation circled around in her thoughts.

They landed the aircraft in silence.

"We're here for two nights," Carlo said as he glanced at her.

She nodded and got out of the aircraft to lower the air stair and open the hold.

After they'd locked the aircraft, they got into the waiting game drive vehicles and took the short trip to the camp.

As they arrived at the Carlevaro Seronera Camp Simone eyed the group of Maasai warriors doing the jumping dance in welcome. No chance in hell she'd be able to slip away from this one. A waitress shoved a breakfast cocktail into her hand and she joined the circle of in-house guests enjoying the show.

Kevin Jenkins, the lodge manager, nudged up to her. "We don't have a staff room available for you. Michael is flying out later, but we gave the pilot room away ages ago to a guide who is traveling with a group of Americans. We didn't know you'd be here and availability is tight as it is."

She searched Kevin's face, her mind racing. After the Ngorongoro Crater she'd be happy to sleep in the kitchen.

"Don't panic," Kevin said. "I put you in a guest chalet as requested."

Simone swallowed. "A guest chalet?" She couldn't

imagine this being authorized by the reservations department. "As requested?"

"To accommodate the Carlevaros we swapped two guest couples around to go to the Grumeti Camp first. We have enough rooms available, with the brothers sharing."

She raised a hand in protest, but Kevin hitched his shoulders.

"That's what Carlo ordered and it's arranged now," he said above the singing of the Maasai.

Carlo. Did he think he was doing her a favor? How was this going to reflect on her? She spent an overnight at this lodge every week, and knew most of the staff by name. Sleeping in a chalet would set the tongues wagging all the way to Dar es Salaam and back.

Poor Kevin—shuffling guests around to accommodate the Carlevaros. He'd made a great effort to show the Carlevaros how important this site inspection was, impressing with his Maasai cultural experience and breakfast cocktails. The big shots from the Carlevaro International headquarters in Rome rarely visited East Africa and he had to make this inspection count. She should be the last person to grumble about something as insignificant as a bed right now.

"Enjoy your stay," Kevin said and he smiled at her as the dancing ended. He left her to catch up with Carlo, Angelo and Dino.

With resignation, Simone picked her bags out of the row lined up by the porters. Natalia came up to her, all smiles. "I wish we could have such a welcome for all our guests."

"I think everyone who does a full itinerary with Carlevaro gets the cultural experience in at some point," Simone said.

"I hope so. It's something we should market more." Natalia turned to the others.

Carlo, Dino and Angelo wrapped up their conversation with Kevin and walked up to them. "I'll finalize with Simone," Carlo said, locking gazes with her. Natalia strode off with the others to follow the porters and Kevin outside.

"We're here for two nights, then Lake Manyara," Carlo said, "Can you arrange to refuel at Arusha the same day we fly to Lake Manyara? Ruaha is able to accommodate us after Lake Manyara."

She nodded, trying to keep her face impassive, untouched by his words. She bit the tip of her tongue to try and control her seething emotions. If she had to sit around she'd much rather do it at home with Sarah. "What am I supposed to do for the next two days?"

His gaze took her in, and for a second, she feared he might read her mind.

He lowered his voice. "Rest and relax. Play the tourist." He leaned closer. "Permission granted. And I'd like a full report on the spa facilities. Bill it to my room." He stepped away but she didn't miss the naughty spark in his eyes.

The situation had become completely unbearable. As if she would spend the day being pampered...on his account! Before she could give him a sharp retort, Carlo strolled off to catch up with the rest of the party.

The Maasai and other guests had dispersed. She'd eaten nothing that morning, in an attempt to avoid the Carlevaros at breakfast. She was ravenous and took the way to the kitchen.

She pulled her phone out to call Michael Flynn,

who should still be at the lodge. The flight to the Selous departed in an hour's time. She paused a second to order her thoughts. She was probably the only innocent pilot currently aware of the poaching and air trafficking situation, and she had no permission to reveal anything to Michael.

The poachers hadn't managed to stow the tusks the night before. What were the chances they'd try again? If the poachers stowed the tusks that night it would prove that they were unaware of the Carlevaros' investigation.

Rubbing her forehead, she was still undecided as she ambled into the staff mess, which was situated behind the kitchen. She pocketed her phone when she saw Michael sitting at a table, busy on his phone, an empty plate pushed to the side.

"Hey Simone, fancy seeing you here," Michael said by way of greeting. "How've things been?"

She grimaced. "Hectic."

He gave her the once-over. "You look knackered. Are those boys working you too hard?"

Michael was the sincere type and wouldn't mean anything other than what his words implied. "No, the situation is difficult."

"Sarah?"

She put her finger to her lips to silence him. "I don't want to bring her up. With the promotion and Ross...I want to keep Sarah out of it."

Michael shrugged. "Your kid, your life."

She walked over to the steam tray and helped herself to some warm maize porridge. It was the stuff she had grown up on and every time she ate it, it took her home. She poured a coffee from the urn, letting go of a deep sigh. This was more her world, and relaxing here in this casual atmosphere was like coming home after a long day, wearing high heels that pinched her feet, and kicking her shoes off. She put her plate down and sat in a chair opposite Michael.

"How long are you here for?" He raised his brow at her. "Are you staying the night?"

"We're here for two nights because they can accommodate us."

"I got kicked out this morning so that they can get the room ready for some guide. Where're you slumming?"

"I…" Simone hesitated. There was no way out. "I have a chalet."

"Woo-hoo!" Michael gave a soft whistle. "Moving up in the ranks? I promise not to tell Ross." He winked at her.

She pulled a face at the idea of Ross. "It was the only available room."

"Lucky you. I wish management would accommodate me like that, and then I'd tag Annie along. She loves the whole spa-thing." He glanced at the staff at another table as they got up and left the mess.

"How's Annie's new job going?" Simone asked.

"She's loving it and neglecting me. All environmentalist, saving the elephants, one at a time, you know." Michael gave her a lopsided smile. "Where're you off to next?"

The other staff had left and Simone tried not to show her relief too openly. They were alone and she could talk to Michael freely.

She told him their plans for the next couple of

nights, and they both fell quiet for a minute. "Stopping over in the Selous tonight? Staying at Rufiji?" Simone asked.

"Yip."

She searched his face. Trust could be such a simple thing, such a dangerous thing. But she'd known Michael for three years and had co-piloted with him many times. In a second her decision was made. "Do me a favor, will you?" She stirred her porridge, ignoring the unease that slid down her spine. "Check the hold before they load the empty food containers and the luggage." She hesitated. "Don't let anybody see you, if you can manage."

"Sure." He raised his eyebrows at her. "Why?"

"I…just let me know if you find anything strange? Anything really. And scratch deeply, not just on the surface."

Michael opened his mouth to ask more, but she shook her head. "Just look, okay?"

He nodded then checked his watch. "Gotta fly." He stood and whispered with a wink, "Mum's the word. I'll see you in Dar."

She grinned back at him. "Thanks."

As Michael rushed off she slumped back and got busy with her breakfast.

Chapter Fifteen

Simone climbed the wooden stairs to her chalet twenty minutes later. It was built on wooden stilts at the foot of a hill overlooking the open savannah. Green grasslands, dotted with acacia and yellow fever trees, spread out as far as the eye could see, along with a few smaller shrubs and the endless grass that lured the wildebeest.

She opened the door and inhaled in a sharp breath as she took in the vast, luxurious space. It was just as she'd remembered it from years ago. *Nothing beats a Carlevaro chalet.* Her bags stood in the corner. A huge four-poster bed dominated the room, with a mosquito net gathered at the posters. Crisp white linens covered a thick duvet and enough cushions for royalty were placed at the head. There was a lounge area with a sofa and occasional chairs. Simone crossed the room and opened the door to the bathroom. A Victorian bathtub stood in the middle with a folding glass door opening to the back of the chalet, and there was an outdoor shower hidden between two boulders. Over the years, trees had grown between the crevices, and their dense foliage provided privacy.

It couldn't be a more romantic place, and memories of her and Carlo spending a night in one of these chalets surfaced. He might have left for the day, but he had a permanent presence in every thought she had, in every beat of her heart and every pulse of her blood through her veins.

She needed this day away from him. Everything had become muddled. The original reasons why she'd wanted to keep Sarah a secret had crept into a corner, where they waited, pouting and whimpering, to make sure she knew they were still there.

Strolling out to the deck she took in the view and forced her shoulders to relax, then sat down with her mobile and dialed her mom, something she should have done two days ago. Already her shoulders were hitching higher. Her relationship with her mom was a ball of snarled yarn that she'd never been able to properly disentangle. She'd cut off the pieces that she could work with, and had let the rest go—one more reason why she'd returned to Tanzania.

"At last, you call, Simone." Her mother's voice sounded old, dried by too many cigarettes.

Simone sank deeper into the lounger. "I've been busy at work, Mom."

"How is Sarah?"

She closed her eyes, her hand curling into a tight ball in her lap. Sarah had sounded fine over the phone, but was she? Her own separation from Sarah was slowly suffocating her willpower. "She's with Ruth. I'm spending a few nights away with work." She told her mom about flying the Carlevaros and her three-week assignment.

"You're leaving her too often with Ruth." Her mom coughed. "I wish you'd come home and let me help with her."

Simone bit down on her jaw. Her mom always made her feel wretched about Ruth. "The money isn't good enough back home, Mom." That was only half a reason but presented the easiest excuse. Her mom, finally, had a job she'd been able to keep, and getting Sarah into the mix would be a bad idea for both her mom and Sarah. Her mom's independence had become a quest, almost unattainable, but something to strive for. Once no longer dependent on her dad, maybe her mom would be able to move on.

"Gabi said the trip to the UK was amazing."

"We had fun," Simone said, glad that her mom didn't push the Sarah button any further. "I'll send you some photos as soon as I'm back home."

"You spoil Gabi too much. She showed me the things you bought her."

Frustration raised its ugly head. "If I don't do it, who will? Gabi works hard."

Her mom was silent for a moment after her little tirade. "It's your money. You should save it for Sarah."

Simone shook her head. "We'll be fine, Mom. We'll look out for each other."

Mom cleared her throat, her voice wavering. "Yes, I know. It's just—" She broke off but Simone could complete the sentence as if it was part of a memorized prayer. *You never know how long it's going to last…*

Simone stared at the trees over the savannah as the old emptiness washed over her again. It meant so many things…how long was the money going to last, how long was he going to be away this time, how long until he phoned, how long was he going to stay this time around, how long until he left again? Her mom's whole life had been one long wait, dulled by nicotine, interspersed with severe drinking bouts that were fueled by depression and hovered on alcoholism.

"Any news from Dad?" she asked, loathe to even call him that.

"No." Her mother took a breath. "Not yet."

"Sometimes—" She paused. As a child, her dad had been absent for months on end, on exploration for mining companies in the era before cell phones and the internet connected the world. He still lived in that bubble of total disconnect. The problem was that the card had been played so often, it was as if the whole deck of cards was a replication of that one, stabbing ace of spades.

"What?"

"You've got a job now, Mom, your own money. You could divorce him, then this waiting game would be over."

"It's not a game, Simone. And a divorce wouldn't help, I'd still wait for him," her mom rasped into the phone. "I don't expect you to understand."

Simone shook her head. Her mom had been waiting forever...and deep down, hadn't she been doing the same thing, waiting for Carlo? *No.* "It's been six months now, how long is it going to take this time?"

"I don't know. Two years was the longest. All I know is that he'll be back."

"I was there. No need to remind me." Why did it still hurt? When her dad had come back after that two-year stunt, the year she'd turned sixteen, he'd had money. Now she was convinced that he'd been into money laundering and corruption, that the money hadn't been a fat bonus as he'd told them. She stopped asking him details about his life a long time ago. But she couldn't stop envisioning the breadcrumb trail of children he'd left across the African continent, pinpointing where he'd been. Little organ pipes in height, from tallest to shortest, with her his firstborn, all of them sporting similar green eyes, like his. *I don't want to know.*

She pressed her palm to her forehead, reluctant to face the reality that she'd been unwilling to wait for Carlo because she hadn't wanted to turn out like her mother. *Waiting, waiting, waiting.* The realization was a painful bruise right under her heart. It had been sitting there all this time, unable to heal.

She understood her mother better in that moment than ever before. And herself. Her own independence, which had been so hard to gain, her mother always leaning over her shoulder, wanting to make sure her daughter didn't make the same mistakes she'd made. Her love of flying had taken her away from it all, and once she had her wings there had been no going back to the nest.

"Mom, I need to ask you something."

"Yes?"

"When I returned home from Carlevaro Air after those first three months..." She swallowed. She hated talking to her about the time when she'd returned pregnant from her first stint in Tanzania, because her mother hadn't been supportive of her having Sarah. The intense fight she'd had with her mother, about her returning knocked up as her mom had predicted, blared in her ears as if they'd had it minutes ago. "And I left again..." She had to take a breath.

"You didn't leave, Simone. You absconded."

That her mother could still conjure that bitter tone and drive the corrosive guilt in her... "I did phone you to tell you I was fine and you shouldn't worry about me," Simone shot back, wishing she could have the conversation without the brutal swordfight that would draw blood. "Did anybody call for me during that time?" She rubbed at her eyes. "You never passed any messages on to me when I was back home for Sarah's birth."

"Call for you? At the house? No."

"I meant a phone call," Simone said softly, scared to face the truth now that she was at the door of it.

"I can't recall. Possibly?"

"Someone from Carlevaro, Mom?"

"Carlevaro?"

Fury rushed through her at the dumb echo. Her mother had probably been in a drunken haze and couldn't remember squat. She no longer wanted to talk to her mom. She'd run out of patience. "I've got to go. I'll call you soon."

"Wait, Simone." Her mom's voice wasn't urgent, but it held a promise of recollection. "A man from Carlevaro phoned a few times. He had a stutter or something, he kept on saying Carle, Carle Carlevaro."

A shiver crept over her as if a ghost had spread itself over her body, pricking her skin with goosebumps. The wet, hot trail of a tear ran down her cheek, followed by another and another that trickled to her neck. Simone closed her eyes. "And?" she whispered.

Her mom snorted. "If I jotted down a message for you, it should still be with the post I kept for you. It's somewhere in the house. You didn't take it when you left."

The last sentence was said in accusation, as if collecting her four-year-old post was more important than anything else. Maybe it had been.

"That's okay, Mom." There was no quiver in her voice, but shivers ran through her. "I'll chat with you again soon, okay?"

She rang off and tossed her phone on the end of the lounger. She drew her legs up in a hug that would never be tight enough.

It was a long time before she had calmed herself enough to go back into the room. She washed her face but didn't feel any better. She had to hear Sarah's voice, so she phoned Ruth at the worst possible time of the day, as Sarah was tired and hungry. They had a short chat, which didn't help.

She slumped down on her bed, almost having come full circle. To close the loop, she had to speak to Gabi.

"You've been too quiet," Gabi reprimanded. "What's been going on?"

She filled Gabi in on the poaching and trafficking investigation and having to work with Carlo at much closer quarters than anticipated. "I think he suspects I'm involved in the trafficking."

"No!" Gabi drawled the word out. "That's ridiculous."

"He knows I'm hiding something from him."

"Sounds like you've been spending too much time together," Gabi said drily. "Besides his obvious idiocy, what's he like? Still same old, same old, or changed?"

"He's the same…but different. Older, wiser," she said, her voice catching on the words. And he was no idiot.

"Falling for him twice as hard, aren't you?" Gabi murmured. "I told you not to let him close."

Her sister was no idiot either. She'd been falling

for Carlo, slowly, paragliding down from the dizzy height of his unexpected arrival back in her life. And the landing was going to be far from smooth. She couldn't lose control now. "I've no idea what to do."

As if Gabi sensed her distress she spoke softer. "About Sarah?"

She didn't want to break down again, but the conversation between her and her mom just gushed out. Carlo *had* tried to get hold of her.

For once Gabi was shocked into silence. There was no jab to follow. "I'm so sorry, Simone. What a mess. If I'd been home at the time..." Gabi had fled to boarding school as soon as she'd convinced her mom that it was the best idea ever. A prestigious scholarship had sealed the deal. By the time Simone had been ready to start flying commercially, Gabi had been out of the house, finishing the last years of high school in Johannesburg.

"There was no way you could've known." Simone wiped at her eyes. "Everything is muddled. I don't know if I should tell him about Sarah or not."

"What can you gain by telling him? What can you lose?"

Sarah. Her fear popped up as if by instinct.

"It's about that fight they had, isn't it?" Gabi said eventually, the pain in her voice so tangible, it pressed down on her own chest, making it hard to breathe.

Flashes of memory burst through her mind and Simone dropped her head into her hand. "Yes. Probably."

She'd hardly turned ten when, for a whole week, they'd huddled together in terror as their mom and dad fought, days on end. She tried to protect Gabi, who was only five at the time. *So little, just like Sarah.* Her dad's words about their mother being unable to care for them… About her mother's drinking bouts, the fact that he had money, and would get custody of the children if it ever went as far as divorce. That he could take them in any case. He should take them now. That her mom had no say and that he knew some pretty smart lawyers. It was real, the fear so intense that it overshadowed most of her teenage years.

Her mom, dependent, intimidated and uneducated, had never stood a chance.

"The problem is, this is not about us, it's not about me," Simone said. "This is about Sarah."

The idea of Carlo with Sarah, being the father that was the missing piece in their lives was the image she hadn't been able to wipe from her mind the whole day.

The idea of being loved and being cared for was something that left her so aching with want, for Sarah's sake. But then…the image of his virile body covering hers made her go limp; the fantasy of them making love had become physically agonizing. The things Carlo had been saying… If only it *was* only about Sarah.

"And you think telling him would do her any good?" Gabi's retort was laden with doubt. "Simone, you don't need him. Sarah doesn't need him. You're fine on your own. You want for nothing."

"I know," she swallowed, "but I can't help thinking that keeping Sarah from him would be the perfect mistake."

Gabi groaned into the phone. "Honestly, that's your call. All I can guarantee you is that he'll disappoint you as much as the average male."

Chapter Sixteen

Carlo sat down with a curse. His day had been a total waste of time. He'd missed Simone. He had missed her for four endless years, and spending just hours away from her had awakened his longing. He should have stayed at Seronera with her and should have lured her to bed. That was where his head had been the whole day, and with the rest of the team gone it had been a wasted opportunity. Simone might have protested, but he would have changed her mind. A touch at a time, a kiss at a time.

He'd given up fighting his attraction to her. To him, it was only a matter of time before they'd make love, and right now, the sooner the better. He grunted his own frustration and raked his hands through his hair. He was going to break this impasse between them, whatever it took.

The sun slipped below the horizon and in the soft blue of dusk, he saw the evening star. The drive to the mobile safari camp had been long and tiring, yet the energy of his resolve pulsed through his veins. As night fell, he sat overlooking the savannah, watching as bats swooped in the darkening sky. In the distance, a hyena howled for its mate.

Voices drifted from the path below the chalet. The wooden stairs leading up to the chalet creaked with the sound of her steps, at the rhythm of her gait as she climbed the stairs. He was surprised at the details he could recall. There had never been a breach, except that there had been, and it gaped between them. He breathed quietly as he waited, his heartbeat leaping.

Her footsteps slowed. He'd turned the housekeeping staff away when they'd come to do the room turndown, and he hadn't switched on the lights. Simone would struggle up the stairs in the dark.

A torch flashed, lighting the steps.

"I'll find my way," she said, then continued her cautious ascent to the deck of the chalet. She reached the top of the stairs and the light switch snapped on. Soft artificial light flooded the deck, blinding him for a second.

She didn't see him immediately, but when she did, she pulled in a sharp breath, her eyes wide. "I'm so sorry, did I get the wrong chalet? I didn't check—"

He stood up, shoving his fists into his pockets. "I've been waiting for you."

Her face paled and she took a step back. She'd walked too far down the deck and as he strode up to her he blocked her path to the stairs. She was cornered.

Wide-eyed and alert she stepped to the side until she hit the wooden balustrade. "Carlo—" Her voice was barely audible, and the soft-spoken plea made a smile twitch inside him. She would plead much louder than that, and quite soon.

He didn't move closer but simply gazed at her. She was so beautiful, flustered, her lips parted. "*Dio*, you're a goddess, Simone. Irresistible."

It would take him two steps to close the gap between them, but he wanted to savor this moment, stretch it out and tease her. He let his gaze travel over her face, lower to the column of her neck where her pulse skipped under the creamy, sensitive skin, lower to the slope of her breasts. Her tank top hugged her curves, but the shoulder and the neckline had slipped to reveal a satin strap and a lacy bit of bra above one breast. Hardly a millimeter was visible, but it was enough to burn a heated pulse down his back to where it burst into his groin.

He took a step closer, his hand raised to touch the little lines of temptation. "What are you wearing?" he mused. He'd never seen her in anything but the pure basics and the idea of Simone wearing seductive lingerie made him throb, burning with the need to bury himself inside her. His erection came hard and fast.

"Don't," she whimpered, her eyes not leaving his face as he gazed back at her.

"Don't what?" he asked, as his unhurried finger traced the satin strap, down to the lace, touching her heated skin and the soft slant of her breast, lightly tucking the fabric underneath the tank top.

She trembled and her chest heaved at his touch, her nipples hardening under his gaze.

"There," he said, his voice heavy, his finger retracing its steps to make sure none of her bra peeked out. How he was going to enjoy taking it off later. His lids had become lazy in his arousal, and when he gazed into her eyes again, she seemed to be fighting for her own resistance by closing her eyes and blocking him out as she bit her lip.

"Don't what, *cara*?" he asked again, dropping his fingers to the side of her breast, where his thumb circled a leisurely trail around her nipple, avoiding the hard tip in a measured tease.

"Don't," she whispered again, but when she sucked in a slow breath he knew he'd gotten her right where he wanted her.

He closed in, putting his other hand on the railing where hers gripped at the wood, white-knuckled. He tilted his nose down to her temple, drawing in her scent and letting his lips glide down her ear before catching the lobe between his teeth with a gentle tug. She leaned into his hand, as he'd known she would, and the pebbled tip of her breast pressed into his palm. He groaned as he let go of a hungry sigh, his mouth searching for that sensitive spot just below her ear. "I need some specifics here, Simone."

She gave a soft moan as he kissed her neck, his thumb massaging her nipple, his fingers lightly squeezing.

He ran his other hand up her naked arm and let go of her breast to reach for her face, cupping her cheeks in both hands. "Don't do this?" he asked softly as he stroked her cheeks with his thumbs, letting his fingers softly caress the curls at the base of her neck.

She didn't answer but had dropped her head back at his touch, her eyes drowsy, as he ran the pad of his thumb over her soft, sensual lips, plump and begging.

Her hands slipped to his sides, her heated palms edging him closer. He grunted at the feeling of her hands on him and at the relief of finally having her touch him. It was tentative, but as he lifted her chin her fingers dug into him, bringing him closer.

"Don't. Kiss me," she murmured helplessly.

His lips touched hers and she sighed as he kissed her once, softly. He didn't pull away, but let his lips moor against hers, then moved them in soft strokes that made her open up for him in a sweet surrender. She leaned into him, her hands edging up his chest. He kissed her deeper and groaned as her tongue intertwined with his in a slow turn that tasted of her soul.

She trembled under his touch and he lifted a leg between hers and pinned her to the railing, taking her more deeply with his mouth. Her mound rested against his upper thigh, and his hands trailed down her back to pull her tight to him in a low rhythmic pressure that would have her begging, feeling exactly what he had in store for her. She was so soft, so delicious.

A saltiness penetrated his mind as they kissed. And then he tasted it. She was crying, her silent tears seeping into the corner of her lips. Her long fingers curled into his shirt, pinching him. He pulled away, soothing the tears with his lips. *"Cara...cara...*why can't you forgive me?"

She sobbed. "There's nothing to forgive. After all this time...there's nothing to forgive." She dropped her head, resting her forehead against his chin. "I just want to go home, Carlo."

"Then let me take you home," he whispered, for the first time realizing that her home was with him. He'd do anything to have her back. Now that he had her, he was never letting go.

"I meant Dar es Salaam." She lowered her head to his chest, her sobs more intense despite what he'd said.

He hugged her close, pressing kisses to her hair. *"Dio,* Mona." He exhaled deeply. "I didn't mean for this trip to be too much—"

She met his gaze, shaking her head. "You don't understand." She bit her trembling lip, fresh tears swelling and overflowing from her eyes. "I lied to you this morning."

Dread curled inside him, and at the despair in her eyes, his desire cooled like a sun-baked stone tossed into ice-cold water. He tried to recall their conversation that morning. There had been nothing that could have implicated her...nothing. "Lied about what, *cara*?"

"About the dependent. In my employee file." She nearly choked. "It's not Gabi."

He frowned, not quite catching her drift. "I don't understand."

She scanned his eyes, and for a long moment, she just stared at him as tears brimmed. "I have a child, Carlo." She sucked in a slow breath. "A little girl. At home. In Dar es Salaam."

He searched her face, but a cold wariness had crept up from nowhere, settling into the marrow of his bones.

"Why didn't you say anything before." It was a statement, not a question. He already knew the answer.

"Because she's yours."

Chapter Seventeen

Simone hadn't anticipated the sense of complete peace that settled over her. Carlo finally knew. She let her hands slip from where they'd clutched his shirt and dropped her head to his chest.

The whole day she'd worked through the downpour of emotions the calls with her mother and Gabi had triggered. She'd been holding herself together by her nails for the past few days, since Carlo had told her he'd looked for her four years ago. Speaking to her mother had caused all the pieces of what had happened to slot into place.

She'd always wished there had been a reasonable explanation for why he'd dumped her. She'd always wondered how she could have been so wrong about his feelings for her, their feelings for each other, that he would have just dropped her without a word of explanation. Even without knowing about the pregnancy he had searched for her, and that was more than enough for her to let go of the past.

But despite thinking it over the whole afternoon, she hadn't been ready to tell him about Sarah. She'd been dead set against telling him since his arrival four days ago, and getting her mind around everything that had happened had been exhausting. When she'd seen him standing in the light on the deck, his dark eyes determined, his body set to pounce, *waiting* for her, she'd known she would tell him.

When he'd touched her, his hands on her breasts feeding her desire like oxygen fueled fire, his lips on her skin setting a smoldering trail upon her body, it had been the notion of him, and the knowledge that she wanted all of him, that had tipped the scale.

The only way she could ever have him was if he knew about Sarah. Sarah was the link that bound them, but that link could also break them. He'd never been angry with her before, but in the tremors that ran through his body as he took the shock of her revelation…of course he'd be angry and she'd have to deal with the consequences of his anger.

****

For Carlo the world had stopped. He groped for the railing as Simone's hands fell to her sides, unbalancing him physically. He leaned into her, reeling.

"Simone?" He mouthed her name, not sure if she even heard him for he wasn't sure he'd actually spoken.

She didn't answer him, and after a moment he exhaled, taking her face in his hands. Her eyes fluttered open, her cheeks wet and warm underneath his fingers, which trembled uncontrollably.

"I—" He broke off when every truth shone from her eyes. He believed her, and that was probably the worst of all. This was real.

He bit down on his lip, for something heavy and unyielding stirred deep in his gut. Running his hands down her neck to her shoulders, he gripped tighter. "We have a daughter?" The words sounded alien. Unreal. "Four years down the fucking line and you tell me we have a daughter?" He had no control over the heat that surged from deep within him. His hands shook and the

189

warmth spread to his neck and higher.

The unmasked fear in her eyes made him drop his hands to the railing, pinning her between him and the balustrade.

"Why didn't you return my calls?" It was one thing not to have called him because she didn't want to be with him anymore. But this…he felt stripped of some fundamental human right. He'd always sensed he'd left a part of him behind in Dar es Salaam, but he'd never thought of it being something physical, another being, a child he had brought to life with her.

He hissed out a breath. Nothing made sense. "Why didn't you let me know?" It was the least she could have done, but he bit back the sarcastic retort.

Tears welled afresh in her eyes, and he cursed under his breath. "Fuck, Simone. I know it was ten weeks, but surely a *baby* justified one call back." He shook his head. "Just one call."

"I never knew you phoned," she whispered, and the agony in her eyes tore at him.

The heaviness shifted and jolted against the walls of his stomach. Something else had stood between them four years ago. It hadn't only been him and those accursed ten weeks when he had been coming to grips with his dad dying.

He'd be damned if he didn't get the reason out of her right now. He raked his hands through his hair, the simmering heat in him ready to boil over. "How is it possible that you didn't know I phoned?" He breathed heavily to calm his anger. "I phoned at least three times before I gave up."

She stood trembling before him, but she didn't drop her gaze. "I—" She choked up. "I spoke to my mom this morning. She never told me you phoned. She thought the call was just someone from the company. She thought you were phoning from Carlevaro Air. Your name—"

He cursed in Italian, balling his fists. She reached for him, took his fists in her cold hands, her fingers clasping around his wrists. "If I'd known you phoned, I would have told you. But it took so long I...could no longer wait." She dropped her gaze. "There might be a scrap of paper with your name and number floating somewhere in my mom's house."

The weight in his chest squeezed so hard, he could burst. Blood rushed in his veins, and he shook her off to press his fingers to his temples. "A misplaced scrap of fucking paper," he hissed out. "Couldn't she have told you, after the third call?" What the hell had been wrong with the woman? "I thought you no longer wanted anything to do with me when I heard nothing from you."

"I wasn't speaking to her at the time. I didn't stay with my mom."

He dropped his hands to his sides. "Where were you then?" It dawned on him that he'd deserted her, pregnant. Instead of trying harder to find her, he'd given up. "Was the pregnancy the reason why you left Carlevaro Air in the first place?"

"I had no choice." She blinked at the tears that hovered. "The contract they offered me at the end of my probation didn't allow for maternity leave or pregnancy."

He closed his eyes, the reality drilling into him. A new anger rose in him. He would have been able to make all her troubles go away, but he'd given up any chance of control when he'd failed to give her his full name, and that mistake had been his.

"I never signed the contract and returned home instead, unsure of what to do. I looked for you...but my mom wanted to know why I'd come home." She paused. "We were fighting all the time," she said in a hollow voice.

She shook her head, dropped her gaze away from his intense scrutiny. "My mom was crazy mad. Her every prediction had come true. She said my life was ruined." She paused. "And when I couldn't find you, I was unable to explain where...who the father was—" She stalled. "She wanted me to have an abortion."

It was as if his blood drained out of his body to pool at his feet.

"I had to go away...I couldn't live with her for a week, never mind the rest of the pregnancy." She exhaled slowly. "She didn't want me in the house; she'd never wanted *me*." Her hands were gripping the balustrade. "I couldn't do it. I couldn't get rid of the baby, not when she was made...the way she was."

He sucked in a desperate breath. *She was made in love.* It was the unspoken truth. The words that had always remained unsaid between them. He'd never felt about anybody else the way he'd felt about Simone. He'd been madly in love with her but had been too much of an idiot to admit it at the time. Four years had taught him that. He suddenly felt old, as if he'd lived more than three times worth of life the past four years.

"Where did you go?" *Dio.* It was too much. He'd left her pregnant and she'd had nowhere safe to go. A thousand times he had criticized Angelo, a thousand times he had forgiven Julia every sin, but this. It outshone them all. Every thought stabbed and his shame was nauseating.

"I found a temp job in Cape Town and sat it out. I have some friends there who took me in. Flight school connections, who were good to me." She swallowed. "I went home to have Sarah, and then...I asked Peppe if he would consider employing me again. And he did." She looked up at him. "So, I came back."

They stared at each other in silence as he tried to make sense of it.

Below them, guests strolled past with an *askari* on their way to dinner. They spoke Italian and he turned to listen to the voices that rose from the path. He cursed under his breath. "It's Natalia and Dino."

She buried her face in her hands and he shoved his hands into his pockets, listening for the couple to pass.

Fuck. "They're looking for you. Wondering if you want to join *us* for dinner." He took a deep breath as Natalia's light footstep trotted up the wooden stairs.

Her gaze pleaded. "I can't," she mouthed.

Neither can I. He didn't step away from her, but lifted his gaze to where Natalia's head appeared.

Natalia's eyes widened when she saw him. She froze in her steps, gave them one all-consuming stare, and then mouthed a "*scusi.*" She turned on her heel and descended the stairs, speaking rapidly in Italian to Dino.

He waited for their footsteps to dull with distance, staring at Simone who had slumped against the balustrade, her eyes closed, pale as death.

"She told Dino you're not here, and that I'm probably already at the restaurant," he said, letting go of a sigh. Natalia's interruption, as unwanted as it had been, had given him a minute to collect himself. He was not the temper-losing kind, but fuck, he was furious at himself, for having deserted Simone, and at her mother.

Anger would solve nothing. He paced the deck once, then unfurled his fists and stretched his fingers in release.

Simone had turned away from him. "I need to sit down," she said softly, as she fumbled for the room key in her trouser pocket. He scanned her face and regret burned like acid through him. He took the key from her trembling hands, unlocked the glass door and ushered her in. Once inside, he switched on the lamp in the corner of the lounge.

When he straightened she stood by the sofa, eyeing him warily. He said nothing, and she slumped down, clasping a throw pillow to her chest. "What now?"

"Who is looking after her?" He made a hopeless gesture with his hands. He sure as hell hoped she wasn't staying with Simone's mother.

"I have a nanny in Dar that has been taking care of her ever since...ever since I returned to work here three years ago."

"A nanny?" he spat out. *Dio*. A fucking nanny, ready to fuck up his child, just like Angelo had been fucked up. It was possibly even worse than her mother.

He stared at her across the length of the lounge. "We'll go to Dar es Salaam," he said, but there was a sharp edge to his voice he couldn't help. "And I'll meet my daughter." He swallowed a curse. "What...did you call her?"

She hesitated, her fingers cramping the corners of the pillow. "Sarah...Sarah Carla Levin."

Her words winded him. "You remembered? You remembered my mother's name? From the one time we spoke about her?" Her words were unbearable. She'd named their daughter, honoring his mother, and had given her his own name...even after she thought he'd abandoned her. He had to turn away from her, from her gaze that was no longer guarded, as it had been the past few days.

He strode to the glass doors leading to the back verandah. He needed to get out, back into the open air and away from the suffocating pressure on his chest, but the reflection in the sliding glass door made him pause. Simone sat in the soft light of the lamp, drained, but no longer bewildered as she had been since that first morning. The calculating glances she'd been shooting at him from that first day were gone too. Yet there was something he couldn't place in everything that had happened the last few days. He kept staring at her reflection. She wiped at her cheeks, slumped back and closed her eyes.

****

Simone leaned back and relief whispered through her. She sighed deeply. It had been the right thing to do. She'd told him everything, but now, with his back to her, the enormity of what she'd done flooded her. She crossed her arms over her chest; cold spread down her limbs.

She tossed the pillow to the side and hugged her legs up to her chest. He wanted to go to Dar es Salaam, and that was what she'd wanted, to be with Sarah.

When he turned to face her again he didn't step closer, but his gaze burnt through her, analyzing, calculating. It sent prickles over her skin that had nothing to do with what he'd done to her earlier on the deck, what he could do to her with a mere whispering breath on her skin.

She'd played all her cards, and in doing so she'd left herself and Sarah exposed and vulnerable. Carlo could seize control in so many ways. She wasn't ready for any of it. She ached to be with Sarah, but to let him in…the knot swelled in her throat. It was what she wanted more than anything, but on what basis? She would rather not have him in Sarah's life at all if it was going to be a one-off. Or a constant in and out, with some vague commitment and money to smooth the sharp edges.

"We can't fly now," she said, hesitantly looking up at him. It was dark, the flight would be uninsured, and she needed time to think.

She'd blurted out the truth about Sarah's existence because she couldn't keep their daughter to herself anymore, but now…she hadn't thought beyond what had passed years ago and how it had ruined their relationship.

"We'll fly first thing tomorrow morning." He stepped toward her, but she put up her hand to stop him from coming any closer.

"Carlo, I—" She broke off. "I don't want to rush into something we'll regret."

Her words were so laden that the room filled with them and every unsaid word that could find a space to breathe.

He paled even more and a twitch took up residence in the line of his jaw. "Regret? Four fucking years, Simone. That's a shitload to regret."

She couldn't let him barge in on Sarah, but Carlo would want to meet her. Her pulse sped up as he checked his watch…he would be in Dar es Salaam now if it were possible.

"I want my daughter. Here. Now," he said, echoing her thoughts. "What were you expecting?"

She wasn't sure what she'd expected. She hadn't foreseen that he would be waiting for her tonight. She hadn't planned anything beyond the decision to tell him about Sarah. And that decision she'd only made in the past hour, whilst on the game drive. When she'd do that hadn't been something she had narrowed down to the hour.

One thing she hadn't bargained on was flying out so soon. She could fly every route blindfolded, and no one would know that better than Carlo. He could override the insurance situation if he wanted to, and her heartbeat pitched in panic. Her fears, borne from her own past, shot to the surface. She closed her eyes, in silent prayer. "Don't take her from me," she whispered. "Please."

There was not a sound, not a breath, and when she opened her eyes he'd frozen on the spot, his eyes wide and horrified.

"*Dio*," he grunted as he covered the space between them, towering over her. "Is that why you kept her a secret from me the past few days?" he spat out. "Do you think so little of me?"

She looked at him warily. His expression said it all; she had overstepped the boundary—her words had been a stab at his integrity. She couldn't retract her words, and now that he knew her biggest fear, he could use it against her. "I did when you arrived four days ago." She swallowed. "Before I knew you'd phoned." She bit her lip because his expression didn't soften. "I have no idea what to think, what to do anymore."

He laughed, bitter, hard. "Stop thinking. You don't need to do anything." His voice chipped like ice, and her stomach cramped at his harsh, bitter tone. "Four years ago, you were happy to trust my lead. You'll do the same now."

The commands were so unlike him; he'd never spoken to her like that before. Her words had cut deep. He glared at her and seconds ticked past.

"Four years ago, I wasn't a single mother with my daughter's welfare at stake," she bit back. She clenched her arms tighter around her legs, pursing her lips into a firm line. This was moving too fast. With Carlo would come the rest of the Carlevaro clan. She wasn't ready to deal with them, never mind subject Sarah to a bunch of strangers who'd pull her in all directions. "I don't want your family to know."

He just stared at her, shaking his head with a scowl. "What Natalia doesn't know she'll soon figure out." He dragged his fingers through his hair. "You try and keep my daughter's existence from Natalia." He dropped his hands to his sides, unclenching his fingers. "What I don't understand is why nobody said anything. No one. Not when I insisted on changing the schedule so that you would fly us non-stop for the next few weeks, not when I pried into your life with James King." He paused. "Nobody said a word about you having a daughter."

He stared at her, his eyes narrowing as the slow realization surfaced. He balled his fists and hissed a curse. "I'll tell you what you can do." He took a step toward her, almost menacing. "You can stop treating our child like some dirty secret."

His words pierced her heart and she shrank.

Sarah was no dirty secret, and yet there was truth in what he'd said.

She rarely talked about Sarah at work and had kept her daughter to herself. It had been, deep down, one of the reasons she'd left for Cape Town when she'd told her mom she was pregnant. The whispers behind her back, the degrading looks from her friends in the small town where she'd grown up…she couldn't stomach them. She had been the ambitious, snobbish pilot-girl who'd gotten knocked up by some random bloke who'd left her. *Served her right.*

She'd returned to Dar es Salaam, where she could live in anonymity, and everybody pretended they couldn't care less. Even so, there had been rumors going around that Peppe had fathered Sarah.

She might have chosen to have Sarah, but she was no better than her mother. Coldness enveloped her at the insight. She was ashamed of having a child with a man who hadn't cared enough to be around, who hadn't respected her enough to marry her. But it was more than simple marriage vows or making an *honest woman* of her. It was the notion of forsaking all others for *her* in love like her father had never done for her mother. She dropped her face to her knees, wanting to hide the tears that burned behind her eyes.

Several minutes passed before he stepped toward her. A hand brushed her hair and she glanced up at him. His anger still brooded shallow in his eyes, trembled in his fingers that stroked her temple and cheek. He cupped her chin in his hand and his thumb traced over her bottom lip. "We seem to have lost all the ground between us, haven't we, *cara*?" he asked, his voice tired. "There seems to be nothing left to salvage."

Carlo was no random bloke. He held her so gently in a grip that could break her. His fingers were cold, but every gesture he made was controlled, measured, sure. Another shudder ran through her as he forced her to meet his gaze. "Go to bed, Simone. I'll sort out our departure tomorrow morning."

His gaze dropped to her lips. For a second, she thought he would bend over to kiss her, and in that moment, there was nothing she wanted more. But he turned and walked out of the room, leaving her alone.

Chapter Eighteen

Carlo shoved his fists into his pockets as he strode down the stairs. He'd been grinding his jaw so hard his teeth ached. He wanted to beat the anger and helplessness out of his being. He should have walked away after the first spurt of anger, after the shock of Simone's revelation, but he hadn't gotten himself that far. Something had rooted him to the spot, forcing him to stay and draw everything out of her.

He had a daughter.

And her name was Sarah.

His gut twisted and he had to pause, looking back down the path that led to Simone's room. He'd rushed down the walkway to get away from Simone, with her inherent distrust. But there was the bigger picture and he finally understood. She'd given up on him, thinking he wouldn't be back. As if those six weeks they'd had together had meant nothing.

He hadn't even asked if she had a photo of their daughter. Did she look like Simone? All golden curls and sea green eyes, wide with wonder, a smile playing at her lips. Simone as he'd known her.

He dragged his hands down his face, inhaling deeply in and out into his palms. He couldn't go back now, not with his shock and anger still scorching, her fear over what he was going to do to her, to their daughter, blatant as daylight in her eyes.

Did she think he was some kind of monster? That he would tear them apart? Fuck. Maybe he was. His anger at not having known, for having missed so much, was so intense it ate him from the inside out.

He passed the stairs that led to the room he was to share with Angelo. Natalia's expression had said everything as she'd seen them on the deck together. The final puzzle piece had slotted into place, the reason why her incessant matchmaking had been unsuccessful. She'd finally recognized in Simone the mystery woman he'd been pining over for the past few years. Natalia with her romantic, idealistic, perfect life, wanting to create the same for the three orphaned Carlevaro children. And all of them so fucked up in their own special way.

He grunted and shook his head with a heavy sigh. Except that Natalia had never been able to have her own children, despite every treatment available. The heartache of several miscarriages and infertility had nearly torn her and Dino apart.

And here he was, a father, and not even aware of it. He couldn't stop Natalia from talking to Simone directly, but he took a slow breath…Simone was right. For all that she'd kept her daughter—their daughter— quiet, his family couldn't know. Not yet. He still needed to get his own head around the situation.

Four years ago he'd tried his best to do the right thing for his dad, family and the business, but in the end, he'd failed Simone and their daughter. Any second chances he'd hoped to have with her had been stalled by her revelation. He couldn't deal with his family too, a bunch of spectators that would howl their opinions from the sidelines.

He stopped as the path led into the reception area and the guest lounge. Beyond the lounge his family waited in the dining room. They expected his surface-calm presence, sure and steadfast. He wavered as he gathered his thoughts, consciously compartmentalizing his emotions. Avoiding his family for dinner would raise suspicions, and he would rather sit through half an hour of torture than a full cross-examination for being missing in action.

He raked his hands through his hair with a deep sigh. At first light, he and Simone would leave for Dar es Salaam. He had to make up some excuse. The others must find their own way to Ruaha. Once in Dar es Salaam, he would know more, and would take action on the information he had.

One thing was certain—he wasn't leaving his daughter in the hands of a nanny for a minute longer than needed.

When he walked into the dining room he spotted Dino, Natalia and Angelo already eating.

Natalia met his gaze briefly, not revealing anything as she took up her wine glass for a cautious sip.

Dino waved for him to sit down. "Sorry, we started without you, but it has been a long day." He lifted a finger to call a waiter.

You have no idea. "No problem." He sat down, trying to avoid Angelo's piercing gaze.

"Julia is looking for you," Angelo said. "She phoned me. She's been trying to get hold of you but you didn't answer."

Automatically he felt for his phone in his pockets. Fuck. He'd switched it off and had left it on the coffee table on the deck of Simone's room. "I must have left it in the office. I got busy with some things."

The waiter stood closer and he ordered the main course, skipping the rest of the five courses on offer. Dino poured him some wine.

"Was it urgent?" Carlo asked Angelo, grateful to have a topic of conversation. "Did she say what it was about?"

"No, just that you must phone her back as soon as possible."

Angelo's gaze burnt on his face, then dropped to his hands, which were trembling slightly. He took a deep sip of his wine.

"What's eating you, Carlo?" Angelo asked as if he could see straight into his mind and heart.

It was strange to be on the receiving end of that question for once. "Nothing much. I did some calculations earlier with Simone. We need to fly to Dar tomorrow to refuel." He couldn't look up, and turned his wineglass around and around. "We won't be back tomorrow. I was hoping to fly directly to Ruaha from here. This means we lose a day."

"We should fit in the Mara while we are on this side of the world," Natalia said. "One less flight, and it would feel less rushed. It wouldn't matter much if you miss one lodge. Makes more sense, don't you agree, Dino?"

She glanced at Dino, but she was consciously rescuing him from a sticky situation.

Dino shrugged. "Sure. I know you wanted to get to Ruaha as soon as possible, Carlo."

"One day won't make a difference," Natalia said. She made a comment on the food that arrived at that moment and Carlo sighed at the reprieve. He ate in haste, the excuse of having to phone Julia too convenient to linger.

He didn't want to go back to Simone's room to get his phone because they both needed some breathing space. Instead he continued to the lodge's back office, where he'd claimed to have left his phone.

He knew Julia's number by heart. He called her a couple of times a day, even though she lived with him and worked in an office one floor down from his.

He walked in on Kevin, who was working on his laptop. "Mind if I make a quick call?"

"No problem," Kevin said as he got up from his desk. He showed Carlo how to dial out to Italy and closed the office door as he left.

Julia answered in the middle of the second ring. "I visited Peppe." She sighed deeply into the phone. "*Dio*, Carlo."

He swallowed at the tone of her voice. "Did you get anything out of him? Does he remember Simone Levin?"

"He is getting better by the day, and there's nothing wrong with his memory." She breathed into the phone. "How much do you know about Simone?"

His pulse was starting to beat heavily. At least he now knew about their daughter. He couldn't imagine hearing about her from anyone but Simone. "Just tell me what Peppe told you?"

"Peppe said she trained with you under probation, then when…Dad got sick, and you left, she was passed around the other pilots for the last of her training. She left abruptly, without any reason, never signing her fixed contract." Julia paused, and he could hear her swallow. "When she asked him to have her job back with a baby in tow...he couldn't turn her away." She sniffed, and a slow chill crept down his back. "Peppe thought she'd been raped at the pilot's digs. By one...or more of the pilots."

His blood stalled and his chest tightened. God help him. *It's worth every cent to me not to be surrounded by a bunch of horny bastards who think all I'm good for is a quick fuck.* As Simone's words from several nights ago surfaced a shudder shot through him. She'd never said anything about the male pilots she'd lived with beyond that rude statement.

Surely she would have mentioned it tonight. After everything that had happened, that had been revealed between them, she couldn't keep something like this from him.

"She never made a case." Julia's voice trembled. "Peppe said he knew she'd be safe with you, but once you'd left..." She broke off.

He closed his eyes, rubbing at his forehead. He was going to disappoint Peppe, who lived his life by the strictest of moral codes. Simone had been *safe* with him until he'd ditched her for ten long weeks. Probably the longest weeks of her life, as she searched for someone who hadn't existed. Anger at his conceited idiocy surged again. If only he'd been upfront with her, if only she'd known Peppe was his uncle. He slumped over the desk. When exactly had he planned to tell her who he was?

Julia's sharp inhale, verging on a sob, broke through to him. "Please, Carlo, tell me this type of thing hasn't been happening at our properties?" Tears edged her voice, and his whole being felt like it had plummeted down an abyss. Julia had interpreted his silence as confirmation.

He wiped his hand down his face. To ask Julia to talk to Peppe, to draw this story from him, had been cruel in retrospect. But he hadn't expected this. "No, I…I don't think so." He paused as his stomach churned. "I hope not." Simone was the only female pilot currently at Carlevaro Air. "Not with Simone…as far as I know." He wouldn't be able to live with himself if something had happened to her when he'd left her, alone and exposed.

Julia gave a shaky sigh. "Peppe no longer employed female pilots, as a rule. He never asked Simone about what had happened and she never brought anything up. She keeps to herself. Very private."

"Yes." What a can of worms. He'd never even considered something like that happening in the pilots' digs. When he'd worked for Carlevaro Air there had been only three female pilots on the payroll. Thank God Simone no longer lived in the pilots' digs.

"Please, can you…check if she is okay?" Julia's voice hovered. "I know she is just an employee I've never met, but if you can somehow make sure—"

He closed his eyes. The opportunity to tell Julia about his aborted affair with Simone was staring him in the face. But he wasn't ready to talk about his daughter. "Yes. I'll see what I can get out of her."

He pressed his thumb hard against his forehead and rubbed. Julia had been unhinged by her conversation with Peppe. He had no more capacity for worry, but Julia was alone in Rome, where she could pick up the phone and get any narcotic she wanted. "Where are you?"

"At work."

He sighed. "What are you doing tonight?"

"Going home to pack for the Tusk Awards in London."

Not that too. He'd forgotten about the Tusk Awards. "Are you going to be okay, Julia?"

She didn't answer immediately. The old unease, which had been overshadowed by everything else these past few weeks, tap-tap-tapped inside him.

"Yes."

He was supposed to travel with her to London for the awards ceremony at the end of the week. With everything else it had slipped off his radar. "Who are you taking with you to London?"

"No one." She hesitated. "You always go everywhere with me."

He dropped his forehead to his palm, suppressing a groan. "Call me, call Angelo...if you need to." He visualized her face, but instead of her smooth olive coloring, her skin was gray, her mouth taut, and her brown eyes wild, desperate, almost black and begging as they had been the night she came to him for help.

He cursed silently. He couldn't be everywhere at once. No matter what he did now, he couldn't be there for Julia.

Just like he hadn't been there for Simone. His own inadequacy was eating at him in short, sharp bites.

It seemed like a long time before she answered, "Okay."

"Promise me you won't cave in, *cara*." He tried to be stern, but it sounded as if he begged.

"I won't." It was barely a whisper.

The weight of worry he'd had over Julia, which

over the years had seemed to become lighter, yanked at him. He had no choice but to take her word. He rang off, wondering what shit storm he'd created.

****

Carlo stared blindly, rerunning the conversations he'd had with Simone and Julia through his mind. Simone had never implied that she'd been raped. Nothing she'd said, nothing in her bearing, had hinted at there being anything that she hadn't been willing to share with him that night.

When he'd kissed her, there had been nothing between them except the secret of their daughter. As she'd kissed him back, there had been no hesitation that would have given him pause.

When Kevin knocked on the door an hour later he shrugged an apology. He arranged with Kevin for a vehicle to take them to the airstrip at dawn and left the office, taking the path leading to the rooms, exhausted.

He couldn't reverse the clock. He couldn't redirect all his anger and resentment toward anybody else, especially not Simone. He'd left Carlevaro Air assuming that she would sign her contract and would be there when he returned. Which he had never done, something he hadn't foreseen at the time. That he had been to blame for her situation left him pulsing with a permanent ache.

Would she forgive the harsh words he'd uttered when he'd lost it earlier that evening? Those words about their child being a dirty secret? His behavior had been unpardonable, given that Simone was a single mother, who'd received zero support from him for the past four years. No amount of money he could hand over now could wash away that guilt.

Eventually, he took the path to her room with a sense of purpose. He'd have to make the best of the situation. Never hurt Simone again. And be the best father he could be. Better late than never.

When he reached her chalet, he took the stairs quietly. The light on the deck shone softer, and he found his phone where he'd left it. As he pocketed it he glanced into her room.

The glass doors were closed, but she hadn't drawn the curtains. From where he stood, he peered past the lounge to the bed at the end of the room. The bedside lamp cast a soft glow on her back. She seemed asleep. He knocked softly on the door, not knowing what he would say, what he would do if she turned around and told him to fuck off, forever. He deserved that, more than anything else.

She didn't stir. He tried the door and it opened without a creak. She hadn't locked it when he'd left, and he stepped inside, feeling indecisive. She stirred, pulling her legs higher to her chest. Light played on her skin with the movement of her shoulder blades. She wore a white camisole top and matching sleeping shorts with her hair fanning over the cushion and her shoulder. Already his blood stirred at the thought of her, with her long naked legs, her creamy skin soft and warm against his. As if she read his mind she shuddered, but didn't wake up.

He moved closer. She was his; she'd always been his. He felt as if he had some right to be there, although he had none. He stopped next to the bed and stared at her. Her fingers had relaxed around her dated cell phone, and a cluster of tissues had escaped from her other hand.

Edging around the bed to the other side, his gaze caressed the curve of her hips. Her breasts rested tight against the silk, her areolas visible through the light fabric. The shadows playing over her body made heat flare within him, and he shoved his hands into his pockets to stop himself from reaching out to her.

For the first time since seeing her again, he could tell she was at peace. Combing his hands through his hair, he sighed. She'd been exhausted and now he understood why. She hadn't been able to sleep while he'd been in the vicinity. Every jolt and hitch of her shoulders, every haunted glance suddenly made sense, and relief poured from deep inside him. She'd been hiding their daughter from him, and not something sinister.

He slipped her phone from her fingers, gathered the tissues and put them on the bedside table. He nudged the duvet from the opposite corner and folded it over her, forming it into a warm cocoon. He burned to lie down and settle her into his arms, nestling her against his chest where she should be. But it would be artificial. Too much was still raw, and he doubted she would want him there.

Tomorrow was going to be a hell of a day. And Simone, for all that she was asleep, was probably gathering her strength for a parental battle of historical proportions. He let the last of his anger slip from him. He would take her lead in this, for she had, after all, been the only parent his daughter had ever known.

He might be a father, but if he were honest with himself the idea petrified him. His few male friends who had ventured into fatherhood had done so with a plan, and a wait of at least nine months, during which they'd gotten used to the idea. Increasing life insurance, updating wills, buying everything babies needed, and being subjected to their partner's pregnancy-induced mood swings. Being catapulted into fatherhood wasn't something he was going to get to grips with overnight.

For a moment he let his hand hover over her head, just shy of touching her blonde curls. Involuntarily his thoughts jumped back to Julia. When their dad had fallen ill, Julia had been unable to deal with the grief and had fallen deep into heroin addiction. Four years down the line and he still didn't know exactly what Julia had been through, but her reaction to her conversation with Peppe made him retract his hand.

He switched off the lamp and left the room, letting Simone be.

Chapter Nineteen

Simone startled awake. Early morning light filled the room, creating quiet shadows, but she could have sworn someone had knocked. She turned and looked toward the glass door. Carlo stood outside, hands shoved in his pockets, his silhouette framed by the undrawn curtains.

In a second everything that had passed the previous night flooded back and she moaned, her relaxed body hurtled back into tense muscles and hammering heart.

She got out of bed and grabbed the hotel robe that she'd tossed to the floor the night before, stumbled to the door and fumbled with the lock. Carlo calmly lowered the handle, opened the door and let the crisp morning air in.

"Did you sleep okay?" he asked, his eyes searching her face.

"Yes." She shivered, out of her cozy cocoon. She couldn't remember getting under the duvet during the night.

"The vehicle is ready. We can go as soon as you are." He was dressed, shaved, smelled divine and was probably...battle fit.

She searched his face. He wasn't impatient—yet. "Okay." There was no going back. His eyes looked drained and heavy. He didn't look in shape for flying.

"Did you sleep...much?"

"As much as can be expected." He dropped his gaze. "I'd like to apologize. Before we get on that plane." He looked up again. "Together."

Together. The way he said it implied so much. An unwanted heat spread to her cheeks. "Don't—"

"I regret some of the things I said last night—"

"Carlo—"

"Let me finish. I might never have the guts to say this again."

She bit her lip to stop its trembling, her hands clinging to the robe's belt, which she'd tied too tight in a rushed knot.

"It was unfair to say you kept our daughter a dirty secret. To think what you've gone through these past years, without any support, I—" He faltered.

She closed her eyes. "There is some truth in what you said," she whispered. The last bit of fear dissolved and she opened her eyes. He looked desperate, lost, and unsure. So unlike the man that ruled Carlevaro and deep down owned her heart.

"I won't take her away from you, Mona."

"I know." The Carlo from those first weeks, who still lurked underneath the layers of stress, would never do that.

"But I want to be involved."

"I understand, but we'll have to talk about that." It was a course she'd chosen, but how was it going to work with him in Italy and her and Sarah in Dar es Salaam?

"Sure."

"Let's just start with today."

"Okay." He shifted on his feet. "There's something else I need to know before we leave here."

Something in his voice made her pause. "What?"

"I had a call from Julia. She spoke to Peppe about the reasons why he re-hired you."

A chill crept down her back but there was no longer any reason why Carlo couldn't dig into anything he wanted.

"Were you ever—" He exhaled deeply, his gaze darting, as he struggled to find words. "Violated?" He almost choked on the word as he met her gaze steadily. "By anybody in the pilots' digs? During the time you stayed there alone? Once I'd left?"

He sounded so pained, almost embarrassed, and she contracted inwardly. "No." She shook her head. "Why? Why would you think that?" She inhaled a shaky breath as the realization hit her. "Are you thinking you are not Sarah's father...and that I'm trying to shackle you with a daughter so that you can pay child support?"

"Fuck, Simone." He gave a frustrated growl. "Stop doubting my every intention. Distrusting every question." He raked his hands through his hair. "That's what Peppe thought and why he set you up as he did, in your own apartment. A result of his guilt trip, for which I am grateful. Just the idea—"

She raised her hands to stop him. She had to pick up the pieces of her broken trust in him. He was back in her life; he was going to be with Sarah today. Tomorrow. Possibly as often as he could manage. At some point, she was going to have to trust him with her daughter, alone.

"I'm sorry." She swallowed and met his gaze. "I'm still edgy."

He rubbed at his forehead. "Julia is scared

that…stuff has been happening here."

"I was careful, once you were gone." She hadn't lived in the digs for more than a month after he'd left. "But I wouldn't put it beyond some of the guys who stayed there." Who were still staying there.

He nodded with a shift in his shoulders, a heave of relief. "I wouldn't be able to live with myself if something like that had happened to you…to any woman in our employ."

She closed her eyes. "I told you how she was made." She barely whispered the words. She no longer knew how to make things better, to find the clean start she'd been craving.

He inhaled in a slow breath. "Yes."

Without thinking she stepped forward and wrapped her arms around his neck, pulling herself up to his hard body in a hug. His arms circled her and he drew her tightly to him with a sigh. He dropped his head, inhaling into her curls, his nose resting against the sensitive skin at her temple. She could have stood like that forever, soaking up his quiet strength.

They could kiss things better. A shudder of pleasure rushed down her body, settling in her core, where her need for him had been quietly keeping beat the past few days.

His hands traveled down her back in a soft, lingering caress as if he'd read her reaction to him, to the mere idea of him. "Get going, *cara*. I'll wait for you at the car."

She stepped away and nodded, suddenly shy. He walked away, but when she returned to her room she found her cell phone next to her bed, the used tissues in a little pile on the bedside table. She hadn't put them there.

Carlo. He had been there during the night, tucked her in and cared for her. Salvaging what was left of their relationship. She wished he'd gotten in bed with her, but the time hadn't been right.

****

Simone landed the aircraft without a bump. They'd flown in silence for most of the flight to Dar es Salaam; the intense atmosphere between them had been replaced by cautious anticipation. There was much to talk over, but everything hinged on Carlo meeting Sarah.

As she taxied the plane to the parking on the apron Carlo wiped at his brow for the hundredth time. During the flight, he'd kept checking his watch and the instruments as if it would make them get there faster.

She turned to him once she'd parked the plane, and they took off their headsets. For once she had the upper hand in the situation. "Nervous?" she asked him.

He chuckled. "Yes. Believe it or not."

"Just be yourself." It sounded cheesy, but under all those layers was the man she had fallen in love with.

"That's not very encouraging." He sighed and rubbed at his forehead as if he could rid himself of the etched lines on it.

"No." She laughed and he shot her a wry grin. "Stop scowling. And relax. She'll see right through you. Kids are like that."

"I'll follow your lead, then."

"Come. I'll get them to refuel so that she's ready to go…when you are." She didn't want to think too far ahead. Carlo might be here now, but he would be gone again pretty soon. One more reason to approach the day with caution, to make sure her already grappling heart didn't cave in completely. She couldn't cope with him leaving her a second time, once she'd given in to him.

They walked in silence to the Carlevaro Air offices, the wheels of their luggage protesting against the rough tar. The office was situated at the end of a dark corridor in the terminal building, with its windows overlooking the apron. It was a busy satellite office with twelve employees who managed the administration and maintenance of the Carlevaro Air fleet.

"When will they refuel?" Carlo asked.

"They'll do it later." She checked her watch. "After lunch. I'll put in a request when we hand in the keys."

They stopped in front of the security gate at the door, and Simone rang the bell. She glanced at the coveted corner office, where the fleet manager sat at his desk, busy on a call. Now that Carlo knew about Sarah, it could spoil her chances of being promoted. Or would Sarah be the weight that tipped the scale in her favor? Ross would be so pissed off she'd never hear the end of it. Maybe it was time to move on.

The gate buzzed open, and she led the way, saying hello to the staff who were busy at their desks. They all smiled and were glad to see her, which was heartwarming. She didn't miss any of the gazes that jumped from her to Carlo and back again. The whole office drew in a quiet, apprehensive breath.

"So you want to spend your days in here?" Carlo asked as they navigated the clusters of desks.

"I'll still get to fly occasionally. I need to diversify."

"It's a desk job, and long hours." He didn't sound pleased.

Was he thinking of Sarah? She'd been a working mother out of need, but also choice. Reduced hours would be great, but it was the overnights she really needed to ditch. Maybe she could negotiate that, with him backing her, if the promotion fell through. She didn't want to abuse the situation; it would make her feel weak after she'd come this far on her own.

"If I don't make the move now it's only going to get harder."

"True. Still working on that five-year plan of yours?"

For the past few years, her own plans were made in relation to Sarah's needs, and her ability to afford what her child would need next. She recalled his words to her that first night. "That was your five-year plan."

Carlo chuckled. "Those tend to go for a tumble. I should know." He sighed. "Arrogant assumption that we can have it all planned out. We're all at the beck and call of something."

They stopped in front of an administration assistant's desk. Behind her was a large wall-mounted electronic safe. Inside the open, upright box were several rows of pegged keys.

"Hey Rebecca. Keys for the DHC Twin Otter. It's parked on A3." Simone handed over the keys. "If you can arrange for a refuel and maintenance check today still?"

"Sure." Rebecca pushed a logbook toward Simone. She watched as Simone signed for the return of the keys.

Simone glanced at Carlo. "I'm not sure when we're leaving again, but she must be ready for us to fly out at a moment's notice."

"You won't be flying," Carlo said drily.

Confused, she turned to him, but heat crept up to her neck. He was dictating her life already. "What do you mean?"

"You need to be at home." His tone did not invite any further discussion. "One of the standby pilots will fly with me."

She frowned and he glanced at her. She couldn't stop the angry heat that rushed to her cheeks.

He searched her face. "We'll talk about this later. You're due a day off, so don't fight it."

She could spare herself a tiff in front of the whole office. But if she didn't say something now, he might think he could rearrange her life as it suited him, like he had a couple of days ago. "There are hardly enough pilots to fly the high season schedule. There's no room for shuffling things around as it pleases you."

He sighed. "You don't need to do the overnight flights, Simone. That's all I meant." He shifted on his feet and raised his hand to touch her, but dropped it again.

Inside her the sudden anger cooled. She'd been overreacting because the day ahead was stressing her out. She didn't need to be up in arms with him when they arrived at her apartment where Sarah waited, totally oblivious.

She dropped the discussion. "I need to get a few things from my locker."

Carlo glanced toward the fleet manager's office. "I'll wait for you here."

Simone strode off, trying not to fume. She buzzed out of the admin office and continued down the corridor to the pilot's lounge.

Michael sat in the lounge, his phone in his hands, thumbs furiously tapping on the screen, his one knee jerking. He looked up as she walked in and froze.

"Simone." His gaze dropped back to his phone.

"Hi." She didn't have time to chat and was glad to see he was engrossed in some game. But then she recalled their conversation the previous day.

He avoided her gaze as she walked to her locker. The staff room was empty, almost dead if it weren't for the creaking of the old sofa as Michael shifted.

"Did you…?" she asked.

He inhaled. "Did I?"

"Find anything?" She eyed him, but caught him staring at her with a strange light in his eyes. He had her attention now.

"What?"

How couldn't he know what she was talking about? "In the hold? After the flight back from Rufiji?" She swallowed. "Did you find anything…suspicious?"

He glanced around the room, making sure they were alone.

"Yes?" She was in a hurry.

He got up and strode to the door, checking up and down the darkened corridor, then leaned closer. "What exactly are you looking for?"

Her pulse quickened. "What did you find?"

"Nothing."

He'd said that too quickly and dread weakened her muscles. *He's lying.* How much had she messed-up in trusting him? She went with her instinct. "Bullshit."

"Bullshit?" he whispered. "You want to know about bullshit?" He took a turn in the room, caged. "One bloody elephant tusk," he hissed as he held up one finger, then put it to his mouth to indicate silence.

Goosebumps spread over her arms, the sweat in her pores cooling. *Fuck.*

She had to force down the rise of bile, which rose with a slow turn of her stomach.

"My question is, Simone, what exactly do *you* know?"

She should never have ventured down this lane. "Was it—"

"Packed in a special food crate, strapped against the wall of the hold?" he asked in a sarcastic whisper. "Yes! I nearly missed it, to be honest. Well disguised. You've been busy."

"I haven't been flying poached tusks around," she hissed, their eyes clashing in equal wrath.

"Neither have I," he said, with some menace, but after seconds he broke their locked gazes.

She wanted to go back to some neutral ground with him, to go back to the Michael she knew and trusted. "Maybe we both had." But that look she'd seen in his eyes…she stepped away from him, no longer sure what to believe. That Michael could be the culprit was an uncomfortable reality. "Only one tusk?" she whispered, her head spinning.

He nodded.

"Where's the other one?"

He almost growled, but turned away from her, glancing at the door. "Why the hell do you think *I* should know?"

She went to her locker, the sound of the screeching metal eerie with their hushed, deep breathing. Only one tusk…it made sense to fly the tusks one at a time. One tusk's weight wouldn't throw the weight and balance calculations, given the fuel left for the last stretch between Rufiji and Dar es Salaam. *Damn.* Whoever had set this up knew his shit.

"Who else knows?" she asked, unable to take stock of the things in her locker.

"Fishing, are you?" he murmured angrily.

"No!" Freaking hell, he'd think she orchestrated the whole syndicate.

"Annie."

"How?" She could not keep the shock from her voice as she glared at him. "You told Annie? Why?"

"Fuck, Simone." He rubbed his face with both hands and when he looked at her she could almost not meet his gaze. "She dragged it out of me this morning, when I spoke to her over the phone after my…discovery. How dare—"

"But Annie works for the African Elephant Specialist Group," Simone hissed, referring to the American-sponsored NGO that had local government connections that fought the illegal ivory trade. Tremors ran through her at the impact Annie could have if she chose to open her mouth. Annie might be her friend, *might have been* by the sounds of it…but to Annie, Carlevaro East Africa meant nothing.

And Michael? God, she'd put her foot right in it. Still, this was no proof. Nothing was proof.

Male voices followed by laughter filled the corridor, and Michael's gaze darted between her and the door.

"You're on your fucking own, Simone. I'd watch my back if I were you." He stomped out, going in the opposite direction of the voices.

Staring at the contents of her locker, everything

blurred. Were his last words a warning or a threat?

The other pilots ambled in and she greeted them shortly, then scrambled for her stuff and made a quick exit. But Michael's last words were not going anywhere as they swam in the fog in her mind.

She walked down the corridor and she took a deep breath, forcing herself to calm down and focus. Yes, she was essentially alone, but Michael didn't reveal that he knew about the investigation…and Carlo was with her now, and later…she couldn't let her thoughts wander down that lane quite yet.

Annie was a problem. Hopefully, Annie wouldn't be so indiscreet as to let anything slip at work. Not while Carlo and Noel's team was still busy with their investigations. Something must come up and soon. Should she tell Carlo about Michael?

She slowed down her strides and stopped outside the admin office. What to do? There were too many balls in the air, and right now they all seemed turned to stone, ready to hail down on her head.

She had no idea what to make of her conversation with Michael, but she had to make a decision, now.

Sarah.

This day was not about a crisis that had gone on in the company for months. It was about the crisis of her life for the past four years. It was about Sarah, and Sarah had always been more important than anything else.

She wouldn't do anything.

Chapter Twenty

Carlo glanced through the office. There were security bars on the windows and two cameras in the corners that filmed everyone that entered the room and everything the staff did.

The fleet manager, who'd seen him with Simone at Rebecca's desk, approached him.

"There's more security here than when I flew for Carlevaro Air," Carlo said, following the man into his office.

The manager indicated that he should sit down, but Carlo declined, going to the wide window, which overlooked the tarmac, instead.

"We had a petty cash theft last year of more than ten thousand dollars. Sometimes we need to fork out cash for fuel, otherwise we don't keep such large amounts," the fleet manager explained. "Peppe installed the cameras as a preventative measure."

Carlo remembered Peppe had mentioned the theft in his quarterly report, and that the issue had been resolved. It still didn't sound legitimate, but he would give anything to have a mere petty cash theft to deal with right now. "Do you ever review the camera footage?" He hadn't noticed any cameras on the outside of the building.

"We'd only do that in the case of an incident. We've had no incidents since the cameras were installed."

Carlo sighed. "And you are going back to Canada?" The manager had cut his two-year expatriate contract short.

"Yes. Can't stand this weather." He laughed. "I'm leaving in three weeks." The manager settled his hands on his hips. "Ideally I would like to do a proper handover to the new fleet manager."

"I know. The new executive team must ultimately decide, but," Carlo paused, "you can take Simone Levin off your list of candidates."

The manager nodded, but passed him a searching glance. "She is the best candidate for the job."

"Probably." He shoved his hands in his pockets. "I've another position in mind for her. In the interim, make sure Simone no longer flies overnight flights."

"Sure," said the manager.

Carlo turned to see Simone come through the security door. She stopped by Rebecca's desk, briefly talking to her, checking something in the logbook.

He wished the manager well and met up with Simone.

"Let's go," Simone said as she met his gaze, her voice tense.

He glanced again at the contents of the safe. It was a neat little setup. Rows of single keys, sometimes two, hung on hooks. There was one hook with a key that looked out of place, but then the pattern continued. Labels above the keys indicated the aircraft to which each specific slot belonged.

He took his suitcase and followed in Simone's footsteps, but something made him turn back and look again at the safe. Rebecca had closed the safe and twisted the knob to lock it.

He swore under his breath. He couldn't blame Simone for being on edge; he couldn't focus on anything, except the day ahead.

****

Carlo helped the taxi driver with their luggage and scooted in next to Simone on the synthetic fur that covered the seat. He leaned back with resignation. It was like being in a sauna, bar the smell of cheap car deodorizer, which dangled on the rearview mirror. Sweat started trickling down his neck.

Simone leaned forward and in Swahili asked the driver to close the windows and put the air conditioner on.

"Your Swahili is very good," he said. "You've made an effort."

"I know enough to get by." She shrugged. "I'll never be a native speaker like Liz or Ross. I took some lessons for a while and that helped."

He sensed she was unhinged. The rings under her eyes were darker, and she bit down on her jaw.

"It's going to be fine, Simone," he said, as much to calm her as to calm himself.

She stared out of the window, and after a moment, she exhaled a slow breath. "You should hear Sarah speak Swahili. She's too cute."

His stomach contracted at the small detail she'd shared with him. They hadn't spoken much about her, and he hadn't asked Simone for a photo yet, as he was about to meet her in person. Imagine a daughter that spoke Swahili.

"She's learning from the nanny?" he asked, trying to sound neutral about the inevitable nanny situation.

Simone nodded.

"What else can you tell me...about our daughter?" he asked softly, hoping she would relax enough to let the floodgates open.

She stared at him. "Please start calling her Sarah. I know it must hurt like hell, but that was all I had to go on."

He swallowed at the intense powerlessness he felt. He took hold of her hands, which were clamped together in her lap. "This will be real when I've met her, seen her."

She allowed him to take her hand but pulled away after he'd held it for a second.

"I would have insisted on calling her that, in any case," he added, then cursed inwardly; the name would just not come up when he spoke.

They drove in silence for a while.

Simone stroked some wisps of hair from her face and checked her watch. Her fingers trembled. "We should be there in ten minutes."

"What else can you tell me about...Sarah," he forced her name, "that would make this smooth sailing?" He had no idea how to deal with children; it was a program in his system that had never been switched on, and one he'd consciously avoided. His siblings were still a handful, as it were.

She turned to him. "She is bright, a chatterbox, loves hugs and cuddles, and is a pure blessing." Her eyes begged the words she hadn't allowed to leave her mouth.

Don't fuck her up.

He shifted in his seat. The stakes were high, and he held the weakest hand here. He was going to have to fake it until he made it. "What are her interests?" As soon as he asked the question he felt stupid, as if he was trying to ease into a blind date.

"Princesses, of course. Flowers. And fairies. And castles and…the idea of a prince." Simone skipped a beat. "I've tried not to disillusion her."

His spirits sank lower.

"She's a little girl, Carlo."

Right. Despite the air conditioning blowing full blast in the car, the sweat trickled faster down his back.

"No dragons or witches. Don't even mention dinosaurs."

He nodded. No dragons. No witches. Zero dinosaurs.

He had a shitload to catch up on.

They sat in silence for the rest of the trip, and he got trapped thinking about dragons and dinosaurs, and the last time he'd been this nervous. It was the first Carlevaro International directors' board meeting he'd led after his father's death. The bunch of first generation directors had, systematically, torn him to shreds. That initiation was a walk in the park.

The taxi pulled up to the solid security gate outside of a four-story apartment block that had been in the foundation phase when he'd left. It was well kept, freshly painted with no telltale signs of tropical rust or city dirt clinging to the walls. Windows blinked in the sharp sun. The exterior of the building reassured him. At least Simone didn't live in a dump with his daughter.

"Ours is on the third floor," Simone said as they got out of the car and collected their luggage.

"Sea views?" It was obvious from the location, but he needed some idle talk.

"Yes." Simone called the security guard through the gate and as he recognized her voice he wheeled the gate open.

"Lifts?"

She laughed. "Yes, the generator kicks in during power cuts."

There was a glimpse of a paved driveway, some grass, some palm trees and a fenced-in pool as the gate rolled open. He followed Simone, carrying her backpack and pulling their suitcases, as she rummaged for her apartment key in a bag she'd extracted from her backpack.

They entered the property and he took a deep breath, readying himself as they headed to the lobby.

"Mommy!" It was a high-pitched burst, followed by the sweetest laugh he'd ever heard. Little feet pattered over the pavement and a ball rolled to his feet. He dropped the suitcases and turned. There she was, unmistakably his little Sarah. Her blonde curls bobbed wildly with each step she took, and she all but leaped into Simone's arms as Simone crouched down to catch her.

Simone laughed as she straightened and hugged Sarah close. Little arms circled her neck, chubby fingers disappeared into Simone's curls, and a pink princess dress puffed around Sarah's legs. "I missed you, my darling," Simone whispered, her voice strained.

"Missed you too, Mommy," Sarah said, straddling Simone's hips. After a long hug, Sarah pulled away and took Simone's cheeks in her palms and nudged her closer. They rubbed noses, Sarah clumsily, and he melted at the tender intimacy of the moment.

"Ekimo kiss," Sarah giggled, and Simone chuckled with a sniff, before breaking the bond.

"I've got someone you need to meet," Simone said. Sarah hadn't noticed him, and at Simone's words, his hammering heart did double beats at a time. Simone turned to him, settling Sarah more comfortably on her hip.

Panic shot through him. He hadn't discussed any of this with Simone. He would loathe being introduced as anything else than what he overwhelmingly wanted to be in that moment, a father, a knight, a first prince.

As he got a full view of Sarah for the first time he had to blink. She was a little Julia, a miniature version of his mother, staring back at him, with eyes so gray it was like staring into a mirror at his own.

"This is your daddy, Sarah," Simone said, "and his name is Carlo."

Sarah's gray gaze took him in, her expression going from happy to bland, to a slight measuring up as her eyes narrowed and her lips pouted just a bit. "Really?"

"Yes, darling," Simone said firmly, her voice stripped of misgiving and doubt.

After a few infinite seconds, Sarah said, "You *very* late," while staring him straight in the eyes.

He could not help the grin, and his heart opened up all four chambers to fill with something he couldn't define. "Frightfully," he said, as he bit down his nervousness. "I'm sorry, too many dragons to fight, and a wicked wizard cast an evil spell over my sister, Julia." He raised his hand to twirl a rogue curl of Sarah's hair between his fingers. It was so soft, like an angel's. "She's a princess like you, and I had to free her from

231

his evil spell."

Sarah's eyes had widened with every word, and he could feel how his estimation rose, bit by bit.

"Really?" Sarah asked, unquestioning belief shining from her eyes.

He nodded solemnly, grasping in the same breath that every word had been dreadfully true. "It took longer than I ever imagined." He dropped his hand, amazed that Sarah had allowed him to touch her. "But here I am."

"Tell *all* about it," Sarah said. And just like that she struggled from Simone's arms to the ground and grabbed his hand. "Come. Ruthie's said it's snack time."

His fingers clasped the small hand in his. Hers was warm and soft, and as her hand disappeared in his much bigger one, he was as lost forever as he'd been found in one moment.

He met Simone's gaze; her eyes were moist, but her lips smiled. "You're a natural," she mouthed.

He glowed at her words, with warmth he hoped to never shed. Sarah tugged him toward the pool, and he had to drop the backpack.

A tall African woman hovered a couple of meters from them. Nothing about her said British nanny. She wore a dress made from colorful local fabric, her braided hair twisted in a bun. Her whole face smiled as Sarah rushed toward her, calling, "Ruthie, my *baba*!" as they drew closer.

My *baba*. My father. His two cents' worth of Swahili was worth a million dollars in that moment.

Ruth smiled and stuck out her hand. He shook it with a swallow. Not sure what Simone had told Ruth about him, he said, "Carlo Carlevaro, nice to meet you."

Ruth's eyes told him nothing, as she'd dropped her gaze.

Before anything else could pass, Simone drew Ruth into a quick hug. "Thank you for taking care of Sarah."

"It's always a pleasure." Ruth laughed, a true, sweet laugh as she stooped to tickle Sarah on her belly.

Sarah giggled back and that almost settled it for him. Ruth didn't seem to have a wicked bone in her body.

"I'll help you with the bags and be on my way." Ruth picked up Simone's backpack and suitcase where they had dropped it.

Sarah tugged at his hand, gazing up at him earnestly. "When Mommy work, Ruthie's here. Mommy here, Ruthie go home."

"I see," he said. "Sounds like Ruthie needs a break."

"Mommy too."

He would have laughed if Sarah hadn't nailed it. He took his suitcase; Simone had Sarah's ball in her hand and together they went into the lobby. As they took the lift Sarah still clung to his hand. "We bakeded cookies."

"Just baked, darling," Simone corrected gently.

As they reached the landing Carlo leaned closer to Sarah's ear. "Maybe we can make Mommy a cup of tea," he stage-whispered. "And you can put some cookies on a plate for her."

Sarah's eyes, bright and full of life, shone at him. "A tea party!"

Chapter Twenty-One

Simone stepped out of the shower, feeling almost human. After a very thorough cup of tea and a tower of cookies, a makeshift lunch, and lots of time spent with Carlo and Sarah on the carpet in the lounge, some of the knots and creases in her stomach had ironed out. Sarah had been all over Carlo like an entire nest of ants, but he'd taken to it as if she was water, and he the desert.

Eventually, she'd relaxed enough to leave Sarah with Carlo while she took a shower. The shower wasn't exactly solo, with Sarah barging into the en suite bathroom every two minutes to ask her something. Could she show *Daddy* this? Could they play that? Could she paint his nails?

She rubbed her hair dry, then wrapped the towel around her breasts and knotted it in place. As she strolled out of the bathroom her ears pricked. Sarah's chatter echoed in the lounge. She took a quick peek out of the bedroom door, down the short corridor to the lounge.

Carlo sat with Sarah, the picture books she'd left them with discarded, his fingers outstretched. Sarah held the red nail polish in her hand.

A smile played around Carlo's mouth, his eyes not shifting away from his daughter.

Simone watched, smothering a chuckle, as Sarah twisted the bottle open.

"Hold still!" Sarah's excited voice filled the lounge, and Simone bit her lip to stop a giggle. Carlo would learn soon enough how to defend himself.

She went back to the room to rummage for some fresh clothes in her closet. She envied Sarah, who had taken to Carlo with enthusiasm and unquestioning trust. Sarah had warmed to him within minutes...but children were like that, especially when trust had never been broken. Carlo had been completely into Sarah from the first moment and had looked into her eyes like she was the most precious child in the world. Who could resist that, never mind a little girl who wanted nothing more than to have a father?

She took a pair of cut-off jean shorts and a strappy top and tossed them on the bed. Hopefully, there was more to Sarah's immediate infatuation and adoration. Maybe it was those eyes that were so similar to her own, which gave Sarah no doubts about where she came from or belonged. Maybe it was Carlo's voice, which had taken on a gentle, warm tone she'd never heard him speak in before.

Her hand hovered over her underwear drawer. Her boring basics stared back at her. At the back of the drawer was one lost pair of lacy underwear—washed once, never worn.

Maybe it was the fact that there had been no other men in her life, no constant flow of male strangers that had ousted Sarah from first place. She'd never exposed Sarah to unstable or uncertain relationships, making it easier for Sarah to accept Carlo for who he was. Three and a half years was a hell of a long time to wait for a knight in shining armor. For Sarah it might seem shorter, the equivalent of a couple of weeks.

She no longer needed to find excuses for Carlo's absence from Sarah's life and the relief was almost palpable.

Her fingers caressed the soft edge of the lace and she had to bite her lip. She was all sexed up inside, melting, hot and contracting with longing. Because he was here, in her personal space, being more than she'd ever hoped he would be to Sarah. It had only been a few hours, and yet it was as if everything had fallen into perfect harmony, leaving her craving the one last thing that would spin her world into an orbit of bliss.

There was no way she'd say no if he made the first move.

She plucked the seductive underwear from the drawer. She wasn't going to prance about in them, giving him a catwalk show. They'd been wasting away long enough and her other underwear were gray from too many washes. She really needed to do some shopping. What did other women call it? *Me time.*

Laughing at the notion, she stepped into the satin knickers, the soft touch of the fabric a pleasant caress against her skin. She dropped the towel and strapped on the bra, her nipples hardening against the delicate lace. She glanced at herself in the full-length mirror. One baby down she'd managed to keep her figure, but the sheer triangle of lace in the front revealed a shade too much pubic hair. *Ugh.* She should have made better work of that, but with Sarah popping around like a champagne cork on speed…it would have to do.

She paused. Who the hell was she trying to fool? Shaved and scrubbed and all but begging for Carlo Carlevaro. Just like day one, all those years ago. Sure as hell no other man had ever been able to do this to her.

Resigned that Sarah's presence wasn't going to kill her body's needs, she pulled on her shorts. She put on the tight top but on seeing every trace of lace embossed on her breasts, she hesitated. He couldn't have it that easy.

She pulled another top from a hanger and dressed in what could only be called a demure, loose-fitting T-shirt. She was far from battle fit, not that it mattered. Her body begged to surrender to invasion, occupation, and annexation by what used to be, just days ago, the enemy forces.

****

Carlo glanced up from where Sarah was busy painting his thumb. Simone had walked into the lounge and leaned against the kitchen counter. Laughter sparkled in her eyes, and she suppressed it by chewing her lip. Seeing her in something other than the Carlevaro pilot's uniform made heat spread through his chest and lower. He had to peel his gaze from the sexy shorts she wore, jeans cut off close to her groin, her legs tanned and endless as they stretched to her bare feet. He longed to run his hand down those legs and up her inner thigh, feeling her shudder at the touch, the goosebumps on her skin prickling his fingertips.

His gaze shot back to his hands. It was a slaughter. Sarah's tongue stuck out of the corner of her mouth as she worked on his thumb. It was the last of his fingers that still needed a blotching; the rest looked as if they'd had a rough meeting with a cheese grater.

"That's lovely, darling," Simone said, then coughed a laugh as she shifted to switch the kettle on.

He stared at Simone openly, which was much easier when she had her back to him. Her butt was something in those shorts and the T-shirt was just the right fit to allow copious free roaming of his hands. *Dio*. He wanted to press her hips to that counter, trap her with his body and let his hands tease her breasts until she begged him to touch her sex.

"All done!" Sarah called out and shot him a gorgeous smile.

His pulse slowed as he inspected his manicure. "I love it," he announced. *Geez, can one even get this stuff off?* He could live with it for now if it kept that smile on Sarah's face.

Sarah shoved the little paintbrush back into the bottle with a severe thrust, then gave the cap a twist and dropped it on the couch. "Don't touch nothing," Sarah said. "Smudges."

"Okay," he nodded, then burst out laughing. "This is a first."

Sarah clambered over him and he automatically shot his hands into the air to keep her from touching his wet nails. She took up a half-eaten cookie on the side table, took a bite and offered him the other half. He opened wide, and she popped the cookie into his mouth.

"Yummy," Sarah said, crumbs on her lips as they chewed together.

Carlo looked at her and leaned back on the sofa with a grin. She was the most vibrant little person in the world. He might have missed much, but he sure was going to make up for it. Something in Sarah reminded him of Julia, of Angelo, when they were little and their mom had still been around. Life had had no jabs then.

It was good to be away from his family. Sometimes the responsibility he felt toward Julia and Angelo seemed weightier than the whole of Carlevaro

International. It wasn't something he could divide and entrust to other people. His family didn't come with a board of directors.

Simone opened the fridge and he watched as she rearranged some things in it, shaking a milk box and sniffing at something in a plastic container.

"Do you want to go out for dinner?" he asked. Outside the sun was setting, and its warm glare filtered in through the floor-to-ceiling windows, turning everything a shade of diluted gold.

Her hands stilled when she didn't answer him. Had he crossed some line? "We don't have to. I just thought it might be easier for you?"

She closed the fridge and turned. "Sarah missed her nap, and I don't want her to get cranky in a restaurant."

He didn't believe that was the whole truth. From what he had read in her eyes, he sensed she wasn't ready to be seen with him and Sarah together in the outside world.

He couldn't blame her. Most of their expatriate staff lived on the Peninsula; the pilots' digs were two blocks away. Someone would be bound to recognize them if they had dinner in one of the local joints. He'd subjected her to enough in his years of absence; he couldn't open the field for more speculation by being suddenly present. Not until they'd figured this out. "I'll go get take out."

"Pizza?" Sarah chirped. She'd made herself comfortable, head on the armrest of the couch, using his thigh as a footstool.

He brushed a curl from her forehead with his forefinger. "I would love to think that's your Italian blood speaking, sweetie."

Sarah yawned.

She probably hadn't understood a word he'd said. "Pizza it is, if Mommy says yes."

"Yes, please, Mommy." Sarah struggled up and slipped to the floor, clutching her groin.

"Go to the toilet, Sarah," Simone said, "before it's too late."

Sarah pattered down the corridor and disappeared into the bathroom.

Simone met his gaze and folded her arms over her chest.

"Pizza?" He didn't want her to dash his hopes of having dinner with them. At least dinner. Only dinner. He'd take whatever she wanted right now.

"Pizza Margarita for Sarah. No green stuff, like basil or rocket, otherwise she won't eat it."

He nodded. No green stuff.

She dropped her gaze, first to his lips, then lower. "You know what I like." She was perusing him, her gaze wandering, and a soft blush tinged her cheeks. "Nothing's changed in that department."

Her words could go two ways, and inside him the heat glowed. He let go of a slow, inaudible breath. She looked up again and they stared at each other for a moment. Simone glanced toward his suitcase and laptop bag that stood in the corner of the lounge.

He was welcome, but possibly not *that* welcome. He suppressed a sigh. "I'll go check in at the hotel. Take a shower. Fetch the pizza." He wanted to give her a last chance to opt out. She could tell him now that he needn't go stay somewhere else that night.

"You can take my car, no need to bother with a taxi. For now." She didn't move away from the counter but reached to pick a key from a row of hooks on the kitchen wall.

He went to her. "Thank you."

She held out the keys. "First parking bay on your right when you walk out of the lobby."

He aimed for the key, but instead took her hand in his. She didn't twist her hand to drop the keys in his, or pull away, but held still. He unwrapped her fingers one by one, until the keys lay flat on her palm. Her skin was warm, her fingers so willing to uncurl at his quiet command. He took the key, but kept a hand on hers, tracing circles on her palm with his thumb, then running his fingertips over the back of her hand, slowly, back and forth, determined, lengthening the distance with each feather-light stroke. He leaned toward her, the soft brush of her breaths that had become shallower, faster, flowing over his skin. "Is there anything else you need, besides the pizza?" he murmured. "Milk? Wine? Condoms?"

He was moving in for the kill, but had never feared a rebuff more. If she showed him the door now...the way the tension had been burning in him for the past few days, he'd combust. When he looked into her eyes she appeared dazed; her mouth had opened slightly and he wanted to melt those lips further, in a languid kiss.

"All of the above," she whispered, her focus on his mouth. "For what it's worth, with our track record."

He chuckled softly, but didn't let her sobering words overshadow the moment. Instead he let his fingers trace all the way to her elbow, which he cupped in his hand, and drew her toward him. He bent over to kiss her, and her lips met his without hesitation, willing, wanting and opening in time with his. He deepened the kiss, and she softened against him.

"I pooped." Sarah's voice rose like smoke between them. "Wipe my bottom."

He pulled away but caught Simone's fingers in his, staring down at Sarah. "This is surreal." He chuckled, the heat that the kiss had ignited cooling.

"You've no idea." Simone let go of his hand, and took Sarah's in hers. "Daddy is going to fetch pizza."

"You come back?" Sarah gawked at him with eyes wide.

"Always, sweetie." He jingled the car keys. "Won't be another minute if I could help it."

Simone took another key off the hook. "House keys, just in case."

He took them from her with a slow grin. A band of triumph jammed in his chest. "Thank you."

"Buy some nail polish remover too, if you know what that is." She shot him an innocent grin as they ambled off to the bathroom.

"Do you think the hotel's spa will know how to deal with it?" he called after her. He honestly had no clue.

"Deal with what?" Sarah asked. "Dragons?"

"Nothing serious, darling," Simone said. She paused at the bathroom's door. "Sure, that would be better, because I'm not dealing with that."

He strode out of the apartment with a chuckle and with a new concern for his fingers. He stuffed them in his pockets and took the stairs, not sure he wanted to look at them either.

Chapter Twenty-Two

Simone studied Sarah's profile in the bedside lamp's soft light. Sarah had had a meltdown within half an hour after Carlo had left. She hadn't expected otherwise, given the busy day they'd had. She'd managed to keep Sarah going through a quick dinner, which Sarah had halfheartedly poked at.

Sarah was calm in her sleep, angelic, but still so small. Carlo was tall, and Sarah had hardly reached a head higher than his knee. She wanted to hold Sarah close, assure her everything was going to be fine, but deep inside she couldn't quite settle her own unease. She hadn't had time to discuss anything further with Carlo, and at the speed things were happening, nothing was going to be discussed that night.

A knock sounded from the front door, and she lifted her head to listen. The turn of the key echoed down the corridor.

"Simone? Sarah?" Carlo called as he entered the lounge, but she didn't reply. She hadn't switched on the lights in the lounge, but he should be able to find his way in the moonlight that shone in through the windows and the light from Sarah's bedroom.

He put some things on the kitchen counter, the keys jangling as he hung them back on the hooks. His footsteps sounded soft on the carpet as he came down the short corridor. Already her heart had sped up at the thought of him, but she wanted to have this last moment with Sarah. Life was never going to go back to what it had been before.

She heard him hovering in the door of Sarah's room, his presence as palpable as the promise of heavy rains in the air, the scent of him as earthy as the first drop. She glanced toward him, and beckoned him inside.

"It took longer than I anticipated," he whispered with apology.

"She wouldn't have made it, either way," she whispered back. She lifted the sheet higher over Sarah's chest, hugging her legs closer, tighter to her daughter.

Carlo sat down on the edge of the bed, in the corner made by her drawn-up legs. He leaned over and propped up on his hand, which he'd nestled between her and Sarah. His wrist and inner arm touched her thighs, skin to skin, kindling the warm flame in the depths of her body. "Was your hair as blonde as hers when you were young?"

"Probably." She sighed. "There aren't any photos of me this age."

They were quiet for a moment.

"You've done an amazing job, Mona—she is…beautiful, in and out. I—" He broke off and she turned to face him. Emotions flickered over his face as he studied Sarah. "She looks like my mother…just like Julia." His voice was strained and when he looked back at her there was a cutting regret in his eyes. "I hope I can make up."

She smiled. "You're off to a good start. Thank you for being so wonderful and just…nice." She touched his hand. "Did you get the nail polish off?"

"Yes." He chuckled. "Definitely not my thing."

She inspected his fingers in the dim light, his touch gentle against the uncertain trembling of her own.

His gaze traveled over her and he rested his hand on her hip. "How does she sleep?"

Simone bit her lip. "Very well." She tried not to laugh. "That is, until she wakes up."

She watched him digest this information. "And when would that be?" he asked, and from his expression he was expecting the worst, that Sarah woke up several times a night like a newborn.

"Around seven tomorrow morning. With any luck around eight."

"She sleeps all the way through the night?"

"Yes."

"Well, then." The lamplight shone in his eyes as he met her gaze. He shifted his hand to rest on her ankles. From there he caressed her naked leg with his fingertips, lightly, slowly, with gentle intent. He hovered at the crook of her legs, rubbing the tender skin behind her knee with his thumb. As he grazed her thigh with the back of his hand, tremors of pure lust hit her in long, languid waves. He spread his fingers over the top of her thigh, at the ragged seam of her shorts, his thumb tailing his fingertips, which reached inward, to the apex of her thighs. He leaned over her as a lone finger traced the inner line of her legs back to her knees, and she burned to open for him, so that he could reverse to where she needed him most.

"Hungry?" he asked, his voice a husky whisper.

"Very."

"Then let me feed you." He stood and held out his hand. "Until you've had your fill."

245

She switched off the bedside lamp and placed her hand in his as she swung her legs off the bed, and he helped her up. She circled her arms around his neck and he kissed her, softly. His hands were on her butt and he lifted her to his erection. He heaved her higher and she wrapped her legs around his hips, pressing her sex against his as he kissed her.

He walked with her, turning into her bedroom. He paused at the bedroom door. "Do you close this?" he whispered between kisses.

She pulled away and lowered her legs, touching the tips of her toes to the floor. He loosened his hold, letting her settle against him. "I don't know." In the soft light she stared at him. "I've never—" God, it sounded lame. "With Sarah…I've never been with anyone else."

"Really?"

Heat spread over her cheeks at the astonishment in his eyes. "Now you sound just like Sarah," she accused. "And that after spending only one day with her."

His gaze softened, and her battering heart slowed at the tenderness in his eyes. "All this time and you're still only mine." He stroked down her body, cupping her tightly. "I haven't been able to get off without thinking of you, so technically there's been no one else for me either," he murmured in her ear, the words echoing his obvious physical desire. "Let go, *cara*. You'll hear her if she wakes up."

He closed the door behind them. As he drew her back into his arms and lifted her off her feet, time lost its meaning and it felt as if they'd slipped right back to where they'd left off four years ago.

The bedside lamp she'd left on earlier cast a soft glow in the room. Centre stage was a high-raised, king size Zanzibari-style bed, with a mosquito net covering its carved wooden frame like a veil. Cozy with cushions scattered over it, it was a nest within a nest.

"You always wanted one of these beds," he said as he plopped her down on the edge, between two falls of the mosquito net.

"Hmm," she murmured as she closed her eyes. "It's not much fun alone."

He kissed her, tenderly exploring her mouth, as they shifted deeper into the bed. His hands stroked up her arms, pinning her down as he pressed his leg between hers. The weight of his thigh made her moan in anticipation, and she moved against him, relishing the intense desire the pressure fueled.

"I could tie you up at the corners and fuck you all night," he murmured as he released her arms, running his lips down the column of her neck, nipping at her sensitive skin with his teeth.

His words let the image vibrate like an electric current through her. It sounded rough, but in Carlo's hands it would be the sweetest torture. She didn't move her arms as potent memories of past exploits ran through her mind's eye, of Carlo in charge and making her body respond to his every whim. "I wish you would," she murmured, regretting that she had no stash of silk scarves for him to pick and choose from.

He chuckled as he knelt between her legs. "That's a bit wild, for starters, don't you think?" His hands got busy with her shorts' button and zip, and he tugged them off her hips. "I think we should leave that for dessert. There is no need to rush our meal."

His comment made her smile. It was a glimpse of the old Carlo, the way he'd teased her before. He shifted and stripped the shorts from her legs. She lay in front of him, legs slightly bent and open.

The way he stared at her made her feel utterly desirable and needed. She sat up and pulled her t-shirt over her head, and they tossed her clothes to the floor. As she lay back his hands rested on her shins; his gaze wandered over her body before it came to rest briefly on her breasts.

His eyes met hers. "You are so beautiful," he murmured as he stroked his hands up her legs to her lacy underwear. His thumbs were on her inner thighs, and she shuddered as he traced the elastic leg of her panty with his fingers, down, then higher, his thumbs grazing the lips of her sex. "And this is very pretty." His fingers made lazy patterns, imitating those of the lace, in feather-light touches that made her crave his fingers, deep inside her.

Her breathing halted as he brought his thumbs together and upped the pressure on the downward caress. The lips of her sex opened wider in wet heat, her swollen clit brushing against the crotch of her panties. A heated wave of pleasure shot through her. "Carlo."

His touch was hypnotic, gentle, and rhythmic as he stroked her body with his fingers, his lips, and his nose. His breath stoked the fire that flamed under her skin. She longed for him to touch her breasts, but as if he knew this, he went everywhere except there. Her nipples had puckered into almost agonizing hard peaks and were jutting up through the lace of her bra.

She reached for his hair, trapping her fingers in the thick strands, wanting to urge him up to kiss her nipples.

"Slow down, Simone," he whispered against her

hipbone, his other hand pressing lower as he fitted his warm palm over her mound.

At his touch, every part of her caved into a wanton mess and begged for him to possess her.

She arched her back as his mouth trailed to the curves of her breasts. "You don't understand," she whispered, her voice sounding as desperate as she felt.

"Oh, but I do." He chuckled as he sat up, took her hand and palmed it to his erection. He filled her hand and felt like jean-clad rock. He wanted her as much as she wanted him.

"Don't let go," he groaned as he reached for the sculpted border of her bra. With slow intent he traced the edge with his fingertips, and she snatched a short breath at the rousing trail his fingers left behind. He licked his lips, finally cupping her breasts in his palms, thumbing her nipples in a gentle pull that shot desire to her core.

When he pulled away the intensity of the absence of his touch was almost as heady as having his hands smooth over every bit of her begging skin. Shooting her a wry smile he unbuttoned his shirt. He peeled it off, revealing the strong contours of his shoulders, the dark patches of hair around his nipples that came together in a trail that disappeared beneath the waistband of his jeans.

He looked at her pointedly and she rubbed his erection through the thick fabric of his jeans, but it wasn't enough. Her hands fumbled with his belt, her gaze glued to her fingers, which were unwrapping what she'd been craving since she'd seen him standing in the door that first morning.

He waited, watching her hands as she popped the

buttons, his breath stalling when she liberated his erection from the constraints of his jeans and jocks. An intense swell of desire spread through her body at seeing his rigid cock jut up toward her from the silky nest of black hair. She cupped him in her hand and he groaned out a slow breath, straightening up, pushing his hips toward her. She traced the veins running the length of him with her fingertips, following their pulsing to the tip. He dropped his head back as she rubbed up and down, increasing the pressure of her fingers, spreading his pre-cum over his sensitive head after every few strokes. She licked her lips at the thought of taking him in her mouth and pushed up on her elbow.

He laughed as he tossed his shirt to the floor and covered her hand with his, stopping her movement. "Slow down, Simone. *Dio*. I'm too close."

She dropped back with a grin, quietly thrilled that she hadn't lost her touch. He took some condoms from his back pocket and slid his jeans off. His muscular body was beautiful in the soft light, which caught the shadows playing on his arm muscles and torso.

His gaze burned into hers as he rolled on a condom. "You, *cara*, have been sorely missed," he said as he propped on his arms next to her shoulders, and dipped his head to kiss her mouth. Every last bit of love that hid away in unknown corners brimmed from her heart.

She caressed the smooth skin on his sides, his back. His heat radiated through her fingers to her core as he kissed her, pressing his hard length against her clit, smoothing up and down, in the rhythm of his tongue.

"We're not slowing down, are we?" he murmured as he reached for the crotch of her panties, hooking it to the side.

"No...please," she whispered back. Knowing she was dripping wet, she opened her legs wider.

He grunted his approval as he slipped a finger into her drenched sex, then two. She moaned as he stiffened his fingers against the front wall of her channel, rubbing hard.

"God, Carlo, please..."

He swore in Italian as he extracted his fingers, and in one slow thrust entered her. He was gentle, but already her orgasm tried to break through the barriers of her resistance. He kept thrusting slowly, yet hard and deep, meeting each throb of her budding orgasm at its head. She dug her fingers into his buttocks to hold him still against her, wanting to prolong the sweet sensation of going over the edge.

His own control was hard to contain as sweat pearled on his upper lip and beaded on his forehead. He locked gazes with her and stilled against her. "Fuck," he mouthed, his breathing strained but motionless.

When he pulled from her and thrust back again, she tipped, as if in slow motion, his slower thrusts calculated to draw out her pleasure. She moaned as she came, each rippling contraction extracting his orgasm. He dropped his head back, grinding deep into her swollen sex as he vibrated his release into the core of her body.

He breathed heavily, and she stroked her hands up his chest and reached for his face. When he gazed at her he looked drugged. He said nothing as he rolled to his side, pulling her close, not breaking their intimate connection. Her hand on his chest felt every beat of his heart as it slowed down, the heat on her skin cooling with his.

His lips rested against her forehead. "It has always been like this between us," he murmured. "Nothing has changed."

She couldn't respond, the intensity of the moment too tight in her throat. It was true. It had always been easy between them, the rise in their desire so quick and mutual, the release as quick or as leisurely as they'd wanted it to be.

He slipped from her and got rid of the condom. He gathered her in his arms, chest-to-chest, so close, as if they'd never been apart. His knuckles stroked down the length of her arm, rousing the thick stirring of anticipation in her belly, the slow rise of her pulse at knowing they weren't done. Knowing Carlo, he'd just started.

He shifted and his fingers fiddled with the back clasp of her bra. "How did you manage to keep this on so long?" he murmured, kissing her neck as he released the clasp.

"Someone said it is *very pretty*," she teased as she wriggled, and he eased off the bra and tossed it to the floor.

"What an idiot," he laughed. "He hasn't seen you naked...for a long time." He trailed kisses over her collarbone to her breast, her nipple, which was begging for the warm, wet heat of his mouth. He licked her skin, a teasing circle around her breast, blowing over the damp trail, a slow spiral as he aimed for the peak, making her tight nipple ache in anticipation. His fingers were tracing a similar pattern on her other breast, and when he finally took her between his lips, gently rolling her other nipple between his fingers, intense desire jolted to her core, leaving her panting. He sucked, tenderly, then harder as she moaned and dug her fingers into his hair.

He let go, and she breathed in quiet reprieve. Her body was an instrument that he had mastered four years ago, and he clearly hadn't forgotten how to play her. He tugged at her panties, rolling them down her thighs, and let her kick them off. She stilled next to him, under his gaze that drifted from her breasts, lower, his hand following suit, but stopping abruptly at the scar lining her pubic hair.

He rested his hand on the faint line, a question in his eyes. Her heart contracted…he'd never seen this before, never been with a woman who'd had a baby by caesarean.

"Sarah got stuck." She paused, sure she couldn't laugh at the expression on his face. "So, I had an emergency C-section."

His brows shot up, consternation flooding his face as it hit him what type of scar it was. "I'm sorry…I didn't know." He frowned. "I thought…" The weight of his hand on her stomach increased the slightest bit. "I'm sorry for not being there." His voice sounded hollow, as empty as that chamber of memories that should have been full with the birth of his own daughter.

She caressed his temple, his gray hairs springy against his softer black ones. She'd wanted a guilt-free night but from the look on his face it was as if he was staring at the physical reminder of his absence.

She tried to ease the shift between them. They'd left Sarah in her room, and there she would stay. She'd hoped to leave everything else behind too. "Gabi was there," she whispered as she trapped his hand in hers.

"And Sarah was healthy, which was the most important thing." She drew his fingers to her mouth, kissing them, then guided his hand to her opening thighs, letting him slip his wet fingers inside her.

He stirred to life against her hip as he stroked her, and her body responded in turn. She felt for his cock, gathering his sack in her hand, feeling him harden.

He kissed her, but there was a change in him, in the way he touched her, his palm resting tentatively on her clit, his fingers moving languidly, with reverence, as if she would break under the rougher touch she now craved. He knew her too well, but he was hesitating.

She swallowed as he turned away. He could read her body, but in that moment, she could read his mind. "Tell me what happened," she murmured against the stubble on his chin. "Tell me about the wicked wizard and Julia." She said the words so softly, wanting him to hear them, but scared of what they would release.

He dropped back, covering his eyes with his arm. As he breathed out, he shuddered. After a minute, she propped up on her elbow, gently tugging his arm from his face. He didn't open his eyes, but gripped her hand tightly, the tension in his hand echoing the strain in the pull of his mouth. He was quiet, but the muscle in his jaw twitched, his nostrils flaring as he breathed. He was battling with his emotions, trying to subdue them.

"Carlo…" She didn't want to beg him to open up to her, but there had been more to those ten weeks when he'd gone missing than she'd anticipated, and she had to know.

"I never talk about my dad, Mona." He glanced at her, then cupped his palms to his eyes, as if to block out all light. "I think I might need to get drunk to talk about him without…breaking down."

She dropped her gaze, focusing on the softness of the hair on his chest, his breath that hitched faster, the strain building in him, evident in the fact that he didn't exhale completely.

"It's okay," she murmured, cursing her own absence from his life, and the scar on her belly that had caused the atmosphere between them to change.

"Those ten weeks…" He broke off, playing with the mosquito net. He switched off the light, enclosing them in darkness. "My dad knew he was ill, but he hid it from us as long as he could. By the time I got that call, things had started to spin out of control." His voice was heavy with despair. "There was nothing we could do." His voice broke, and he swallowed. "Nothing."

He lay still, and she pressed against him, trying to alleviate some of the pain the memories carried. He circled his arm around her shoulder and nudged her close. She relaxed against him as he sighed deeply, seeming almost relieved. "Julia got roped into some really bad relationships at the time. She got addicted to heroin and zombied through everything. Oblivious." He sighed. "She's clean, for now, but I still don't know how to keep her that way." His fingers were in her hair, lost as he entwined a curl between his fingers. "I've been taking care of her ever since she decided to get clean."

"How long has she been clean?"

"More than three years. To get her to come to her senses…took a lot of energy. Then one day she just came home." He shook his head. "It seems like a long time, doesn't it?"

She had no clue about addiction and couldn't

comment, except that three years was a long time to be without something, someone.

He let go of her hair, and rubbed at his forehead with his thumb, as if he could iron out his frown. "After my dad, after that hopelessness…it has been the hope, the notion of having some control over her addiction, that has kept me going."

She didn't need to hear more. He didn't say it, but the unsaid words rested on his chest. After his mom, after his dad, he couldn't bear to lose Julia too.

"Does Angelo help?"

He grunted with a nod. "Yes, but Angelo has his own addictions."

She didn't want to pry further, sensing the territory could be more slippery.

"Women. Humping and dumping. Angelo's specialty." He reached for her cheek, stroking it with his finger, cupping her chin and lifting it so that their lips could meet. "I was quite worried that first day, introducing you to him." He paused as he peered into her eyes. "Knowing him, and the way he stared at you…" He hissed out a breath. "As if he would have you before the day was done."

His hand, which still rested on her cheek, slipped lower, his thumb stroking her bottom lip. His lips replaced his thumb and he kissed her as he caressed the column of her neck, then lower, teasing a path to her breast, which he kneaded possessively. He'd gone hard against her, his erection pressing against her thigh as he moved to suck her nipple into his mouth, shooting a shock of desire right down to her womb.

His lips retraced their path to the curve of her ear, and he whispered for her to roll onto her stomach. His lips pressed warmly against her neck, her shoulder. She tried to breathe as her skin responded to his hungry kisses.

His movements grew harder, more urgent as he massaged her back, squeezed her hip, pulling her lower on the bed. She bit her lip as she recalled how good he could make her feel, every inch of her skin heating up at the thought of the pleasure to come. She splayed her legs and raised slightly on her knees, her breathing labored in anticipation. He grunted his approval as he kissed her spine, lower, to the dimples above her buttocks. His hand stroked her back, his touch possessive. His knuckles followed the split of her buttocks, deeper, until his fingers caught her sex, and he slipped his thumb inside her. His rhythm was slow and tentative at first but she moaned at the intense sensation deep inside her, every stroke reaching further. He pressed harder, and she edged up higher on her knees, almost feeling the need to crawl from him as he deepened the thrusts with his thumb, his fingers bent to catch her clit with each heave of her body. The pressure built so fast, she was going to come apart.

"Carlo—" she whispered. He released her, leaving her burning, swerving on the edge of the cliff.

She heard him tear a condom wrapper between her rapid breaths, and then he was on top of her, pressing her down onto her stomach and nudging her legs wider. "Touch yourself, *cara*," he whispered against her hair behind her ear. She didn't need to. He slicked himself on her, rubbing his cock over her clit and entrance, then penetrated her with a single hard thrust. He rested against her back, his face right next to hers, his hand settling on her throat. He nuzzled her ear, his lips caressing the sculpted rim. "Touch yourself, Simone."

She opened her eyes, smelling him right there with her, breathing in the same breath as him. "No," she murmured.

"The honor is all mine," he whispered as he edged his hand under her, clasping her clit with his fingers. He hadn't tied her up, but in that moment, he had bound her to him. She could go nowhere but where he planned to take her.

He entered her, again and again, his weight bearing down on her, his hand wrapped around her throat in perfect pressure. He thrust so deep, right to her womb, and as he pressed closer, she knew he owned her. At the thought her release came, drenching his fingers. He paused for a moment, his breathing ragged as he kissed the corner of her mouth, nuzzled the side of her nose with the tip of his. She lifted her cheek to his, caressing his rougher one. She couldn't see him, but felt him as if they were one, the urgency of his desire, the need to make her his, and only his. She'd never been so close to him. When he came, he stilled, his hand on her neck tightening, then slacking.

She had been thoroughly claimed.

Chapter Twenty-Three

Carlo studied Simone's face. She was asleep, her features barely illuminated by the light that fell through the windows. She glowed, still flushed from their lovemaking the previous evening.

Being with her during the night had made it clear to him how lonely he'd been. For the past four years, his life and time had dragged on forever.

She stirred against him again, nestling her sweet ass to his hard cock. His erection had woken him up and he groaned. He had no idea what the time was, but outside the pitch black had slipped into a kinder hue of indigo blue. Simone was on her side, her knees pulled up. She'd always slept like that, and he had always cupped her perfectly.

Her hair spread over the pillow and his chest, and he pulled the strands away to expose her neck. Kissing her softly, he inhaled the sweet scent of her skin, which still held a trace of sex. With a sigh she leaned closer and he stroked her arm, letting his fingers wander to her side and to the hollow of her hip. He nibbled at her ear as he caressed her butt, wanting to wake her up.

She purred, and he slid his fingers over to her perfectly exposed pussy.

"How are you feeling?" he whispered in her ear, dropping a kiss on the curve of her shoulder, studying her face, and her lips, which showed traces of having been thoroughly kissed.

"A bit tender," she murmured.

He slipped a finger between the lips of her sex, finding her wet and deliciously warm.

"Let me kiss it better," he murmured, watching her lips as a smile tugged at the corners. He pushed his finger into her. She hadn't opened her eyes, but stretched lazily and rolled onto her back, forcing him to extract his hand.

He breathed into her neck, relishing the scent of sleep still on her. She turned toward him and hooked a leg over his leg and hip as she opened her eyes, and kissed him on the mouth.

"What did you say?" she murmured against his neck, her hand stroking his chest.

He propped up on his elbow, his other hand on her hip, teasing the soft swell with his knuckles. "Let me kiss it better."

"Hmm." Her hand reached for him, and she clasped her fingers around his begging cock. "And what do you propose we do with this?"

The tightening of her hand around his cock made his innards pool inside and all he wanted was to lie back and let her suck him dry. She slowly teased him, her fingers unfurling to get a firmer grip, and he gasped. "Whatever pleases you, *cara*."

She chuckled as she tugged the duvet away, shifting lower. She took him in her mouth, and he jerked as the hot, wet heat surrounded him. It was almost unreal to feel his cock engulfed in her mouth, and he gathered her hair from her face to watch her. He sighed deeply, the intense pleasure relaxing. She shot him a glance, arousing him more as her own pleasure in the act reflected in her eyes.

He wanted more, he wanted to plunder her mouth and claim this part of her like he had claimed her the night before. He exhaled in an attempt to gather his wits. When it came to sex he had a few rules, and he liked to stick to them for good reason. Once Simone was done with him he would need a nap. "Ladies first, Mona."

She pulled away, but instead of looking at him she tipped her head, pointing her ear in the direction of the bedroom door. "Shit," she whispered and sighed.

"What?"

"Sarah." She closed her eyes, shaking with a quiet laugh. "Your more official welcome to parenthood." She climbed over him to the edge of the bed, rubbing her pussy against him en route. "You might want to deal with that in the shower."

He laughed as he grabbed her ass. "I was planning to eat you out for breakfast."

She got off the bed, picked up and put on his shirt. "There's plenty leftover pizza in the fridge." She winked at him as she slipped out of the bedroom, closing the door behind her.

He stared at the mosquito netting that spread over the frame of the Zanzibar bed as his laughter died down to a soft curse. Through the closed door, he could hear Simone soothing Sarah's cries. Sarah clearly only slept until seven on blue moon Mondays every leap year.

Twenty minutes later he strolled out of the bathroom, showered and in his jocks. He paused in the door, the picture in front of him making him skip a breath. The pillows were heaped with golden curls as Simone lay with Sarah in bed, cuddling her close in a semi-doze. Sarah's chubby fingers played with some of Simone's curls; a soft toy lay squashed between them. Simone lifted a finger to her lips, indicating that he should be quiet.

But Sarah must have sensed the exchange because she turned toward him, not letting go of Simone's hair, peering at him wide-eyed. As if he was part of the furniture, she turned back to Simone.

He edged around the bed and got in with them, spooning Simone's body with his, resting his hand on her hip. He stared at Sarah over Simone's shoulder, and Sarah paused for a second before she closed her eyes and carried on rubbing a curl between her thumb and forefinger. Simone searched for his hand and laced her fingers with his.

"This is the prettiest picture I've ever seen," he murmured in Simone's ear. It was true. He'd never beheld a more breathtaking image than Simone and Sarah in the natural morning light, so close, in bed. He wanted to see this every morning. More than ever. He wanted photos of them, all over his walls at home. On his desk, in his wallet.

"Just wait," Simone whispered back, laughter hiding in her voice as he dropped a kiss on her temple.

"Wait for what?"

"For Sarah to wake up completely."

Her words were hardly cold when Sarah tossed the long-limbed teddy to the side and started kicking at the duvet. She let go of Simone's curls, but her fingers got stuck and by accident she yanked some hairs.

"Ouch!" Simone cried out.

Sarah sat up. "Sorry, Mommy." She gawked at him, and it was as if she recognized him for the first time, and noted that he was there.

He walked his fingers over Simone's hip to Sarah's leg. She giggled as they reached her leg and ran to her tummy, which he tickled. Sarah laughed, and crawled away from his hand. She got up and, as if by instinct, started to jump on the bed.

Her curls bounced with every jump, shooting up and almost touching the mosquito-netted ceiling.

Simone groaned. "Not on the bed, darling."

He laughed as he slipped off the bed, picked up his jeans and pulled them on. "Where else?" If he were a midget he would join Sarah in her antics. He must remember to order a trampoline.

Simone had covered her face with her hands and was wobbling with every jump Sarah made. Both were laughing, and a surge of love flowed over him in an unstoppable wave.

"Simone." He reached for her, his hand on her arm, ready to spill his heart at her feet.

Sarah paused, and Simone peeked at him through her cupped hands. In the second of silence, a phone rang somewhere in the apartment.

"My phone." Simone sat up. "Nobody ever phones me at this time of the morning." She frowned at him. "You need your shirt." She got off the bed and rushed from the room. "Give me a minute," she called back.

He winked at Sarah, who'd continued to jump on the bed, but something was out of place. The moment had passed, the magic diluted within a breath.

He tried to listen to Simone's conversation over Sarah's giggles. Her voice echoed down the corridor, normal in greeting, then strained as she answered the caller. Dread filled him from the bottom up, as if the previous day and night and this morning had been too good, and he hadn't deserved them.

"Best you get down, Sarah." He grappled for her hand, but she ignored him as she jumped on.

She was flushed red, her eyes bright with laughter.

"*Cara-cara-cara*," he remonstrated, "get down now before you fall and break something." The bed was high, and just the idea freaked him out. He grabbed her by the waist and swung her off the bed, setting her on her feet. She shrieked playfully and pattered out of the room.

In the moment of quiet reprieve, he heard Simone's voice. "No…no. I've no idea where he is." There was a pause. "Of course, I can go to the hotel and check…I'll let you know. Yes. On this number."

He cursed and picked up his shoes. When he straightened Simone stood in the door, his phone in her hand.

"It was Julia."

His blood stalled and his toes curled.

"She's looking for you." She held his phone, which he'd switched off, out to him.

Anxiety for Julia surged through him. "Thank you. Why did she phone you?" *Did she sound high? Did she make sense?*

"She can't get hold of Angelo or Dino. Apparently, she's been trying to phone you for the last couple of hours. She tried the hotel, but you're not there." A steady blush spread to her cheeks. "Since she knows…we've been flying together she wondered…if I knew where you were." Sarah pattered in and grabbed Simone around the leg and Simone rested her hand on her head. "She found my number in the company directory."

He cursed in Italian as he switched on his phone. Twenty missed calls stared at him from the screen. Most were from Julia but the other numbers he didn't recognize. He doubted Julia would be able to phone him twice if she had used drugs, never mind twenty times. She wouldn't care to hunt him down via every avenue on a high. Nothing made sense. He met Simone's gaze.

"You'll need your shirt," she murmured and turned toward her closet as she unbuttoned his shirt.

She could have passed her phone to him, and he could have spoken to Julia directly, but he didn't need to ask what she'd told Julia. *She didn't know where he was.*

He closed his eyes for a moment, breathing down the cold disappointment that flushed through his chest. The outside world had invaded their cocoon with brutal force. He opened his eyes, and stared at her naked back, how gracefully it sloped down to her rounded butt, to her legs that carried on forever. Sarah clung to Simone, nagging to be picked up.

"Not now, Sarah," Simone said as she plucked some beige underwear from a drawer. She turned, just enough so that he could see the edge of her breast. "Your shirt." She held it out toward him.

He took it from her with a sighed thank you and walked out of the room as he pulled it on. Once in the lounge, he dialed Julia's number, dropping onto the couch and preparing himself for the worst, already plotting how to get the rehab centre to collect her wilted, wasted body from home.

"Thank God, you finally picked up," Julia

answered.

Nothing in her voice gave away that she'd used, but the adrenaline was pulsing through his veins. "Are you okay, Julia? Sorry, I only switched my phone on, I—" He broke off.

"God, Carlo, I don't know what to do," she said, then added as an afterthought, "I'm fine, I'm one hundred percent fine."

He swallowed and dropped his forehead to his palm as he breathed his relief. "What's wrong?" He couldn't imagine anything else warranting all her calls.

"Alan Kaan and Brett Winser phoned me, on the old landline." Her voice trembled. "In the dead of night...freaking me out."

The phone rang in his mind, its menacing ring echoing through the tomblike hall of their old family house. He shook his head, trying to place the names in the unexpected turn of the conversation. Brett Winser was the CEO of the East African Wildlife Society; Alan Kaan was from the African Elephant Specialist Group. His chest tightened. Both Alan and Brett had been in the conservation industry for decades and had been his father's friends, but closer friends of Peppe's. "Why did they phone? Is this about Peppe and the Tusk Awards?"

"They would have spoken to Peppe but knew about his heart attack. They wanted to talk to you." Julia paused. "Since you didn't answer your mobile, they phoned dad's old landline. Imagine, they still have the number." She sighed into the phone.

Few people still had that number or bothered to phone it. His blood was pulsing at his temple, and deep in his gut, he knew where the conversation was going. "Why?"

"The poaching and trafficking have leaked." She didn't quite sob, but her voice broke. "They wanted to know whether there was any truth to the rumors." Julia groaned. "Carlo, I—"

"What did you say?"

"Denied all knowledge of anything and denounced it as impossible." The tears, which had been thick in her voice, broke through, and she sobbed.

He got up from the sofa and started pacing the lounge, raking his hand through his hair.

"God, I lied to them. Was it the right thing to do?"

"Calm down, Julia. What exactly do they know?"

"They seemed to know everything. That we have a network flying tusks from our concessions out to Dar es Salaam and onward to Southeast Asia. That Carlevaro Air is directly involved."

"Fuck." The word popped out. For a second there was nothing else to say. That the information had hopped so undistorted from its origins to the ears of the highest players in the East African conservation industry gave him the chills.

"Alan Kaan asked me if we were responsible for the container of tusks they've discovered in the Mombasa harbor."

He swore under his breath. By the sounds of it, Alan Kaan knew more than he did. "We're not responsible for the bloody stowed tusks in the Mombasa harbor. We don't even fly to Mombasa?" Suddenly he was uncertain, as everything zoomed out of focus. He paced the room again but stopped short on seeing Simone in the corridor, wide-eyed and pale. She shook her head.

"Carlevaro Air doesn't fly to Mombasa." Julia

never cursed, but strings of Italian swear words slipped from her mouth. "I don't understand, it's only been two weeks and Alan Kaan knows. How did he find out?"

"I've no clue. We took pains to keep it quiet." He paused. "Noel Peters and his team—"

"They're from Kenya," Julia interrupted him. "They could be involved."

"No. Noel Peters—" He sighed and raked his hand through his hair. "He can't possibly be involved."

"Everybody has their price, Carlo." She swallowed. "Who else could have leaked it to them?"

"I don't know, but heads are going to roll once I find out." Carlo stopped to think. "Where are they? Alan and Brett?"

"They're already in London for the Tusk Awards."

Sitting in some pub and tearing Carlevaro International down brick by brick.

"I'll get on my laptop and see what I can do from here," he said, searching the room for his laptop. Then he recalled he'd left it at the hotel, and exhaled deeply. "You're going to have to give me ten minutes. I'll call you back. And stay calm, Julia."

He rang off, just in time too, as Sarah bolted down the corridor, past Simone, and into the lounge. "Daddy!" She held several dolls by the hair, their legs protruding in awkward directions.

Simone grabbed her around the waist and stopped her from going further. "Not now, Sarah."

Sarah cried out, kicking her legs in protest as Simone picked her up.

He met Simone's gaze. Her face was even paler than it had been minutes ago.

"I need to go to the hotel for my laptop. Somehow

the poaching leaked to some of our major conservation stakeholders." He shoved his phone in his pocket. "With the big shots of those two NGOs knowing, it's only a jump to the Tanzanian Government." He tried to gather his thoughts but they'd scrambled.

"Carlo, I—" Simone started, trying to talk above Sarah whining that she wanted to be put down.

"I don't know how this is going to pan out. Alan Kaan and Brett Winser phoned Julia," he explained, but from her expression, Simone knew whom he'd discussed with Julia over the phone.

"I've flown them a few times," she said, putting Sarah on the floor. "Sarah, be quiet."

Sarah was by his leg, looking up at him and holding out her dolls.

"I've got to go," he said, "but I'll be back later, okay?" He walked over to where Simone leaned against the kitchen counter.

"I'll drive you to the hotel?" she offered. "It's only five minutes from here."

"Dad-dy!"

His gaze dropped to Sarah, who'd followed him and hadn't stopped calling for him, her voice rising with each attempt to get his attention as she tugged at his jeans. "No, you best stay here. I'll grab a taxi at the Slipway. It's only a minute's walk." He dropped to his haunches and brushed Sarah's curls from her face. "I'll be back later, okay?"

"No dragons!" she cried. "Play Barbie!"

"Oh sweetie, these dragons are tame." He bit back the lie and stood. He reached for Simone, but she'd folded her arms over her chest. He squeezed her shoulder, and would have kissed her, but she looked flustered and closed her eyes as he searched her face.

"I'll call you," he said and marched out of the front door.

****

Simone didn't move from the kitchen counter. She stared at Sarah, who in turn stared at the closed front door, on the verge of throwing a full-blown tantrum. She wanted to tell Sarah that now was not a good time, but her voice was gone.

What the hell had just happened? Nobody knew better who'd set that ball rolling than she did. Her gut twisted, and her blood hammered in her temple. She swallowed at the tightening in her throat, willing the sting behind her eyes away.

Heads were going to roll, and hers was first in line. She cursed Michael, but it didn't help. Annie had obviously told Alan Kaan, her boss at the African Elephant Specialist Group, about the tusk Michael had found in the Carlevaro Air plane. If she hadn't asked Michael to poke around in the first place, this would never have leaked.

"Mommy, where Daddy go?" Sarah whimpered, tugging at her shorts.

"Work," she whispered. She hadn't told him that she'd leaked it, indirectly. There hadn't been a chance.

She turned to switch on the kettle, to do anything that would take her mind off the past disastrous half hour. She had to tell him that she had asked Michael to check the hold and that he'd spoken to Annie about finding that tusk.

Carlo was going to be furious. She wasn't sure he'd ever forgive her. But that wasn't all of it. Beyond the poaching leak stood everything else that had happened that morning.

"Do you want some cereal?" Her hands were shaking and she'd do anything to avoid thinking beyond Alan Kaan and Brett Winser and the silent storm she'd stirred up.

"Daddy go work, Mommy stay home?" Sarah asked, her eyes wide, her bottom lip trembling.

"Something like that." Simone blinked. How was she going to explain anything to Sarah? She knelt and hugged Sarah close.

"Does daddies stay?"

She sniffed and rubbed at her nose. "He'll be back. He said he'll phone."

She'd heard that one before. She blocked the whisper in her head.

His face when she'd handed him his phone, telling him to call Julia, flashed in her mind's eye. Her stomach clutched tight, and a cold sweat broke out on her forehead.

She should have passed him her phone.

Something in Julia's voice, unexpected warmth, had reached to her like a hand through the phone. She could have explained to Julia that he'd been there, in her bed, making love to her and ignoring his phone for the past twelve hours because of her. She could have rewound every clock and could have made it easy for him, for them.

But she'd told him she didn't want his family to know, and he'd respected her wishes. She'd denied any knowledge of his whereabouts first, and he'd taken her lead. Carlo had walked out, and she had no idea how he had interpreted her actions that morning. It made her feel horrible, the idea that she might have made him think that she'd shown him the door. And that after the day before and the intimacy they'd shared.

"Why you crying, Mommy?" Sarah asked, her voice thick with tears.

She closed her eyes. She'd clogged up everywhere, and her shoulders shook. "I don't know, my darling."

Chapter Twenty-Four

Simone stretched the duvet tight into the last corner, running her palm over the clean linen to smooth it as she made up the bed. Sarah had helped her, but she'd been more in the way than anything else. Sarah's chatter was one thing, but it didn't help her pluck her courage together to pick up the phone and call Carlo.

An hour had passed since Carlo's swift exit, and still he hadn't called her. Every event of the morning kept circling in her mind, and she found she was not quite ready to tell him she'd inadvertently caused the whole fuck-up.

Her fingers trembled, and when her phone's ring echoed down the corridor, she jumped. She'd been expecting it, and yet, she didn't want to answer the call.

She rushed down the corridor to grab the phone from the kitchen counter, her pulse slowing down as she saw it was only the office administrator phoning her. She took a deep breath before she answered.

"Would you be able to fly today?" Rebecca asked. "One of our standby pilots is already standing in for Ted Barker, who has called in sick. Mr. Carlevaro asked if you would be able to fly with the DHC to fetch Mr. Angelo and the Viggios from Seronera?"

The anxiety, which had curled around her throat like a cold hand the past hour, clutched tight. Carlo hadn't bothered to phone her directly with this request but had asked the office to phone her. She ignored the tug in her stomach.

"I know you have a day off, Simone—"

"Of course I can fly, Rebecca." Her voice croaked over the line and she had to clear her throat. "I just need to arrange for my nanny to take care of Sarah. As soon as she's here I'll be on my way."

"Thank you. How long do you think you'll take?" Rebecca asked.

"I'll leave as soon as the nanny arrives." She checked the time on the kitchen clock. "I should be there in less than two hours, if the traffic to the airport isn't a disaster."

"Thank you. Ross is on standby to fly with you. He already signed out the keys."

Simone closed her eyes as she hung up. Ross O'Connor of all people. She should have spared herself any flight in his company.

She dropped her head back, taking a deep breath. She became aware of the almost unnatural silence in the apartment. She looked around and found Sarah staring at her. She stood in the middle of the carpet, two dolls hanging from her little hands, her face dejected. "You fly today?"

Every weight dragged her down and she had to wipe the tear that crawled down her cheek. Now was hardly the time for another emotional breakdown in front of Sarah.

"I'm sorry, darling. Someone is sick and can't fly, so I have to go in his place." She tried to smile, but it felt like a grimace. "I'll be back tonight."

Sarah frowned and Simone sensed her thoughts ticking over. *You said that the last time, and you were gone for days.* Sarah dropped the dolls to the carpet as her shoulders slumped in automatic acceptance. "Ruthie?"

Simone looked away, unable to face Sarah's disappointment. "I'm calling her now."

Ruth was available, and Simone thanked her accursed stars as she went to the bedroom, Sarah trailing behind her.

Her bedroom almost looked strange, neat, without a trace of anything that had happened there during the night. It was as if Carlo had never been there, leaving her feeling empty.

She rushed her shower, whilst Sarah rummaged through some old toiletries. She paused in front of her closet, taking in the space where her uniforms usually hung, all ironed and ready. It was empty. All her uniforms were in the wash or still drying.

She still had some old Carlevaro shirts and cargo pants somewhere from the first cycle of uniform handouts three years ago. She looked through the drawers one by one, searching for where she'd packed them away. The drawer she'd packed them in was empty, and she swore under her breath. She was sure they'd been stashed away there, but then she hadn't spring-cleaned her apartment since she'd moved in.

She shrugged. *Say hi to casual day*. She sighed at the thought. It was the Carlevaros; they were no longer strangers but they were still the owners. Even if the Carlevaros forgave her the slip in attire, she didn't relish the idea of appearing unprofessional. She pulled on a T-shirt and jeans, just as the doorbell rang. She heard Ruth letting herself in, calling a cuckoo to Sarah, who crawled to the bedroom door and peeked out to the

275

corridor.

"Cuckoo!" Sarah called back.

Some of the tension slipped from her shoulders. Sarah didn't throw a tantrum and seemed fine, despite their day together having gone down the drain. She didn't want to think of Carlo's promise of being back later. It had thinned to mere words.

She met up with Sarah and Ruth in the lounge. "Thank you for coming, I hate doing this to you last minute." Again.

"No worries, I had nothing planned." Ruth crouched down to Sarah. "We'll have fun, won't we? There's still time to go to nursery school if you want to go play, Sarah?"

"If Carlo comes by, you can let him in," she said, not sure why she'd bothered to mention him. "But I'm definitely back tonight." The clock on the wall beckoned her. "I'd best get going."

She roped Sarah in for a quick hug and kiss, but Sarah lifted her arms to block the hug and turned her cheek away, forcing her to kiss her temple instead. The pang that shot to her heart at the rejection was almost too painful, and as she closed the front door behind her she leaned against it for a minute. That was the first time Sarah had done that to her.

Driving to the airport gave her time to think. She weighed the pros and cons of telling Carlo about her involvement in the leak sooner rather than later. The option of not telling him flitted through her mind, but she shook her head. He should find it out from her, rather than from anybody else. Whichever way, it didn't look good. She parked her car at the second terminal and took her phone from her handbag. Carlo still hadn't phoned her and she shuddered to think about the morning he must have had since marching out of her apartment.

She dialed the number he'd given her a couple of days ago. It rang a few times before he answered.

"Carlo?" Her throat constricted.

"Simone? Hold on."

She heard him typing in the background and closed her eyes, resting her head on the steering wheel.

"Where are you?" he asked.

"At the airport."

"Sorry to do that to you," he said. "But someone needs to go fetch Angelo and Dino."

He sounded stressed, and the tapping on the keyboard didn't stop.

"Don't worry about me." The guilt was suddenly too heavy. "I—"

"Is Sarah okay? Ruthie is with her?"

"Yes."

"Good, we don't have a choice right now."

She sat up again, putting her fist to her mouth. The way he talked, it was as if they were in this together.

He groaned. "This is spreading so fast, Mona. It's a fucking cock-up. To think the whole bunch of them are sitting in London for the Tusk Awards. I should've known this morning. They always go for meetings beforehand. I just got an email from the marketing director of A&K, one of our biggest clients for East Africa and a sponsor of the awards." He paused as she heard him click-click-click. "Listen to this email—"

She knew who A&K was, and it didn't help. Her stomach cramped. "I know how this got leaked, Carlo," she whispered. "I'm so sorry."

"What?" He was silent for a moment. "How?"

She cleared her throat. "It's my fault." She took a deep breath. "Michael Flynn's girlfriend, Annie Smith, works for the African Elephant Specialist Group."

She told him about asking Michael to check the hold, and how he'd found the tusk. "I didn't tell Michael to keep his findings to himself...I counted on his discretion."

The silence on the other end of the line was deafening and she filled with dread.

"Annie Smith is a real climber, she's moved from one NGO to the next in the past five years, always going higher up, using whatever she can to...be promoted." She was rambling on now just to fill the silence with her own voice.

He sighed into the phone, his breathing hardly containing his fury, which was palpable. She shrunk into her seat, wanting to get away from whatever he was going to say. She could see him clenching his teeth, rubbing his forehead.

"Say something, please." She didn't want to beg, but there it was.

After seconds that ticked on like days, he sighed. "What do you want me to say? That it's okay? I told you that first night that you were the only person I trust, Simone."

The jab was piercingly sharp, and she closed her eyes. "I know," she whispered, but her voice broke and she wasn't sure he'd heard her, as he said nothing.

He murmured in Italian and the tone of his voice made her shudder. "At some point, this would've come out despite our efforts to keep it under the carpet. I would've preferred to have some progress in our investigations first. Having something concrete to report when such allegations are made makes us look in charge, whereas right now, we look like we don't know what the fuck we're doing, that we are unable to manage our own company." His anger was stressed with each word he pronounced, his Eton English almost biting in the hauteur of his pronunciation.

This wasn't the passionate Italian from the previous night; neither was it the man who had fathered Sarah—this was the CEO of Carlevaro International. She didn't know what to say and her chest tightened as he started typing again.

"Where are you?" she asked to break the heavy silence.

"I'm at the office. Sitting at Peppe's desk," he barked. "Someone should be here."

"I'm sorry, Carlo. I didn't—"

"I need you to fetch Dino," he interrupted her. "I'm thinking of going to London. Fuck. These stakeholders were my father's cronies. Friendships and *trust* that were forged over decades."

She swallowed. "Yes, I understand."

A heavy silence ticked past. "When my dad and Peppe started Carlevaro East Africa, they had a plane and two bush camps in the Serengeti. That was forty years ago. Every cent of profit was pumped back into the company, into conservation." He paused as if to give her time to digest his words as if she didn't understand. "This can't go down in flames under my watch, Simone."

Her throat contracted at the thought that the company could go down, and that she would have had a hand in it. She would never be able to forgive herself if it came to that. "No," she managed to whisper.

"Dino needs to be here to deal with the Tanzanian government. At this point, I'd be surprised if they don't already know." He resumed his typing. "I'll talk to you later."

He rang off before she could say anything. Tears threatened to spill over as she closed her eyes. She pressed her fingertips to her eyelids, forcing the tears away. The least she could do was to contain her emotions and get on the plane to fetch Dino.

She unbuckled and got out of the car, grabbing her handbag and locking up. Entering the terminal building, she did her best to calm herself, but deep down it was a façade.

She found Ross slouched on one of the sofas when she walked into the staff lounge.

"Let's go," she said, wishing she could be as relaxed as Ross.

He gave her the once-over as he pocketed his phone, his eyebrows hitching as his gaze hovered over her breasts. "You're flying dressed like that?"

His open inspection gave her the creeps. "Yes." She sauntered away from him, not caring if he followed her or not. Of course he would make some stupid comment about her attire.

"Not once I'm manager," Ross said, right behind her.

"Don't count your chickens before they've hatched," she spat back.

Twenty minutes later they were taxiing to the runway. She cringed and wanted to squirm as Ross's hand covered hers. His fingers were rough with calluses on them, his skin scratchy. His touch stirred a revolt in her stomach, because her body still tingled with the traces left by Carlo's lovemaking. Carlo's palm had been gentle, his fingers long and manicured; hands whose hard labor only involved making a woman come. Heat crept up her cheeks at the memory and the thought of the bed linen that was probably hitting the rinse cycle in the washing machine at home.

This was why she could never get over him. Carlo was etched into her whole being, more so now than ever. Was this feeling all that remained of the night?

She sighed in relief as Ross let go and they climbed into the sky.

"So how was your trip with the Carlevaros?" Ross asked some time into the flight.

"It was fine." She didn't want to talk to Ross.

"I heard you got a chalet at Seronera." Ross's voice drilled through the headset to interrupt her thoughts. "Must've been fun?"

"Yes." She sure as hell hoped Ross hadn't gotten that tidbit from Michael Flynn.

"Why?"

"Because it's high season and the staff accommodation was full with private guides." She rolled her eyes. Everything had to be explained and justified. "Kevin had to swap some guests to the Grumeti to make space for the Carlevaros."

He didn't respond. She might just as well get to the point. "Listen, Ross, I'm not in the mood for small talk." Sometimes things had to be spelled out.

"Rough night, Simone?" He didn't turn to her, but something in the tone of his voice, more than the vulgar smirk in it, made unease slink down her spine.

"If dealing with a mountain of washing is your idea

of a rough night, yes." She prayed that her voice sounded normal, aided by the distortion of the headset and the microphone she spoke into.

"I'd love to show you my idea of a rough night." He leaned over and put his hand on her thigh. It was so sudden she hardly had time to register the move before he pinched her leg. She jolted but his hand jumped to her groin. He clasped her mound, pushing his fingers down to grope the soft lips of her already tender sex.

She choked on the breath of air she inhaled. She tried to close her legs, but only managed to catch his arm between the yoke and her knees. She grabbed his hand and peeled it off her, jerking his fingers back until she saw him wince, then she yanked some more.

"Fuck you, bitch!" He yanked away, forcing her to release his hand.

She let go, hoping she'd broken his finger. She leaned away from him, wanting to run. But she was strapped in the pilot's seat, sky-high, the yoke of the aircraft bobbing listlessly in front of her as if nothing had happened. Her whole body burst out in pins and needles, and vomit pushed up her throat. She gulped, her heart beating so fast it felt as if it would jump from her chest.

By instinct she checked the instruments in front of her. Everything was as it should be. From the corner of her eye, she saw Ross with his hand resting on his leg, rubbing his filthy fingers against each other. He said something but her ears buzzed. She pulled the headset from her head, breathed deeply, trying to step back from what had happened.

After a minute she put the headset on again. He chuckled and she wanted to punch him so hard that his blood would splatter over the airplane's windows.

She waited for her heart rate to calm down, clenching her jelly legs together. When she could control her voice, she turned and glared at him.

"If you want to go down in this plane today, touch me again. It will give me great pleasure to see you die, even if it's the last thing I do. I'll also remind you that the last guy who tried this with me not only got a few weeks in a Tanzanian prison, complimentary of Peppe's influence, but also lost his job and left with a criminal record." She took a deep breath. "Don't fuck with me, Ross O'Connor."

"Justin was stupid enough to get caught on camera. Who's going to believe you now, Simone? Peppe's gone."

She'd always had an uneasy feeling around Ross, and her instincts had been right. "I'm reporting this as soon as we get back to Dar es Salaam."

"Are you now?"

Of course she was going to report it. How could he think otherwise?

He was quiet. She checked the instruments in front of her. Thirty minutes to go before they arrived at Seronera.

The atmosphere was laden with something unsaid. It dawned on her that he was neither scared of her, nor of her threats. She took a sideways glance. He seemed indifferent, possibly faking concentration, probably searching for words to throw her off balance. A smile played on his lips, and the idea of him laughing at her made her stomach turn afresh.

"So tell me, is he a good lay?"

She froze. "What?"

"Carlo Carlevaro, did he ride you hard last night?"

Blood drained to her feet as the implication of his words hit her. "I don't know what you're talking about. Shut up, will you?"

"Come on, Simone, I saw him go into your apartment and he didn't leave until this morning."

"What the hell? Are you stalking me?" As soon as the words were out she wanted to kick herself. She could just as well have admitted he was right.

"No, mere coincidence. But useful to know, all the same." He glanced at her. "He did leave in a hurry early this morning. No bad feelings, I hope?"

Her whole being reduced to ash. She didn't know what to say and stared out of the window at the landscape, which swept away underneath them.

"You slept with Peppe. Moving over to the new boss would be no surprise." He sighed into the mouthpiece. "It's a pity you aim so high, some of the lads are crazy about you."

Anger washed over her like a tsunami. "I did not sleep with Peppe Carlevaro!" she spat at him. "And the new boss is Angelo Carlevaro! Get your freaking facts straight, asshole."

"So you're not denying it?" He was so calm his words chilled her inside and out. "This wouldn't look good if it comes out," he continued, his voice sympathetic in a monotone, reprimanding way. "Imagine if you get the management position. Everybody will say it's because you slept with both Peppe and Carlo Carlevaro. Especially if you go and smear my name, the only other successful applicant."

She swallowed. She trusted Ross to spread the news bit by bit, insinuating seeds of untruths. He was the type to use anything against her to get what he wanted.

"Withdraw your application for the management position, and this will all go away."

She laughed, but it sounded a bit hysterical. "Are you blackmailing me? What you did doesn't *just go away*." Fury rose like bile in her throat.

"No, not really. I'm trying to convince you to keep some sort of reputation intact."

A frisson of hate rode over her. "Go to hell."

She should ignore his words, but they'd struck the old chord inside her. For years she'd tried to convince herself that the rumors about her and Peppe didn't affect her. The idea of being seen as a slut had always been abhorrent to her…it was so far from the truth. Sarah's absent father had compounded it, and even though things might change with Carlo's return, Ross had the ability to play every emotional weakness she had.

She burned to tell him that Sarah was Carlo's daughter and that Carlo had the right to be at her apartment for that very reason. Instead she closed her eyes and bit her tongue. Revenge against this dickhead who had made her life a subtle hell over the past few years would be great, but it was none of Ross's business. Ross would have a field day with that information and he had no right to know, not when Carlo's family was still out of the loop, and about to board this very plane.

She chewed her tongue the rest of the flight, which couldn't end quickly enough. The stripe of dust of the Carlevaros' vehicle approaching the airstrip was visible from the air. They were only a minute away from the airstrip. On landing the aircraft she breathed out her angst. She released the throttle, closing her eyes. Ross snorted as he pulled off his headset, unbuckled his harness and got up to open the air stair.

She wanted to stretch her legs, but they felt too heavy. Anger overpowered all other emotion and she pulled herself out of her seat, clinging to the railing as she descended the stairs, not trusting her legs. She unlocked the hold for the luggage. Ross smoked a cigarette some distance away, his back toward her, relaxing with not a care in the world. She switched on her phone, wanting to report the incident immediately, if only verbally to the fleet manager, but it searched for a network for some time, finding no reception.

The tension in her shoulders had escalated to a painful cramp. She breathed out a sigh of relief as Angelo, Natalia and Dino arrived and got out of the vehicle. She suppressed the need to run to them.

Ross went to help the driver with their luggage, and carried some bags to the airplane, in conversation with Angelo and Dino.

Natalia came up to her. She had dark half-moons under her eyes, which accentuated her worry lines and wrinkles. "Thank you for coming to fetch us. If we knew yesterday that this was going to happen we would've left for Dar es Salaam with you."

"You couldn't have foreseen this."

Natalia shook her head, drawing her mouth in a grim line. "That's up for debate. You're pale, are you okay?"

"We had some turbulence. I felt nauseated earlier." Simone couldn't meet Natalia's penetrating gaze. Natalia was the type of woman she could tell anything to, but not now, not here in front of all the men.

"Oh dear, that's not Dino's cup of tea either."

"Sit in the front row; it sometimes helps." It wasn't true, but she wasn't flying back with Ross O'Connor at groping distance without Natalia and Dino breathing down his neck.

She greeted Dino and Angelo and soon they were in the air, heading back to Dar es Salaam. With the other three on board Ross didn't even look at her. He was such a coward.

Chapter Twenty-Five

Simone wiped her hands on her jeans when they'd parked the plane on the apron next to the other aircraft. She pulled her headset off as Ross got out to let the air stair down for the Carlevaros. She opened her door for fresh air and pulled the paperwork from between the seats. She took up a pen, but her hand hovered over the log, as she relived Ross's earlier assault. Her fingers trembled, a solid cold enveloping her at the memory.

How to phrase what had happened? Putting it down in words was impossible. The cockpit voice recording, captured on the electronic flight data recorders, would have been the perfect evidence, but the most recent flight data would have wiped it out.

She closed her eyes for a moment, trying to make some sense of what had happened. *Simone Levin was sexually harassed during the flight by Ross O'Connor.* Her mind repeated the words yet her hand didn't pen them down. By pinching her leg. By groping her groin. It sounded stupid although it had felt far from stupid. It had been intrusive and demeaning.

She glanced back to the cabin. The others were unbuckling. Angelo was already on his phone, talking in rapid Italian. She had no idea how much Dino, Natalia and Angelo knew, and if Carlo had told them of her part in the whole mess. During the flight, the three had tried to talk, breaking off in silence as the aircraft was too noisy for any decent conversation. Angelo slumped back into his seat again, nodding his head as Dino and Natalia disembarked.

Angelo leaned over and held his phone out. "Here, it's Carlo. He wants to speak to you."

Her heart raced, and her nervous fingers dropped the pen between the two pilot seats. "Thank you." She took his phone.

"Simone?" The strain of the day was concentrated in his voice. "How are you?"

She closed her eyes. "I'm fine." Too many words burned on her tongue. The need to tell him she was sorry, again, the need to tell him about Ross and what he'd done to her earlier. But this morning still hung between them, and Angelo sat behind her in the otherwise dead quiet, empty cabin. "How are you?" she asked instead.

"I'm in the international departures lounge next door," he said. "My flight to London departs in half an hour."

She suppressed a sigh. "Okay." This wasn't exactly news, but it wasn't exactly painless either.

"I'll have to see how it goes tomorrow. I've scheduled meetings with everyone who is in London."

"Have you managed to speak to Alan Kaan or Brett Winser?"

"I got hold of Alan," he sighed. "The conversation convinced me to go to the UK."

"Oh," she managed.

Ross ambled up to the open door on her side of the aircraft, staring at her, waiting. She shook her head at him, her stomach fisting in a cramp.

"I managed to speak to Michael Flynn." Carlo took

a breath but didn't elaborate. "Can you check the aircraft Michael flew on the day he found the tusk? Find the container he refers to? It could still be there."

She reached for her door and closed it, so that Ross could no longer hear her side of the conversation. "Sure." Michael had flown the CC 208, number 583. She'd checked the log after her conversation with him the previous day.

She'd do whatever she could to patch this up. "I'll check if the airplane is here." She glanced over to the other aircraft, which were parked next to the DHC. Most of the planes were back for the day.

"Thank you." He hesitated. "Is Angelo still there? Natalia? Dino?"

"Angelo is here, I'll pass you back to him." Her heart had sunk to somewhere below her knees.

"No, wait." He paused. "We never had time to talk about Sarah." His tone was softer.

She closed her eyes. "No."

"This day didn't pan out as I hoped. When you get home, please give Sarah...a hug and a kiss from me."

She almost choked up at his words and bit on her tongue to stop the surge of emotion. "Will do," she whispered.

"I've got to go, we're finally boarding." He rang off, saying nothing else, and the void he'd left almost swallowed her whole.

Angelo had waited for her to finish the call. She turned to hand Angelo his phone. He didn't blink as he caught her gaze. He'd followed the whole conversation, and with it, her rollercoaster emotions.

Leaning down she picked up her pen from the floor, wiping at the lone tear that had escaped.

"Let's get out of here, this heat is suffocating," Angelo said, getting up from his seat. Stooping, he scooted down the narrow aisle toward the back exit of the aircraft.

She took a deep breath, grabbed the flight documentation, got out of the aircraft and locked her door. Ross was talking to Dino, Angelo and Natalia where they were waiting.

Angelo came up to her. "Is the plane Carlo referred to here?" He waved toward the other Carlevaro airplanes that were parked on the apron.

"I'll have to look," she answered, clutching the flight documentation under her arm.

Ross was hovering close, listening to their conversation.

"Do you have time to show us around? I think we should look at more than one plane," Angelo continued as Dino approached them.

She didn't bother checking the time. She wanted to get rid of Ross and the immense guilt that had overrun her every thought since that morning.

"I'll deal with the flight admin," Ross stepped up to them. "You can get going, if you need to, Simone." His voice was friendly, helpful. He held out his hand for her to pass him the clipboard with the flight log still attached to it. "You should leave the clipboard in the plane, you know, but no worries, I'll deal with it."

It was so simple, it was so much easier, to just let it go. She took the pen, signed the document and handed it over to Ross. He held out his other hand and she dropped the aircraft's keys in his palm.

She couldn't deal with Ross, the Carlevaros who lingered expectantly, with gazes on her, seeming to gleam with knowledge about her part in the leak, and the whole fuck-up at the same time. "Thank you." She managed to gather some manners together for show.

"No problem," Ross said, signed where he was supposed to sign on the log, and then winked at her.

Heat rushed to her face. With the documents now signed without his assault documented it would be game, set and match. She wouldn't have hesitated to raise her complaint to Peppe, without it being logged. There was no proof, nothing in her own demeanor during the flight or after, that would help tip the scale in her favor if she mentioned this later.

"I'll catch you later, Simone. Mr. Carlevaro, Mr. and Mrs. Viggio."

With a nod to the rest of the group he set off for the terminal building, and Simone exhaled in relief.

She took a deep breath and focused on the moment. "If you'll wait here, I'll check if the plane is back." She searched around the other planes, spotting the CC 208.

She returned to the group. "It's parked there, but I'll need to get the keys to open the hold. Bring your luggage, we'll leave it in the office."

Picking up one of Natalia's suitcases, she led the way to the terminal building. She walked slowly, hoping to give Ross time to take care of the paperwork so she could deal with the Carlevaros without his supervision.

As they buzzed into the office she spotted Ross in the fleet manager's office, his back turned to the door.

The Carlevaros put their luggage behind the security gate, and Simone walked to Rebecca's desk, Dino and Angelo following in her wake.

"Can I sign out the key for the CC 208, number

583?" Simone asked. "We want to go check something."

"Sure." Rebecca turned to the safe behind her back, taking the key off its hook.

"Do you always keep the safe open like this?" asked Dino, as he eyed the situation.

"I always lock it." Rebecca handed the key to Simone, her eyes downcast. "Ross just handed back the keys for the DHC."

"You'll have to wait for us," Simone said as she signed for the key. "We won't be long." The other staff in the office had been chattering, like birds at the end of the day. It hadn't taken much for them to go quiet, staring at her where she stood surrounded by Team Carlevaro. She shifted on her feet, averting her gaze from those prying pairs of eyes. It was ridiculous, but she couldn't shake the feeling that everybody knew she'd messed up.

She couldn't get out of the office quick enough.

"What do we keep in that safe?" Dino asked her.

"The keys to all the aircraft and their spares," Simone said. "As far as I know."

"Why do they keep the spares there? It would be better to have them in a separate safe where no one has access to them, except in an emergency," Dino said.

Simone frowned as the implication of his words sank in.

"Do you think the other employees could have access to the keys?" Natalia asked.

"Well, if they can get the spare keys, they can unlock the aircraft, and put whatever they want in the hold," Dino replied.

"But we have the log book, all keys must be signed

out," Simone said.

"Which is great as long as everybody follows procedure and no one has an ulterior motive." Dino sighed, wiping a drop of sweat from his temple.

Simone led the way to the Cessna Caravan Michael had flown two days ago. That someone would take a key, or sign it out for any purpose other than flying, had never entered her mind. But a spare key would be perfect for opening a stationary aircraft at any of the lodges, especially at night, when no one was watching.

"There she is," Simone said, guiding the group to the plane. The last of the flights from the islands landed and parked some distance from them on the apron. The sun had dropped and soon it would be dusk. They needed to be quick if they wanted to see anything in the twilight.

She unlocked the hold of the aircraft, and everybody peeked in with anticipation.

It was empty.

"What does this crate look like?" Angelo asked. "Was Michael specific in any way?"

"No, only that it was strapped to the wall of the hold, camouflaged."

"Let me get in." Angelo hoisted himself into the hold and felt around the inner walls.

"There are no straps or anything here, but this wall feels like it's carpeted," Angelo called out.

Natalia stared at Dino, then glanced at her. "Carpet?"

Simone shrugged. "I've no idea."

"Rough or soft carpet?" Natalia called.

"Fuzzy, black. It's covering the whole wall."

Natalia's eyebrows shot up. "Help me up, Dino."

Dino frowned but helped Natalia into the hold. After a few seconds of inspection, she peered down at them. "It's the loopy side of industrial Velcro."

"*Merda*," Angelo cursed. "Are you sure?"

"Yes," Natalia said. "On a surface this size, it would be secure. If you stuck something with the other side of Velcro to it nothing would budge the entire flight from the Selous. We use the stuff when we attend travel conventions."

"It would hold something as heavy as forty kilograms?" Simone asked.

Natalia nodded. "Yes, if the bottom part of the container rested on the floor of the hold." She sat and let her legs hang from the hold. Dino took her by the waist and helped her down.

"Well, now we know." Dino sighed, wiping the sweat on his forehead and temples. "Container gone, proof gone, carpet intact. Great."

"Sounds like whoever's involved had something custom made." Angelo jumped down.

"And they're organized." Natalia picked up her handbag from where she'd dropped it on the ground earlier.

Simone closed the latch door and locked it. "How did this go on unnoticed?"

"Collusion, without a doubt," said Dino.

They strolled back to the terminal building. Inside the office, the last of the staff had switched on the lights, which now threw a few beams over the apron.

"Are there any other lights? It's very dark out here," noted Natalia. "Are there no lights on the runway?"

"No, we don't fly at night," said Simone. "This

terminal is used only during the day and only by small aircraft. The office opens at six in the morning; at this point we only have a skeleton staff manning the office."

"What's security like after dark?" asked Angelo.

"I can't say. I've never stayed around to see." Simone felt seriously misinformed for someone who wanted to take up the fleet management position at Carlevaro Air.

The group exchanged glances, taking the few stairs to the building.

"Airport security has the usual strict luggage checks when you enter the terminal for check-in during the day, but as for other times and around the perimeters of the terminal, I don't know."

"Our insurance covers our planes for standing outside like this, and not in a hangar," said Dino. "I must read through the policy again to understand what airport security we need to comply with. For now, it seems like as little as possible is implemented."

"Passenger safety overrides everything else," Simone said. "They are more concerned with what goes into an aircraft before takeoff from here, than what comes out once a plane lands. Especially since our return flights are all domestic and from our reserves."

"Clearly an oversight on our part." Dino wiped at his brow again.

Rebecca was one of the few staff left in the office waiting for them. The fleet manager was in his office, and Simone glanced around to see if Ross was still around. There was no sign of him. She signed the keys back in and Rebecca locked the safe.

"If I run now, I'll still catch the last staff shuttle home," Rebecca whispered apologetically.

Rebecca was in a hurry but trying not to show it in front of the Carlevaros.

"I'll let them out," Simone said, knowing Rebecca could be stuck otherwise.

"Thank you," Rebecca whispered as she picked up her bag. "He'll buzz you out," she said as she nodded toward the fleet manager.

Dino turned to Simone as Rebecca rushed off. "Who keeps the office keys?"

"The fleet manager and Rebecca. They work on a rotation basis and have access keys and the code to the safe. Whoever gets here first in the mornings opens up the office and signs out the keys for the first flights out."

Dino nodded as he glanced around the office, spotting the security cameras, inspecting the window with the view over the tarmac.

"Let's go, Dino," Natalia said. "Carlo wanted you to get onto those calls and emails."

"Maybe we can do it from here," Angelo suggested. "See what goes on here at night."

Simone shifted on her feet. Sarah was at home, and she owed her a hug and a kiss.

"How are you getting home, Simone?" Natalia asked. "You've just missed the last staff shuttle."

Simone sighed inwardly. Natalia really did miss nothing. "I'm here with my own car."

Angelo raised his eyebrows at this information. "Can you stay? We might need some help as we go on."

"I—" She broke off. "I have plans for tonight, I'm sorry."

"Surely nothing the fleet manager can't help us with, Angelo," Natalia said, killing the direction of the conversation. "Carlo mentioned earlier today that we mustn't abuse her. Simone has been working day in and out."

She blinked at this information. Nothing in Natalia's demeanor gave anything away but she was solidly in her court, prompting Angelo to back off.

Angelo shrugged but Simone was not convinced that he agreed she needed a break; after all, she'd only been shuttling them from one lodge to the next for the past few days, seeming to lounge about for the rest of the time.

"How are you getting to your hotel?" Simone asked Natalia.

"I've got the number of a taxi service. I'll call them now, or the fleet manager can help us." Natalia dropped her gaze before it shot back up to her. "Go home, we shouldn't keep you any longer."

She took her leave and buzzed herself out of the office, using the little button hidden at the secretary's desk closest to the door.

Walking down the empty, dark corridor she clasped her handbag tighter. A prickle ran down her spine, and she took longer, faster steps.

She walked past two security guards who chatted by the entrance leading out to the parking lot. There were no officials at the x-ray scanners for luggage; the terminal building was locked up for the night. One of the guards unlocked the door and let her out.

The door shut behind her and she gave the parking lot a once-over. Her heart rate slowed. It was a good hundred meters to her car and the sun had gone. A few figures were stalking in the dusk, and the honks and the buzz of the ever-present traffic on the other side of the razor-wire fence seemed far off. There were no more taxis waiting at the exit, and there were no streetlights.

She felt for her car keys in her bag, pulling them out with a jingle that sounded surreal in the close silence that surrounded her. She took a breath, ready to bolt to her car.

Ross's painful pinch on her leg, and memory of his fingers on her sex, echoed on her skin, spilling adrenaline into her bloodstream and causing her heart to thump in fear. She recalled that he'd been watching her.

I'll watch my back if I were you. Michael's words rang through her mind.

She turned back to the door and knocked. A security guard opened the door again, and she asked him in Swahili to escort her to her car.

The man took a flashlight from underneath his desk, and the other guard let them out.

She thanked him when they got to her car and she locked her doors, then buckled up. Relief seeped through her as she sped away straight to the exit, weaving through the odd car that still stood in the parking lot.

An hour later, Simone couldn't help feeling that she'd escaped as the gate rumbled open at her apartment block. She parked and took a moment in the dark to gather her thoughts. She glanced in the rearview mirror, observing the gate. How did Ross know that Carlo had come in and had only left the next morning?

She got out of the car, slamming the door harder than intended. There was no way he could have known, unless he'd seen them entering the gate. He must have seen them when the taxi had dropped them off outside. She mumbled to herself as she entered the lobby, trying to shake off work and everything that had happened that day before seeing Sarah.

Sarah deserved her undivided attention, but ever since that email with the changed flight schedule had landed in her inbox her life had been an absolute mess.

She leaned her head against her apartment door for a second. It wasn't that easy. That Ross had groped her was still hard to stomach and freaked her out, but she was safe at home now, and tomorrow she would put in a complaint against him, for what it was worth.

But her hand in revealing the poaching was not so easy to shrug off; the new rift between her and Carlo felt almost as deep as the first one had been.

In the silence of the corridor the beeping of her phone, signaling a message, was almost ominous. She sighed and dug her mobile out of her handbag.

A message from Liz blinked on the screen, and she paused to read it.

Beheaded dik-dik waiting for me this morning in the kitchen. Female and pregnant at the end of gestation. Blood everywhere as if they slaughtered it on the spot. I just want to run. This is clearly aimed at me. They want me to leave.

God. Her heart hammered as she read the message again. She leaned against the wall as the image of the tiniest gazelle overwhelmed her thoughts, dead with such cruelty. Someone had his knife out for Liz and was getting serious.

She had no idea what to say or how to comfort Liz. She still tried to formulate a response with quivering fingers when a message from Carlo beeped through, popping up on the screen.

After London I'm needed in Rome. Not sure when I

can be back. Will see how this situation develops and get it under control first. C

She had to read it twice before the full meaning sank in.

He was gone, indefinitely.

Her fingers trembled so much she couldn't respond, and her phone slipped from her fingers. It dropped with a clang on the tiled floor, echoing everything inside her.

With a curse she dropped to her haunches to pick it up. The screen showed a webbed crack, stretching from the corner over the screen. She pressed some buttons, getting away from Carlo's message. The phone was still working, but her heart was a chipped cup that had fallen again and shattered into a thousand pieces.

She gathered herself, knowing she couldn't respond to Liz right now with anything that would help her feel better. In the end she only messaged her back that she hoped James reported it and that they should take care.

When she entered the apartment, she exhaled the breath she'd been unconsciously holding. Ruth and Sarah were playing with Sarah's dolls on the carpet.

Sarah looked up and her face split into a sweet smile. She hopped up and pattered over. When she hugged Sarah close she forced out the last of her day.

She had Sarah. Her daughter had kept her going through some tight spots in the past and she would do so again.

Chapter Twenty-Six

Carlo leaned back in the business class seat, signaling for the flight attendant to take away the food he'd hardly touched. His flight had been delayed by a good three hours for no apparent reason, and his irritation was gnawing at him.

Ever since the flight had taken off, and he had been forced to switch off his internet connection, he had been stalked by some weird feeling. He'd forgotten to do something important, but couldn't recall what. The notion would surface briefly, but would disappear into his subconscious as soon as he tried to put his finger on it.

Carlevaro East Africa's precarious position had thrown everything else out of the picture, and all he could see was bloodshed as his father and uncle's company was bulldozed to the ground. If it would have a ripple effect and spread to their Southeast Asia operations...

The flight delay had annoyed him, but had given him time to work out an action plan with Dino over the phone. He'd rung Dino as soon as the delay had been announced and they'd barked at each other for a good ten minutes. Then their mutual anxiety over the leak had given way to reason, and they'd gotten back in the same court.

He hadn't told Dino about Simone's part in

exposing the poaching and trafficking. He had sure as hell been mad and disappointed, but the emotions had already passed. Simone didn't have a malicious bone in her body and had acted out of her own sincere care for the company, with no other intention than to help him solve the mystery. He didn't want her name linked to the sordid affair.

Either way, it was only a matter of time before the whole scandal came out, as it always did. And it was likely to get messy. He had no idea how big the syndicate that they were dealing with was, or how far they would go to protect their scheme. He didn't want Simone involved anymore because he wanted to protect her and Sarah.

He also wasn't in the mood for Angelo's insinuating comments or disparaging remarks from Dino. If he'd known about Sarah, about the whole fuck-up of their relationship four years ago, he would never have assigned her to this investigation in the first place.

She wouldn't have been in Dar es Salaam. She would have been in Rome. He cursed. She hadn't replied to his last message about him going back to Rome. He didn't expect her to be happy about it, but he hoped it would only be for a few weeks. He should have phoned her while he was still able to. Shifting in his seat, a pang of guilt shot through him. This whole thing reeked of déjà-vu. He slumped back in his seat. Not phoning her had been cowardly, an action fueled by his shock at her revelation about the leak and everything else that had kept him busy that day.

He groaned and waved the flight attendant away as she approached him with an offer of coffee. He'd phone Simone as soon as they landed at Heathrow.

He closed his eyes, forcing himself to relax. Dino and Angelo would get no sleep that night as they surveilled the second terminal. Alan Kaan and Brett Winser were no puppies, and the day ahead might be one long cockfight. It wasn't only Carlevaro East Africa's reputation that stood to be shredded by the poaching and trafficking allegations; every conservation shareholder had their head on the chopping block.

****

Simone stared at the mosquito net spanning the ceiling of her Zanzibar bed. Sleep was very distant as she still tried to formulate a response to Carlo's message. It was fine for him to flee to Rome...she was sorry again...she would wait for him? In the bigger scheme of things, it didn't matter. He had gone and whatever they'd needed to discuss could be resolved over email.

Her phone rang and she froze at the unexpected noise. Liz's name appeared on the cracked screen and she braced herself. She didn't have the energy to debrief the morning's events with Liz, but Liz probably needed someone to talk to.

Could the poaching leak have reached the other managers? She braced herself to feign ignorance, in case Liz mentioned it. "Hey, Liz, are you all right?"

Liz breathed into the phone. "God, Simone, never mind this morning. I don't know what to do. I'm spotting."

She sat up, brushing her curls from her forehead. "What?"

"I'm bleeding."

Her heart jerked in her chest at the implication of

Liz's words. "Oh God, is it heavy?"

"No, just a smudge or two." Liz's voice trembled. "I can't help wondering if this morning…" She gulped. "This morning might have triggered something. It was too much."

Simone wiped the image from her mind, trying to focus on her friend's distress. "Have you phoned the doctor?" She closed her eyes. Liz was stuck in the middle of nowhere and was possibly losing her baby.

"I'm waiting for the clinic to call me back. It's after hours, and the doctor on call is busy with another patient."

It would be killing Liz not to be able to do anything. She glanced at her bedside clock. It was past ten at night. "Is James with you?"

"Yes, he told me to lie down." Her voice quivered. "He hasn't left my side since this morning. Carrying his freaking handgun." Her voice croaked. "He hasn't done that in years."

What a mess. Of course, James would make sure nobody got close to Liz. But that was no way to run a lodge, never mind giving his wife some comfort. Hanging around Liz with a gun would probably have freaked her out more, making her think someone was about to jump out of the bushes to strangle her. She ignored her train of thought, focusing on the problem. "Lying down is good for a start, but you must see a doctor."

"I know…I…" She broke down. "I don't want to lose the baby, Simone."

Simone swallowed. No. "Have you done a symptom search on the internet?"

"Yes," she sobbed. "It just freaks me out. I'm so

scared."

It would freak her out too, and it wouldn't help much either. "Tomorrow is Friday, there's a flight from Selous to Dar es Salaam. James has the schedule and can see if there's space on the flight. Get on the plane and go to the clinic. You can stay with me."

"The lodge is at one hundred percent occupancy, Simone, I can't drop everything and run."

"Oh, for God's sake, Liz." Simone shook her head. "Someone is threatening you. It's enough excuse to leave mid-service. And this is your baby!" Carlo's words returned to her in a split second. *I would hate for her to risk her health and that of her baby because of work.* "Carlo told me that—" She cursed under her breath. "Just trust me on this one, okay? I have it from the highest authority that you can drop everything. Just do it. I've nothing scheduled for tomorrow and I can take care of you. You'll be safe in Dar."

Liz was sobbing uncontrollably. Her too-comfy-with-the-boss glitch had gone unnoticed. "Don't upset yourself more. Let them eat bread, Liz. You've got assistants. They should be able to keep the kitchen going for three or four days without blinking." She hesitated a moment. "I think you need to get out of there, either way."

Liz paused to blow her nose. "You're right. They'll have to get someone else if…if…"

Simone closed her eyes, praying that Liz wasn't having a miscarriage.

"I'll call you tomorrow when I'm at the clinic." Liz blew her nose.

"I'll come fetch you at the airport and take you there."

"Thank you," Liz said with a sniff.

"Lie down, put your feet up, and don't move until you have to. I'll see you tomorrow."

Her pulse raced as she rang off. Her fear for Liz overshadowed her own problems. She had no idea how far whoever was stalking Liz would go, but if she lost the baby... She breathed, thankful for her uneventful pregnancy with Sarah.

Minutes later her phone beeped a message. She wished it was Carlo, but there was no chance since he'd be flying.

We're both coming tomorrow. James isn't leaving me, bless his soul.

Yes, bless his soul. She got up and straightened the linen and plumped the pillows. If the Kings were coming she would sleep with Sarah. That way she wouldn't have to change the linen again in the morning. It would calm her to be next to Sarah; it would probably be the only way she'd be able to sleep. She sent Ruth a short message asking her to come and take care of Sarah early enough that she could pick up Liz and James as soon as they'd landed.

Sarah was still asleep when she left for the airport the next morning. As Simone waited at a gridlocked intersection her phone rang. She picked it up but didn't recognize the number. "Hello?"

"Simone?"

She would recognize Angelo's voice anywhere. It had the same deep, sexy tones as Carlo's but he had a thicker Italian accent.

"Hi, Angelo. How are you?"

"Listen," he said, not responding to her niceties. "Dino and I are at the airport office. Can you come in for a meeting?"

She frowned. There was a strain in his voice, which unsettled her.

"I'm on my way to the airport to pick up Liz and James King. I should be there within the next thirty minutes." She checked her watch. "With any luck."

"Good." He rang off without any further conversation and she dropped her phone in her lap. Why did he sound so tense? The call was unlike Angelo; he'd never been so curt with her before, almost to the point of being rude. Had James told Angelo about the killings in Liz's kitchen? Surely it had come to the point where he should share this with executive management.

As the traffic crawled forward, foreboding settled in her stomach. What the hell had that been about?

She checked her watch as she drove into the terminal's car park. In the bright morning sun it appeared innocent and harmless. Liz and James arrived only in half an hour so she had enough time to track down Angelo. As she got out of her air-conditioned car the heat hit her. She'd put on a mini skirt and a tank top, not anticipating a meeting with Angelo, but now she felt naked.

Screw it. She tossed her car keys into her handbag and lifted her shoulders back. If they wanted her dressed for the occasion they needed to call her in a timely fashion.

As Rebecca buzzed her into the office, people stopped talking and heads turned toward her. They weren't used to seeing her like this—her curls wild and bouncing loose, her tanned legs bare. Everybody's eyes traveled to the juncture where Carlo had been two days ago. Had Ross already spread his poison that she'd been sleeping with the boss?

"Mr. Carlevaro is waiting for you in the office," Rebecca said, her usual smile absent.

Something was wrong, and it wasn't just her dress. "What's going on, Rebecca?"

Rebecca didn't meet her gaze. "I'm not sure, but they've been here since I arrived this morning. I'm not sure they ever left last night."

Simone walked past Rebecca's desk to the fleet manager's office, knocking on the closed door before going in.

Angelo and the fleet manager sat behind the desk, staring at two computer screens, whereas Dino stood by the window, hands in his pockets, his gaze on the apron and the aircraft taking off. Another man, with the logo of their security company on his breast pocket, stood behind Angelo. The men looked up as she entered and Dino turned around to face her. All four pairs of eyes shot daggers at her, and she recoiled under their scrutiny.

"It seems a perfect match," the security man murmured to Angelo, almost absent-mindedly, as he turned to Dino.

"Hello, Simone," Dino greeted her before turning his back on her again. He looked exhausted, almost gray in the sun that filled the room.

"Why are James and Liz King coming to Dar es Salaam?" Angelo asked.

She glanced at the fleet manager, who ignored her, typing away on his keyboard. It was such a warped situation, such a weird question; her breath stalled and she forced herself to inhale.

She had no right to divulge anything about Liz's medical condition, but something told her the truth was important. "Liz is pregnant and I believe she might be miscarrying."

"And?" Angelo snapped back.

He wanted more, but she didn't know what to give him. They must know about the dead animals that had been planted in Liz's kitchen. "A dead dik-dik was waiting in Liz's kitchen yesterday morning. But you know about that?"

"Yes. We also know James King is a bloody fine shot and used to work as a ranger before he went into lodge management." Angelo stared at her, the silence unbearable as he waited for her to respond.

Simone shrugged. That James had been a ranger wasn't news. "I don't understand."

"I won't be surprised if he is the one threatening his own wife to keep us all confused."

The idea had never even entered her mind. "That's ridiculous. Why would James even threaten Liz? To the point of triggering a miscarriage!"

"So that's their reason for traveling here, is it? And what else?"

"What else is there?" She was unnerved by Angelo's harsh tone. "I'm not a doctor, she's coming to see one."

"So you say." Angelo voice was dry, angry. "Are you sure their little impromptu visit has nothing to do with the poaching that's been going on, now that the cards are on the table? I mean, best get out of the country while you still can."

She suppressed a curse. "What are you talking about?" Simone asked. "You're going around in

310

circles."

"Get to the point, Angelo," said Dino, without turning around. "Liz and James King will be considered separately. We don't know the full backstory yet."

Angelo stood from where he sat. "Noel Peters reported to us yesterday that the cameras they've installed malfunctioned on the day the tusks were flown from the Selous to Dar. How convenient. Also, they failed to follow the tracks you discovered at the plane that morning to anywhere significant." He glared at her. "We've been studying the recorded footage from the security cameras in these offices. Carlo mentioned it and we thought last night that there could be footage linking the tusk delivery from Rufiji two days ago."

Prickles rippled down her spine. "And?"

"See for yourself," Angelo said, gesturing to her to take his seat.

She went around the desk, stepping over wiring and equipment from the security company that cluttered the floor, and dropped into the chair. The fleet manager shifted the screen slightly so it faced her. On the screen was a paused video clip.

"We made a copy of the salient part," Angelo said. "The lighting isn't great, but it's good enough."

Her heart throbbed at her temples, and she clenched her hands together to stop them from trembling.

Angelo leaned over her, brushing against her shoulder as he shifted the mouse to click on the play button. The touch shot a foreboding tremor down her spine, and she shifted in her chair to get away from him. She had no reason to be anxious, but as if Angelo sensed her agitation he straightened up and stepped away.

The video started with a noiseless, motionless, dead visual of the Carlevaro Air office's desks. The footage was not very good, with a haziness about it, which was caused by the lack of light. The clip indicated that it was eleven o'clock at night, seconds ticking past in slow motion as nothing happened. A clang sounded first, metal against metal, a key turning in a lock. The office security gate swung open, and the back of someone's head appeared on the screen.

A cap covered hair that was only barely restrained. Despite the black and white image there was no doubt that the person in the clip was a blonde. And had curls that escaped from the hole made by the strap at the back, and at the sides, effectively hiding the ears. The figure ambled into the room, back to the camera, revealing a tall body, the waist dipped in with a jacket of sorts that had been tied around the hips. The person wore a long-sleeved, female-cut shirt and cargo trousers that looked like Carlevaro Air's standard issue. The dip in the waist and the curve of the hip that was covered by the jacket...made it look like a woman. Her right hand reached into the pocket of the jacket around her waist.

Simone peered closer at the screen, her eyes taking in the small details that were fuzzy to the eye. She snatched a breath and almost laughed. It was her—or at least it looked like her. Even worse, as the woman pulled something from her pocket, the footage had caught glimpses of a logo on the jacket's arm. She didn't need to look twice; she knew that logo by heart. "Aero Club South Africa." It was the club where she had done her training and had completed her commercial license.

She chuckled, incredulous, trying to warm over the cold dread swamping her innards.

The woman moved to the safe, where the aircraft keys were kept, punched in the code, hung up a set of keys, and took one set out, which she pocketed. She closed the locker again and made sure it was locked by twisting the handle back and forth.

"Her hands look weird," Simone said, her voice almost inaudible.

"We think she is wearing skin-colored surgical gloves," the security guy said, his voice gruff.

"Why?" Simone could kick herself as the word slipped from her mouth.

"Fingerprints." Angelo had leaned over her again and rested his hand on the back of her chair. "Which is pointless, given the footage, don't you think?"

Simone bit her tongue as she watched the clip to the end. The woman didn't turn to walk out, but retreated a few steps, turning her head to see if she'd left everything as she'd found it. When she reached the door, she slipped from the frame, but just in time for the video to catch the top of the cap. It was a plain cap, except for the classic Carlevaro logo embroidered on the front, the stock standard thing tourists could buy at all their hotel boutiques. Nothing gave the cap's owner away, but inside her every cell liquefied. That cap was hers—for some reason she just knew it. The cap had been in the same drawer her old uniforms were stored in, and that drawer had been empty.

The whole clip was less than forty-five seconds long. It was quiet in the office. Her own heart pounded in her ears. Feet shuffled and she became aware of the droning of the air conditioning.

"Must we play it again?" Angelo's voice was like a rough shake of the shoulders.

"That wasn't me," she said, her words falling into empty space.

"I'll be damned," Angelo hissed.

"Calm down, Angelo." Dino's voice was level but higher pitched than usual.

"That wasn't me," Simone repeated, wanting to say the words until they believed her. "What's the clip supposed to prove?"

"The footage was taken two nights ago, Simone, when you came back from Seronera," Dino said. "You were in Dar es Salaam that night. The rest we will figure out pretty quickly."

She closed her eyes. She had the perfect alibi. Two nights ago, Carlo was thoroughly fucking her at around eleven o'clock at night. A smile crept up her throat but, at the same time, every muscle contracted with helplessness. She couldn't blurt out that truth right now, right here.

She drew in a slow breath. They really thought it was her. They didn't know about Sarah, they didn't know about her and Carlo, and she was not going to be the one to tell them because that responsibility rested with Carlo. She sure as hell was not going to reveal to Angelo and Dino whom she'd been with in front of the fleet manager and some random security guy to save face. At least not without Carlo by her side, for how would that make her look? Ross's words about *trying to convince her to keep some sort of reputation intact* had been haunting her, despite every effort to shrug them off. "I tell you again, it's not me in that video."

"What proof do you have? A *trustworthy* alibi, maybe?" The fleet manager, who until that moment hadn't said a word, shook his head at her. His disappointment was almost tangible.

"None that I would like to share." She got up, and the men stood back in unison. "Excuse me, I must find Liz and James. I'm taking them to the clinic."

She walked to the door, but Dino called her back. "We need to complete our investigation, Simone. There will be criminal charges."

She turned to Dino, then to Angelo. She lifted her hands in a 'so-what' gesture. There was no reason why she would be charged with anything. "Go for it. But please do yourself a favor and dig a little deeper before you start randomly accusing people."

"We're suspending you until this case is solved, Simone," Angelo said. "We are appointing Ross O'Connor as the new fleet manager."

She stared at him as his words sank in. In a few words Angelo had killed everything she'd worked for. Every minute she'd spent learning the ropes to manage that office had been reduced to nothing.

"It's not only the video footage, Simone," said the fleet manager, scrutinizing her face. "Carlo Carlevaro instructed me to take you off the candidate list."

Carlo? Anger surged through her, hot and ready to burst. How dare he do this to her? How dare he interfere like this? She stared at the fleet manager in shock, her gaze jumping to Angelo, who stared at her blankly before looking away. Dino kept his back toward her.

She closed her eyes for a second, taking a deep breath. There was no way that she'd ever work under

Ross O'Connor. "Why bother," she said, barely controlling the anger that wanted to spill from her mouth. "I'm resigning with immediate effect."

"Simone—" Dino broke off with a sigh as if the fight had gone out of him.

"I'll vacate my apartment once Liz is fit to travel back to work. They'll only stay a couple of days with me."

There was nothing left to say. She took her mobile out of her handbag and put it down on the table. Her locker key followed, and she shrugged as it clanged on the table. There was nothing of note in her locker. "This is all I have that belongs to the company."

"We'll need your resignation in writing," the fleet manager said, without looking up from his desk, his jaw tight. "Don't leave Tanzania without notifying us."

By the sound of his last words she wouldn't be able to leave at all.

"Sure." She turned and walked out of the office, back straight and head held high. She didn't turn to see the men's reaction, but walked out of the office, the security door buzzing open as if by magic.

Chapter Twenty-Seven

Once outside the office, Simone strode down the corridor, grappling with the surreal situation. Resigning like that was about as immature as it could get, but she'd been fuming. Between the dubious video footage and Carlo's interference into her life, she didn't know what had angered her the most. Her head spun and she leaned against the wall for a moment to gather herself.

Passengers from the Selous flight filed through the door to the baggage claim area. The Kings were on that flight and would be there in a minute. God. She wiped at her face, brushed her hair back and breathed into her palms. She couldn't believe she'd resigned, even if only verbally.

Liz and James came through the glass doors. Did they know what the Carlevaros thought of them? She wasn't going to inform them of their budding status as criminals. There was no way she could tell them what had happened; it would only add to their distress. The last thing she wanted them to worry about was her impromptu resignation or untrue speculation. Forcing her emotions down she met up with them.

"It's okay," James said as she offered to take one of the bags he carried. He had dark circles under his eyes and a frown etched on his forehead.

"How are you?" Simone asked Liz. She was almost yellow with pallor, and had lost weight in the few days they hadn't seen each other.

"I'm not any worse," Liz said. "I'm more worried than anything else. There has been a little more blood, but I don't know if it's the start of something. There's not enough to indicate—" Her voice broke off as they continued down the corridor. "I'm so glad to just be gone from Rufiji, even if it's only for a few days."

Simone didn't want to think that far ahead. "Did you get an appointment with the doctor?" she asked instead. Her own worries had shrunk to nothing.

"They told me to come as soon as I could get there."

"We'll go there directly then," Simone said, leading the way to her car. They got in silently, and she put the air conditioning on full blast. The atmosphere in the car was heavy, and as both James and Liz had their problems on their minds, she didn't bother to make small talk.

When she parked at the Peninsula Clinic forty minutes later James jumped out to help Liz out of the car.

"Good grief," Liz said, giving Simone an exasperated look. "You'd think I'm about to break in two."

"He's right. It's better not to do anything stupid." Simone turned to James, relieved that they could be there for Liz. "Please take my car. I'm not sure how long you'll be, and then you won't feel pressed."

"You're sure? How're you getting home?" he asked, glancing up the empty road that was lined with frangipani trees and tall walls that hid the houses of the well-to-do neighborhood.

"I'll walk, it's not far." Simone hooked her

handbag over her shoulder.

"In this heat?" Liz stared at her with big eyes. "You must be mad."

"Don't worry, chances are I'll meet a tuk-tuk en route."

"You're not needed at work?" James still hesitated.

"Nope. She's all yours," Simone reassured him as she patted her car on the roof. "Go see the doctor. I'll see you back at the apartment."

"Thank you, Simone." James gave her arm a thankful squeeze before walking with Liz into the clinic.

She started down the road. The impact of her resignation hit her deep in her stomach and shivers rippled over her skin. She slowed down to a standstill. What had Carlo been thinking, telling them not to consider her as the next fleet manager? Why would he even do that to her? She was jobless, but that was not the biggest issue. She could get a pilot job anywhere in the world and had some savings that would see them through. But she had Sarah, and probably the worst thing was that Sarah's little world was going to collapse. Dar es Salaam was the only place, and Ruth the only other person, Sarah really knew. They saw her mother and Gabi as often as they could, and spoke often enough, but they were not part of Sarah's daily existence.

She'd hoped that Carlo would become part of Sarah's life, but she was unsure how things were going to unfold. There was no way he could see Sarah every day with him living in Italy, traveling for work, and them living...who knows where. Her unknown future was too overwhelming to contemplate further. Even if the storm that Dino and Angelo had kicked up blew over by Monday, by which time they would hopefully have nailed the real culprit, it wouldn't matter. The bottom line was she couldn't work for Ross. The time to leave Carlevaro Air had come.

Minutes later her apartment lured in the distance. A sense of peace, which had been eluding her for years, settled deep inside her. All these years she'd been waiting, hoping to meet Carlo again, to get some closure over what had happened four years ago. Maybe it had been the real reason why she'd returned to Dar es Salaam, living for the faint hope that they would cross paths. Now they had met again she could get on with her life.

The relief was not mind-blowing, but the closure was something she'd needed. Hot tears burned her eyes. She would have to break the news to Sarah over a space of days. She couldn't just pack up and leave on the next flight. It wasn't fair to Ruth either. The least she could do was find her another nanny position before she left, but knowing Ruth's capabilities it would hardly be an issue. The rock in her throat scratched. She'd manage one step at a time.

The Kings. Suddenly she wanted to avoid them at all cost. Adding their stress to hers and vice versa...her apartment was too small. Fleeing north to Carlevaro Kilweri Beach Camp, her weekend haunt whenever she could manage it, was the perfect solution. Sheila, the manager at the Carlevaro camp was one of her oldest friends, and saying good-bye to her would be on the to-do list in any case. Sheila wouldn't mind if she just pitched out of the blue.

When James knocked on her apartment door two

hours later she was packed and ready to go. Sarah bobbed up and down with excitement to go visit Auntie Sheila for the weekend.

"Where's Liz?" Simone asked as she let him in. "What does the doctor say?"

"The baby's heart is still beating. Liz seems to be fine, pregnancy-wise. They've put her on progesterone and bed rest." He looked strained and she ushered him to the lounge, where he collapsed onto the sofa, Sarah following suit, staring at him. "They're keeping her at the clinic for now. She's dehydrated, so she's on a drip." His voice caught on some of the words and his hands trembled as he scrubbed his face. When he registered Sarah was there, he managed a weak grin, "How are you, Miss Moppet?"

Sarah grinned back. "Fine."

Simone's heart went out to him; he loved Liz deeply and was worried. "I'm sorry, I'm sure she's going to be fine. And the baby too."

"We're going Aunt Sheila," Sarah confided in James.

He nodded absentmindedly. "I just can't help wondering, if I'd taken action earlier, if we would be here right now." He shook his head in dismay. "Liz has been so exhausted with work, and everything that's been happening at the lodge."

There was nothing she could say to make any of it go away. "I'll put the kettle on, and there's some lunch if you're hungry."

"I...thank you, Simone, a cup of tea would be great," he said, looking at her. "I left because I wanted her to sleep. She really needs it. And with me around, she won't rest. She's worried about me too, for some reason I can't quite get."

She understood, and if nothing else, Liz needed a break from everything she'd been subjected to.

Sarah got off the couch and took some toys from a box in the lounge's corner to show James.

"Not now, Sarah," Simone said, "James is tired." She glanced at him. "You might like to have a nap yourself, after lunch," she suggested. She and Sarah would be gone by then, and he could have some peace and quiet.

He didn't respond, but stared in front of him with a blank expression. "Sorry," he said, shaking his head, "I think a shower would help clear my head. Since yesterday—" He broke off. "I've been running non-stop."

"Sure," she said, sensing he wanted a moment alone. "Lunch can wait."

He took his bag and disappeared down the corridor and into the second bathroom.

She went to the kitchen to switch the kettle on, and took the sandwiches she'd made earlier out of the fridge.

When James ambled back into the lounge twenty minutes later he looked marginally better. He had his phone in his hand, and she wished he would just let things be, but he was staring intently at the screen.

"I've got so many calls. Can't they get on with it and leave me alone?" He sighed as he put his phone to his ear to listen to his messages. "The place won't fall apart in one day. Although lately, with all the shit that has been happening…" He leaned against the kitchen counter with resignation.

Simone watched his face as he grimaced.

"Bugger." James turned away and paced the lounge. She frowned, but he had his back to her, brushing his hand through his hair. He continued to listen, pressing buttons on his phone to save messages.

"What's up?" Simone asked as she put the cups on a tray.

"Blimey," he almost laughed as he turned around, "you think a day can't get any worse, then this." He met her gaze, shaking his head. "It was my assistant manager at the lodge. The Tanzanian army has blocked our airstrip. They pitched and parked an army truck in the middle of it."

Simone stared at him in disbelief. "You've got to be kidding me."

"Why would they do that?" James stood frozen, his gaze almost haunted. "Fuck me, and excuse my French, but the only reason they would do that—"

Blood had seeped from her face and she felt almost dizzy. "The trafficking."

"Did word get to the government?" James shook his head. "It's impossible. How?"

Her stomach cramped and she couldn't reply.

"I should be worried about the guests," James said, a faint blush rising to his cheeks. "But all I can think of is that we got out this morning." He closed his eyes for a second. "Imagine being stuck there, with Liz, with the baby…with everything else that had been going on."

The idea was harrowing. Being stuck in the bush was no joke, not when you needed urgent medical attention. And now with the army blocking the airstrip the only way out would be a very long and bumpy ride.

Thank God Liz was safely at the clinic. "Who could be planting those dead animals? It's sick." James must know something.

"No clue. It has been going on for almost a month now, but it has escalated the past week." He shook his head. "Liz has been freaking out and I can't blame her."

"Could there be any link to the poaching?" She had no idea where the question came from, but it slipped straight from her mind off her tongue.

He threw up his hands. "I don't know. The poaching has been going on for months, and this…only recently." They stared at each other, not knowing what else to say. "All I know is that they know their business, because every time they don't leave a trace."

He was as flustered about the whole situation as she was. She couldn't sit around with him and dissect everything again and again. "James, I—" She paused. "I'm going away for the weekend. I think you need your space. I…phoned Sheila at…Carlevaro Kilweri Beach." It was a lie, but who the hell cared. She'd had no phone to call with. "Sarah loves it there, and after everything that has happened Liz needs to rest, which she won't with us around."

"I doubt they'll discharge her today. The doctor said they might keep her for the night." James stared at her. "I don't want to kick you out of your flat."

She shook her head, and for a moment they both said nothing. "You're not kicking me out. I'm kicking myself out." She laughed at the truth.

He blinked. "If you're sure."

"As long as you are all right. You know there are taxis about a hundred meters from here."

"Yes, we'll be fine. But don't you need to work?"

"I'm…off." She glanced away to where her bags were packed and ready.

He brushed his face with his hands. "With this mess...guests are going to miss their international flight connections, it's going to snowball. I should be there." He frowned. "Is Carlevaro Air insured for this type of situation?"

"Of course." That was the least of her problems.

"They might need extra flights, more flights. They might need you."

"I'm around, just a phone call away," she said, her tone level, non-committal.

He gave her a queer stare at her blasé answer, but she walked away.

With a certain determination, she extracted herself and her daughter from her flat, giving vague promises of being back on Monday. With Sarah strapped in the back, she slipped the key into the ignition. She couldn't curb the wave of sadness knowing she would only come back to pack.

Chapter Twenty-Eight

Carlo rushed toward the meeting point he'd arranged with Julia the previous evening. Ever since he'd gotten off his flight at Heathrow hot bursts shot through his core, making him short of breath. When he'd switched on his phone after landing, he'd wanted to phone Simone, but messages had beeped through in an avalanche. Some warped connection had caused some delays, but what he'd read had left him stone cold. He'd switched over to his emails and when he'd read Dino's latest his stomach had coiled into a pit of nauseating acid that threatened to surface. The Tanzanian army was blocking the airstrip at their Rufiji Camp. He hadn't bothered to read any more messages but had phoned Dino instead. The connection had broken up and then he'd had to disembark.

He cursed as he still couldn't see Julia. The phone in his hand vibrated and he glanced at the caller ID. It was Angelo.

"The situation has exploded, Carlo." Angelo spoke as if he stood next to him.

"Clearly." He edged to the wall to get out of the fray of people. "What the hell is the bloody army doing on our airstrip?"

"They're blocking our planes. We've been unable to get a response from anyone in the Tanzanian government." Angelo sighed a curse. "James King is in

Dar and not at the lodge to manage the situation. We can't get anything out of the staff. The guests are going crazy, calling up their bloody travel agents, thinking they are in the middle of a political coup."

Fuck. "Why the hell is James King not at Rufiji?"

"His wife had a miscarriage or something," Angelo said. "I'm not sure how much of it is true, but they left for medical reasons."

Carlo dropped his head in his hand. "I see." Could things get any worse?

"So far they haven't tried to flee the country, so their reason for leaving the lodge seems valid."

"What do you mean?"

"Apparently Liz King has been the object of a stalker. The type that leaves dead animals on the kitchen counter."

Shit. That was news.

Carlo wanted to probe further but Angelo interrupted him. "Did you watch the video clip I forwarded you?" he asked. There was a moment of silence, the scraping of a chair in the background.

"No," he said, the irritation bubbling up in him. "I haven't had time to open some stupid YouTube clip in the middle of a—"

"It's not a stupid YouTube clip, Carlo," Angelo spat back. "It's footage from our security cameras at the airport offices. It shows our poaching culprit, caught red-handed."

"What?" It was hard to believe. A wave of relief surged through him. Something was happening at last. "Are you serious? Tell me?"

"We caught Simone Levin on camera putting airplane keys back in the safe in the dead of night."

Carlo frowned. "Simone?" On saying her name his pulse sped up. He hadn't kept his promise to phone her first thing on landing.

"Yes."

It couldn't be true. "When?"

"The night you flew from Seronera to refuel. The footage shows her hanging up the spare keys for the Caravan, which flew in from the Selous with that tusk. Well, we assume it's that aircraft's keys."

He was stunned to silence as he digested this information. "I'll have to watch the video, but it can't be Simone."

"We've got footage of her, Carlo. I've suspended her—"

"I don't care what you have on camera, Angelo, it can't be Simone." He sucked in a breath. "Why the hell did you suspend her?"

Angelo cursed and then spoke to someone else. "Carlo says it can't be Simone. Wait, I'll put you on speaker." It couldn't be Dino, because Angelo had spoken in English.

"No," he groaned, "don't put me on speaker, please. Who else is there with you?"

"The fleet manager and the security manager."

Prickles of sweat pinpricked his brow; his stomach tightened. "Make this call private. Get the others out of the office."

There was a shuffle in the background as Angelo ushered them out. "Dino's not here, he went to grab a coffee. We worked through the night."

Carlo swallowed. He'd arrived at a fork in the road, and he couldn't turn back. "It can't be Simone, Angelo."

Angelo sighed, his annoyance evident in the soft curse that followed. "Why the hell can't it be her?"

He exhaled but it did nothing to relieve the hammering in his chest. There would be serious damage and he doubted he would ever be the man his brother looked up to again but the rift was unavoidable. "Because I spent that night with her."

For a long moment there was silence. "You mean to say you fucked her after you preached to me to keep my distance? With the *staff*?" Angelo spat out a curse.

He'd gone cold at Angelo's rude description. "It's not like that, Angelo." He sighed as he looked up at the ceiling as if help would fall from it. "Let me explain. Simone and I—" He broke off. He had no idea how far he wanted to go with this conversation.

The moment had given Angelo enough time to digest his sin, without the bigger picture. "Hell, Carlo, you screwed her, after you told me to back off. Double fucking standards. Go fuck yourself."

The phone went dead as Angelo killed the call.

He closed his eyes, breathing, telling himself that Angelo had worked through the night and was tired.

On the other hand, it was the fight that had been brewing, waiting to happen. Maybe it was a good thing it had finally imploded. He could shake off the invisible shackles Angelo had tied to him, leashing him to some brotherly perfection he'd never aspired to.

Maybe Angelo would do him a favor and start sorting out his own shit.

He shrugged off his anger at Angelo for suspending Simone—Dino could fix that mess if it ever came to that. He pulled his cabin bag to a seat and sat down. After a minute of collecting himself he phoned

Dino. Leaning back, he inhaled deeply as Dino answered. "Please make sure Liz King gets the medical treatment she needs. If they can't accommodate her, evacuate her and James to South Africa."

"Sure," Dino said. "And what about her stalker?" Nothing in his voice indicated that he'd spoken to Angelo yet.

"This is the first I've heard of it. What has been going on?"

Dino in short terms explained to Carlo what had been happening for the past month, and that James had been studiously reporting each incident to the head office but that it had slipped under their radar.

Hearing the grim details, Carlo sighed. He had no other choice. "Close Rufiji River Lodge, cancel or transfer all our bookings there for the next two weeks and move the current in-house guests somewhere else, unless they want to get out of Tanzania."

"Yes, we're already driving vehicles down to move guests or get them back to Dar es Salaam."

Trust Dino to take charge. "Where are you?" Carlo asked.

"Walking from the cafeteria. The coffee is like mud," Dino said drily. "I've asked Peppe's nurse to try and get the name of a Tanzanian government official who can resolve the issue at our camp."

"I'm not sure how you're going to manage that over the phone." He paused. "Is Angelo still there?"

"He just barged out of the office and walked straight past me. What's going on, Carlo?" Dino's voice was calm, but searching.

He hesitated, a cramped moan escaping his throat of its own volition.

"Are you aware that Simone resigned today?" Dino probed.

Carlo dropped back against the seat. "No, I thought Angelo suspended her."

"The footage—"

"She's been set up, Dino. Get the police in and figure out who the hell posed as Simone on Wednesday night."

Dino didn't answer immediately. "You spent that night with her, didn't you?"

He said nothing, but it was answer enough.

"I'm not blind, Carlo." Dino sighed. "I'll see what I can do." There was a short pause. "You told the fleet manager to take Simone off the list of candidates for the fleet management position?"

The question came from the side and he had to recall that he'd had that discussion with the fleet manager. "Yes, a few days ago."

"Well, she is livid about that. Seems you may mess around with her, but you can't mess around with her life."

As Dino rang off he searched for Simone's number. God, what she'd been subjected to. He'd had no bad intentions when he took her off the promotion list, he'd only been thinking of Sarah. Surely Simone would understand that. In any case, there was no way she could continue working there when he wanted her in Italy. He bit his tongue as the phone rang. The longer it rang, the more he shifted in his seat. Was she ignoring his call? He stood, wiping his hand over his face as it went to voice mail.

He rang again, and this time someone answered. "Mona?"

"It's Dino."

Anxiety spread in his stomach like a warm flood of dread. "Where's Simone?"

"She left her work phone with us when she resigned this morning. I wouldn't have answered but I saw it was you."

Carlo's chest constricted as panic rose to his throat. "Where is she?"

"I don't know. At home? Where does one go when suspended from work? When one has resigned?" Dino's dry tone was biting back at him. Had Dino digested the news that he'd spent the night with Simone and hadn't liked it?

They could all go to hell; they didn't know the truth and he had no desire to explain it to them.

"Dino, you need to find her. I need to talk to her." Everything else evaporated before the visions of the events four years ago, when he'd been unable to get hold of Simone with no idea where she'd gone. The same feeling of utter loss engulfed him. "I need to talk to her," he repeated.

"I'm at the airport, Carlo." Dino had lost all sense of humor. "I don't even know where she lives."

He gave him Simone's address. "Please, Dino. This is urgent." He was begging, but his world had shrunk to nothing but the need to talk to Simone. "Please give her back her mobile. No woman should be without one in Dar es Salaam. Tell her I'm waiting for her call." He balled his fist and bit into it to contain the rising panic that was audible in his voice. He breathed. "Please."

"Not just a stray fuck, eh?" The comment was so out of line with Dino's usual contained self, it sent shocks through his guts. The situation was getting to

Dino as well, and for the first time in his life he wanted to shake Dino by the shoulders to make him understand.

"No offense meant," Dino continued, a slight drop in his tone. "I know you're not Angelo. I'll see what I can do."

Dino had rung off before he could make any further comment.

He slumped back into the chair. People were rushing past, ignorant of his inner turmoil. He couldn't get hold of Simone, and he'd left her again without a clear message that he loved her, that he wanted to be with her. He should never have left Dar es Salaam; he should never have left her again. His own idiocy dawned on him, and a weakness crept up his legs, to settle in his bones. He didn't know what to do beyond that he had to find her, and Sarah.

The ringing of his phone drew him from his reverie. It was Dino, and he closed his eyes before he answered.

"I got someone from the Peninsula office to go to her apartment," Dino said. "She's not at home, and her car is gone."

Carlo's heart plummeted and a new wave of anxiety hit him. "Do they know if she has a private mobile?"

"No. She doesn't seem to have one." He sighed. "The person spoke to her neighbor. She didn't know what time Simone left or where she went." Dino skipped a beat. "By the looks of it, and I quote, she took her daughter with her."

The world around him had spun to a standstill.

"Sarah. Her name is Sarah," he whispered as he drew his hand over his face. "Someone must know where they are." He was praying aloud.

Dino had gone silent as if he was waiting for his confession. Damn him if he was going to give it to him now.

"I tried to call James King," Dino said, breaking the standoff. "Simone did mention they'd be staying with her tonight."

Carlo ignored his last sentence. "Did you get through to him?"

"No, his phone isn't even going over to voicemail. His message box might be full. He could have switched off his phone, with this disaster at Rufiji and everything else. Highly inconvenient."

"Fuck Dino, I—" He couldn't think.

"I'll keep you posted," Dino said and rang off.

Carlo lowered his phone, staring at the screen, which trembled in his hand. Dino was pissed off at the situation, and he didn't even know the half of it. His stomach knotted in a painful twist. He'd lost all control.

Slowly he became aware of someone watching him. He looked up and met Julia's gaze. She stood some meters from him, as people flittered between them. He'd totally forgotten about her, and that he was supposed to meet her.

He hardly recognized her. Her long auburn hair shone in thick strands around her face, and her skin was sun-kissed with radiance. He had to blink—she seemed so well, so different from the woman he'd left at home just over a week ago.

Inside him something broke and it was as if he was waking up from a long, drug-induced sleep. Julia was fine, and she'd most probably been fine for a long time. He hadn't spent enough time away from her to notice how well she looked, or to look beyond the broken girl who had come home that night years ago, begging him to help her get clean.

She took a tentative step toward him. He stood, for a moment wanting to hug and cling to her, to soak up her strength, but he checked himself. Julia hated to be touched.

"What's going on, Carlo?" Her voice was uncertain.

"I've made a terrible mistake," he said, and it was swallowing him up. "I need to go back to Dar es Salaam."

She closed the distance between them, gazing up at him. "This will pass, Carlo. It's going to be tough, but we'll make it."

"It's not the company, Julia." He raked his hand through his hair. "I've left the woman I love behind for the second time." And he didn't know if she'd forgive him.

Julia searched his face, reading something in his gaze, because the frown melted away from her forehead and her gaze softened. She was so much like the woman she'd been before she'd fallen into addiction, so much like his mother...so much like Sarah, that he wanted to weep for what he'd lost in losing his mom, and for what Julia had gone through. He'd almost lost her too.

His resolve tightened in his chest. He had to find Simone and Sarah.

"Let's get you on the next flight back then." She took her phone from her handbag and dialed. Her instructions were rapid and clear as she spoke to someone in their travel department. She asked them to book him a flight on the first connection available from Heathrow to Dar es Salaam. She paused, listening, then glanced up at him. "The quickest connection is via Qatar in two hours' time."

"I'll take it."

"You'll arrive at four in the morning."

"That's fine." Suddenly he couldn't get there quickly enough, and his palms prickled at the thought of something going wrong to delay him getting back to Dar, back to Simone and Sarah.

Julia finished the call and slipped her phone back into her bag. "You depart from this terminal. Let's check you in and then we can grab a coffee."

He was grateful for Julia's clear-headedness at that moment when everything had overwhelmed him. After he'd checked in he had only half an hour to spare. They sat down at a coffee shop, and he sighed in relief.

"Thank you. I felt a bit stunned earlier." He met her gaze, which held no judgment. Julia wouldn't delve into his private matters, not until he decided to reveal something to her. She had too many of her own secrets that she'd chosen not to share, and it was a gulf they wouldn't bridge. Not as they were now.

Why had he come to London in the first place? "I'm supposed to meet with Alan Kaan and Brett Winser later today. I'll cancel with them once I'm on the plane." He took a sip of his coffee. "You don't need to go to the Tusk Awards tonight."

"I—" She pursed her lips together. "It will look like a total admission of guilt if Carlevaro isn't there tonight, Carlo."

"Possibly, but that doesn't mean we need to feed you to the wolves to save face." That he could be so indifferent about Carlevaro East Africa's fall from grace was liberating. For some reason, reconnecting with Simone overpowered every other priority.

"I'm not sure how widely the rumors have spread. It might be all right."

"Or everybody will give you the cold shoulder," he said as a matter of fact. "You can't sit through an award ceremony for conservationists while tusks are being loaded into a Carlevaro Air aircraft somewhere."

The idea was cold and sobering.

"I'd hate going alone," she whispered.

Alone. Julia never went anywhere without either him or Angelo in attendance. He exhaled deeply. Julia had taken the flight from Rome alone, and she looked well, but putting her in a social environment where everybody would be ready to stone her would be beyond cruel. "Don't go. Hopefully not many people will notice our empty seats."

She checked her watch. "Your flight's almost boarding."

He ground his teeth as he searched her face. He hated leaving her like this. A week ago, he wouldn't have dared. "Where are you going now?"

She met his gaze with a sigh. "I'll go see Granny. I haven't seen her for years and...I've come all this way."

He wanted to reach for her hand and shifted his hand toward her. "Swapping the pack of wolves for a lone one?" He tried to smile with the comment, but there was nothing humorous in the situation. "You can fly home, you know."

"I think it's time, Carlo," she murmured.

Her words shot unexpected warmth through him.

The time to break this unnatural connection as caretaker to Julia had been looming on the horizon, but he'd never realized that the break needed to come from her. "I'm always here for you," he promised, helpless. If Julia was ready to walk on her own, he had no right to hold her back, even if it took all his strength at that moment not to tell her to fly with him to Dar es Salaam.

"I know. I'll call Angelo if there is anything." A smiled tugged at her lips. "I can't wait to meet her, she sounded lovely over the phone when I spoke to her the other morning."

His heart jolted. Julia had spoken to Simone over the phone only once but had already put two and two together.

She smiled at him. "Natalia told me something was plotting between you and Simone."

They stared at each other and the flood of words could no longer be contained. "I met her four years ago, when I worked at Carlevaro Air...I have a daughter with her." The pent-up worry spilled from him, and he felt empowered for the first time. "She called her Sarah. After Mom. I never knew, Julia. I'm such a fraud."

Julia closed her eyes, emotions tugging at her mouth. She opened her eyes and stared at him. "You're no fraud, Carlo. You're the best man I know." She wiped a stray hair from her cheek. "Go make it right while you can," she said. "And bring them home."

The final boarding call for his flight sounded over the intercom. He got up but she stayed seated. He wanted to lean over and kiss her goodbye, but instead thanked her softly and walked off.

He turned around some twenty meters away to wave a final time. Julia never judged anybody and the relief at finally having told someone in his family, even if it were only the barest of details, swept through him.

Chapter Twenty-Nine

Simone lay in bed, listening to the waves, which broke a few meters from her verandah. The salty tang of the ocean was heavy, penetrating the gauze-covered windows. The chalet had no glass windows, with every space being open to the ocean. The only protection from the elements was mosquito netting.

It was dark outside. Sarah curled close to her, deeply asleep. With the images of the video clip rerunning in her mind, as sharp as if it was one of her own memories, sleep was very far away. Someone had posed as her and she still couldn't figure out who it was.

The woman in the clip was Caucasian, which didn't help much as she was the only white woman on the team. The perpetrator had to be an insider, and therefore...a man. She gasped at the realization—the playing field had just widened with about thirty more options.

She stood and took the flashlight from the bedside table. The generator ran only at certain hours, from sunset until ten at night and in the mornings. It was past midnight and the unnatural hum of the engine had long since ceased. By torchlight she pulled the stack of graphs she'd worked on with Carlo from her suitcase. She'd squashed them in as an afterthought but the answer could be there.

Flicking through the papers, she studied the graphs but learned nothing new. Going through the names of the pilots that flew the route again and again proposed no new solutions—Michael was always the logical conclusion, since he constantly flew that route. She'd struck all the Tanzanian pilots off her list.

In frustration, she tossed the papers down on the bed; some missed the bed and drifted down to the floor, but she left them there and strolled out onto the beach and into the waves. She needed to clear the fog in her mind. The water licked to her thighs, just shy of wetting her pajama shorts. Compared to the winter wind that blew in from the sea the water was warm. She shuddered, suppressing the desire to strip and swim in the dark. Sarah was alone, and already she was too far from her daughter.

Back in the chalet, she washed the sand off her feet in the shower. When she padded back into the bedroom she stopped to gather up the papers that had fallen on the floor. She picked them up at random, shuffling them together, then paused. Two sheets had similar graphs on them, but they were not graphs of the same thing.

Sitting down on the bed, she looked closer. One was the graph plotting the circle route Carlevaro flew, with the overnights in the Serengeti and the Selous. The second graph was for another route that stopped in Ruaha, then in the Selous. The second part of the second graph matched the circle route graph—the plane would fly to Rufiji and stop only to offload guests and pick up those leaving.

There was scope for manipulation there, if the pilot had a plan of action and knew what to do.

She stared at the names of the three pilots who

were plotted on the second graph. Stephan Botha was an older pilot from Namibia who'd started with Carlevaro Air six months ago but he hadn't flown the route for the past three months. Michael Flynn and Ross O'Connor were the other two pilots. A shiver ran through her and the papers in her hand quivered so much she had to put them down on the bed. She compared the graphs with those that had Michael's flights plotted on it. For the past few months, he'd flown those two routes almost exclusively. The longer route with the overnight in the Selous, and the shorter route that flew to Ruaha and then Rufiji. That meant he flew to Rufiji four times a week.

Ross O'Connor flew the Ruaha and Rufiji route on alternate days to Michael, and spent the rest of his time island hopping between Zanzibar, Mafia and Pemba, or on standby. The island flights were short, giving him enough time to slump around the lounge at the airport…keeping an eye on things.

The day she'd come back from leave rose in her memory. Ross and Michael had been sitting together in the lounge. Michael had never pretended to be a friend to Ross; he couldn't stand the guy. Was that the perfect screen?

She paused. Whoever flew the flights from Ruaha to the Selous would have the time to plant spare keys at the airstrip. Keys the poachers could use to open the specific aircraft that would fly the next day and overnight at the Selous. Those keys would need to be returned at some point.

The night they had parked the DHC Twin Otter at Rufiji a plane had been parked on the Rufiji airstrip, but it had been the wrong one. The poachers had had the wrong key and somehow their communications had failed. They hadn't known it was a charter plane parked that night but had tried to stow the tusk in the aircraft anyway. The scratch marks around the keyhole…the empty hold, the multiple footprints they'd read like a book… The poachers had tried to get in, but hadn't been able to.

Her pulse sped up. It wasn't a final solution, but Michael and Ross could be working together. She still hesitated to believe that Michael was involved. To have misjudged him for three years…and his girlfriend Annie was an environmentalist. But nothing else made sense.

Planes were assigned to flights based on a rotation schedule, because Peppe had always insisted that any pilot should be able to fly any airplane to any destination. Nobody was allowed a comfort zone. Getting the key for the aircraft that would be parked the next night required the code to the safe and keys to the office. Bribes could have paved the way for getting the code out of Rebecca. She blinked. Did Ross or Michael have a hold over Rebecca, or had they intimidated her into giving them the code? Did Rebecca even notice the missing key or did she choose to turn a blind eye to the glaring hole in the safe?

She took several deep breaths to calm down. Whoever had taken the photos had done Carlevaro a hell of a favor. She spread the papers out on the floor to get an overall picture, wanting to double-check her theory. Nothing else matched so clearly. She sighed, gathered the papers and put them on the bedside table. It was four o'clock in the morning. She had no phone and there was no way she could wake Sheila up to call

Carlo. It would be light soon enough.

****

Carlo tried to rush through the customs process on arrival in Dar es Salaam, but at that time in the morning, it didn't pay to rush anything. He pursed his lips in frustration as he hailed a taxi and gave the driver the address to Simone's apartment. It was past five-thirty in the morning and the traffic would be building up. Hopefully he'd be there in thirty minutes. He wished it could be quicker. Every minute on the plane had been an eternity.

With resignation that he couldn't escape the drive through the city centre, he sat back and watched the city come to life. It was much busier than he'd anticipated, the roads crowded with pedestrians on their way to work, dala-dalas packed with people hooting as they crossed intersections. Cheeky tuk-tuks wove through any gaps, always faster, always getting ahead. He cursed. With a tuk-tuk his trip could have been faster.

"Please wait," he said to the taxi driver as they arrived at Simone's apartment block. He got out of the car and called to the security guard at the gate. He tried to explain to the guard who he was, but the man recognized him. In half a second, he darted across the paved driveway and to the lobby, taking the stairs to her third-floor apartment two at a time.

Taking a deep breath, he rang the doorbell, but it wasn't working. He knocked, harder than he'd intended. A moment later the door opened. James King stood before him with a cup of coffee in his hand. "Mr. Carlevaro!" he blurted out as his eyes widened.

"Thank God you keep to your safari hours," Carlo said by way of greeting.

"Yes, my internal clock. Always up at this hour." For a moment James was flustered. "Come in."

They shook hands and Carlo followed him into the apartment. "I'm looking for Simone?" His heart begged, and he held his breath. From the look James gave him he must look desperate.

"She's visiting Sheila." James searched his face. "She left yesterday."

"Sheila?" He knew so little of Simone's circle of friends and the life she'd built for herself over the years. "Where is she?"

"Sheila McKenzie, she's the manager of your Kilweri Beach Camp."

Sheila was one of their oldest employees and had been working for Carlevaro for more than thirty years. Relief rushed through his body, and for a moment he wished he could collapse on the sofa. Sheila would take care of Simone and Sarah. "Did she get there safely?"

"I think so." James gave him a quizzical stare. "We can phone Sheila to check? There's no network coverage on the island so you'll struggle to get hold of Simone on her mobile. Sheila has a satellite phone."

Carlo raked his hands through his hair, dropping into a chair. "Simone no longer has a mobile. You have Sheila's number?"

James frowned. "Sure. I'll get my phone."

Carlo's heart beat in his throat as James reappeared with his phone pressed against his ear.

"Hi Sheila, yes, yes fine, did Simone and Sarah arrive yesterday?" James asked.

Carlo stared at him, clenching his fists. James looked at him and nodded.

He let go of the breath he'd been holding. *They're*

safe. He raked his hand through his hair and strode to the window overlooking the sea to hide his emotions from James.

"She's at the end of the row of chalets? That's too far," James continued. "It's okay, no need to talk to her, thank you."

"Please tell Sheila to keep Simone there. Don't let her leave." Carlo turned toward him. "Keep her safe until I get there. And make sure the boat waits for me. I'm leaving now."

James repeated his words to Sheila and then James rang off. "I'll forward you Sheila's number."

"Thank you," Carlo said. "Someone came around to look for Simone last night, but no one was here."

"I was at the clinic," James said.

He studied James's face. "I forgot about Liz. How is she doing?"

James shook his head. "She spent the night at the clinic…I…she's pregnant and there have been some issues."

Carlo nodded. "I'm sorry to hear that. Is everything all right?"

"Yesterday evening everything was still fine." James paled, and for a second Carlo's gut twisted. If something had happened to Simone during her pregnancy with Sarah she would have dealt with it on her own. There was nothing he could do for the Kings. "If necessary you should evacuate to South Africa."

"Thank you. The doctor didn't think it necessary yesterday. I'll see what he says this morning." He heaved a sigh. "At least Liz has been able to get a good night's rest."

"I heard about the other incidents at Rufiji. I wasn't

aware of them until yesterday."

James huffed. "It all was rather petty until the last one. It upset Liz that it was a pregnant dik-dik that was slaughtered."

"Understandably. It seemed to be aimed solely at her." He met James's gaze steadily.

"Why are you looking for Simone, Mr. Carlevaro? It sounds serious."

Carlo told him what he knew, about the video clip and Simone's consequent resignation.

The color drained from James's face. "She told us nothing yesterday! Resigning!" He gulped. "I thought she'd be promoted to fleet manager."

"The other candidate will be promoted," Carlo said, not wanting to share private details of Simone's life or future.

"Ross," James said blandly. "Ross O'Connor is the other candidate." He cursed under his breath. "At least he'll stop harassing Liz now. Ever since you arrived he's been phoning Liz to find out what Simone's doing, where you are flying next."

"Why would he phone Liz?"

"They're brother and sister."

Carlo digested this information but shrugged it off. The safari business tended to be nepotistic, and he couldn't point a finger at that, heading a family business.

"He never phones us, we hardly see him, but this past week—" James shook his head. "He's anxious about the promotion. It's a bad time to have everything in shambles, now with the army blocking Rufiji and—" He looked at Carlo. "Have you heard that they also parked an army truck at our Ruaha airstrip?"

Carlo frowned. "No, this is the first I've heard of it."

"Angelo sent out a message last night about Ruaha to the other lodge managers—"

"The email must have gone through while I was flying," Carlo said. It was more likely that Angelo had chosen not to let him know. "For all I care, they can bulldoze both lodges at the moment. I need to get to Simone."

James raised his eyebrows at his response. "But…this video…do you suspect Simone is involved in the poaching?"

"No, she's been set up." He glanced at the door.

"Mind if I walk you to your car?"

"Not at all."

They walked out of the apartment and James closed the door. "Liz has been skittish. As much as I hate to say this, I'm glad we had a valid medical reason to leave the lodge yesterday."

"What has been happening at the camp would have been valid reason enough for me." He blew out a deep sigh. "I wish you'd raised it during our initial meeting," Carlo said as they took the stairs.

They stopped in the empty lobby.

"On Monday it was the shock of having you all on our doorstep, days after Peppe's heart attack, that got to me. And then seeing the photos." James swallowed audibly, staring through the glass doors that led out to the parking lot.

From James's nervous stance there was more. "Fair enough."

"It wasn't the right time or place." James didn't move, and he waited for him to carry on. "As you know, we've been tracking the poaching ever since we noticed the increase." He paused as if he wasn't sure he should go on.

"Yes?" Carlo prompted him, sensing James had something important he wanted to share.

"One full moon when we thought they would strike I went out with one of the rangers. Trying to find a needle in a haystack. After four hours we were on our way home when we ran into some Land Rover trouble close to the airstrip. We didn't think much of it and got busy fixing the problem."

"As one does," Carlo said drily. Only the mad and the cocksure would get out of a vehicle in the Selous in the dead of night to fix an engine issue.

"As one does." James grinned as if he'd read his mind. "I only became aware of the unnatural silence around us when the other ranger shushed me and we doused the torches. It was after two in the morning, but we heard talking, subdued and at intervals. Whoever approached us was unaware of our presence as we'd been there for some time. The wind carried their voices to us before they could notice us. There were four of them, speaking Swahili, and they passed without seeing us, about fifty meters away. They carried something heavy, curvy. We were too shocked to move, them being so close to the lodge and to the airstrip."

"And that's when you started suspecting things were happening there which we were previously unaware of," Carlo said as the picture unfolded in his mind's eye. "It was you who took those photos that were sent to Peppe anonymously."

"Yes." He paused. "It took me two weeks after that initial sighting to get a photo opportunity. I tried to get it to Peppe as soon as possible, and Liz's check-up at the clinic in Dar was the perfect opportunity." He wiped at his brow, where a fine sheen of sweat had settled between the furrows on his forehead. "Peppe's heart attack…I regret—" James dropped his head.

Carlo nodded with a sigh. "The photos were not the sole contributing factor." He gave James a comforting squeeze on the shoulder, because he was so devastated. "Why didn't you reveal yourself sooner?"

"Liz doesn't know. She's too chatty. I didn't want her to know about what we saw or the photos, in case she let something slip." He rubbed his forehead and sighed. "The stalking started right after we spotted the poachers. I had to be careful, dealing with criminals. That they would try to get to me through my wife!"

"It wouldn't be the first time that happened."

"And with her being pregnant…it added another dimension to the issue." James drew in a sharp breath. "I suspect the poachers might have seen us that first night, despite our keeping quiet and hiding. It must have been when we drove home two hours later. We had no idea where they went after their visit to the airstrip, but they must have seen us."

Dread coiled in his stomach. How far would the poachers go to protect their scheme? "The hunter becomes the hunted."

James nodded. "Something like that. Liz thought those incidents were linked to a disgruntled employee, someone I've given a written warning…or fired, who perceived it as an unfair dismissal." He glanced away, his mouth pulled in disgust. "But this gazelle yesterday morning. It had gone too far."

"I agree," Carlo said as he shook his head.

"Someone is warning you to back off."

"Yes."

"But who?"

James shrugged. "I hate to think that a pregnant gazelle was put there on purpose." He dropped his gaze. "You see, the only people we've told about Liz's pregnancy are her family and mine."

Carlo said nothing. Simone had known Liz was pregnant, and he had overheard Liz's comments in front of the kitchen staff. Liz was too chatty, indeed. James's notion that no one else knew about Liz's pregnancy was far-fetched. "Liz told Simone."

"Which makes her the only one outside our families who knows."

That James was insinuating that Simone was involved in stowing pregnant kill in Liz's kitchen was wasting his time. Carlo shook his head and checked his watch, getting anxious to leave.

"That's everything you know?"

James nodded.

"I've got to go."

James held out his hand and they shook briefly. "I hope this gets resolved soon."

"The lodge is closed for two weeks to sort this out," Carlo said, his focus returning to Simone and the need to find her. As he got into the taxi he shot a last glance at James, but he'd turned away and was heading back to the lobby.

As the taxi drove up the coast out of the northern suburbs of Dar es Salaam his mind kept on coming back to everything James had said. How far had the news of the poaching traveled? Had the insider at Carlevaro Air heard that they were investigating the matter? Right now, the only information the staff could have was that their airstrips were blocked, not the reason why. He had sworn Michael Flynn and his girlfriend to silence, for what it was worth. The fact that Michael had flown that tusk two days ago was proof that, at that point in time, the poachers didn't know their cover was blown. He checked his watch; it was past seven in the morning and the fleet manager would be at the Carlevaro Air office. He dialed his number.

"Has any pilot called in sick today? Or is anyone absent without leave?" he asked the fleet manager. If the insider were aware of the leak, he would have disappeared by now.

"No. Everybody is accounted for."

"Ross O'Connor?" Carlo asked.

"He clocked in as usual. He's on standby today. We'll probably start the handover process later if nothing comes up."

"Good," he said and rang off, not quite sure if that was the information he was looking for. Only one thing was for sure—time was running out. He took his laptop bag and pulled out the stack of graphs he'd worked on a few days before to go through them again.

Chapter Thirty

Simone sat up and gazed at the aquamarine waters through the gauze-covered windows. Sarah was waking up, and soon she'd be able to go to the main guest area and find Sheila. The need to phone Carlo was reaching a boiling point. She'd already decided to phone Dino, in case she couldn't get hold of Carlo.

Sarah whined, and she tucked the bedcover tightly over her tiny shoulders. The wind blew in from the sea, and it was cool for an early morning. The sun lay in promise on the horizon, and she could see a handful of *dhow* boats going out for their morning's fishing.

In the past, she'd always stayed with Sheila in her chalet, but Sheila's daughter was here for a week. Luckily there had been a chalet available for them. The knowledge that this would be her last stay at the camp settled and regret washed over her. She drew her legs to her chest, wrapping her arms around them.

Someone whistled and she saw a figure strolling on the beach. A dog bounded into view, chasing crabs into the surf, followed by Sheila, who took wide strides toward her chalet.

She shot a glance at Sarah, who had gone back to sleep. She got up and opened the door as Sheila came up the short path to her veranda.

"How did you sleep, honey?" Sheila asked as she met her gaze.

"Not very well, but it's okay." Simone felt exhausted but gave Sheila a hesitant smile. Sheila had acted as substitute mom these past three years, and she'd told her everything about the poaching, the video clip and her resignation.

"I'm switching the generator on in ten minutes if you want to come over for some coffee? Also…" Sheila stopped mid-sentence, glancing away.

"Yes?"

"James King called." Sheila looked up, almost apologetically. "The Carlevaros are searching for you. They're coming to fetch you this morning."

Simone frowned, shaking her head. "I'm not hiding, Sheila. I've done nothing wrong."

"I know, honey, I believe you." Sheila sucked her lips, which accentuated every wrinkle on her sun-ravaged face. She took Simone's hands in hers. "But what if the police throw you in jail? You know how they can react if something is not to their liking. Just see how they parked those army trucks on the airstrips."

Simone squeezed Sheila's hand and then let go. "I'm sure it won't come to that." Maybe she was projecting overconfidence, because her heart dropped an inch at the thought. The Carlevaros…Carlo…wouldn't do that to her, not once she'd explained her findings to them. But Carlo wasn't here, and he had for some unknown reason scrapped her for the promotion. She had no idea what his intentions were.

If the police did come, or if the other Carlevaros came, what would happen to Sarah? They hadn't listened to her when she'd told them it wasn't her in the video clip, and there was no reason to believe they would listen to her any better now.

"From what I understood they left Dar already, so they should be here within the hour."

"Did James specify who was coming?" Simone asked.

"No, he just said he had Mr. Carlevaro with him."

It had to be Angelo. Carlo was in London. She closed her eyes, wishing it were anybody else. After her dealings with Angelo she wasn't sure she could make him listen to her for five minutes, let alone long enough for him to understand what she had discovered.

"Okay," Simone said. "I'll get dressed."

Sheila sighed. "I've got to oversee breakfast. Come have some when you're ready." She ambled off, whistling for the dog to follow her.

Angelo would be there soon enough. Whether he had the police with him or not, she wouldn't let go until he had listened.

****

Simone strolled with Sarah on the beach away from the row of chalets. The rising sun dazzled the early mother of pearl waters into a translucent aquamarine. A breeze blew in from the east, lapping at the hem of her white dress and taking the edge off the promising heat of the day.

Every nerve in her body was wound tight and Sarah had picked up on her mood. Sarah had been quiet, holding her hand, letting go every now and again to pick up a shell to add to her collection.

"This one's for you, Mommy," Sarah had said with the first shell, then they'd run through their circle of friends with her subsequent finds. When Sarah stumbled across a beautiful clamshell, still intact, opening and closing like a little purse, the radiance in Sarah's smile had been catching, until she said, "This one is for Daddy."

Her throat tightened at Sarah's words, but she held out her palm, taking the delicate gift from Sarah. She hadn't had the guts to ask Sheila for her phone to call Carlo. She might have told Sheila a lot, but she hadn't told her everything. Maybe, after her interrogation with Angelo, and her explanation of who Sarah was, he'd give her his phone to call Carlo.

The camp's guests slowly surfaced, scattered over the wide stretch of beach, climbing the rocks that created a natural pool away from the breaking waves, gathering shells or swimming.

Simone continued to stroll on for about three hundred meters. She didn't want to face Angelo with guests within earshot. If nothing else, she wanted to avoid a scene. She swept a wisp of hair out of her face and turned to face the sea breeze.

Sheila's dog ran in her direction, with Sheila following, waving frantically. She rushed toward Sheila, who held her phone out.

"Carlo Carlevaro," she said between gulping breaths. "He wants to talk to you. Urgently."

Her heart lurched in her chest. He was phoning her. He hadn't forgotten. He'd tracked her down. She closed her eyes for a second, listening to Sheila catching her breath, trying to gather her own emotions.

"Here honey, you just press the dial button," Sheila said between heavy heaves. "Good grief, he shouldn't do that to an old woman like me."

"Thank you," Simone said, taking the satellite phone from Sheila.

"I've got to run, I've two guests departing. Everything always happens at once."

Simone nodded and watched as Sheila trotted toward the main guest areas.

With a pounding heart she dialed and Carlo answered almost immediately.

"Simone, I need to make this quick while I still have network coverage. What do you know about Ross O'Connor?"

"I—" She swallowed to get a grip over the unexpected question and his skipping the niceties completely. He sounded so far away, but his voice was serious, if no longer angry. Part of her was thankful that he hadn't mentioned their last conversation, when he'd been furious with her about leaking the poaching.

She wanted to tell him how sorry she was about the whole mess, wanted to demand why he'd sunk any hope of her being promoted, but something in his voice told her he didn't have the time for that right now. "I think he is involved in the poaching ring, with Michael Flynn. What's going on?"

"I've been looking at the graphs," Carlo said, the urgency in his voice palpable. "Between Ross and Michael, they are at Rufiji almost every day."

"Yes, I figured they would be able to plant the aircraft keys at the airstrip for the poachers to stow the tusks in whichever plane flies the next day."

"Yes, but Michael isn't involved," Carlo said. "He's the only other pilot who knows we're investigating the poaching syndicate. If he'd spread the word, the guilty parties would have fled by now. And if he was involved he wouldn't be sticking around to find out what happens next." He sighed into the phone.

"Help me make sense of this."

She dropped her head, the need to tell him about Ross's assault overwhelming her. "Ross tried to…intimidate me the other day on the flight." She broke off as the memory rushed back, crystal clear. Ross's hands were on her as if he'd groped her minutes ago and she shuddered.

"What did he do?"

As she told him about Ross's assault and his threats regarding the promotion, Carlo cursed over the phone. "But there it is!" he called out. "The fleet manager position." He spoke fast. "As fleet manager he'd be in control of our planes, he'd be able to set up the whole operation so smoothly no one would be the wiser."

A shudder rushed down her spine. "Of course," she murmured. "God, I never thought about that."

"He must have a team of locals working for him at the lodges." He cursed. "We'll smoke them out."

She couldn't believe it. Ross wanted the fleet manager position so he could carry on his poaching and smuggling. As fleet manager he would have command of everything…could expand his horrid operations to every lodge they flew to.

The video image came back to her, and she inhaled sharply. In the dark blur of the footage the body shape had been misleading, disguised by the loose wrapping of her club jacket around male hips. The way he'd retreated, never showing his chest to the camera, hiding his lack of breasts, now made perfect sense. "The person in the video has Ross's body shape." She pressed down on her excitement in realizing she was right. "Ross has been to my apartment. He rummaged through my clothes, probably took my jacket, my missing uniform. I—"

Carlo said something, but the line was breaking up on his side. "I'll phone Dino...go back a few kilometers...Simone...won't be long—"

The network broke up and she glared at the satellite phone's screen. The call had cut off by itself.

An hour later she was still on the beach, waiting for Angelo's arrival, holding on to the phone in case Carlo phoned back. Why had his phone cut the call like that? Surely the network coverage was better than that in the UK.

When the phone started ringing she checked the screen. *James King.*

Without thinking further she answered, "It's Simone, James. How is Liz? How is the baby?" She'd been praying that everything was still fine.

James breathed heavily into the phone, "Simone, thank God I get hold of you. Liz is gone. Is she with you?"

She froze in her tracks, her blood stalling in her veins. "No? What do you mean she's gone?"

"She left the clinic early this morning, she wasn't discharged but just walked out. She left me a message—" His voice broke, his agony obvious. "I didn't see it until later, when I left the apartment to go to the clinic."

"What did it say?" Simone asked, dreading his answer.

"It wasn't what she wanted, it got out of control, that Ross won't stop, that she only wanted to help their dad." The words spurted out, mangled in his distress. "I have no idea where she is."

"Her phone?" But as she asked, the answer was

obvious. Liz wouldn't be taking any calls.

"She left it at the hospital. Any idea where she could be?" He sounded desperate.

With Ross. She couldn't stomach the thought. "Have you tried to get hold of Ross?"

"His phone is switched off."

There was some hope. "Ross must be flying. I'm so sorry, James, but I really have no idea where she is."

"Ross isn't flying today. Our baby—" he wailed, and the sound tore at her and she had to blink. He must have come to the same conclusion as she had. Ross and Liz were operating the poaching and trafficking syndicate. She didn't want to believe it.

"You know what this means, Simone?"

Yes. They were on the run. Her shock was too raw and she didn't know how to comfort him. She closed her eyes, speechless. In the silence over the line she could feel his heart breaking. "Don't believe the worst, please, James. She loves you. She will contact you. It sounds like she's been intimidated by Ross...and only wanted to help their dad—"

He sobbed into the phone. "I don't know."

"Where are you now?"

"At your apartment."

"Have you spoken to anybody else?"

"No...I've been hoping to track her down...by myself, before—"

He didn't need to elaborate. The police would get involved now.

"I'm going to the airport," James said, "Maybe I can find out if they've flown out to somewhere."

It was unlikely. It would be easier for Ross and Liz to disappear in Dar es Salaam, or flee by road, skipping border crossings and avoiding police. Especially while they still had time on their side. It would take the police some time to get a search party going, once the Carlevaros alerted them to search for Liz King and Ross O'Connor.

"Keep me posted if you find out anything, okay?" Simone begged.

As James rang off she stepped away from Sarah, who was busy building a sand castle, to calm down. She wanted the criminals to be caught, but that Liz was involved was hard to stomach. With her being pregnant…Liz didn't make any pretense of that, too? Did she ever really know Liz? Her heart ached at her friend's duplicity.

Half an hour later she still couldn't get her head around what had been happening. She had returned Sheila's phone, and had helped Sarah decorate her sand castle with little enthusiasm. She kept glancing back at the main lodge, waiting, anxious to hear from Carlo. Did Angelo know about the call between them? Or about Ross and Liz? She didn't understand why he would waste his time coming all the way here if he knew about the call. It didn't make sense.

There were more guests on the beach now, lounging around and swimming. Between them the tall figure of a man, jeans rolled up to his knees, a white shirt with sleeves scrunched up, strode toward her with such determination, he was totally out of place.

She looked again at the fast-approaching figure and had to blink. *That purposeful stride…that body…* Her heart bolted and she turned to face him, just as Sarah saw him too.

"Daddy!" Sarah called out, running toward him.

He laughed as he grabbed his daughter, swinging her into his arms as she shrieked with joy. Simone closed her eyes and tried to bite down on the flood of emotions that broke free. His breath sounded in her ears as he drew her to his chest, and his free arm circled her body.

"Thank God you're safe," he whispered against her curls, his own body quivering against hers. He kissed her cheek. "*Cara*...Mona." He found her lips.

She kissed him back, relief seeping through her. He had come for her. He had *found* her.

He let Sarah slip to the sand in order to take her fully in his arms. "I thought I was going to kill Ross with my own hands when you told me he'd molested you," he murmured in her ear.

She pulled away to look at him. "What's happened?"

He cupped her elbows in his hands and searched her eyes. "Are you all right?" The intensity in his gaze made her knees weak. "Promise me that the incident on the flight with Ross was the only one."

She nodded. "It was. I should have known he's the type."

He searched her face, then he dropped his forehead to hers with a sigh. She leaned into him, sensing his relief in his fingers that loosened their grip to stroke her arms. "What's been happening? Have you heard about Liz?"

"James phoned me." He locked his gaze with hers. "Seems we all got taken for a ride on that one. After our call this morning I asked the fleet manager to search Ross's locker. He found your aero-club jacket and a cheap blonde wig." He shook his head. "He's gone. He

362

clocked in early this morning, as normal, but nobody has seen him again."

"James phoned me to ask me if I knew where Liz was. She'd walked out of the hospital and left everything behind."

"They're on the run together." Carlo sighed. "James took the photos. He didn't speak to Liz about it, wanting to protect her, unaware that she was involved. I can't help thinking how it would have panned out if he'd told her about the trafficking when he made the discovery."

Sarah clung to her leg and they looked down at her. Inside her the love for her daughter drew to a sharp point, and she held her breath for a second. How far would Ross have gone to get what he wanted?

"Ross intimidated Liz." But she couldn't stomach that Liz had been involved in the first place. She dropped her head to Carlo's chest and he pulled her close.

"The stalking…I won't be surprised if that whole business was set up to stop James from investigating further, or to intimidate Liz into silence."

"Ross stalking Liz? With the dead animals?" It was hard to believe he could sink so low. "Do you think she knew it was him? Her own brother?"

"Possibly, we'll find out," Carlo replied. "But the pregnant dik-dik…he gave her something to give her the gap to leave the lodge legitimately."

Simone frowned, feeling even more uncomfortable with misjudging Liz. "Do you think Liz's pregnancy was a hoax?"

"Who knows."

"I don't think so…James have been with her for

the scans, there was a little heartbeat—" Her voice broke.

"The miscarriage was a hoax then," he comforted her.

It didn't help. Pretending to have a miscarriage was even worse and she found she couldn't reply.

"It will be resolved soon, *cara*," he said in a softer tone. "Dino is getting the police involved, they'll catch them at the borders. If not soon, eventually. And we'll get the whole story out of them."

For a long time they stood, digesting what had passed. She shifted on her feet, snuggling closer. "I thought you were in London," she whispered against his neck.

"I was, but then..." He claimed her mouth and kissed her so possessively that she molded against him, letting go of every other thought, except him.

When he finally pulled away he gazed at her. "I thought I'd lost you." He hugged her so close she could hardly breathe. "Please, *cara*, don't ever disappear on me like that again."

"I didn't disappear, you had to go slay dragons." She dropped her gaze. "I thought Angelo would be coming this morning. Sheila's message..." Had been very cryptic.

"Angelo is in Dar, hopefully learning how to wield a hefty sword." He cupped her face, tracing a line down her cheek. "I don't care, to be honest, what Angelo is up to right now."

He kissed her again, even more deeply, setting desire alight inside her.

Sarah giggled and Carlo lifted his head. They both looked down to where their daughter was happily anchoring them to the ground, an arm around each of their legs.

He took her hand and they walked along the beach, with Sarah running ahead of them, chasing tiny crabs into their holes. She breathed in the humid air, the saltiness of the water starting to cling to her skin. The heavy weight had slipped off her shoulders.

Except… "Carlevaro Air will be without a fleet manager soon, and I heard that you took me off the list of candidates?"

He heaved a sigh. "Are you going to hold that against me forever?"

"I might. Messing with my career," she said, then added, "Mind you, that's not the first time you've done it." The last time he'd made her pregnant, but she got Sarah in return, and wouldn't give her up for anything in the world. She glanced down at her daughter, who was picking up shells and forcing them down a crab hole. Maybe letting Carlo mess with her career wasn't all that bad.

He started to say something, but stopped. After a few seconds, he said, "I was hoping you'd come fly my Cessna 206 that's standing at the Rome aero club with me. I still need to do some hours this year to keep my license." He faltered. "There are private charters that fly from Rome, if you want to carry on working. If that's not enough—"

She looked at him, slow heat curling up to her heart, where the beats picked up pace.

He took a deep breath and turned, taking both her shoulders in his hands. "I'm such an idiot. I'm never leaving you again." He rested his forehead against hers. "You've always been the one, Simone, always.

Yesterday, this morning…I was lost, going crazy not knowing where you were, whether you were safe with everything that has been going on. Not being able to get hold of you when I needed you." His voice broke, and he hugged her tighter. "And Sarah…"

At the thought of Sarah and what they shared her heart almost burst. Simone had to swallow her emotions. "This whole mess, Carlo, I never thought, never knew it would spin out of control so fast."

"It's over now. We know who the culprits are." He brushed her windswept curls from her face. "It doesn't matter."

"Of course it does. The company—"

"You mean more to me, Simone," he said simply. "And to think I nearly made the same stupid mistake twice." He shook his head. "To have left you again…please forgive me."

She reached for his rough cheeks, his stubble deliciously scratchy under her fingertips. "There's nothing to forgive. You are here now, that's all that matters."

He held her for a long time, nuzzling her hair. Simone pressed her nose into the smooth skin of his neck, savoring his manly scent. The tide was coming in and water pooled around their feet.

He took a deep breath and pulled her even closer. "If you can bear to marry me, we can fill that old Carlevaro house with so many children that there will be no space for the shadows of the past."

She melted under the intensity of his gaze.

"I love you, Simone, I always have. Marry me, and fly with me to Rome."

Her heart hammered in her chest, her mouth dry

with the sudden fulfillment of her dearest wish. "Can't we fly first? It seems rather rushed."

"Is that a yes?" he asked, a smile playing on his lips.

She chuckled, kissing his neck. "It's been yes from the first time I saw you."

He kissed her and she knew she would finally be flying home.

A word from the author...

I've always loved to read romance and wanted to write my own book since I was thirteen. Life took various turns in the wrong direction but inadvertently supplied me with writing fodder for quite a few books.

I lived in East Africa and worked in the luxury safari industry for a few years, precious time which was the catalyst for my novel, *Perfect Mistake*.

Thank you for purchasing
this publication of The Wild Rose Press, Inc.

If you enjoyed the story, we would appreciate your
letting others know by leaving a review.

For other wonderful stories,
please visit our on-line bookstore at
www.thewildrosepress.com.

For questions or more information
contact us at
info@thewildrosepress.com.

The Wild Rose Press, Inc.
www.thewildrosepress.com

Stay current with The Wild Rose Press, Inc.

Like us on Facebook

https://www.facebook.com/TheWildRosePress

And Follow us on Twitter
https://twitter.com/WildRosePress

CPSIA information can be obtained
at www.ICGtesting.com
Printed in the USA
LVHW04s2326150618
580538LV00007B/13/P